Anthony Antinucci is a high school history teacher. He graduated from the University of North Carolina at Charlotte with a degree in criminal justice and has experience as a law enforcement officer. He and his wife, Lauren, live in North Carolina and have been happily married for almost three years. *As Though Nothing Could Fall* is his first novel.

To my Grammy and Poppy, for recognizing my love for writing ever since I was young.

To my father, who believed in my talent and showed me the confidence to achieve whatever I set my mind to.

To my lovely wife, Lauren, who assured me of my passion and helped keep the dream alive.

Anthony Antinucci

As Though Nothing Could Fall

AUSTIN MACAULEY PUBLISHERS™

LONDON • CAMBRIDGE • NEW YORK • SHARJAH

Ordering Information:
Quantity sales: special discounts are available on quantity purchases by corporations, associations, and others. For details, contact the publisher at the address below.

Publisher's Cataloging-in-Publication data
Antinucci, Anthony
As Though Nothing Could Fall

ISBN 9781643789491 (Paperback)
ISBN 9781643789507 (Hardback)
ISBN 9781645365716 (ePub e-book)

Library of Congress Control Number: 2020908935

www.austinmacauley.com/us

First Published (2020)
Austin Macauley Publishers LLC
40 Wall Street, 28th Floor
New York, NY 10005
USA

mail-usa@austinmacauley.com
+1 (646) 5125767

I want to thank my entire family for supporting me through this process and believing in my ideas. Special thanks to my cousin, Elizabeth, who provided many resources that proved to be instrumental in my publishing process.

I wish to thank one of my favorite authors, Dennis Lehane, especially his work on his novels, Gone Baby Gone and Mystic River, both inspirations for my novel.

A special thanks to the Huntersville Police Department who employed me during my time as a police officer. There, I learned the importance of the job and the great service police officers provide for their communities.

I wish to also thank my criminal justice professors at the University of North Carolina at Charlotte for helping me acquire the knowledge for the source material used in my novel.

Of course, I must thank Austin Macauley Publishers for giving me a chance on my novel and senior editor, Ashley Pascual, for assisting me in the process.

When the truth is in front of us
We hold our strength like sand
As though nothing could fall

Chapter 1
Michael

"The water was cold, wasn't it? Like the ice seeping down from our house in the winter. Damn icicles that would always fall on my car but never your mother's. How could I remember the cold when...when? Never mind, it wasn't what I wanted. It's about what must have been made. Almost, almost."

After he was done murmuring his usual babble of the night, I looked at my father and saw his eyes resting on the buttons of my shirt. His hazel eyes hadn't moved since he started speaking. In the past, I would try to get his attention but was often met with hindrance. Now I understood that all he needed was to find something to stare at as he talked to me. Since my occasional attire was a cheap suit and tie that I triumphantly acquired through bargain shopping at Brooks Brothers, I realized that my father had a thing for buttons. Since then, my tie would come off right before I entered the Alzheimer's facility.

As my father started to look around the rec. room, my eyes started to wander themselves. The Memory Unit of Massachusetts General Hospital was well kept as the white floors seemed to be well mopped at all periods of the day and night. The majority of my visits were in the evening and the floor never ceased to hide my reflection with every step I took. The walls were covered with inspirational posters that displayed mountain ranges and valleys in places all over the globe. Quotes for the damaged soul covered each one of them as some people truly believed that hope would come popping out onto the floor.

I felt the rugged end of my armrest as I thought of yet again how I never felt comfortable in these maroon chairs of despair.

I looked at my father once again, examining his thin hairline. The gray was finally starting to out-battle the black. The black used to fill up his scalp, almost in its entirety. With every visit, I started to see parts of his head that I never knew of. His olive skin was on its way out as the formation of a pasty white accumulation was starting to move in. His moderate case of Alzheimer's was starting to take its toll, as if his aging wasn't already an issue for him. Three years ago, to this day that phone call still makes my hair turn a little gray.

One of his maids at the time found him wandering around his own office trying to find Maverick, our German shepherd that passed away when I was nine-years-old. He wasn't even fond of the dog when we acquired him from one of our neighbors. I guess it was ironic that the maid found him screaming his name out of anger. Not only that, but the maid found dozens of checks covered in a random series of words and phrases that made no sense. The word "almost" could be found on just about every one of them after I spent an entire night trying to dissect the condition that he was in.

I never erased the call.

Before I let myself sink into another episode of, "How My Father Went Nuts," I felt a hand on my shoulder. I looked up to see Tom, the orderly who supervised my father's care.

"How's Richie doing tonight, Mike?" he said. The fluorescent lights from above shined over his dark skin as his complexion was much darker without heaven's undying light above him.

"Normal, he's still fond of my buttons. Doesn't matter what shirt I wear; he stares at them as if they were his own."

"What happens if you keep the tie on?"

"He looks at my belt buckle."

"Way to remove the gentle signs of awkward gazing."

I gave him a small smirk as my ears dialed in on my father making a humming sound. Since the first day I brought him in, Tom was right there. He's shown more care and sympathy for my father more than I ever thought a devout caregiver could. Most of the time I found myself talking to him instead of my father. Tom, a man of about fifty-five, always had a taste of the excitement as stories of his upbringing as a black child in Boston garnished more attention than any story I could come up with. His own father, a gambler who never knew how to fold his cards, always did his best to attract young Tommy into a life of mischief and determined unlawfulness. Thank God he turned out alright. If not, my father could have had some depressed drunk who owns a rundown apartment in Southie.

It was sad really. The shit so many young kids see from their parents. We live in a world now where parents can't be trusted to be the role model all kids deserve. My father was no saint, but he chose the path of reasonable discipline. Guess I got lucky, so to speak.

"Who's been shaving my father, Tom?" I said.

"Good question. It changes every night. Most of the time it's me but Barbara or Ronny have him when I'm unavailable. Why?" he said.

11

"He's got some fresh cuts underneath his throat, right near one of his blood vessels. Whoever is shaving him needs to be more careful."

"You got it, boss, I'll see to that right away. By the way, how long you been here, isn't this your weekend off?"

"Over an hour," I said with a monotonous tone.

"Why don't you go out, have a drink? Weekends are full of opportunities you'll regret for a lifetime."

"You know I don't drink. People can't smooth all their senses with the bottle."

"Speak for yourself."

"Yeah?"

"Of course. We proud men who enjoy our liquor will go to great lengths to ensure a wonderful time shall be had. Know why?"

"Can't wait for you to tell me."

"It never talks back when you open your mouth."

"Feeling a bit sexist are we, Tom?"

"Please, you know I love Meredith with everything I've got. All I'm saying is that privacy is privacy, ideas are ideas, and solitude is what keeps men stable."

"Well, I guess I agree with you in some sense."

"As you should, Mike, as you should."

My father's knees started to straighten out as he attempted to stand up. Tom quickly saw that his presence was needed as my father stumbled quite hastily. Tom gave me a nod as he held my father's right elbow within the marks of his palm. Orderlies are trained never to put their patient's arms around their shoulders when assisting them as patients tend to get spooked easily, causing a chokehold that requires at least five people for assistance. Tom told me that one of their trainees last spring endured a chokehold so fierce that the trainee was knocked out for several hours. Can't let your guard down anywhere.

"It's about that time Mike. I'll have him ready to see next week. Go do something worthy of relaxation. Have a good one," he said as he used one of his free hands to give me a wave as he walked my father off.

"Take care of him, will ya?" I said.

Without turning his head, he said back to me, "Keep it stone."

"Keep it cold," I said with a smirk.

As I passed through the automatic doors leading me outside, the winter wind was waiting to strike me with a measurable gust. Every streak of hair on my neck shot up as the configuration of warmth surrounding my body quickly went away. I zipped up my jacket and proceeded to walk under the tree line outside of the building. My watch said 9:00 p.m. as I was about to cross over onto North Grove Street when an ambulance, sirens blaring, sped by my feet. The ambulance came to an immediate stop as its back doors flew open right in front of the Mass Emergency Room entrance. I watched as two paramedics were slowly bringing down the yellow-colored gurney carrying what appeared to be a teenage boy with lacerations upon his forehead. Before I had time to observe any longer, the paramedics rushed him through the automatic doors and out of my sight. Poor kid.

As I started to walk up the steps of the parking garage, I looked out upon the sea of cars parked in the visitor parking section with no one in sight. Does everyone have the same Friday night plans as I do?

I found my car on the third floor, parked right beside a gravy-colored Jeep Cherokee and a Volvo. My beauty, a 2004 Nissan Altima, looked exactly how I left it, cheap and ready for exhaustion. It's been with me since my promotion. They gave it to me as the perfect lookout car that would never get spotted, since it looks like every other gas guzzler that Americans pour their savings into. The only difference is the Mopar wheels that were installed for their durability and capacity to withstand hopping a curb without blowing out.

Just as I sat in the driver's seat, my pocket started to buzz from one of the two phones resting inside. I prayed for it to be the other one. I put the key in the ignition and my ears were met with Frank Sinatra's *As Time Goes By*. The track was almost over but the smooth vocal jazz knew how to kick in when the time was right. Ah, Frank.

I gave my phone a few more seconds, hoping it was a wrong number and the person on the other line would realize it was not going to happen. I put my hand in my pocket and unveiled two phones. One was my personal phone. Its gray surface looked brand new as it seemed like weeks since I last used it. The other was my work phone, a more worn-out version of my personal phone. The department opened an account for these which meant I wasn't spending a dime. Unfortunately, it gave them the power to call whenever they liked.

"Shit, Frank."

Chapter 2

"It's bad, Mike, get yourself to Langone Park right away."

Captain Burkes sounded distraught on the phone. His tone reminded me of my father's after he'd arrived home from one of his trials that didn't go well. Richard Bowen's distressed voice was one that I could never forget, even though it was a rarity.

Langone Park was one of the greatest attraction spots for children and young adult life in North End. As I drove down Causeway Street, my mind started to wander towards the child who used to play on the baseball field there almost every afternoon. Back then, I didn't own a phone and my phone didn't own me. Any kid in the neighborhood could go out on the field and run till their legs gave out. The waterfront view gave all of us a search for what we wanted to be. We used to look out across the harbor towards Charlestown and wonder if there were kids out searching for us.

God knows what just happened there.

As I drove through the intersection onto Commercial Street, a flicker of blue and red could be seen emanating from the windows of a few parked cars up ahead. Though patriotic and expressive, the lights conveyed the wrong message as I parked close by.

A few beat cops were taping the road off as my car came to a halt just before one of them. A young officer with rough eyes stared back at me. He paused for a moment, gave me a nod and proceeded to wrap his yellow tape around one of the lamp posts.

I felt my phone vibrate in my pocket as the message revealed only a single "?" from Burkes. That was my cue.

As I emerged from my car, I froze a moment. The night was young but that could change at any moment. Burkes knew I was here. Too often does he like to give me shit if it's not within the ten-minute time zone he believes everyone should abide by. My head hung on my shoulders for a second as I let myself get composed. A deep breath or two never hurt the world. Old tips from pops never die-hard.

As I shut my door, a soft voice echoed my name before it was interrupted by the car door finding its lock.

"Mike?" a woman said from the sidewalk.

I looked to see what I thought was a ghost in a gray sweatshirt.

"Jess? What are you doing here?"

Jessica Clark. She used to know the way she made me freeze in my tracks. Everyone did. Her auburn hair was draped over a sweatshirt that covered half of her upper torso, leaving one of her shoulders visible. I tried to maintain my glance at her eyes.

"I live here actually. I'm three stories up from where your car is. What are you doing here?"

Her voice sounded exactly how I remembered it. All my ears could hear was the peaceful tone that she used to present me with all the time. It's as if college was yesterday.

"I'm here for work."

"Work? I didn't think lawyers worked past five during the week."

"It's been that long huh? A lawyer's suit would be nicer."

I moved my jacket back to reveal my badge attached to the worn-out belt behind it. Jess managed to crack a smile. The only difference from before was flashing lights could not be seen shining at me from her blue eyes. "Oh, well I'm sorry to hear that."

"Don't be. Look, I know this is quite a shock us meeting like this, but do you know anything about what happened over there?"

I pointed to Langone Park where the field lights were on and a dozen of my fellow officers were setting a perimeter. The whole scene looked awry, but I had to ask these questions. Why did I run into her here?

"Nothing actually, I just got back from a run. Is everything alright?"

"I'm not sure. Listen, this may be odd, but do you mind if I come back later and ask you some questions?"

"I guess that would be okay." I saw her look towards the park and her mouth found a pause. Her face still contained the configuration of freckles around her nose that I remembered seeing after walking along Chanley Park with her back when I knew her more than I do now. Her thin figure still remained as her well-fitted jogging pants wrapped around her legs. Memories of Boston University began to flood my mind.

Something took her away from me back then and I never could find my answer.

"It's been a long time hasn't it?" she said.

"Longer than I'd like," I said. "If you're uncomfortable I can just get a patrol officer to come, ask you questions once we are done here."

"No, that won't be necessary. Maybe we can catch up if that's alright with you? Space has come between us for a long time don't you think?"

"That sounds great. Just wait up in your apartment and I'll come by for you."

With that, she put together another smile and walked towards a marble painted door directly adjacent to the passenger side of my car. As she opened it, she turned back to find me watching her leave. I found a straight face as she just looked at me with no expression.

I turned my attention to the scene no less than a hundred feet north from where I was standing. Just before I could step on to the road, a figure quickly ran into me, almost knocking me off my feet. It was actually two boys, both of whom barely even recognized that they had just run into me. Before I could utter a word, one of them said, "Excuse me, my bad." The two boys were already halfway down the street when I decided to look away. At least one of them had manners.

I made my way towards the fence of the baseball field but was pulled to the side before I could enter. I noticed three crime scene investigators gathered around something.

Captain Burkes, in all of his onion breath glory, was standing in front of me. His well-combed hair was slicked back with a shining gel that I assumed was Redken. His tomato-sized cheeks peered over his collar as he placed his hands into the pockets of his oversized raincoat.

"Nice of you to join us, who's the girl?" Burkes said. His voice sounded a little scratchy. Sounds like a cold was in his future.

"Just an old friend," I said.

"Just a friend? I'd get to work on that number. Make her your means of at least talking to the opposite sex. You do know how to do that, right?"

"Very funny, more distractions for me equal less results for you. I'm doing you a favor."

"Crime will always go down in one way or another. Some tweaker will get his fix and there will always be a dealer looking to beat the shit out of someone at three in the morning. You just do a good job thinning the herd."

"You really know how to compliment people, don't you?"

"Been doing it for years."

Now that Burkes had his fun, I had to know what was going on. In the past three years I've worked for him, he never sounded that distressed on his own. He could have fooled me by the way he held himself now.

"Cap, what's going on over there? It's not our usual kill and desert is it?" I said.

"No, I'm afraid not. We found a boy," Burkes said, just before he cleared his throat. "You're not gonna believe this next part."

"A deceased boy on a Friday night? Sounds like Dorchester."

"I wish they found him there. This boy here, his best friend was Thomas Zaccardi."

Chapter 3

Thomas Zaccardi was the twelve-year-old son to Francis Zaccardi, the so-called Don Corleone of North End. Heavyset and molded by the environment he embodied. He was a man that everyone trusted…yet he trusted few.

For over fifty consecutive years Boston has arrested at least one Zaccardi for gang affiliation, brutal assaults, and drug trafficking. A few have been charged with murder but over the years Francis has learned to cover his tracks. He owns a bakery down on Hanover Street, along with his three brothers, Ralphie, Jack, and Richard. Francis, the undisputed leader of the bunch, is rumored to have connections with every known gang in all of Boston. Reports have claimed that he made a guy literally eat a sandwich filled with his own dog's feces just for disrespecting him at a bar once.

After studying him through the police reports when I was a rookie, a young cop like me would end up like a pancake if I ever decided to run him down. My second year in a uniform had me seeing him from a distance. Still fresh in my knowledge of community policing, he struck me as a man who no one chose to trifle with. I couldn't help but wonder why no one had taken him in cuffs. Yet, at the same time, the idea of never meeting him sounded lovely.

I kneeled down over the body. His short brown hair was off to the left side of his scalp as his jaw was angled up towards the lights. His soft green eyes looked frozen in time as his pale skin was falling closer into post mortem lividity. His clothes were wrinkled and worn out. The zipper on his green jacket was only halfway zipped, revealing a cloverleaf imprinted on a white shirt underneath. His neck was covered in purple bruises from earlobe to earlobe. I was willing to bet that forensics has already determined he had been strangled. His arms and legs were spread out across the pitcher's mound. Whoever did this was in a rush or could have been spotted. His right arm was locked out diagonally, with his left leg locked out as well. It was almost a perfect, straight line.

Everything was arranged except his right leg was bent at the knee.

I took a few steps over to his right leg where I noticed that his jean pocket was inside out. The man or woman who did this had to have removed something.

Something felt odd though. Who would murder a young boy and leave him in the middle of a baseball field on a Friday night?

"How did we I.D. him? He doesn't have a wallet on him," I said to our lead forensic investigator, Jeffrey Long.

Jeffrey looked up from his clipboard as he was filling out his report and locked eyes with me. His gray hair appeared to be out of place. Work never sleeps, even on the first night of the weekend.

"Burkes said the groundskeeper found him earlier this evening. I'm not sure what his name is or anything. I'd ask him yourself to be honest," Jeffrey said.

"Not where you wanna be tonight, Jeff?"

"Not in the slightest, tonight was lounge night with the kids. Can't find tranquility anywhere these days, am I right? Your Friday night ruined as well?"

"Can't say it was. The agenda was pretty empty."

"Well, perfect time to make yourself busy. Want the condensed version or the prolonged version of forensic theory and analysis pertaining to how this young man is now deceased?"

"Condensed version, please." Jeff never gets old, even with his gray hair count increasing.

"As you can see, there are several bruises along the neckline, indicating what we have examined to be the result of strangulation. His Adam's apple has been broken, most likely by more than eight pounds of pressure. No traces of fingerprints along the jaw or neckline. It's more likely the suspect used his or her inner forearm to apply maximum pressure. As you can see, his body has gone pale and is experiencing post mortem lividity within the lower region of his body."

"Sounds like someone pretty strong did this."

"Could be, that amount of pressure would explain the discoloration around the neckline."

"Any time of death calculated yet?"

"Yes, physiological time of death occurred relatively five to six hours ago."

"Wait, you're saying this kid was killed in broad daylight?"

"It appears so."

"Who have you told about his?"

"Just you and Captain Burkes."

"Good, let's keep it that way. This isn't our usual body on a Friday night Jeff. This kid was friends with Thomas Zaccardi."

Jeff's face fell flat. His cheekbones sunk as I could tell through his eyes what he was thinking. Most cops on Zaccardi's trail don't exactly get the fairy tale ending seen on *Law and Order*.

"Keep it up, Jeff, let me know if anything else pops up," I said to him as I patted his back and walked towards one of the dugouts.

That kid is never going to get to play ball on this field again. The local girls won't be impressed by his skill. The thrill of adolescence has been stolen from this kid with no sympathy found from his assailant.

Inside the home dugout, was a man dressed in athletic apparel sitting down on one of the benches. Burkes was in there asking him questions as I could tell the man looked to be distressed. As I entered the dugout, I noticed the man was wearing navy blue, Nike sweat pants and a cherry red, Nike sweatshirt.

"Sir, I'm Detective Bowen, you doing alright?" I asked him as I held out my hand. The man shook it firmly and did not lose my gaze until I stepped back.

"Sebastian Walker, I'm the youth baseball coach and groundskeeper for the ballpark here."

"Sorry to have to meet under these circumstances, did you know the boy over there?"

"Yeah, his name is Sam Hatkins. He's on one of the teams that I coach here. Real good kid, this is such eh shame."

"Could you explain where you were prior to discovering the body?"

Mr. Walker put his hands in his sweatshirt and took a deep breath. His cheeks were already formulating a pinkish tint below his eyes. "Well, I've been at the school all day. I'm a P.E. teacher over at James Madison Middle and I have plenty of fellow teachers who can vouch for me. These fields are my responsibility. I'm one of the athletic directors who are in charge of the upkeep and I do a little coaching on the side. Holy shit, I can't believe this has happened."

"We'll handle everything from here. We just need anything you can give us."

Mr. Walker told us about his whereabouts before finding Sam Hatkins. Unfortunately for us, I'm not sure his iced coffee from the local Starbucks has anything to do with the boy's body lying on the pitcher's mound. Walker said he taught the class from seven-thirty in the morning till two fifteen in the afternoon. He told us that nothing was out of the usual in class, except one of the teachers; Mrs. Holly could not help but comment on the sweatpants he was wearing. After class, he said that he had a meeting with some of the staff. He had to leave earlier to come, clean the fields in preparation for the games being played this weekend. Before finding the body, he said he went into one of the offices to find the supplies that he needed. As soon as he flicked the 500-Watt LED lights upon the field, he saw it. Sam Atkins body, lying there motionless with his legs and one arm spread out.

I could see the look on his face in my head. Horror draped over it as if it was the first gust of winter hitting him. I could only assume it was the first time he had seen a deceased body as Walker's voice lowered just before he said, "him lying there." Like everyone else, no one should have to see a child die at such a young age. Youth are the beacons of what is it to come, except this one's light will never grow bright enough to matter.

After Walker told us every descriptive detail he could think of, a few minutes had passed of nothing but silence. I had one more question to ask him before he could go home. Burkes had an officer get his address already, leaving no need for me to ask.

"Mr. Walker, before we let you go home, I need to ask you one more question," I said as I twisted one of the buttons on my shirt.

"Sure, what is it?"

"Do you know anything about Sam's relationship with Thomas Zaccardi?"

Walker's demeanor presented a new stance. He shot to his feet and stared at me. Burkes, who was standing to my left, became startled as I watched him slightly move his hand to his hip.

Walker's eyes looked like he just found out that Fenway Park was being closed. Men knew how to flip their switch. Clearly, Atkins' dead body had jettisoned from his mind as his frustration had peaked.

"Zaccardi? That family, that piece of shit family. They had something to do with this, didn't they?" Walker said.

"We don't know yet, look, Mr. Walker…"

"Do you know what they are? They represent what's wrong with this town. The crime wave in this city is too high and who do you think is surfing on top? The Zaccardis have done too much to the people of North End and taking the life of a kid is just way too far. I knew Thomas's Uncle Richard in high school and I knew he would be involved in everything his family had become. They're like a plague. You can't get rid of it until you wipe them from the ground. Francis Zaccardi and Whitey Bulger would have been best pals, guaranteed."

"Proponent of the death penalty, Mr. Walker?" Burkes asked him.

Finally looking away from me for what seemed like a lot longer than it was, Walker shot a smug look at Burkes.

"Look, Mr. Walker, we're not trying to rustle any bad memories, we just need to know anything you can tell us about the friendship both of these boys had. Do you understand?"

Walker nodded.

"I do, it's just that I don't know much honestly. Thomas and Sam were good buddies. They were attached to the hip any time of the day until they had to go to their separate homes. The only time I would see them, was in passing at school and just about every night of the week here in the fields. I'd go ask Thomas himself if you have any questions."

Thanks for the reminder. My mind had started to drift away from the thought of interviewing Thomas Zaccardi, the heir to the Zaccardi Empire. The last trooper who even entered the bakery they owned "accidentally" lost one of his back molars. It sat off the corner of Fleet Street where a nice boutique was stationed across the intersection. My father took me there to buy my mom some flowers once. I had no clue what sat across from it. As a kid, it was a place where suckers lost their money increasing their belt sizes.

"Mr. Walker, I appreciate you sticking around and helping us out. Let me just get your information and you can be on your way," I said.

He handed me his driver's license and I almost took a step back with the amount of facial hair he once had. He could have passed as a lumberjack.

As Burkes and I both told him to try and have a great evening, we watched as he left down the street, staying on the sidewalk. He didn't even turn around once.

Chapter 4

After another hour of canvassing the area for anyone who might know anything, Burkes had approved the medical examiner transporter to take the body. Atkins was carefully brought onto a stretcher. His arms and legs were still fairly movable as rigor mortis tends to affect the body several days after being deceased. I watched as he was loaded into the van and taken off.

This was my first child case. I was promoted to detective two years ago. I still don't think I've grasped it yet. When someone gets to this position, they never really tell you what to expect. Lives are intruded, trusts are broken, and at the end of every day, everyone looks to where I left them. Victims have thanked me for my work but that doesn't solve the problem as to when they get back home. A home to where someone they love isn't there anymore. Or the money they lost will never be fully returned to them. Victims stay victims for the rest of their lives.

My self-loathing was interrupted as I felt my shoulder pop from Burkes bumping into me. He motioned me over to the caution tape as the pile of restless reporters was scrambling for answers. I didn't even pay them any attention when they arrived about an hour ago.

"I'm not trying to avoid talking to them, but you are the better looking of the two of us," Burkes said as he cracked open a Coke.

"What, being over fifty isn't in these days?" I said with a grin.

"Being over fifty means you want to see your kids more and let their prestigious young guns do all of the trench digging."

"Fine, I'll go give them a quick couple of words and be on my way."

"Where do you have to be besides here?"

Burkes almost looked interested as he took another swig.

"Just meeting an old friend."

"It's that fair-haired auburn wonder isn't it?" I could hear his snarky confidence after each syllable.

"She lives right across the street. She may know a thing or two."

"Listen here, Casanova, if she might have information, you would have worded that differently. Just make sure you stop by Sam's house before you call it for the night, I'm going to need you on this all weekend, but you already knew that. Just let me know when you need help, I'll send you a text tomorrow."

"Hey, Cap, did we get into contact with the parents?"

"Mr. Shoot-first-and-ask questions later had their number and called them. Seems their romantic getaway in Maine got interrupted. Should be in town tomorrow morning or even tonight, I'll get them to call you."

Burkes left through the back way of the crime scene as he avoided any media attention he could. I knew how dark a cop's humor could be, but I never took the time to indulge. I knew Burkes had sympathy for the kid, no matter the dialogue that came out of his mouth. I made my way off the field and stood along the sidewalk, gathering myself before I would be assaulted with questions.

"Need a mint or something?" I heard a voice say from the corner of my ear.

A young officer with a bronze tint to his skin entered my peripheral. His dark hair was combed back, and I could see the streetlight bounce off of the gel that was rubbed over it. I looked at his name tag. Officer Delahine.

"Officer Delahine, I saw your name on the new hires the other month. How are you liking it?" I asked.

"Besides Boston being one of the busiest crime-infested cities in the country, I'd say, loving it aren't you?" he said.

"You'll adapt overtime. Just takes some time you know."

"Yeah, what are you going to tell the most concerned citizens of North End?"

Officer Delahine was smart, I could tell. He looked no older than twenty-five, but age is just a number these days. Not that I can complain, I probably have more freckles than he does.

"Thanks for your work here tonight, Officer," I said, as I put out my hand.

"Just Leo, don't need you losing your breath with Officer Delahine," he said as he shook my hand firmly.

I gave him a nod and walked towards the caution tape where a middle-aged man with a brown sports coat was just about to fly out of his jacket if he could not ask me a question. All I could think about was: let's get this over with.

Short but sweet Mike, short but sweet.

*

After dodging every descriptive question that I could, I informed the media that it was an ongoing investigation and if they have any more questions than to contact my supervisor. Burkes is going to love me.

The crowd quickly dispersed, and I could not have walked faster to my car. Once arriving at my driver's side door, I examined myself in the rearview mirror to see if any stray hairs had come out to play. I felt like a freshman at Roger Parks High School again taking my first date to prom.

Jess was a mere memory until tonight. The last time I saw her was over ten years ago. Graduation was three weeks away and we knew that everything was headed for a change of pace. She was one of the brightest and cleverest of people I had ever met in my life. Through the four years that I knew her studying law at BU, her internship offers, immaculate grade point average, and her extracurricular involvement made her borderline omnipotent. She could have chosen any career and I knew that success would follow her. Astronomy was her golden interest. She could always find her solace among the stars. Honestly, that was one of my favorite things about her.

We decided to spend the weekend in Deerfield as a chance to get away from the stress between our books. The rural side of Massachusetts was just the change we needed at the time when everything came to an unexpected predicament. I remembered feeling a bit drowsy on the ride back, as Jess offered to drive. I let myself slip into a quick nap when the car came to a sudden halt off the side of the road. I jolted myself awake to find Jess sitting next to me with both hands on the wheel. The dust caused by the sudden braking started to encircle the car in a cloud of dirt.

"Jess is everything alright?" There didn't appear to be any other cars around us, thus eliminating the feeling that we were involved in an accident. Yet, she sat there frozen while looking straight ahead.

"Mike, I can't be this me anymore," She said back to me.

"What are you talking about?" She didn't move her head.

"I've been sitting here while you've been asleep thinking about everything going on and it can't go on. We are two different people headed for a different path. I live my life one way and you live yours another," she said as she turned her head to look me in my eyes. "Get out of the car."

"Get out of the car? Wait, what are you talking about? Jess, tell me what is going on with you. This isn't…"

"I can't live this life with you and all that it entails. You're sweet and full of righteousness. No one should mess that up, especially me. Please, just get out so I can let you live the way you should."

"Wait a minute, Jess. Do you love me?"

"Damnit, Mike, I can't answer that right now."

"Do you love me or not? If you do, then this is not worth throwing away. Whatever it is, or whatever you are dealing with, it can be fixed if you just let me in."

"Letting you in is what put us here…"

"Do you love me?"

"Yes, but this can't happen anymore."

"Jess talk to me and let me…"

I heard the car door unlock. I noticed Jess's hand had found itself pressing the button. Something was wrong within her right now that I could not begin to understand. We talked about everything in our lives but now, something had changed. She looked distant, as though something appeared to be lost in her eyes. The fight in me went away, the look of certainty in her eyes was the only hint I could see. The unlocking of the door had signified everything that needed to be said, with nothing further left to say.

I remember reaching for my backpack in the rear seat of her car and looking at her one last time before she drove off. Words became useless as none were coming out of my mouth. The dust had cleared as I opened the door to put my foot out. Before getting out I could hear her gently say, "Don't let it change you."

She drove off after that. The next week, a box full of my things were left at my door. No note, not a letter. If she wanted to be erased, then she succeeded.

I never saw her again, until just a few hours ago.

I walked up to the door of the apartment building and realized that I had no idea which floor or room was hers. On the side of the door rested a box with several buttons with handwritten names attached to each one. As I scrolled the list with my finger, I found Ms. Clark written next to room #302 on the third floor.

I pressed the buzzer twice until I heard her voice come from the speaker box.

"Hello, who is this?"

"It's me, Mike."

"Oh, Mike. I'll buzz you in, just come straight up the stairs."

"Thanks."

After hearing the chime ring through my left ear, I entered the lobby. It smelled of pastries for some reason that I could not explain. The lobby contained two brown leather chairs with a table in the front covered with stacks of the Boston Globe. I found the stairs in the back and made my way up to them. We were about to really talk for the first time since that day. Admonished was the right word. All it took was the murder of a young boy on a Friday night for us to meet again. Tragedy and acquaintances don't mix well.

As I arrived at the door, I could hear the sound of a keyboard and a man's voice singing. It was Rick Davies of Supertramp singing "Goodbye Stranger." Jess's stereo must have been on as I raised my fist to knock on the door.

The door opened before my fist felt the wooden door and I saw her standing there. Jess's hair was wet, and her auburn strands were resting on her shoulders wetting her gray t-shirt she had on.

"Nice tunes."

"Thanks, kind of an oldies girl if you remember."

"Yeah, I remember. Mind if I come in?"

"Sure, hope you can forgive the mess. I don't exactly have a cleaning service hired around here. I could get my records stolen."

I walked into her place and was met with a nice brush of heat hitting my body. It had to be around seventy-four degrees or higher in this room. Her living room contained two beige colored sofas and several paintings on each wall. Each painting had a sailboat experiencing its own adventure.

I moved towards one of the sofas underneath a red sailboat trying to refrain from being capsized by a massive wave. "Couldn't help but notice your boat theme that you have here, it really ties the room together," I said.

"Hey, I like them, leave me alone."

Jess sat down on one of the sofas to which I sat on the opposite one. She seemed happy in this place, I couldn't know for sure, but it looked like she made a steady living here. I just hope the ghost that walked through her door doesn't ruin anything.

"I don't mean to address the uncomfortable nature of the situation but I'm not here to vie for affection, I'm just here to ask you if you saw anything from across the street and that you're alright."

"Look, Mike, I understand. Uncomfortable is not the word used to describe you being here. You have a job to do and... I get that. It's just a strange situation you know, us being back in the same room again. Look I think you should know--"

"Life has moved on you know. I've just gotta ask you a few questions about what happened across the street."

I could see that she seemed put back that I cut her off. I didn't want to know right now; I just couldn't get caught up in those thoughts again. Meeting her right now, of all nights was a wanted surprise but an inappropriate encounter. In better circumstances, I would ask her.

"Okay. What happened over there?"

"Someone was murdered."

"That's, that's horrible. Do you know who it is yet?"

"A young boy, his name was Sam Hatkins. Did you know him at all? I gathered he was one of the local boys around here who always played ball at Langone."

"I don't recognize that name, I see several boys playing ball whenever I come home from work or when I go on my runs, but I've never learned their names. Do you have a picture?"

"Not at the moment. You wouldn't want to look anyways."

"Oh, I see. Well, I was at the observatory down at BU today from eight this morning till about five this afternoon. After that I lounged around the apartment for a while and then I went for my run, which of course is when I met you."

"The observatory? You took a job at the astronomy department?"

"Yes, it was one of the offers I received."

"That's great to hear. Glad you are doing what you love."

"And how about you, are you doing what you love?"

I sat back on the sofa and looked at one of her paintings. After glancing at the boat almost capsizing from a wave, I said, "That's the million-dollar question, isn't it? It has its moments. Every job does."

Jess gave me a quick smirk and then started to rub her thumb across the top of her lip as if she discovered a thought that she couldn't let go.

"Thanks for talking to me, I just wanted to make sure you didn't see anything and check on you." As I started to stand, Jess quickly moved her thumb away from her mouth and stood up with me.

"Mike?" Jess said.

"Yeah?"

"It was great to see you, I mean it."

"Yeah, it was great to see you too."

Seeing her now, ten years after that night, she never lost it. She never lost that attraction that I had for her. She was a memory that became a reality again and I held everything back to not reach for her hand.

"Before you go, let me give you my number. In case you have any more questions or if you want to catch up." She disappeared into the kitchen and, in no less than ten seconds, returned with a blue-colored sticky note with her number written in black ink. I gave her an extra business card that was in my jacket pocket and started to motion for the door.

As I opened the door and took a step out, I turned to see Jess watching me leave.

"Goodbye stranger," I said.

"Don't be," she said, as I shut the door and walked down the hall.

Chapter 5

The roads were clear as I headed home.

For a while on my drive back, I thought about Jess and what she said. Familiar thoughts about her were once again circling around my head like a whirlwind that someone would see in a pond once the wind comes by. I turned Frank's voice up higher on the CD player, but the thoughts hovered for a while. But, just like her, they left. Ready to come by again before I have a chance to notice.

I started to think about Sam Hatkins. His body spread out on the mound that I used to play on as a kid. I wasn't much of a pitcher, yet I remember standing on the mound almost every day after school. I grew up here. This used to be my neighborhood and now some kid that could have been me back in the day was dead. I didn't know Sam Hatkins but I had to now.

Burkes told me that some of the local boys went down to talk to his parents. I figured in the morning, I would head to the station and look them up. Burkes won't be happy. I just hope his parents aren't involved with Zaccardi. The last thing Boston needs is another mafia scandal involving the police failing to do their job. A while back, Zaccardi and his group were at the end of the wire when a coffee shop down on Hanover went up in flames. Zaccardi was known to have coke lying around the place from time to time, but no one could prove it. Things got worse when the body of the local priest from the neighborhood was found upstairs burned from head to toe. Forensics traced coke in his system, may he rest in peace.

I was just wrapping up college at the time, so I had a minimal connection to the case. However, my dad led the prosecution, being the public servant that he was. It was one of the few that he lost. The Boston Municipal Courthouse was flooded with people that day. I remember standing out front with my pops wearing an un-ironed buttoned-up shirt with a tie that was unprofessionally tied. My father so duly pointed out. I could remember Zaccardi walking out with his head held high, acting like his two-thousand-dollar suit could protect him from any unwanted glares. Camera flashes were going off simultaneously to the point where I nearly missed him walking out. His gray hair was running thin across the crest of his scalp and his wrinkles looked deep enough to start a ravine. I remember by the time he walked down the steps standing directly adjacent to me and my father, Zaccardi stopped and looked over at the two of us. After removing his eyes from me, he looked at my father and pointed at himself. Zaccardi lifted his hand and spread his fingers like he was releasing a bird into the air. Something unforgivable was let free that day, and the world will never be able to erase that grin.

I managed to nudge myself out of the daydream, I was occupied with, and found myself parking in front of my apartment. Beat up and classic. City Point has a great view of the water and is far away from the treacherousness in North End. My father told me, "Never live in the place that you work, it changes the way you see everything." After working for the prestigious Boston Police Department for ten years, I think my father meant for me to live in a different town.

After pulling the key out of the ignition, I found myself looking at the blue sticky note with Jess' number on it. Maybe I'll call her now and forget about wasting time thinking about it later. Maybe not.

I decided to put the note in my wallet as a reminder for later. As I reached in my pocket to retrieve my wallet, I felt nothing but the material of my slacks. I looked around the car and couldn't find it in between the seats or the floor. Great, how the hell could I have lost it?

As I quickly got out of the car, I slammed the door shut behind me. I made my way towards the front of the car and bumped my shin into the front bumper. Before I could muster any colorful terms of painful utterance, I pictured my wallet falling out of my pocket somehow back at the crime scene.

This couldn't have been a simple night of murder, it had to get worse. I wasn't going to go back. Hopefully, one of the officers at the scene found it and would leave a message. I've seen enough of that place for one night. All I could focus on was my pillow and the mattress that it laid upon.

Chapter 6

The next morning came with a bright surprise. I forgot to dim the shades and was greeted with a beam of sunlight perfectly angled at the left side of my face. I could hear the hummingbirds delivering their morning concert outside, most likely in the trees located outside of my window. Their sounds reminded me of the thirty-minute showing I watched of popular birds in the Boston area on Animal Planet once. From what I could remember, their sounds are more notably considered to be chirps instead of singing. Their chirps signify their own type of language, as every morning, I feel that their chirps are speaking to me by saying, "Mike, let's see, what curveball will hit you today."

After sitting up in my bed, I checked to see that it was around nine-thirty. Dad was probably being taken in for his morning shower at this time. Unfortunately, it is something that I have had experience with. It's been about three years since we sat together in my living room. Both of us were in my living room, just across the hall, watching the Sox play on a Saturday night. The Red Sox were up by three against the Baltimore Orioles in the top of the seventh inning. Pedroia had just hit a ground-rule double to extend the lead when my father's stomach started to gurgle. It was one of those times where my father was able to slow down and appreciate a good time instead of worrying about his next case. I wish that I thought more of it and acted quickly since he was already diagnosed with Alzheimer's a month before. I remembered the couch cushion from where we were both sitting started to become warm. It took me a few seconds to realize it however, I knew what it meant. My father's bowels had emptied along the couch. When I turned to look at him, he was still watching the game without any thought to the matter. The Red Sox winning became insignificant as I sat there waiting for him to notice. Life seemed to have been reversed. There was a time where my father sat and watched me relieve myself when I was incapable. A father's love is a father's love, no matter what the past says.

After taking a shower, shaving, and putting on a getup that consisted of beat-up jeans, a gray t-shirt, and a navy-blue jacket, I went down-stairs to make some toast. I flipped the TV on to see Sam Hatkin's face covering the morning news. WCVB was doing a full spread on the incident and even had the fairly attractive Faye Richardson leading the discussion. I thought of the publicity that would be in this case, and all the hiding I was going to have to do when asked about leads.

This marked the third Saturday I have been assigned a murder case since making detective three years ago. Typically, the old vets would swoop down and beg for an opportunity to charge some loose cannon drug dealer for murder. Yet, it's still a Friday night and most of them have families that they somewhat get along with. I guess it's alright if the young blood has his weekend thrashed. However, I couldn't shake the thought of Sam Hatkins being strangled in the middle of a baseball field. Somebody would have had to walk by and seen something like that. Hatkins couldn't have been murdered there.

As I contemplated the thought for a few more seconds, I finished up what was left of my two pieces of toast with strawberry jelly and made my way to the front door. My place was in decent shape compared to most. I kept it modern, most of my furniture being grey and colors associated with it. I noticed the pile of dirty dishes resting on the counter just as I was heading towards the door. A proactive thought came across my mind, but I decided to neglect them.

Wallet-less and driven, I placed my Glock into my holster, my two phones in my pocket, and my Red Sox ball cap in my hand to throw in the back of the car if I needed it. When I opened the door, I took one step out when I noticed something on the ground right before the brick steps. There was a small brown box with something written on top of it. I crouched down to see that the word "COP" written in all capital letters.

Not the ideal situation for a Saturday morning. I did not know what to think as I stayed crouched to the ground. My neighbor, Francis Keating, a high school teacher from Southie, was out walking his blonde Labrador retriever and was coming up on his usual route past my townhome. As he approached, I looked up and gave him a quick wave. Please tell me this thing isn't ticking.

I waited for Mr. Keating to pass until I lowered my head down upon the box. I listened for any sounds of ticking. Memories of counter-terrorism courses in college were coming back to me now. Chemically induced explosives could be packaged in just about anything with enough storage space. Scenario upon scenario flooded my mind. A troubled son or daughter's parent who I happened to have arrested was finally plotting their revenge for having their hero taken away. An ISIS-inspired website or any xenophobic pamphlet detailing the precise way to generate a household explosive could easily be to blame for such an action.

32

After waiting for a few seconds, no sounds appeared to be coming from the box. I took another moment to scan the area to see if there was anyone in sight. After seeing no one, I carefully started to open the box.

Inside was a crumpled-up newspaper and something wrapped amongst the sports section. After removing the newspaper wrapping, my wallet became clear as day within my right hand. I was set back as this was too peculiar and odd. Nothing appeared to be stolen as all cash, cards, and my Dunkin Donuts gift card were all accounted for.

After removing all of the newspaper, I found a white notecard inside. The notecard had a note written on it written in black ink that said: 3:00 p.m. 'WATERFALL PAUL REVERE MALL.' More peculiar and odd.

I decided to keep the note and placed it inside of my wallet. Who managed to take my wallet off of me after leaving the hospital last night? I remember having it while walking out of the hospital, passing by several doctors, nurses, and patients. I doubt one of the patients was able to steal my wallet, packaged it all nice, and then mail it to via UPS. Shortly after leaving the hospital, I drove to the Langone Park, got out of my car and saw Jess, who I never even got within one to two feet of. Who could have taken my wallet as I walked to...

Those two kids. The one that bumped into me, geez. A cop getting fooled by a sly move like that would most certainly hurt the rep. His slim face and his short brown hair was all that stood in my mind. Maybe Burkes had a thought or two. But why bring it back?

The Boston Police Department always appeared to me as an office building with no special attributes that would generate any discussion along the street. Located on New Sunbury, the building was covered in red bricks except for the nether region of the building where concrete pillars held up the tremendous weight that looked as if they were about to give. No argument would be found coming out of my mouth when thinking about the working conditions of the officers that served before me.

In 1635, we were just night watchmen and were paid a laughable sum of thirty-five shillings a month. Heck, those officers had to carry a six-foot pole to catch criminals by trying to wrap a thin wire around their necks. In 1838, the general court passed a bill appointing an official police department. Ironic enough, the first policeman to ever be appointed as a Boston police officer was an Irishman and not of American descent. I guess it made since the majority of the city at that time were Irish immigrants. After enjoying several decades of Boston having its own police force, the officers themselves decided to take a stand and demanded pay raises through unionization. Over one thousand officers had their efforts thrashed when Police Commissioner Edwin Upton Curtis denied any attempt to form a union. The pay is what it is and I wish people would understand that the job is not for the money but the service. Maybe it will get back on track one day.

I called Burkes on my way into the police department. I managed to inform him of the note found on my doorstep and the directions to meet at three in the afternoon. I conveniently left out the part of my wallet being stolen.

"What did you do with the box?"

"It's just sitting in my house right now. The card is currently in my wallet. What's the next play Cap? Should I call SOU for surveillance?"

"I doubt this will be anything, probably just some loner trying to get your attention. However, with a dead boy circling around the news, we can't take any chances. If you decided to go, just ask a few uniforms to go with you. Thanks for calling Mike but I've got to get back to my day off, these Kramer re-runs aren't going to watch themselves."

Glad, some still appreciate the classics. I parked my car behind the station and headed inside. The station looked quite empty as most of the clerical and office personnel were out enjoying the weekend. As I stood at the elevator waiting for it to come down, I looked around to see the paint was starting to come off the walls to my left. The light tan color was starting to dilapidate off the wall as if it was begging for a change. I could submit a note within our comments & suggestions box on the counter to notify anyone of the current issue. Like most things around here, it could wait. Lucky for me, the elevator arrived before I pushed myself to do it.

The third floor was assigned to the special services divisions. This included the general detective unit, traffic, and financial crimes. My district, the A-1, was towards the end of the hallway. By my district, I meant two desks that served as the two detectives who worked the North End and anything in the surrounding areas, granted it was not several miles away. There are almost no walls on the third floor, just a vast sea of desks with paperwork stacked higher than my GPA in college. There were a few box offices located in the corners where the captains and lieutenants were. Most of the time their offices were shielded by the dark gray blinds that kept any nosy officer from looking inside or intentionally doing busy work for the bosses to see. I caught myself doing that as a rookie once. I could not even register a glance.

Burkes' office was within close proximity to my desk but of course, he was not in today. I sat down in my creaky bronze-colored chair and let the weight of my back press against the thin cushion. I pulled my notebook out of my pocket and started to peruse the notes that I took from last night. Sam Hatkins was twelve-years-old, he played baseball with the boys from the neighborhood, went to James Madison Middle School, and was friends with Thomas Zaccardi, son of the infamous "Corleone" of North End. Such a young kid, his

34

parents must be in shambles right now. I need to get their number, not to mention stop by their house as Burkes told me to do.

Kids like Sam, I assume, spend most of their time in one place. I went online to find the principal of his school. After patiently waiting through the slow internet connection, I found her, Dr. Rachel Kurtz. The image from the school's website showed a middle-aged woman with black and gray streaks running through her hair. Her cheekbones were thin, as her forehead was furrowed with signs of her age. I sent her an email addressing the matter and requested a time to meet up today regardless of the fact that there was no school today. I wrote her number down, in case she did not reply within the hour.

As for Thomas Zaccardi, I knew where he was. Unfortunately, like the cub that he was, the lion had to be close.

Chapter 7

Francis Zaccardi's bakery was located at the tip of the intersection of Hanover and Charter. Zaccardi's was the name. Simple and not too cliché. What made the situation more unstable was the fact that the bakery generated quite a bit of profit. The Zaccardi family may be some of the worst recorded scum to walk around Boston, but they could whip up a cannoli to die for. I tried to forgive myself for the pun that I just made.

On my drive over, I contacted the watch commander on duty today to request an additional unit in case something went sour. When I told Lieutenant Davey the address, he chuckled and replied with, "Your career as a detective will be short, I guess." Being young in this spot has its disadvantages I continue to discover. From time to time, I hear that the only reason I got this job was because of my father's prestigious career in law. My usual reply generally involved me saying that I was "wicked smart," and that they should try it sometime.

I parallel parked one block away in front of a family-owned real estate company. I looked around to see if the other unit that I requested was around but did not see any blue and white Crown Victoria with the words "Boston Police" around. I clipped my badge to my belt to make sure that they knew who I was as soon as I walked in. It was almost eleven in the morning and a few families were already heading inside.

I was about to cross the street when I heard a whistle coming from behind me. I turned to see Officer Delahine leaning up against the real estate building with his hands on his belt.

"Heard you needed some help," he said.

"Glad to see word actually spreads fast. Not busy today I hope."

"It's Boston, there's always somebody testing the law. What's your game plan here, you know that's the lion's den correct? We, young guys, have been told to steer clear if we know what's good for us."

"Believe me, Davies already chimed in his two cents for the day. I'm just going to walk in and ask to speak with Thomas."

"The prodigal son? He's at school right didn't you know?"

36

"School? It's Saturday."

"Yeah, but remember the snow we had last week? Those ten inches of snow set everything back a bit. They have Saturday school this weekend, believe me, I had to stop by today to walk around. The place is nothing but a morgue. Everybody loved Sam Hatkins, there's already a bunch of flowers and presents by his locker. Shame, kid had his whole life ahead of him."

"I've been thinking about that myself; this isn't right. What kind of motive does a man or woman have to kill a kid that young? Anyways, I figure I should still go in there and at least inform Corleone himself that I'm going to be talking to his son. Can't have disrespect this early in a case."

"There's always going to be disrespect at the start of a case, you know that. Want me to go in with ya?"

"It's bad enough a badge is walking in. I don't think a uniform along with your Batman utility belt will help the situation any further."

"Gotcha, I'll be two stores down in Dunkin then, might get myself a treat while you're in there. Here's my number, try to butt dial me if you need me."

Delahine showed me his phone and I gladly saved his number into mine. I texted him my name and said, "Thanks, hope I won't need ya." Delahine turned around and decided to walk directly down the street towards Dunkin. Guess he figured that they were already watching us.

As I walked to the door of Zaccardi's, a family of four was walking out eating what looked like fresh *pariginas* wrapped in paper napkins. There is always something reassuring about parents who let their kids skip school, yet sometimes it is not always beneficial.

My father used to bring me to Italian pastry shops when I was young. The mixture of cinnamon, icing, and chocolate never ceased to leave my memory. There was this one place in Roxbury, Aunt Maria's Delights, which baked their treats with sweet pumpernickel rye bread. Easily the best I could remember tasting. Today will not be the day where I try something new. The last thing I need is the Zaccardi family poisoning my Italian treat with arsenic.

I pulled open the doors and glanced upon a sea of *savoias*, *cannolis*, *crispelles*, and other assortments of treats neatly aligned in brightly lit glass cases. The fan circling above was doing its best to fill the establishment with wonderful smells. I peered over to the right side of the store finding the register sitting at the end of a metal counter. Behind the register was Jack Zaccardi, one of Francis's younger brothers. Jack was around fifty and had the shortest rap sheet of the bunch. Typically, in a club of bullies, there was one weak link that played the role as the watcher, instead of the beater. Jack fits the bill of the watcher, by the looks of him, seems he's received more punches than giving them.

Back when I was on the road in my uniform, I had a run-in with Jack and some of his friends outside McCauley's Bar in Dorchester. A complaint was called in that some guys were being overly obnoxious after the Celtics won a playoff game. I remember showing up to find Jack along with some of his pals throwing beer bottles against the wall of McCauley's. When they decided to keep wasting more of our time, we charged Jack and his pals with disorderly conduct. Maybe he'll remember me. Probably not.

"Morning, Jack," I said glancing at his waistband hoping there was no bulge attached to his hip.

"First cop we've had in here in a long time. Dunkin is right across the street if you're lost. Wait, how the hell do you know my name?" Jack replied. He scratched the top of his head where his fingers met a thin patch of black and gray hair. The tips of his fingers were stained with yellow traces of an unbalanced smoking habit. His tan complexion definitely revealed his Italian heritage.

"You know us, we know everybody's name. Not trying to waste your time, I've got to talk to Francis, is he here?"

"How old are you?"

"Old enough to see that you understand the words coming out of my mouth. This doesn't have to be difficult; I'm typically known as a nice guy."

"Nice guy, huh? Well, some of the nicest guys have watched their teeth fall right out of their mouths in the back room there. Are you prepared to lose your precious teeth?"

Being a cop makes you a bit sensitive to threats. However, since I'm no longer a street cop with the desire to arrest every rule breaker that I see, there is no need to get my handcuffs ready. "Do you keep forgetting that I'm a cop? Threatening a cop can get you a night in our wonderful deluxe sweet with your own metal bed."

That shook something loose. Jack's jaw dropped a little and then managed to murmur, "Why don't you go back there and figure out just how welcome you are." He waved me back in like a bouncer at a club.

I made my way around the corner and struggled to open the heavy wooden door that led into the room behind. I stepped in to see four men huddled around a table with one light bulb hanging above. There were racks against the wall of what I assumed was the shipment of ingredients from the morning delivery truck. My attention returned to the table where it looked like Texas hold 'em was being played. There were three cards lying in a line on the table along with stacks of blue, green, and red chips. The four men moved only their heads to see the unwanted stranger enter the door. The smell of cigarette smoke filled the air as I could see that at least two of them had cigarettes in their hands. My nostrils struggled with the smell. There was a Marlboro pack in one of their back left pockets, confirming that more would be used today.

"Fellas, didn't mean to interrupt your game," I said, knowing that I looked like a mouse walking into a room full of unhinged lions.

"What the hell is this Francis? Your chowda, head brother out there let anybody walk back here? Not to mention a fucking badge," said one of the men with a white tank top.

The man with his back to me slowly turned his head around to lock eyes with mine. It was him, Francis Zaccardi. Remarkably, being over sixty, he still had a full head of hair. Some miracle must have caused it to grow a lot over the years since the trial. It was mostly black instead of gray too. Guess he was a man who lived with a lack of stress. Makes sense, as he is the top gun.

"Ooo, a young one. We haven't had a cop back here in what Tommy, a year?" Francis managed to say while chuckling. He glared at me for a few more seconds and said, "This must be pretty important. Guys, I think we really need to hear what he has to say."

After looking into his green eyes for a few more seconds, I thankfully realized that he had no idea who I was. That day on the courthouse steps seemed to be a far-off sailboat for him.

"I'm Mike. I'll keep this clear and short. I need to speak with Thomas, is he around?"

Francis's attention had shifted. "Thomas? What the hell do you need to see my boy about?"

"The kid that died last night at Langone, he was one of Thomas's friends. I came here to ask you personally if I could speak with him before I started to step on anybody's toes."

"That kid, huh? Yeah, I heard about it. Rumor is that we have another serial killer on the loose. You know anything about that young gun?"

"I'm not going to speak about the case with you. I need to see your son so that I can figure out a timeline." *'Did I just say I need to, to this guy?'*

"You what? Wait a minute, do you know what North End stands for?"

"I have a feeling I'm about to find out."

"North End stands for north of the shit. When someone *needs* something from me, a guy doesn't waltz into a man's place of business and demand information. Everyone has their own shit. A man needs a promotion; I help fire the guy ahead of him. If some aspiring fisherman wants to be the new ace of Boston Harbor, I sink his competitor's boat. Do you know what they have in common?"

After a few seconds of silence and ignoring my phone buzz once in my pocket, I said, "I'm sure you're going to tell me anyway regardless of what my answer is."

"Damn straight I will. It's called a favor. The economy is tanking, and the price of freedom can't be left to those clowns in Wall Street. You make your own way, or you fall your own way. The young guys around here have to put in the work to get where they are today. Making the green is what most men want. Information is the secret to success and shit, the young ones like you have no right to demand from the elders who helped build the ground you are walking on. Now, before you piss me even more off, what can *you* do for me?"

"Cops don't make deals with reputations like you."

"The good ones do."

Cops get assistance all the time I knew that. To enforce the law there is a thin line that must be walked on. I've been on it my whole career, yet, the offer to fall off a few times has always been there. Morality always has to be at stake.

"Thomas may have pertinent information, if he's just upstairs it will only take a few minutes."

"Thomas is nowhere, wait, he might be over there or even a few places down. Damn, I can't remember where I left him."

With that sarcasm and malcontent, I knew I was not going to get anything out of him.

"Looks to me that our young daredevil here isn't about to sell himself. Murdered children are no joke, be a shame if someone found out that you failed to do everything that you could to find this boy's killer." Francis said.

"Sorry, Francis, I'm not like the other boys in the neighborhood. Respect was supposed to mean something nowadays, guess self-interest still outweighs proper judgment," I said, making my way out the door. There was a big Boston Red Sox "B" hanging next to the door that I did not see on the walk-in. Before putting my foot across the threshold, Francis opened his mouth again.

"You paint a strong image, kid. I admire the respect you showed coming in here. It's a shame you didn't want to talk business. Your father was the same way."

I paused at the atom bomb Francis just set off. His mind was sharper than I thought. My feet remained still as I could feel my neck start to turn. I left without giving it the chance.

Chapter 8

Moments can get away from you once you think you have it all figured out. It is human nature to feel that once everything is going right, we become numb to the possibility of falling into something worse. Even in the academy when we trained for every scenario we could think of, it was impossible to study everything. Just like it's impossible to study how to go through life. We all forget that life is not the one word we seem to forget: predictable. I've been doing this job for eleven years and the hair on my back has never stiffened like that before.

'Your father was the same way.'

Francis's words kept repeating in my head like a movie reel operator forgetting to change the reel of film to move on to the next one. The bright ray of sunlight that hit my face, as I exited the bakery shop, failed to wipe my brain of the voice in my head. I looked across the street to see Delahine sitting down at a table with a coffee in his hand. As soon as he noticed me walking out, he proceeded to clean up his table and head for the exit.

I met him at a street lamp in front of the Dunkin Donuts.

"Glad to see that you don't have a limp," Delahine said, as he tried to clear his throat.

"Yeah, I'm really thankful. Not much help I'm afraid."

"You alright? You look a little odd."

"What? Yeah, he just tried to make a deal with me and I refused. He formally is not allowing me to speak with Thomas, which, for this case, does not matter as that could be considered an obstruction of justice. Already pissing someone off I suppose."

"You know that comes with the job. Need me to do anything further? I can go with you to the school if you want."

"I'm alright. I think I can handle a few middle school educators on my own. I appreciate it though. You could ask around the neighborhood if they know anything."

"Sounds simple and not too complicated. I love it. You've got my number. Hit me up whenever you need me."

With that, Officer Delahine walked towards the alleyway where his car was parked. He seems like a man to trust for a case like this.

Everyone hears the stereotype that cops just sit around waiting to bust somebody for speeding violations. We've become more scrutinized now with the officer-involved-shootings taking up most of the nationwide news coverage. Charlotte, Baltimore, Chicago, name the city, there's been some kind shooting that CNN has covered. It's the new controversy in the world. The American people are too focused on the outliers located in their municipal police departments when they forget to realize that the majority of cops do their job, just like Officer Delahine. Like all fads and hot topics, officer-involved-shootings will falter, and another concept of controversy will arise in a society where the news lacks the capacity to report the true altruism going on in the country, yet the world.

Not much to do but fight the necessary fight.

*

James Madison Middle was a quaint establishment. Located off Boston harbor, about twenty minutes from the police station, it's been around since the early 1900s if I remembered correctly. The bricks that held the school together were derelict and suffering from many shades of discoloration. There was fresh moss on a few that I could see. However, the parking spaces appeared to be freshly painted, an odd thing to improve when the actual school is suffering. The appearance is honestly dumbfounding when Massachusetts has the number one ranked public education system in the country.

When I got in my car back at Zaccardi's, I checked my phone to see that Principal Kurtz had emailed me back saying that she was available anytime today. Maybe this interview will go better than the last one.

I parked next to a gold sedan whose front right tire was parked on the line. Pet peeves can only tick a man off so far. Not only did that tick me off but all of the other spots near the front were full, forcing me to park near the buses.

I walked towards the front steps of the school and checked my watch to see that the time was 11:15 a.m. The majority of the students were probably at lunch at this time. When I arrived at the front door, I was reluctant to discover that the front doors were locked. I felt quite embarrassed as I remembered that most schools had heightened their security over the past couple of years. I pressed the electronic doorbell where the receiver located above the doorbell button started to ring.

A female voice, with a high pitch tone, answered saying, "Hello, what can I do for you?"

"Hi, I'm Detective Bowen with BPD, I'm here to speak with Principal Kurtz."

"I'll buzz you right in."

"Thank you, ma'am."

After hearing the door unlock from the inside, I entered through the right-hand side door. I looked to see a long hallway with several connecting hallways. A map of the school hung directly to my right and I saw that the structure or foundation of the school was in the shape of a trident. Each separate "spear," so-to-speak, was labeled with each individual grade.

I heard a door open to my left and met eyes with a short, stocky woman with long curly hair standing in the doorway.

"Hi, Detective, I've already informed Miss Kurtz of your arrival. Please, follow me."

After gesturing her with a nod, I followed her into the main office of James Madison. The place had an interesting odor, despite its nice paint job and modern office equipment. I guess the budget is more focused on improving the interior than the exterior of this place. Several of the desks were made from redwood with a nice gloss over it. I noticed that the fax machine that we walked past in the hallway was made in 2017. The gray carpet seemed like a cloud beneath the soles of my shoes as I was escorted to the principal's office. Haven't been to the principal's office in many years, thankfully this wasn't for disciplinary reasons.

Dr. Kurtz looked almost identical to her photo on the school's webpage, as I was expecting the photo to be less than up to date. Her face was petite. Though aged, her apple cheeks were brighter in the right angle of light. Her eyes were small, yet evenly spread apart. After standing up to greet me inside, she revealed to be wearing a black skirt accented with a gray blouse with her sleeves rolled up. Her figure appeared to be thin and well managed.

"Morning Detective, sorry, I guess I should have been expecting you," Dr. Kurtz said as we both sat down.

"No worries. Sorry that I even have to drop in at all, Doctor. I assume you go by Doctor, yes? I read that you got your Ph.D. in Education from BU," I said.

"Occasionally, most of my employees just call me Miss Kurtz, except for a few of the athletic teachers who joke around and call me Doctor."

"Nice to see another eagle, I know that I look like I graduated yesterday but I'm also an alumnus."

"That's nice to see. I'm sure you are enjoying the wonderful catalogs being sent to you every year asking for donations."

"Can't live without them. Not meaning to darken the mood, but, I'm sure you know why I am here."

Miss Kurtz's fingers started to tremble as she combed some strands of her gray hair behind her ear. "Sam Hatkins. Yes, it's been hard to grasp. He was well respected here. I've already called his parents to give my condolences. The call went straight to voicemail."

"I haven't heard or spoken to them yet either, not sure how I'm going to go about that actually. Anyways, I was coming to speak with you directly about meeting with Thomas Zaccardi. According to my sources, he was one of Sam's close friends and it would be paramount that I speak with him."

"I would allow it but, unfortunately, Thomas called out sick today. We tried to call his father, but there was no answer."

'Can't say I'm shocked to hear that,' I thought to myself. *'I would hope, Miss Kurtz has no knowledge of Mr. Zaccardi's reputation.'*

"Did Mr. Zaccardi call in to say that Thomas was sick?" I asked.

"No, actually, Tracie at the front desk said that Thomas called. She said that his voice sounded a bit muffled and scratchy when he called to say that he was under the weather. With the loss of a close friend, falling ill is not uncommon I suppose."

"It can't be easy for him, or anyone at this school who knew him. Do you happen to have Thomas's cell phone number by chance?

"The caller I.D. picked up an unknown number when Thomas called, I'm afraid. He may have been calling from another a number which is strange, I have seen him with his own cellphone. It seems like most kids who shouldn't have one, have one these days. However, we have no record of that. Just his father's number."

"I see. Who does Thomas hang out with and I guess…who did Sam hang out with here at school?"

"Rich Pritt and Tommy Stephens, the four of them were inseparable here. I'm not saying they were the most behaved but those four were always together. Sam was the nicest of them all, and Thomas had his moments."

"Is there any way I could get their information, home address, phone number, anything of that nature?"

"Sure, just let me search for them. But detective, can I ask you something?"
"Of course."

"Thomas, Tommy, Rich, and Sam are only middle school kids. Why on earth would someone murder a twelve-year-old boy with a bright future? It's like the Sandy Hook shooting, those children did not deserve to die but

44

some…some horrible person had to ruin their families with such a horrible act. Since Sam is dead, do you think the other boys might be in danger?"

Miss Kurtz's hands were now in her lap. I could see the tips of her thumbs circulating as she appeared to overlap them by swirling her fingers around and around. I could tell she had a real passion for her work and was not a principal focused on their direct deposit at the end of every month. I respected that, but she was worrying herself more than she needed to right now.

"I do not believe so. I will personally inform you if anything occurs that you need to know. However, if there is anything that you find out would you let me know?" I said to her as I reached into my wallet and handed her my business card.

"Absolutely, thank you, Detective. Is there anything else I can do for you?"

"Yes, is there any chance that I could look into his locker? According to state law, only the principal of a school can access the locker of a child."

"Yes, I'll even bring Officer Warner with us. He's the school resource officer here and his office is right next door."

"Perfect. Let's see what we can dig up."

Miss Kurtz stood up from her chair and led me back into the hallway. She took a few steps to her left, knocked on the office door next to me, and asked for Officer Warner to come with us to check out Sam Hatkin's locker. After hearing a chair scoot back, and some papers being placed on a desk, a tall man with a slightly larger build than mine walked out of the room wearing a dark blue uniform with a BPD patch on both sides of his deltoids. Officer Warner's belt was brightly shined, along with his badge that hung on the left side of his chest. He looked to be in his upper forties, maybe even in his low fifties with the number of wrinkles above his brow.

"Officer Warner, I'm Detective Bowen, nice to meet you," I said reaching my hand out.

"Pleasure, it's a shame you have to be here for this kind of thing," he replied after nearly crushing my hand with his hefty grip. His left hand revealed a wedding ring. Definitely in his forties.

"Alright gentlemen, I'll lead you right this way," Miss Kurtz said as she lifted a key out from behind her back.

Officer Warner and I followed her through several turns until we found ourselves walking through the center spear of the trident shaped school. I observed classrooms to my right and my left that was quite full of students who were almost completely unhappy to be here. Some of their projects, papers, and other miscellaneous activities were hung up on the walls. One section was dedicated to the New England Patriots with what appeared to be an impressive drawing of Tom Brady. The kid even included his five o'clock shadow. The kid has some skill with a pencil.

After walking to what would be the middle of the spear, we arrived at a set of lockers numbered from one to about three hundred. Miss Kurtz lifted the key and made her way to the locker located directly next to Officer Warner. It was not that hard to miss, as the locker was covered in notes and pictures dedicated to Sam's memory. It was a collage of sadness if I knew how to describe it. There were notes with Sam written in pencil on each one. Three sets of different colored flowers lay at the base of the locker. A teddy bear with an "I miss you" t-shirt sat in the middle of them.

"Sam's locker was number 236. As you can see, the kids all got together and showed their love for him in their own creative ways. It's a shame, one of the sixth graders came up to me today and said that Sam was in a better place where no bad people could hurt him. I almost started to cry right then," Miss Kurtz said as she used the key to open the locker.

After moving some of the flowers and the teddy bear with my foot, I opened the locker to see what I could find. Nothing of any value appeared to be inside. A brown coat and a gym shirt were hanging inside, along with a few pens and pencils spread sporadically at the bottom. A white piece of paper was folded on the top shelf.

"Most kids do not use the lockers anymore. They see it as a waste of time, compared to just heaving their backpack around all the time," Miss Kurtz added.

"Yeah, my middle school days were a little different. Guess the new millennium brought stranger changes than we could expect. Let me just check something real quick," I said, as I walked closer to the locker and proceeded to search the coat pockets of anything. Nothing. I looked back up to the paper and took it. As soon as my fingers felt the weight and smoothness of its texture, I realized it wasn't notebook paper, it was a photograph.

Four smiling teens looked back at me after unfolding the photo. In the middle was Sam, it was hard not to recognize him. His face was fuller and tanner than the first time I ever met him.

"It's just a photo of the four of them. Not sure how it helps," I said.

"It was worth a shot," Officer Warner added.

"Yeah, you're right. Figured there would be a note or his phone, if he had one."

"His phone was not with him?" Officer Warner asked.

"Not even a pair of headphones or anything that would lead to him having one. I'll ask his parents when I speak with them." I shut the locker and then faced Miss Kurtz.

"Alright, well, there is no more sense in me wasting any more of your guy's time. I'll walk myself out, thank you for everything," I said.

"Please, I'll escort you out. Got a few questions about the department, I haven't stepped foot in the building for almost a year now. Nothing like hearing about whose been fired and who's still moping around."

I said goodbye to Miss Kurtz with a shake of the hand a sincere nod. Her eyes looked a little red as she started to walk back to her office. Her footsteps echoed in the hall as Officer Warner and I watched her until she was out of our sight.

Chapter 9

This case was not biting at all. Most people know, thanks to the A&E show, *48 hours*, that the first two days of a case are crucial. I'm almost to hour twenty-three with no suspect, or possible suspects to show for. Burkes is going to have a field day when he calls me later. To make matters worse, Thomas Zaccardi appears to be missing. His murderous father most likely has him locked up in his room above the bakery playing PlayStation until he lets him out. Sam Hatkins other friends might be able to offer more insight. His parents were the concern right now, it's almost twelve in the afternoon and I still have not heard a word. I managed to get their number from Miss Kurtz as I walked out, hopefully, they will pick up when I call.

I almost tuned out with my own thoughts of the case when Officer Warner asked about my father. I found it easy to drift during his thoughts on the department and the politics involved with police work.

"Your old man, how is he doing? I met him a few times down at the station when I was walking a beat. Hell of a prosecutor, I almost quit my job to become one of his personal investigators," Officer Warner said. His badge was so impressively shined that the sun was reflecting off of it, catching my eye with every other step that I took.

"He's been better. He's over at mass in the Alzheimer's wing. I visit him when I can. I forgot how much a celebrity my pops was back in the day. I was too busy being nagged by him to get good grades so I could go to law school as well. Northwestern was the place he never shut up about me going to."

"That's a shame, he's a good guy. Hope he's being treated well."

"He is. How long you been here?"

"Bout three years in March."

"Damn shame, he was one of the best. Seems like just yesterday I was where you are, investigating leads and arresting the bastards responsible for damaging the reputation that Boston has. My clearance rate wasn't the highest, but I managed. Guess I figured a consistent day time duty would be a nice way to retire. If I did not have two kids, I would have never left. How come you chose this over law school?"

"More of a lashing out attempt towards my father, I guess. Plus, I wanted to make a name for myself doing something else. It's a long story honestly."

"I get it. My old man had his stipulations as well. The great ones are usually the ones with the most issues. I…

Officer Warner paused to check his pocket. His phone was buzzing as he lifted his head to stay, "Hold a sec, it's the wife. I'm sure she's confused about what to buy for dinner again."

I watched him walk behind one of the buses. We had made it to the bus parking lot, just over a hundred feet from my car. Since Officer Warner mentioned being an investigator, I tried to remember what unit he was with. I probably should have told him that I had to leave but having manners is apparently a virtue the job has not taken from me yet. My father had his manners for a while. They typically were forgotten when he lost a case. His career was prestigious, but there was always that night at the harbor. The night he…

"Sorry about that, looks like I'm having pork chops tonight," Officer Warner said as he quickly walked back over to me.

"Nice to know that you have well-cooked meals."

We proceeded to walk towards my car again by walking in between two of the James Madison buses parked near my car. They were spaced apart by about ten feet or so. The air started to feel a little restrictive.

"Anyways, I hope that your dad is peaceful throughout the time he has left. A fellow like him doesn't need his demons coming back to him so late in life."

Before I could respond back to him, I felt my work phone buzz in my pocket. As I reached in to retrieve it, I heard a whistle throughout the air when suddenly a wire-like substance wrapped itself around my neck. I felt my body jerk back when I noticed that Officer Warner was forcing me backward with some kind of wire. I found myself choking on my own saliva as the wire was severely being stretched underneath my chin.

The distance in between the buses felt smaller as I could not understand what the hell was going on. I tried to grab the wire and pull it off my throat, but Officer Warner held a tight grip. I forcefully stepped backward and managed to shove Warner's body into the side of one of the buses. His strength was overpowering mine as I once again tried to pull the wire off my throat. I could feel my body failing as the chokehold was affecting my vision. The world had become dizzy until I shook my head quickly and decided to ram Warner's body back into the bus, while also repeatedly jamming my elbow into his ribcage. The weight of the wire had lightened greatly as I was able to partially breathe again. I could feel Warner's presence again as my body was forced forward into the side of the adjacent bus. He quickly spun my body around and delivered a jab to my gut. A great deal of pressure punctured my stomach as I quickly returned with thrusting my forehead forward catching the brim of his nose.

As a slow stream of blood started falling from Warner's nostrils, I reached for my Glock attached to my hip. Warner's hands also found my Glock as I struggled to lift it from my holster. Warner's upper body strength far surpassed mine as I could not find the edge. I rushed to figure out what to do when I decided to thrust the heel of my shoe into his ankle causing Warner to lighten his grip. I managed to lift my handgun and before I could think about my next move, there was a loud pop.

The sound had penetrated my eardrums to the point where a constant ringing began. It sounded like church bells from my old church constantly ringing until suddenly they started to fade away as if I was driving away from them.

I looked down to see Warner's body on the ground, along with a stream of blood roaming across the cement.

'What the hell was going on here?'

*

Captain Burkes had showed up no less than twenty minutes later dressed in jeans and a worn-out Celtics t-shirt. Never before have I seen him dressed so unprofessionally and inconsiderate of his appearance. As usual, he was in control of the situation, delegating tasks without a care in the world that he was not in his proper uniform. A dozen officers had arrived and taped off the scene. Including, Officer Delahine, who was currently speaking with some of the James Madison teaching staff. The whole scene was a mess.

The children had to stay inside as it would be too much of a commotion to have their parents clog the parking lot. The teachers who had classrooms facing the bus lot had to shut the blinds and made sure none of the students had a clear sight of the scene. I could only hope that none of the students had seen what happened. Not the best way to spend your Saturday at school.

I played everything in my head over and over again, like a hamster continuously running in a wheel. The only time that I have been in a physical altercation was once in middle school, several one-on-one brawls in the academy, and when I had to apprehend Jimmy Collins from beating up a bartender outside of Fenway. This was my first time shooting my duty weapon. Of all the years that my bullets rested within my magazine or when fired for practice at the range, this was the first time that one of them was officially utilized.

I thought about the sixth commandment for some reason and when I learned about the full ten in one of my Sunday school classes. It's been a long time since I've thought about that.

"Bo, you okay?" Burkes said as he crouched down next to me. I was moved up against my car after everybody arrived. I wanted to stay away from forensics that way they could get their procedural photographs for the record.

I found myself running my fingers through my hair when I said, "Yeah, just pondering if killing somebody means I'm to be cursed forever now."

Burkes put his hand on my shoulder, giving me a look I'd never seen before. His eyebrows looked relaxed, along with an enduring grin. "Listen to me. You did not murder that son of a bitch. You defended yourself, and that is all there is to it. Look, we checked his phone and the person who called him was not his wife. His call history laid out that his wife hasn't called him in two days. The number that called him was blocked. We called TTS and are trying to triangulate the exact location of the caller. However, you know how long that takes."

The Technological Tracking Service was a special tax-funded entity ran by the state that took as long as several days or even a week to get back to law enforcement about a cell phone's location. I knew who called him, maybe not him exactly but I knew who caused this.

"It was him, Burkes."

"Who?"

"Zaccardi, I don't know how he got Warner to do this but it's him."

"What? That's an accusation that would make the chief choke. You know how many cops point the finger in his direction, would be like another fly wanting attention."

"I'm serious, who the hell else could hire someone in this town to take out a cop?"

"Look, I'm not trying to say that you are not a desirable young detective, but why would Francis Zaccardi order a hit on you by a cop that he supposedly 'paid' off? It's not like the dead kid was his son and you were screwing up the investigation."

"I visited him this morning cap. I must have pissed him off."

"Yeah, Davey told me about you going over there. Brave or stupid, can't figure out what you are yet."

"Be a shame if you thought less of me cap, I thought we were just starting to get along."

Burkes released a chuckle and stood back up. "Look, you've got to be cleared before you can get back on this case, you know that right? This is your first shooting and the press is going to be all over this. As you can see, the sea

51

of trickery and illusion is already out there with their cameras plugged up. I'll try and have you cleared Monday so you can get back to work. Do you understand?"

"What about my note from this morning, could be something, I can't let anything to chance on this. We've got more press on this than before. A dead boy and now a dead cop, this is more than I have ever been a part of and I want to do it right."

"A young guy in this kind of light can lose it and this investigation has already been screwed. We'll have Riosky and Dalworth on this with you. They'll take over from here so you can have the rest of the weekend to recover."

"Listen to me, keep me on this. Look at me I'm fine," I said as I stood up to face Burkes. I swiped some dirt off my shoulder and looked at him as stern as I could. "I can't tell you what to do but I can ask. This boy needs justice."

"Mike, you know I can't."

Burkes was serious. His eyes did not budge. It was like beating a dead horse to get my way and I knew the more I pleaded the more of a rookie it made me look.

"Forget about it, I know what your answer is going to be anyways. Call me if anything happens. I'm going home."

Chapter 10

"Drive... Drive until the pain has run its course. Take control of the road and use it to heal whatever is wrong. Trust me, you will be tested. Just remember where you can go."

My dad used to tell me that all the time. Anytime I was struggling with a class at college or when I lost a basketball game back in my AAU days, my dad always knew how to calm me down. I still drive to calm my nerves now. I drove the day that Jessica left me. That drive could have gone better, now that I'm thinking about it.

After one of the officers let me out of the scene, I decided to drive for a while to loosen up. Burkes offered for an ambulance to take me home but I refused. After some of the paramedics evaluated me, they cleared me to drive as there was no sign of any hearing impairment after the gunshot. I was honestly shocked by how fast I got out of there. Guess it would have been different if I took a bullet myself.

I did not know what to do. This boy's investigation had to be put on hold because some sleeper agent of Zaccardi's tried to take me out. Maybe he knew that I might survive the attack and that I would have to be put on a temporary leave from duty. Does not matter, dead or not dead, Zaccardi was getting what he wanted. What if Warner was not even on Zaccardi's payroll? What if Warner killed Sam Hatkins for some reason...? That doesn't make sense as Sam was not killed with a wire. The killer used their inner arm to suffocate him. Still, it could have been him.

I looked into my rearview mirror and lifted my jaw. I could see a purple line stretch across my neck right below my Adam's apple. My neck ached as it looked as if I just survived a hanging in the Old West. Death tried to get me for the first time and I guess he was ticked so he left a mark.

I checked my watch to see that it was past two in the afternoon. The message from the box said to meet at three. I should still go, except Burkes knows that, which is why he most likely is going to send Riosky or Dalworth if he is seriously considering the note to be a lead.

As I approached a stoplight, I saw a white Tahoe almost run a red light right beside me, but the driver narrowly made it through the yellow. I checked my phone to see that Delahine had sent me a message asking if I'm alright. I was going to text him back, but everything felt like it was moving at the pace that couldn't be avoided. Even as I'm sitting in my car, it seems like this case is throwing Boston onto a moving treadmill and I just feel like it is up to me to stop it. Zaccardi is hiding something and I can bet he will not speak a word to anybody besides his own people. He seemed pretty adamant or unwilling to reveal Thomas's whereabouts. There had to be something there.

This case was too important to let go. Sorry Burkes, time to put the rule book down for once.

*

The Paul Revere Mall was more of a tourist attraction than a shopping complex compared to the urban giants within places in New York City. Freedom Trail links everything together as it stretches all the way from Hanover Street all the way to the Old North Church. There were trees along the sides of the path with mulch surrounding each of their foundations. Most of the mulch found its way along the stone path, most likely from kids playing in it or the wind having its fun.

To commemorate Paul Revere's famous midnight ride from Boston to Lexington, a statue was built on the trail signifying his true act of patriotism. Thankfully, it was a Saturday with at least eighty people walking around.

I managed to position myself along Unity Street behind one of the old apartment buildings overlooking the trail. I was in a perfect spot, as an old tree that had lost all of its leaves was directly in front of me. I looked around to see if Riosky and Dalworth had arrived, if not, I was planning on making my way to the fountain and wait for my mysterious messenger. After waiting a few minutes and checking my watch to see that it was two minutes past three, I could see the average build of Dalworth show up without his partner. He was dressed in his casual civilian attire. His brown zip-jacket did not flatter his rather obtrusive figure already. He had his badge attached to a chain necklace that rested on his chest. Poor guy really needs to shave that mustache off as well.

I guess Burkes has the chief crawling up his ass about this case. It's not like him to assign somebody to a probable wild goose chase. Yet, here Dalworth was.

Dalworth was one of the vets of the department and most likely felt like a cog in the wheel with this assignment. The last bust I remember him having were two boys from Southie who had armed a convenient store at two o'clock in the morning. The man was a methodology guru, a straight by-the-book guy like me. Today did not seem like one of those precautionary days.

Dalworth arrived at the fountain and waited a few minutes before sitting down. He pulled his smartphone out and started to occupy himself with it like a young teenager. I looked around to see if anyone was approaching him or showing indication that they were the person who sent me the message. I doubt the four-year-old playing with a few pigeons could have pickpocketed my wallet.

About twenty minutes had passed with no one standing out. Dalworth appeared to be impatient as he was on the phone with someone. I could hear his voice all the way from behind the corner of the apartment building. With no one showing up to see Dalworth made something clear. Whoever sent the message only wanted to see me and no one else. Who could this be? I would hope it's not somebody trying to get me out into the open to show me a bullet. Sure, I've made my enemies over the past few years but hopefully nothing worthy of a murder attempt. I wish I didn't know what it felt like.

My dad always had a gun in our house, tucked right between his pressed shirts and his work slacks. A Smith & Wesson revolver that only saw the light of day for just five seconds every morning. His revolver always seemed to be the topic of conversation whenever violence came up. He spoke of his gun as an opportunity for self-reputation. Everyone has a reputation that others know about, in that, there is a certain opinion about a person that follows them because of the choices they make. My father always spoke of self-reputation and how someone sees themselves, regardless of what everyone else thinks. The gun represented a chance to prove himself when the time came around. It made me think about what happens when a person is faced with an altercation and how they will react. Act or fall, is how my father put it. Look at me now pops.

Dalworth looked to be at a dead end. I decided to get back in my car and head back when my phone buzzed. Burkes was calling.

"Mind telling me why you're not home Dirty Harry?" he said, sounding a bit irked.

"Feeling overprotective today, Cap?"

"Don't play with me. You know why I'm calling. You just shot someone Mike, you should be home, watching the tube. The Sox are on, getting the shit kicked out of them by Tampa but you should be watching. Where are you?"

"I can't go home yet."

"I'm not asking."

"I refuse to be cooped up letting my thoughts take control."

"Mike, when a man sees another man die in front of them, the feeling isn't anything that can be expected. Your father never knew this feeling, but I knew him well enough to understand that he would have needed time to get himself together. His cases were not easy to handle, as you would know. But you were there, you killed a man. Mike, go home and at least put my mind at ease, for him."

I could feel the grip of my phone become tighter when it occurred to me, maybe he was right. It was not like an 80s movie where the hero could kill and then remain clear in the head the rest of the day. Images of Warner have been flooding my mind over the past few hours. His clean-shaven face harbored by the bluish veins protruding from his forehead and neck as he tried to break my own. What if he had overcome me? What void would have I left behind? My father would have nothing…

"Mike? Did you hear me?" Burkes said.

"Yeah, I heard you. I'll be home soon."

Chapter 11

Maybe Burkes knew but perhaps he didn't. Home was not an option yet. I felt bad for going behind his back, but this case could not be left stranded. He has to understand.

I arrived out front of Sam Hatkins' house on Endicott Street, a narrow space with overpowering brick apartments that made it feel like the walls were closing in. According to the Hatkins' housing record, I found back at the station, Sam's home was a mid-income apartment with rent being just over a thousand a month. After committing a questionable parallel parking job, I got out of my car and headed across the street.

There was a BPD cruiser in front of the apartment building. Crime scene protection was paramount with a case like this and hopefully, the officers on duty had not been informed of my recent leave. I jogged up the steps and came to Apartment 314. The hallway smelled of cigarettes and some odor that I could only relate to expired milk. Crime scene tape had been cut off into the shape of an "X" on the door.

After taking a deep breath, I proceeded to give it a knock.

"This is a crime scene for the Boston Police Department, if you are not police personnel step away from the door," a sharp and roughish voice answered from behind the door.

"It's Detective Bowen. Did they inform you that I'm the lead?"

"Detective Bowen, sir, come on in."

The voice sounded more familiar now, and my assumption was clear after the door was quickly opened.

Officer Gonzalez was standing in front of the door in his impeccably shined uniform. Weighing close to 250 pounds, Gonzalez was a prolific athlete as he served as a right guard on our department's football team. His cheeks were on the chubby side, but still managed to reveal sizable dimples. Thankfully, he didn't seem too shocked to see me. Burkes must still be busy looking into Warner's background connections to Zaccardi. Plenty of rap sheets to go around, I probably should be looking into those as well once I'm done here.

"Gonzalez, nice to see you again, how's the wife?" I said, after entering what appeared to be the Hatkins' living room.

"Full of complaints and beautiful as usual, thanks for asking. Thought you would have made your way over here last night, the media is all over this one," Gonzales said, after stumbling with his words from the start.

"Yeah, I got caught up following a few leads. A case like this requires all the attention, being my first child murder and all."

Then came the question I was waiting for.

"Hey, Mike?" Gonzalez said, as a hint of confusion followed his words.

"Yes, sir?"

"Shouldn't you be at home or something? Dispatch called a shooting over the radio and my patrol sergeant told me you were involved. How are you still on this right now?"

"Only one shot was fired, struck the guy in his liver. Just a bruise around my neck. Nothing tragic enough to take me away. Besides, I heard you were over here contaminating the place, had to preserve my crime scene ya know?" I lifted my neck to show him my bruise.

"Shit, I can't even imagine. Well, check anything you like, nothings been touched too much."

With that, I turned my focus to the apartment. It looked homey enough, yet still uninhabitable for my tastes. The floor was covered in a mustard-colored carpet, along with brown furniture that looked to be almost a decade old. Photographs were in an unorthodox fashion as whoever took the time to place them in their frames did a lackluster job. A picture of Sam was crumbled in one corner, leaving one corner showing the white background of the frame. Next to it was a photograph of his parents. His father had a crooked smile with a mole right below his left eye, along with a full head of brown hair that covered his earlobes. His mother, looking more petite and thin for her age, had long blonde hair with several freckles splattered around her cheekbones. His mother's eyes were painfully gray below the lashes. Parents appeared to be nice people, judging from the fact that they weren't wearing baggy clothes nor had any visible illegitimate tattoos.

I made my way through the back hallway and found myself opening the door to Sam's bedroom. The creak of the door matched the damaged hinges to my left. His carpet, thankfully different from the living room, was some shade of tan. His room was covered with movie and video game posters. It seemed that Sam had a knack for action movies as John McClane, aka Bruce Willis, was staring back at me from a 'Die Hard' poster hanging above his dresser. On top of his dresser was a miscellaneous assortment of pocket change, homework, and some candy. After examining the rest of his room, it dawned on me that I had no clue what to look for.

Sam Hatkins was a twelve-year-old kid who barely got to experience life. He was in the coasting phase where he did not have to deal with the monotony and hardworking turmoil of adulthood. He had no receipts, no planners for me to discover what his next move of the day was. Most of my other investigations led me straight to a victim or a suspect's calendars that helped me obtain the groundbreaking circumstantial evidence I needed for a case.

I sat down on the bed and decided to bury my head into my palms. Just as I lowered my head, Gonzalez had appeared in the doorway. Just as I heard his footsteps, I looked down to see a black substance sprinkled about towards my feet. Pencil shavings?

"It true that you have a clearance rate as good as Humphrey Bogart?" he asked with a chuckle.

"Depends on what constitutes the success of a case. I definitely don't have the dames dangling at my fingerprints like he did."

"Still, you caught Britt Stogner last year. The smug office equipment salesman who beat the shit out of his wife and strangled the man she was cheating on. He almost moved to New York until you found the storage unit, he was hiding out in. Nice justice that day."

"Yeah, I remember. Not like this though, seems everything has changed with this."

"Teens die every day. Though…," after shifting his position and scratching the back of his neck, "not all of them are strangled in the middle of the day."

"Just keep doing your part. That's all anyone can ask."

Gonzalez nodded and went back into the other room with his partner. Thankfully, there were many good men working for the department. The problem is, manpower isn't enough sometimes. Intuition was favored here, and hopefully, a colossal load of luck.

Sam Hatkins seemed to be a smart young kid. His collection of books was far advanced for the typical middle school student. His pieces of literature included *Catcher in the Rye*, *Moby Dick*, even a copy of the poem *Iliad*. It was like sifting through a library full of books that were read by my literary analysis professor back at BU. I could only assume his grade point average ranked high compared to the other students in his class. After examining a few more of his books, I tried to push one of them back into the bookcase but felt a bit of resistance when doing so. After trying to wiggle the book a few times, I noticed that about three of the books seemed to be sticking out a few centimeters more than the others.

After removing the three books from the shelf, I noticed a wad of green paper shoved towards the back of the bookcase. The wad was revealed to be several hundred-dollar bills and a few fifties crumbled up. Quite a lot of cash for a twelve-year-old, as there appeared to be over a thousand dollars sitting here. Maybe there was more lying around somewhere. It appeared that he and his friends had some outside interests rather than playing ball going on. There were a few local restaurants that pay kids under the table for work. Might have to ask around.

Whatever he did, his friends were somehow the key to this. If I could talk to them, his whereabouts before he died would be put into perspective. All is next is to find...

A loud cracking sound, then a sudden thud entered the room with great volume. Before I even knew it, my service weapon was already out and being pointed straight at the window directly next to Sam's bed. A large crack in the glass could be seen towards the bottom left of the window. After jolting over Sam's bed, I made my way over to the window and looked outside onto the street after almost slicing my hand lifting the sill upwards. A few people were already observing the broken window by the time I looked out.

"Mike! What happened, are you okay?" I could hear Gonzalez say as he entered the room.

His words barely crept into my eardrum, as I was too focused on looking around outside. After looking around my car and Gonzalez's cruiser, my neck jerked to the right to see a pair of feet running towards an intersection. The figure appeared to be a boy with jeans but any chance of seeing his face was lost after he hung a right down another street. Could that have been?

"Mike, hey, Mike."

"I thought I could catch a glimpse of the guy."

"And?"

"Nothing promising, he ran into another intersection before I could get a look. Have any of us who are nearby to be on the lookout for a young kid in jeans running around. Have somebody check the cameras for any of the shops on the street and next southwest of here. Now, hurry!"

Gonzalez's partner quickly ran out of the room relaying the message through the radio. His footsteps could be heard until he left the apartment.

"What was that about Mike?" Gonzalez said, as he holstered his Glock. I didn't even notice that he had it out of his holster.

"Can't say I know," I said. Might as well start with what was thrown in Sam's room. I moved towards the end of the bed and found something on the ground. It was a brick. Two ends of duct tape were pressed to its side, leading me to believe that something was attached to the other side. I lifted it to find something particularly familiar.

"COP" was once again written on a piece of paper within my possession. The word 'cop' was followed by:

'Last chance, don't send someone else this time
Dock at Prince Street Park...8:00 PM
You don't need my name yet'

Pretty persistent. *You don't need my name yet*. What did that mean?

"What is it?" Gonzalez said, after taking a few steps closer to me.

"A message from our runaway. Seems that someone wants to talk to me pretty badly," I said while simultaneously crumpling the note up and placing it into my wallet.

"Not the best way to make a house call. That thing could have clocked you and put you in a bed for a few hours."

"Must be lucky." As I turned to face Gonzalez, I noticed more of the black substance on the white panel of the window. Definitely not pencil shavings.

"When was the last time you were in this room?"

"Probably an hour. Why?"

"Somebody's been in here."

"What? What makes you think that?" Gonzalez's complexion went from suntanned to a reddish pigment in a matter of seconds.

"Black substance on the window and the floor looks to match the fire escape outside. The crime scene would have picked that up by now and marked it. It has to be recent. Did you or your partner go out on the fire escape by chance?"

"Dammit. No, no we did not. Want me to contact Burkes to tell him we have a breach?"

"Mark it in your report and I'll let him know. Also, call crime scene to come back to see if they can get any trace evidence on our perpetrator, if there was one. Depending on how bad this is, I'll put in a good word for ya. You're a good cop, people mess up. It's what we do."

"You're telling me, let me ask you something."

"Whatcha got?"

"You going to hold off from telling Burkes about the note as well? Heard you're not even supposed to be here."

I froze. Burkes must have reached him somehow and informed him that I should be nowhere near here. Time to see if a suspension is coming.

"Guess the gig is up huh?"

"Look, Mike, I get it. A kid's dead and you feel like you need to do something about it. If I was in your position, I would be doing the same thing. Both of our asses will be on the line if I go through with this, but this kind of thing helps the conscious."

"Duly appreciated. What about the rook who knows I'm here?"

"Training officer has its perk sometimes. It's simple."

"That is?"

"Baffle with bullshit, my friend."

Chapter 12

Men like Delahine and Gonzalez were a godsend these days in police work. Walking a beat or patrolling a neighborhood used to be and is most certainly still to some cops, a monotonous routine that warrants the worst kind of apathetic behavior. Most of the time the media and the public believe we are crooks. I wish for one second, they could observe the work, men like Delahine and Gonzalez do. Then they will see how true courage works.

After checking my watch, I still had a few hours until it was around eight. Gonzalez was unsure whether Sam's friends lived nearby or not. The issue at hand seemed dangerous. I could not determine if his friends were in any danger or if they were the danger from this recent crime against their friend. Most kids would be scared; however, this was Boston. Young boys here develop their own sense of pride and belief that they are untouchable. Unfortunately for me, I did not grow up feeling that way.

As a young boy growing up in Boston, I had my friends just like any other. Baseball and basketball were the roots of friendship. Companions and enemies were made on the field of sport whenever a catch was made, or an unruly foul was committed. The best kind of time spent was late at night when our parents did not know where we were. Parental punishment was certain, yet we still disobeyed. We snuck out, just to sneak out. The thrill of the night air, the sense of disobedience fueled our longing for a chance to getaway. We had questions that could not be answered by our parents. We could only wonder of what was to come, what kind of future waited for us when we graduated school. Except, different from all of my friends, there was a deep anxiety that rested within me. No matter how much thrill I would find in the night, something always told me that it would not last. Time would evolve, catch up, and take it all away. The times that I enjoyed the most were just a blink of an eye. My feeling would settle after every night, the feeling of something holding on and revealing itself just as I was at the peak of my happiness. I just hope that Sam enjoyed his youth more than I ever could.

My youth tends to creep into my mind sometimes. This case is...something different. The field might offer some more insight. Many times, I've ventured back to the scene of the crime in hopes of catching something I missed before. I looked towards my car and started to head that way.

As soon as I took one step onto the sidewalk, I heard the whistle of the wind blow and the sound of two car doors opening and then shutting. To my left approached two men in some beat-up gym clothes that consisted of Adidas workout pants and some off-brand zip-up jacket. They looked like they were set to appear in their own show.

"Detective Bowen," the man with a widow's peak haircut said.

"Yes?"

"Not to make your day any worse than it has been, but its time you came with us."

Taken back, I glared at the man and felt my fingers brush against my jeans towards my waist. The other gentleman with a poor dress sense took notice and revealed a bulge coming from his right-side jacket pocket. Message received.

"Not sure what you mean. My ride home is right over there. Think you have the wrong handsome detective."

"Swing and a miss smart ass, Zaccardi said you might be like this," he said after wiping his nose for a moment.

"Now that you know who sent us, sounds to me you better nip your little ass together and hop in the car."

"Well, you guys are really nice. The offer is tempting and hard to pass up. What are the odds that you'll *whack* me once I get in there?"

"Depends on how smart your mouth keeps running."

"Good point."

Widow's peak motioned me towards their black sedan that had a cracked windshield and several dents sprouted upon its hood. It looked as if their car was continuously bombarded by acorns whilst sitting underneath the world's most dangerous oak tree. Once inside the car, I found myself sitting directly behind the passenger seat with my friend widow's peak to my left. Just as the other man sat in the driver seat, the world had gone black.

"Really, a mask? What are you guys trying to pull?" I asked.

"Look, we may dress poorly, doesn't mean our brains work the same," widow's peak replied.

As my eyesight adjusted to my newfound darkness, I could not help but wonder if my father was ever taken in this type of circumstance. His cases lead up to the brink of sanity, where every case brought upon a new line that might be crossed. It wouldn't surprise me if it did, nothing made that man quit his job. This could have happened to him every week and he would still show up to work every Monday morning smelling of aftershave and a fresh bravado.

"Will there at least be some entertainment?"

After a quick pause, the no-name driver took a left turn headed down some unknown street. Just as I reached for my sock and I heard him speak for the first time. "Sure, the Red Sox are on the radio. They're still getting the shit beat out of them by Tampa."

"So, I've heard."

"Anything else you would like to add?"

"Not really but thank you, at least you guys know how to…

The impact was quick and unexpected. My cheek felt it first as I found myself crashing down into the seat.

*

The field was radiant. I could see fresh lilies growing from the brightest grass I had ever seen. The sun was bright, much brighter than the one tucked behind the clouds that constantly surrounded Boston in the fall. Non-polluted air filled my nostrils as I continued to walk up the hill. No cigarette smoke, no body odor from the local inhabitants of the neighborhood made everything perfect.

At the top of the hill stood a figure. After several more steps, my eyes caught a glimpse of what looked like a woman standing in the middle of the field looking up. Jess?

I found myself starting to run. My pace was light but steady. Jess's auburn hair mixed wonderfully with the plethora of flowers at her feet. My jog remained steady until I felt my foot bump into something. When I stopped to look down, nothing was there. The grass went dark and turned into shades of blue. The day had quickly become night. Jess was still standing there looking up. Her eyes were beautiful as almost every star in the sky reflected off of them.

"Remember doing this Mike? We used to look up here and ponder what it all meant. Remember what it was like to sit here and match everything together?" she said, her voice was as calm as the wave of an ocean.

"How could I forget, not a single moment was wasted looking up at the stars."

"When was the last time you did this?"

"Not since you. Not since you left me that day. Tell me, what happened that caused you to…

As I looked down from the stars, Jess was gone. The star-crossed sky was gone. The lovely hill sprinkled with flowers and grass had dissipated. My feet felt hard now, the soles of my shoes were now pressed against concrete. My toes felt nothing but air as I looked to see that I was on the edge of a dock. A body of water rested below me as I quickly caught my balance and took a step back. The temperature took a sudden drop as the wind blew most of the hairs on my neck all the way up. Coldness had leaked into my veins as I could feel myself, and what felt like the whole area around me became tenebrous.

The water below was as black as the darkest ink. I saw no reflection, no sign of life, just a riveting sense of mortality. It was calm. The kind of unnerving calm that felt like something was coming. Before I could fathom what came next, several beams of white light appeared around me.

I turned to see a pair of headlights as it rapidly became dark once more…

I woke up to another light. A single bulb hanging from the ceiling. The room was a compact space with a few sewage pipes protruding from the wall to my left and a desk with several piles of unorganized documents across the top. It smelled of oil and liquor, such as if a bottle of tequila had been spilled somewhere and was never mopped up. My mind raced to where I could be. The basement of Zaccardi's shop? Perhaps some forgotten room in a bar that Zaccardi owns?

I attempted to get up but did not even recognize that my hands were bound and tightly knotted around the back of the chair. The texture of my binds felt like the type of rope used to open and detract sails in the Boston Harbor. Tight and relentless the ropes were, as I discovered after attempting to free myself. Before I decided to tug at them again, I could hear a door open behind me.

In walked a shadow. It was long and thin as it made its way closer and closer to me. As the footsteps became louder, I could feel their presence to my right as someone was getting closer. I chose not to turn my head. Another blow to my face did not sound appetizing. Then the shadow spoke.

"'Bout time you woke up. Haven't you taken a hit before? I mean, Jesus, you've been out for quite a while. Could have sworn you police-type knew how to take an unexpected blow. Being that you are in a profession of unexpected shitstorms."

The voice of an unwanted familiarity.

Zaccardi entered my peripherals with a yellow grin. Quite the opposite of a long and thin shadow, his somewhat large size never felt as intimidating as it did now. It remained in decent strength despite being over fifty-years-old.

"What's the matter? No smart-aleck remark this time?" he said, as he entered his hand into his side pocket.

"Hold on, I'm thinking. This art takes a bit of work," I replied.

"There it is! The boys said you were a chatterbox. Not the annoying kind, don't get me wrong, just the right kind of amusement."

"Glad that I can still impress."

"You? Impressive? I'd say lucky. Lucky as in our mayor stepping in dog shit after a long day of screwing the people over using below average diplomacy. But, if anything, I would say that you have shown you can handle yourself."

"Warner was yours?"

He didn't seem fazed when I changed the topic. "One of mine? Ha, you make it sound like I lead a cult. Yes, I'm planning a big night where we all drink Kool-Aid and we all die in hopes of a better destiny. Warner was not one of mine. He just did as he was told."

"He was a cop, a man with a family. It's hard to believe what you are telling me."

"You speak of cops as if they are not flawed in their nature? Geez, Mike. You can't be that stubborn and naïve. Your father taught you better than that. He breathed police corruption in like a new air freshener for that unmarked cruiser of yours. He was aware of it, dealt with it, and even used it to secure himself as one of the best criminal lawyers Boston had ever seen. Even a guy like me, who dealt with the lower-class of our society, knew about him."

"Leave my father out of this. What did you do to Warner's family?"

"His family? They are sitting on a nice donation from yours truly. Warner and I had a little chat. I sat him down, in a room quite like this and told him exactly the way life works."

Zaccardi decided it would be a good idea to pause and show off the opposite of an amiable grin.

"Are you going to make me ask you?" I said.

"You could beg? Hell, I might even confess if you do. But I'll take a pass. Warner was a good sport about it ya know? I told him flat out, if you kill this guy, I won't kill you or your family, plus you'll have a nice retirement fund waiting under your pillowcase. No tooth, no money. We're supposed to work hard for our everlasting wealth am I right? Damn, I'm good."

"You sure are full of yourself, aren't you? Sorry, I meant with your personality and not the cannolis stuffed underneath your waistline there. I know how much you don't like to be confus..."

I found myself falling towards the floor. Zaccardi had charged towards me and knocked me clear across my cheek. The quick pain remained for what seemed like several minutes.

"Shit, you fell over. Let's hope your legs work as well as your mouth."

Chapter 13

"I can do this all day."

Zaccardi repeated the phrase several times before leaving out the same way he came in. Lucky for me, he decided to flip the light switch covering the room in black. He left me on the floor, laying in what he hoped was a state of weakness. I did feel frightened after all. I've never been in this type of predicament and it felt quite surreal that it was happening. My mind wandered to Maverick and the time my father locked him in the pantry for excusing himself in the house. The darkness of that room and this room had to be synonymous. I felt like I was in a scene torn from a novel where the villain tries to leave his malevolent mark on the hero. Impressions make a difference; patience means no difference here.

I tried to think of why I was even here. The coldness of the brick against my face made it easy to think. He tried to kill me…for what reason? Could one of his men have killed Sam and Zaccardi was trying to cover for him? He was a kid. Kids are not supposed to die so young. What could he have possibly done to disrupt Zaccardi's life of criminality?

My bounds felt tighter with all of the pressure falling to the ground. My body felt trapped by the chair but my mind felt hindered by the darkness of the room and the horror of the unknown. Escape was of definite concern.

Just as I attempted to roll around to dismantle the wooden chair, the door had busted open. Zaccardi sped through the door, flicked on the light, and began speaking with an upbeat tone.

"Dammit, look, I'm going to have to switch gears for a moment. You need answers and I was almost too late. You should be dead right now but you're not. However, suddenly out there, something hit me. What's that word?

"An…"

"An epiphany! That's it! As you know, since you asked about him. Thomas did not go to school today and though you must have thought he was home, he was not. My son, though troublesome and precious to me, is having a hard time revealing where he is. It seems that I have something here, meaning you, that might help me."

"Parents lose kids all the time, maybe he's hiding from your parental control."

"Damn, still acting smart even though I'm offering you a way out. Never thought I'd agree with a man who almost put a dent into my cheek.

"Okay, okay. You need me to find your son?" I said.

"Bingo."

"Why would I do that for you?" My neck was starting to become strained from the uncomfortable angle I was in. It was leaving me quite unsatisfied.

"Now, listen carefully because I know you won't believe it, but let it settle in that college-educated brain of yours. I had nothing to do with Thomas's friend being killed. I'm not into that kind of business. Kids are too young to be maturely punished. Thomas might be in the same kind of danger. You do this for me, I'll never send another person to try and you know…end your time in Boston."

Zaccardi's beady eyes did not flinch. His wrinkles did not twitch nor did his mouth pitch a grin. My mind fought itself from believing him, but my defenses were failing. Nothing was true without facts, but I tried to label it as an assumption. Zaccardi could be on the opposite side of wrongdoing for the first time in a long time. I couldn't believe where my mind was taking me.

Look at me now dad.

"Alright, where do I start?"

*

Widow's peak and his friend dropped me off right back at Sam's apartment. Remarkably, I was not kidnapped for as long as I thought. That felt 'weird' to contemplate.

Zaccardi told me that Thomas and his friends generally scattered themselves all around North End. He claims he's sent several of his men to look for them but failed to generate any results. My first thought was to contact Burkes and let him know of my rather quick kidnapping experience. Yet, if I did that, any attempts to look for Thomas would be shut down.

Zaccardi mentioned that Thomas and his friends were as rebellious as modern-day teenagers could be. Spray painting cop cars, confiscating cigarettes from any storeowner they could persuade, and playing ball at any of the parks around, were just a few of the activities they indulged in. Some of the places that he listed were: Langone Park, an alley near Regina Pizzeria, Zaccardi's own shop, and Prince Street Park.

Prince Street Park, what if? Thomas. The park was directly next to Langone, an interesting coincidence.

I checked my pockets for my keys and found them. As I sat down, started the engine, while also ignoring my scalding hot seats, I felt one of my phone's buzz. My work one buzzed and a number I did not recognize appeared. Strange as in most of the numbers that I have, are saved because they are fellow officers or other work associates.

"Detective Bowen," I said.

"Mike?"

It was Jess. After everything, her voice could not have been more welcomed.

"Yes, hey, Jess. How are you?"

"I'm doing well. I got your number from the card, didn't know if you remembered."

"Of course, is everything alright?"

"Well, being is it that today I'm off from work. I was watching TV and saw that there was a shooting today involving an officer. I'm embarrassed but I was just calling to see if it was you."

I caught a natural smile coming across my face.

"No, no, you shouldn't feel embarrassed. I appreciate it. I'm not really supposed to talk about it."

"That's right, it's probably classified. I thought it was a weird question."

"It was me."

"What?"

I took a few moments before saying it again, "The shooting, I was there."

"Oh, my goodness, Mike. I don't think I have the words to say how horrible that must have been. This is probably foolish of me to ask, but how are you feeling?"

"Today's been a day. I don't have the words either. The world felt like it was here one second and then I never knew if I was going to see it again during the whole thing."

"BU feels like another lifetime huh?"

"No kidding. Surprised you even remember that time. With how successful you are, I was sure that time was nothing but an afterthought for you."

"Hey Mike, you never did get an apology for that day... It honestly was the hardest thing that I've ever had to do."

"Jess, I know that I felt like I knew you pretty well back then. But whatever it was, you had to get out. I know that I was difficult, please, don't feel like you have to apologize. I enjoyed my time with you more than you could ever know but I had to swallow the pill that you wanted other things."

"You were great. Don't let what I did fool you. Listen, Mike, is there any way we could meet tonight? There is something you need to know."

My stomach felt like someone's hand had taken hold of it and turned it upside down.

"Tonight? I have a lead on my case. But if it does not last too long, I will definitely stop by. That didn't sound too desperate did it?"

"No, not at all," she said with a chuckle.

"Great, I'll give you a call. Any place you want to meet or is your place fine?"

"My place is fine. Remember where it was?"

"How could I forget?"

"Now you're coming off as a little desperate…"

"Yeah, that thought probably should have stayed in my head."

"Good luck with your lead tonight."

"Ha, thanks. Hey, Jess?"

"Yeah?"

"Thanks for calling."

"Well, I did tell you not to be a stranger."

With that, we said goodbye. I heard the click of her ending the calling and instantly wished she didn't. I could feel her warmth through the phone, a sense I haven't felt since we were together. This damn case. I would be with her right now if it was not for this insufferable thing.

Sam. He was important, this case had weight. Not just the weight it has on the public, but the certainty that those who choose to harm the harmless should be brought to a justifiable end. I had to fight for him, if not who? His parents have not returned any of my calls and were nowhere to be found. I could not fathom the conversation that I would be having with them as soon as I meet them.

Jess was back in my life but, she had to wait.

Chapter 14

I called Delahine while I was in the car. I needed his help as I'm sure Burkes had somebody from the Crime Reporting Unit monitoring my clearance. I needed to check if there were any calls for service during the time Sam was allegedly strangled. Routine alarm checks or any officer notes related to any kind of call for service near Langone could be crucial. It was old school, but my old training officer relied on the basics. With all the new databases open to officers, there has to be someone who recorded something of use.

Delahine agreed to print out everything he could find and would meet me a block away from Prince Street Park in an hour. He was smart, and I hope there is something for him to find.

I parked my car in an un-too-familiar place. The parking lot across from Mass General unsurprisingly hasn't changed a bit. The routine was all too common. The smell of freshly mopped floors, pseudomonas, and the all too common bowel movements filled the air as I walked past the front desk. Several families were in the lobby, sitting in the maroon couches where more have been before. Two Samsung TVs were attached to the walls where a few people were trying to distract themselves from the predicament before them. I noticed the magazines along the shelves were untouched. Before I made it to the front desk, I noticed a man sitting in a maroon chair facing the opposite direction towards the door. His skin was pale, a color closely related to the walls in the room. He wore a gray suit, recently ironed with an impressive stitching pattern across his shoulders. My attention went to his fingers as all of them were interlocked except for his thumbs. His thumbs continued to rotate around each other. His reservations could be seen with every rotation of his thumbs. I recognized that fear, that sense of unknowing what the next few moments had in store. I remember that feeling. I remember the chair where he now sits.

Margery was working this afternoon. She was a pleasant woman in her forties, with whitish blonde hair and a peaceful smile. Like most days, she joyfully welcomed me back as if she was meeting me for the first time.

"Afternoon, how's he doing today?" I said.

"A gentleman like always," Margery said as she waved me past the double doors into the Memory Unit. Her wave was cut short as I assume, she noticed the cut surrounding by bruising right under my eye. Not to mention the bruise that stretched across my neck. Not the image of a person who has everything put together.

"Everything alright today Mr. Bowen?"

"Just another day cleaning the streets. Tom working today?"

"Yes, he should be leaving soon. Hope you catch him!"

I thanked her and proceeded down the next hallway. A few nurses passed me carrying thick folders that I assumed were patient history files. Each nurse looked to be in a hurry, despite wearing their colorful scrubs which are supposed to be distinctive. I hung a left turn towards the rec. room and noticed Tom kneeling near one of the checkerboards laid over a wooden table. Several of the pieces had been knocked off.

"You know, the key is to keep them on the table, not scattered on the floor where someone could throw out their back picking them up," I said, picking up a few red pieces.

"Haven't you heard of fifty-two card pick-up? Takes a smart man to invent a new version of it," Tom replied.

"That rough today, huh?"

"Every day is the same. Ordinary isn't something I stumble upon much here. You?"

"Could be better."

"Least, you're not that poor officer involved in the shooting at the school. It's a shame, the resource officer tried to kill one of you guys. On school grounds, that's all kinds of psychotic. The worst part of it is, I guarantee that wasn't the first time those kids heard a gunshot."

Both of us got up at the same time and Tom froze before putting the pieces back on the table. I found his eyes falling below mine as I must have given him a tell-tale sign that something was wrong. "What happened to your neck? Wait, Mike. That wasn't you was it?"

The bruise across my neck must have been the reveal.

"Afraid so, pal."

"But why? What on earth did he try and kill you for?"

"You know that boy that was murdered yesterday?"

"Yeah, oh, God. You're on that case?" he said as he scratched his head a few times.

"Technically, I'm not supposed to be sharing any ongoing investigations with you but…

"But, it's me, the fearless orderly who takes care of your pops. Shit's heavy."

"You got it. Today's been a long day. I thought maybe seeing dad for a bit would clear me up before I get back out there."

"Out there? You were just involved in a shooting, isn't there some protocol where you can't be on active duty until you are cleared."

"Hawaii Five-O or Law and Order give you that?"

"The Wire. Don't lowball me like that."

"Ah, I see, might have to check it out. Anyways, where is he?"

"Right where you left him, he's still in his chair. Pretty quiet today, he was one of the calm things about today's storm." He pointed to my father sitting calmly in his chair.

"Do me a favor Tom. Try to get some good sleep tonight, can't be easy with your oversized forearms to get comfortable."

"An arm wrestle might teach you a lesson someday."

"Looking forward to it, my friend. Keep it stone."

"Keep it cold," he said as he started to head towards his locker room to pack his things.

My dad did not move a muscle as I approached him to sit down in the chair across from him. No cuts today after his shave, Tom must have been on it today. The stillness in his eyes was there. After almost a minute had passed, he looked right at me and formed what looked like a smile. His condition had worsened more rapidly than most here at Mass General. His doctor, a thin-waist graduate of Harvard who never ceased to show off his fraternity-like-stature, told me a few months ago that my father's case was one of great severity. Mr. Fraternity stated after my father's diagnosis, that he may live either four or eight years longer. If we were lucky, our signs would not be pointed in that direction. He could live up to twenty years longer. Also, he did inform me that my father's tendency to drink over eight times a week most likely increased his chances of contracting the disease. Reinforces my non-alcoholic behaviors. As soon as my fellow officers found out that I've never taken a swig of anything, it's been nothing but bar invitation after another.

"Hey, pops. Maybe you can understand what I'm saying, maybe not. I've got a pretty big case on my hands here. His name was Sam, he lived off of Endicott. His parents have been a no show ever since yesterday. I don't know what to make of it, it makes me want to knock the father's teeth out. Hear that? Sounded like you didn't it? I wonder what you would say if you could understand what I was going through. *Follow your leads, trust the facts.* The gut is a powerful ally if you utilize it correctly. I remember, you always used to say that. Well, my guts are telling me this will end how it ends. Murder has always been a random act, based on materialistic desire or human savagery. Shit…sounds like I've given up hasn't it?"

I looked out the window to see another building instead of the Charles River which rested on the other side. My mind raced to different conclusions. This case could be a random killing, even though the facts didn't support that. Sam's body was left out on the pitcher's mound of an incredibly visible baseball field. Hundreds of people walk by it every day. If Sam was murdered between three or four in the afternoon, someone would have seen him. Mr. Walker said he found the body around 8:30 PM, about an hour after the sun goes down. How did no one else see him?

Dad made a low grumbling sound that caught my eye. His inability to form proper sentences started several months ago after he progressed to the moderate stage. It hit hard. One day he was speaking to me like he did when I was a kid and then the next, he could only generate fragments. Fragments of thought. Tom told me he could still remember things but his ability to vocalize them was deteriorating.

Richard Bowen, criminal prosecutor for the Suffolk County District Attorney's Office, a man who used his mouth to convict hundreds, could not formulate a single word. His voice was one of the consistent variables of my life. When my mom left, he was the one I went to. As a kid, teenager, eager college student, and when I was a rookie, I sought his advice daily. It was just when he lost the ability to talk is when I figured something out. He taught me many things about how to go through life. It's just that there was one thing he or I never really brought up. I never learned how to live without him. I felt like a clock that lost its big hand leading the little hand to the next hour. Yet, with all of the trust and care I have for my father, I had to ask him about it.

"I know you don't understand what I'm saying but I have to ask. Why did you let it happen? What could have possibly been going on in your mind when you saw me there? Not once have you ever brought…

My phone started to go off repeatedly. I felt compelled to finish what I had to say but I knew nothing would come of it. He was too far gone. Delahine's name appeared on my phone after lifting it from my pocket. I answered after the fourth ring.

"Any overtime in stored for me after this?" he said, sounding like he was out of breath.

"Only if we solve it, I'm afraid. You sprinting over there or something?"

"Nah, just trying to make it out of records before any of the night shift see me gallivanting around the department with a bible of paperwork. I'm supposed to be off, remember?"

"Yes, you've managed to remind me twice in less than twenty seconds."

"Damn, didn't know we were keeping score. Anyways, I'm about to head to the spot. I'll park my car near the corner of Prince St. It's a black Altima with a Sox sticker near my left rear light. Feel free to compliment the wax if ya like."

"Gotta love cocky heroism, I'll do my best to notice it even if the sun is about to go down."

As Delahine hung up the phone, I was just about to stand up when my father decided to speak.

"Cold… I'm sorry for the cold."

I tried to decipher what he went but I assumed it was his usual erratic way of speaking. His shoulder felt bony as I rested my hand on him to say goodbye. I still say it aloud, makes it feel normal.

Chapter 15

"Zaccardi is one tough piece of steel. He's spent more time at Suffolk County Courthouse than most lawyers. If he's not there for his own doing, he's bailing one of his brothers out. How is it that our system lets these guys out after they've started more bar fights, drug overdoses, and family heartbreak than the curse of the Bambino?" Delahine said.

"I'm sure a baseball curse is behind this. Besides, our system is as flawed as the people in it. Just gotta wait for the right change to come," I said, flipping through another page of the call log sheet from Friday night.

"Guess that's a conversation that could last an entire career."

Quoting Delahine from earlier, he did bring what appeared to be a bible of paperwork just on the Zaccardi family. Their criminal history dated back to grade school. I told him about what happened earlier with Zaccardi. Delahine was too sharp to listen to any fabricated story about another fight that I've been in today unrelated to the case. Fresh bruises meant new problems. He already saw me at James Madison. He knew something else was going on.

His car was tidy. The sun was setting but I could make out the wax job. Inside smelled of apple and cinnamon, given there was car freshener mounted on one of the driver side air vents. His seats and floor were recently vacuumed. The man takes care of his car.

"When's the last time you washed this thing?" I said.

"Two days ago, when's the last time you washed yours?" Delahine said.

"I'd rather not say. Just wanted to check to see how well you wash your car. You know the spot that's most commonly missed?"

"Enlighten me, Detective."

"The fuel tank, most forget to pop open the gas cap and clean the inside."

"Ah, not a bad idea. Well, since we're getting personal here," he said, while motioning in his seat. "You got a girl?"

"Quick with the questions future detective."

"Hey, work isn't always just talking about work. Personality has to show some time."

"I agree," I said. "Had one before, just dating every now and then. You?"

"Haven't found anyone interesting yet."

"You sound pretty upset about that."

"Wouldn't mind having someone to talk to all the time. The way this case is going, I'll have to call you all the time. What happened to the one before the dating?"

"Left me back in college I'm afraid."

"You're kidding, damn. What happened?"

"Couldn't tell ya, it happened quicker than a snap. One of those things where you think you're happy and then it ends."

"Sorry to hear that. Any word from her since then?"

"Not till last night. She happens to live right across from Langone. Believe that?"

"Geez, you've got two things going on then."

"What do you mean?"

"Not only do you have this case to worry about, but the love of your life is back in the picture. Can't say that you're not under stress."

"Yeah, not sure how to feel about this one. The case keeps my mind busy."

"Distractions only last for so long."

I gave him a quick smirk and proceeded to look through the call log. He was right. Jess continued to roam my mind ever since I saw her. What a weekend this might be.

All department issued cruisers have a dispatch system that assists cops from call-to-call. The dispatcher takes a call from a citizen, records the information, and then assigns it to a car. Nifty system. That's what I thought when I first started, plus, whenever I was on patrol; I discovered that one could open up their own call for service without waiting for dispatch. Also, once a call was completed or transferred to someone else, I could type my part to show where I was and what I did. A built-in alibi recorded and ready for defense.

As for tonight, I was looking for more proactive policing, hopefully, one of the patrol officers recorded some helpful information in their notes. All I could find, near Langone Park, was a few larcenies from vehicle calls and one-armed robbery that occurred near Charter Street. An Officer Gibbins recorded chasing a white male, wearing a red sweatshirt and baggy pants, stealing a person's handbag while armed with a switchblade. Gibbins stated that the man took the handbag on Commercial Street but ended on Charter. Along with the assistance of Officer Royce, the two officers were able to wrestle him to the ground despite the heavy downpour of rain.

"Did it rain yesterday? Geez, it feels like Friday was such a long time ago. The robbery occurred around three-thirty, around the same time Sam would have been killed. Yet, no one saw this?"

"I never want to go near Ralphie Zaccardi, this mug was accused of sexual assault and possession of coke on the same night. The case was dismissed on a count of insufficient evidence. Somebody had to have been paid off," Delahine said while forming quotation marks with his hands in the air.

"Believe me, if the Zaccardis have anything to do with this I'll be the first one knocking on their door. Anything about Thomas in there that's interesting?" I said.

"Nothing. Says here he is a registered United States citizen and was born in Boston."

"Great, no juvenile reports or anything from DSS?

"Nada. What are you hoping to find?"

"I don't really know, honestly. I just feel like there is something missing. Something that will help us narrow the search."

"We might have to knock on the door of every sex offender within a five-mile radius to start. A young kid like Sammy Hatkins would have been a pretty nice prize for one of those sick pricks."

"Yeah, but look at how we found him. No signs of sexual abuse. No bruises around any other part of the body. No skin underneath the fingernails or lacerations of any kind. All Sam had was one thick purple line of bruising across his neck. Thicker than the one across mine right now."

"Sam could have resisted so much that the guy may have gotten spooked. The only way to fix the problem was to kill him before anything could happen. Depending on where he did it."

"But why leave him in the middle of the field? He must have dragged him out there later at night when it got dark. Forensics didn't find any trace evidence near any dumpsters or anything nearby where he could have been dumped for a few hours. But still…why was he displayed on the mound? Perhaps a message of some kind?"

"Is this how you got, Detective? You ask a lot of questions," Delahine said as he reached down into a small bag below the steering wheel. He presented a Coke within his hands as he offered me one as well. "Want one? We might be here a while, might as well caffeine it up."

I rarely drank soda, but he was right, fatigue was slowly catching up to me and I needed some kind of kick. "Sure, thanks."

"Don't worry about it, what are fellow crime fighters for?"

After taking a refreshing sip, I looked towards the street where a steady stream of cars was going by. The dock mentioned in the note was directly behind an under-developed school. There was no visible sign of the dock, but I knew where it was. I remember running along the crest of North End as a kid, exploring everything that I could find. Funny how some things just come full circle when you least expect it.

"You read much, Detective?" Delahine said, as he took a swig of his Coke.

"For recreation and not for work? Sure, I do when I make the time."

"Yeah, what genre?"

"Crime fiction mostly, or the occasional drama, I like to think that maybe one day I'll be as good as the fictional detectives who always catch their guy."

"Didn't know we had a Philip Marlowe in the house."

"Nice, what about you?"

"Uh, history from time to time, and the occasional mystery thriller like you."

"What kind of history?"

"Typically, anything to do with war. World War One, Two, the Vietnam War, the Korean War, and yes, even the lovely recent war in Iraq. I like to examine the cause and effect of such a man-made manifestation. It's easy to become hooked to issues that could have been prevented. But, what's truly surprising is how war starts. Most of the time someone gets assassinated or some territory is illegally obtained. I just don't get what kind of person can start such a calamity that costs the world thousands or millions of lives."

"It seems to me that you like to know answers as well. Wars are started for much of the same reason that someone is murdered here. Human hypocrisy. Greed, the thirst for some form of control feeds the heartless men and women who choose not to live like everyone else. Except everything changes when they do live with everyone else, no one expects a thing."

"I like where your heads at. Look at us rambling on like a few politicians. We could run for election the two of us. I'd say we have a pretty good shot, anybody can be president these days."

"Yeah, politics is a construction zone on the highway. There is too much caution and hard work that is only abused."

Delahine re-adjusted in his seat and closed the file upon his lap. He tinkered with his radio a bit, roaming from station to station. A nice jazz song that sounded like Sinatra came across, but he skipped it after a few moments. I almost interjected but I was in another man's car. I looked into the rearview mirror to see that I had a stray strand of hair running along my forehead. I combed it back with my fingers when I paused at the thought of my mother doing the same when I was young. Not many memories surround her but there are things that remind me of her from time to time. Anytime I was about to leave for school or get ready to play across the street, she would comb my hair with a smile. She left sometime in between my younger days.

"You know the crazy thing about war?" Delahine said, pulling me out of my train of thought.

"What's that professor?" I said.

"That's funny," Delahine said with a chuckle. "I always became fascinated with how they started, like what event or person was at the root of it all. I mean there are several people to blame but there are few stories that generate a lot of attention. Hitler and his Third Reich were undoubtedly the cause of the Second World War, but I always liked researching the first one."

"Why's that?"

"Well, World War Two was caused by a group of men who had families, jobs, and several years of manual labor under their belt. They were distinguished military officers that followed an ideology developed by one of the most infamous humans in world history. All were men, who later fostered the youth to follow in their ways. The first was started by an assassination."

"By a Serbian nationalist group, right? All of them were men too."

"That's the thing. They were all young, like eighteen and nineteen-year-olds. They were boys who were still in school and had no idea how the world worked yet. These boys were able to band together, unite against a common goal, and were somehow able to coordinate a plan that would plunge the world into its first world war. Hard to believe that's all."

"Eighteen is technically an adult if you think about it."

"Smartass."

"Hey, somebody's gotta speak up. But I am impressed, I felt like I've learned something new today. Pretty incredible actually."

"Makes you think doesn't it? Anybody can do damage, it just takes action."

Delahine fell quiet. He leaned towards the edge of the window and stared out towards the school. He couldn't have been a few years younger than me, but he seemed to ponder complex concepts that university-tenured professors thought about on a daily basis. Before I could open my mouth to ask him more about it, there was a quick pop that fluttered through the air.

It was a gunshot.

Chapter 16
Thomas

The field was dry. The air was crisp, and the sun was starting to set under a configuration of pink and orange clouds. Each looked like a structure trying to encompass the next. It was a marvelous sight, a rarity from where I live in Boston. There were not enough open fields to gaze upon a sight such as the one before me.

The tall grass beneath me appeared to be moving. I was being thrust forward by some unrecognizable force. My feet were moving but not on my own accord. I heard what appeared to be galloping from behind. I turned to see a figure approaching. It was on four legs and approaching at an increasing speed. I could only make out its head bobbing up in down until I was able to put a name to it. The fur upon its back stood straight up and remained stiff with every leap. It was a panther.

I tried to speed up, but my pace remained constant. My neck began to sweat down into the collar of my shirt. I shuffled my arms back in forth to see if any momentum could cause me to run faster. Nothing was working as the galloping became louder and louder. I turned, expecting to be pounced on when…when nothing happened. The panther was gone. I looked all around the field and could not find it. After an endless number of glances, I found my head becoming heavy as if my brain was replaced with a giant boulder. The weight turned to pain as if the boulder and sprouted needles. The pain became overwhelmingly infectious that it lingered to my hand. As I reached to apply pressure in hopes that it would stop, I felt a knot where my hand should have been.

I saw two yellow eyes staring back at me as they were devouring my hand.

"Thomas, hey Thomas," a low voice said. I felt someone push my shoulder and then another voice filled my ears, much louder than the first.

"Mr. Zaccardi, do I have your full attention?" Mrs. Alvarez said.

I found my body jerking up to a bright light and several faces looking in my direction. It came to me now. I was in Mrs. Alvarez's class, apparently dozing off during her lecture on *The Outsiders*. The front board was covered with new notes that must have been added while I was asleep. Mrs. Alvarez stepped in front of my field of vision and once again asked her question.

"I'm afraid you've lost a little of it," I said. A few classmates had started to chuckle until they looked at Mrs. Alvarez whose face did not appear to be budging.

"Must be brave cracking jokes in class. I remember when I was in middle school. We had a kid, named Sammy Junior who labeled himself as the class clown. Know where he is now?"

"No, ma'am."

"South Bay House of Correction. You're smart, Thomas. Try to show more of it for a change. Fall asleep again and you know where I'll send you. Now, open your book to chapter ten or you will see yourself headed that way quicker than your wit."

To that, I nodded and opened my book as quick as I could. Some of the pages were folded from the last student who had it, but the binding was still in a rather good condition. Mrs. Alvarez had turned and was asking Bobby Meramec on the front row a question about some part of the book that I know I was behind on.

"Shame, I thought you were one of her favorites," the low voice from before said to me. It was Sam. He sat adjacent to me where I could see the outline of his nose from my right peripheral. He was wearing a green zip-up jacket, the same one I owned myself back at home. Although, his blue and white Nike sneakers were much dirtier than mine.

"Yeah, the funny thing is, I actually enjoy *The Outsiders*. What were we doing so late that has me all tired?"

"Well, Tommy and Rich thought it would be fun to steal one of the broken-down cars in the neighborhood and take it for a spin. Lucky Thursday nights aren't flooded with the cops or I probably wouldn't be sitting next to you right now."

"I didn't think it was that late. Must have been past twelve by the time we got back. Anyways, where were you?"

Sam held up his book and flapped it around. "Educating myself, something's gotta get me out of this town one day."

"Leave? Why would you wanna leave this place? Basketball, freedom, and everything that's nice and green. I mean you…"

It was then that gravity took its effect and sunk the mood of the room.

"Mr. Zaccardi and Mr. Hatkins, it appears I don't have your complete attention. Please, inform us of the reason that you are whispering and not listening to my lecture," Mrs. Alvarez said.

I turned to Sam and gave him a quick nod, to which he only smiled and looked away.

"It's simple really. You don't have my full attention."

*

I wonder if Mrs. Kurtz's office was any different from the last time I was in there last week. I'm sure at this rate I could earn a suspension for insubordination or whatever defiant term the school system had for students like me. I don't mean to come off as I do, part of its hereditary, but most of the time it's because I can. My grades are above average, so, I often think to myself, why not have a bit of fun?

The lobby outside of Mrs. Kurtz's office smelled of lavender. The source of the smell came from an air freshener dispenser releasing a chemical in the air every ten minutes. I timed it the second time I was sitting in this exact chair. The last few times I was sent to the office, was directly after or an hour or two past lunch. Causing trouble before lunch was undoubtedly a mistake as my stomach was already starting to rumble. Mrs. Stacy, one of the office attendants sitting at her desk to my left, had to of heard the noise but made no indication of it.

I leaned my head back against the ice-cold wall and stared up at the ceiling. Sam had gotten off "Sam" free, with no threat of a trip to the office. I still managed to make that joke to myself regardless of how dull or cliché it is. Makes a good laugh for me though. Let me take that back, Sam almost got away clean if it wasn't for Mrs. Alvarez making a comment about how he should cut ties with our friendship, stating that it would help him focus on the more important things in life. She may be young and stern, but Mrs. Alvarez knows how to make a statement.

"What did you do this time?" I heard a familiar voice say as I lowered my head. It was my U.S. history teacher, Mr. Fletcher. He was wearing his typically khaki pants, an oddly patterned sweater vest, along with a pair of cognac loafers that matched his age. I've never asked him but with his hair being more gray than black, I would have to say mid-forties to about fifty.

"Mrs. Alvarez doesn't like me. At least, if she did, she sure shows it in a strange way," I said.

"Not sure if she's the problem bud."

"It's just so easy ya know? I do my work and try to have a bit of fun at the same time. What's the harm in that?"

"Remember what they taught you in elementary school? What's the word, oh geez, it's so hard to remember sometimes. Respect, that's it! You know what it means. You just have to show it. Manners make for memorable students."

"So, do the funny ones."

"True, but being a smart ass doesn't help either."

"Yeah, maybe I'll see you next period?"

The door to Mrs. Kurtz's office opened as I could hear growing laughter coming from inside. Mr. Walker and she were chuckling about something until he walked outside and locked eyes with me. His smile started to wear off as he gave me a quick glare. He then smiled at Mrs. Kurtz and said goodbye.

"Gotta go, don't look into her eyes," Mr. Fletcher said as he moved towards the office exit, passing by a wall of art projects hanging proudly. Mrs. Kurtz came out of her office, looking like she heard what he said.

"Turning my own student body against me Tom?"

"I wouldn't dare, God, save the queen!" He said as he scooted out of the door as if he was late for an appointment.

Mrs. Kurtz's office looked exactly the way it did last week. Menacing and old fashioned. The only new addition I could find was a painted picture of a cow on a field hanging behind her desk. I assumed it was her daughter's work of art. The ceiling fan above was rotating at an alarming pace that it may fly off at any moment. I could see the sky as I made my way to the chair in front of her desk. Rain clouds were moving in, yet the sun was still shining bright for a little while longer.

"Well, Thomas, it's unfortunately nice to see you again," she said as she sat in her much larger black chair, covered in leather and a far more comfortable material than my rear was currently on.

"Mrs. Kurtz, this isn't my fault I was only..."

"We've gone over this. You call your teachers Mr. or Mrs. For me, you should use the proper prefix."

"Oh, Principal Kurtz, sorry about that."

"Thomas, I don't understand your behavior. You are exceptionally bright when it comes to academics, but when it comes to respecting your teachers you appear to have none. Anything to say about that?"

"I just get cooked up being in a classroom all day. I lose interest."

"Well, that's normal for students. However, you must find better ways to interact with Mrs. Alvarez or you will be suspended. This is the third time in the past two weeks you've had some sort of complaint against you. The second from Mrs. Alvarez. She said you were sleeping and responded sarcastically instead of owning up to it."

"I didn't get much sleep from last night. It wasn't entirely my fault."

"Then who is to blame for your lack of sleep?"

I remained silent. My feet were now crossed together as I tried to maintain eye contact with her without saying anything.

"There's part of the issue Thomas. You have to own up to your own decisions and not transfer the blame elsewhere. You're still a kid I understand but making a decision and owning up to it is something you need to learn. Maybe your father can help, do you have a better number for him, he hasn't responded to my last few calls?"

"I just know the one you have. Sorry, he works a lot," I said in a low voice whilst scratching the back of my head. My hair's been dry for two days, probably should take a shower tonight.

"It's just crucial that he knows what is going on in your life. Parents are so instrumental in their child's educational careers and I'd hate to see you waste your time away here. The attitude needs to stop, and you need to set the example."

"What example are you referring to?"

"Not the attitude I hear right now. It's time to grow up and act like the mature adult I know your father would want." What should mean a lot to me is that she actually does care. However, it's not that I don't care for her. It's who she is trying to connect me to. If only she knew and what I couldn't possibly explain to her is that the fact is.

He'd have to care first.

Chapter 17

No suspension, that's a win. Although I could do without having to clean Mrs. Alvarez's room twice a week, I just don't see the need. I hooked a right leaving the main office and started along the 7th-grade hallway back to my class. As I walked along the hall, something wretched filled the air. The janitor had left his mop in the bucket and its repugnance was noticeably present. Science projects galore took up most of my vision, as there was a plethora of pie charts, hand-drawn sketches, and any other kind of representation of climate change all over the wall. One of the posters had a rather impressive illustration of the carbon cycle being depicted with trees and their roots in the ground.

As I was about to turn another corner, I came to face-to-face with Sam leaning against the wall. He had his bookbag along his left shoulder with his right leg propped up against the wall.

"Twenty minutes, not too bad. Last time you were in there, it was almost an hour. Did you smooth her with your charm again?" Sam said. His eyes were equally spaced apart, even though at an angle it appeared that his jawline seemed crooked.

"Yes, my lower lip works wonders when I stick it out far enough. What's the deal, where are we meeting Rich and Tommy at?"

"They're already at the court, Rich faked a stomach cramp and had to go to the nurse while Tommy actually got his Ma to come pick him up."

"Wait, his Ma is letting him skip today?"

"C'mon, you know her. She never cared about school as a kid, what makes you think she's strict about it now."

"Maybe she can sign us all out tomorrow, nobody wants to come to school on a Saturday."

"Yeah, too bad, I'll probably be here."

We managed to sneak out the back door of the school and circled around to get our bikes hooked to the racks near the gymnasium. A few students wearing our school's designated gym attire noticed us to which I replied with holding my finger against my mouth. The two boys looked at each other. One shrugged his shoulders and gave us a thumbs up.

Sam and I made our way through the neighborhood, staying on the sidewalks as much as we could. North End was hot today. The sun was blinding us from the west as we rode our bikes. After looking behind a few times, I saw some storm clouds approaching but appeared to be well off. I couldn't help but think how unlucky it would be if we skipped school to play basketball only to be ruined by some rain.

We passed several men and women dressed in casual business attire, each of whom looked at us strangely. They were most likely out for an early lunch and were not expecting to see two handsome middle school boys skipping school. As I trailed Sam, we found ourselves on Prince Street. Lucky for us, it was a straight shot from here to DeFilippo courts.

Prince Street was a few blocks from my house, or the shitbox located above my dad's bakery. My father, a man who earned more money than his tax forms revealed, was no stranger to bending the laws of society. As a kid, he was the hero who brought gifts only a rich boy from Cambridge could appreciate. I never asked, he just bought them. It was impossible for me to know why until I became a bit older. I watched movies and TV shows depicting criminals who earned their money with intimidation. My father fit the bill. He never hit someone in my presence, but my uncles knew how to run their mouths. I'm still young so I don't exactly know what he does but, I am almost positive our hand-made cannolis don't bring in the money that he boasts.

I remember one-night last year, it was a little past two in the morning when I heard a door shut hard. It startled me as I quickly jumped out of bed to see what was going on. Even though our apartment is directly over the bakery, our walls and floors are thin. I could not make out what it was but all I could hear was a welting sound coming from below. There was no distinct pattern, just the same kind of sound over and over again. Some sounded weaker than the others until I could hear what my mind probably tricked myself into thinking that it was an egg being cracked over a pan. There was a light protruding from the door at the bottom of the stairs as I slowly crept closer down. A voice, which matched my uncle Ralphie's, said something that I did not understand.

As I reached the bottom of the stairs, I leaned my ear against the door and one more welting sound cracked off until there was nothing but silence. Everything seemed still for a moment, as if nothing had been going on at all. Maybe I was still asleep or hoping that I still was. Thoughts of dreaming had vanished when the door opened, and my stomach had sunk me to the ground like an anchor. My uncle Ralphie stood there, glaring at me from his six-foot-three stature. His biceps, the size of two professional league footballs, were covered in bluish-green veins running along them like icing upon a pastry.

"Hey, Tommy," he said, holding his large finger against his mouth. "Your dad wouldn't want you to see this. It's bad for business to get the boss all riled up during a meeting. However, you need to learn somehow."

I felt his hand press against the swell of my back as he lightly pushed me into the doorway. My eyes caught the foot of someone sitting in a chair. As soon as I saw it twitch in an unnerving fashion, I thrust myself backward. I unconsciously found myself shaking my head back and forth. Ralphie looked perplexed but expressed a look that seemed as if he understood.

"Ah, still acting like a little shit. It's alright. You're probably making the smart decision by not looking. Don't worry, it runs in the family. Your Uncle Jack was just as anxious when we brought him into the loop." He paused for a moment and gave a quick nod to someone else in the room. I could hear someone move around. The desk drawer in the room could be heard being opened and something being pulled out of it. My uncle held up his hand and then proceeded to look back at me.

"Tommy, it's like this. The world is filled with deer, right? You know, bouncing around with antlers and jumping around their own shit they leave on the ground. Then there are animals that go around and stop the deer from leaving their shit everywhere. Leopards, lions, tigers, right? Well, your father and I like to label ourselves as panthers. We are as black as the night. No one sees us coming. You know what I mean?"

Once again, I could remember that I shook my head again, trying to panic at whatever was going on inside the other room. My shoulder felt heavy as my uncle rested his hand on it.

"Go back to bed, one night you'll see what I'm talking about," he said. He looked back into the room and waved his hand around towards the guy he signaled to earlier.

I heard a man scream and then the door was shut. I can't remember anything after that.

"Thomas look out!"

Sam shouted to me as my bike was headed directly towards a tree. I quickly corrected my steering and narrowly turned away from it, almost hitting my back wheel against a mailbox in the process.

"Where are you, man? Haven't said a word in at least five minutes," he said.

"Just daydreaming, you know how we scatterbrained people are," I said.

"Well, you managed to keep yourself busy the whole time 'cause we're here."

DeFilippo courts consisted of two types of courts. A basketball and a field hockey court that were seasoned with sun-burned paint, poor fences, and a lack of adequate basketball nets. Yet, it was home. I grew up playing on these courts with Sam, Rich, and Tommy. It was a connection that we all had and no matter the condition the courts were in, we always wanted to play. What made these courts unique was a giant Italian flag that was painted on the wall adjacent to the basketball court. Italians aren't known for their basketball, but it was nice to see another sport flourish.

Rich and Tommy were already tossing the rock around the court. Tommy missed an easy layup when we rode by. After he saw us witness his blunder, he yelled out to us, "Check out these moves Sammy! The ladies always come back for more."

"Your mom asking about me again or something?" Sam said, as we set our bikes against the charcoal-colored benches next to the gate entrance.

Sam and I walked onto the court and were greeted by the rest of the group. Tommy's extremely recognizable grin shined back at me with its crookedness representing how his brain worked. He was the chatterbox of the four of us, always cracking one off when we needed, or didn't need a joke to clear the mood. His baggy clothes always helped people peg us as the uncontrollable youth that roamed North End. His shirt today illustrated a baseball player wearing a Boston hat pissing all over a New York Yankees helmet. "Like my shirt? I feel that it represents our classy society," he said as he dribbled the ball around.

Rich was not that different from Tommy. He had a better-kept physique and had shorter brown hair, rather than the mop of curls resting on Tommy's head. Rich had smoothness about him, something that the other middle school girls found mysterious but lovable. Everybody is a character.

"What took you so long this time? Flirting with Miranda Keyes again?" Rich said.

"Nah, Mrs. Alvarez was on my case again," I said, watching Tommy take a shot from the free-throw line.

"Ah, the pretty senorita! What Tommy and I would do to be in that class with you."

"Trust me, you'd be transferred your first day. Sam's the only reason I'm still in there, he keeps bailing me out."

"Somebody's gotta do it," Sam said.

For a few minutes, the four of us messed around and shot the ball successfully for the most part. We enjoyed the ability to get away when we wanted. We knew our truancy was going to get back to us one day but all we could think about was how it could wait. Each of us had our own familial struggles. Tommy's dad is a coke addict who claims he is "cutting the habit" every year. His mom, bless her heart, has to deal with the both of them while she's working hard at Eastern Bank. Rich's mom left when he was young, but his dad works as a mechanic up in Charlestown. He's a good man. He lets us stop by from time-to-time to educate us on the foundation of our nation's greatest achievement: the automobile. I burned my hand once trying to change the oil in an El Camino. It's one of my favorite scars.

Sam's parents take the cake for the worst parents of the decade. They neglect him every chance they get, always disappearing on their own adventures across the Eastern coast. They once left him for a week straight to fend for himself. Alcohol is the only medicine they've ever been prescribed if I'm being honest. It makes me sick, it does.

With all the crap going on at home and the struggle with school, how could we be expected to be in school on such a great day?

The four of us were about to start a game of two-on-two when we heard several sneakers hitting the court. I turned to see four boys, with a stunning resemblance to the four of us, looking around the court. Each had on basketball shorts, worn-out t-shirts, and twenty-five-dollar sneakers you could find at any corner store.

Each of them looked around as if they had never been here before. While three of them started to stretch their legs, the boy farthest to the right spoke up.

"We're from the Southside, wanna run it?"

Chapter 18

The Southside boys knew how to play ball. We agreed to play to twenty-one, the winner had to win by two points. Anything in front of the three-point line was one point, while anything behind was two points. It made the games go by longer.

The one who spoke first, his name was Gerard. He played point guard, against me. Sam lined up as my shooting guard, while Tommy and Rich just went with the flow of the game. Gerard and his group had the basketball IQ of an analyst on ESPN. Anytime a foul was committed, they were the first to say something. We weren't dirty players, we just liked to play.

Southside scored five straight baskets in a row, putting them up seven to zero. We started to catch up after Sam nailed a couple of three-pointers from the corner. Tommy was the rebound king as he aggressively fought everything that came his way. Gerard took notice and put his larger friend, who was wearing a Donald Trump t-shirt, to guard Tommy. For a while, it worked, as Tommy struggled to recover the ball for us.

The score was a little closer after twenty minutes at eighteen to seventeen, them. I found myself dribbling the ball down the center of the court on a fast break when I saw Rich near the base of the basket. Gerard was in front of me as I picked up the ball to pass to my right where Tommy was but delivered a bounce pass under Gerard's legs. The ball found Rich who scored an easy layup, tying the game up. Gerard looked discomforted as he now had the ball heading down the court. As soon as he approached the tip of the three-point line, I pressured him for the ball. As he tried to move around me, I managed to cut him off to the right where I caught an elbow to the forehead.

I stumbled a few steps and heard the ball stop dribbling.

"Oh, shit you ran into my elbow," Gerald said.

Rich and Sam approached me, but I waved them off. "Everything's cool, everything's cool. Just a little handsy. Be nice if some of our refs here could call that," I said.

Play resumed as Gerald received the ball from an inbound pass. Once again, he dribbled around the top of the key and failed to find someone to pass it to. Rich was covering his guy well, as Sam was pretty much orbiting his guy's entire atmosphere, cutting off any chance of being open. Gerard decided to stop along the edge of the three-point line, step back, and take a shot. I was too late to give pressure as I could hear the ball sail through the net, making a bittersweet swoosh sound. Twenty to eighteen.

"It's alright, champ, douchebags get their way most of the time anyway," Tommy said, as he fed me the inbound pass.

I took the ball down the court, trying not to look directly into the sun that was beaming down. The clouds were almost to it but not yet. As I approached the top of the key, I decided to dribble head-on towards Gerard. He started to back up quickly, as I hurried towards him. Instead of faking to the right for a pass, I drove the ball straight passed him and made a layup. Down by one.

"Nice! Let's go bud!" I heard Sam say as we ran back to our side. Once again, Gerard looked unhappy to see me. He decided to pass the ball off to one of the boys of Southside who was dribbling around Rich. As the boy who had the ball dribbled at midcourt, Gerard quickly hurried towards the free-throw line and was met with a pass. I sprinted towards him as Gerard was raising his hands up for a layup. Just as I was right behind him, I jumped up and swatted the ball from his hand, blocking his shot.

It was almost too quick. Gerard abruptly turned to me and spat in my face as we slowed down near the fence. For a second, I thought it was just my sweat, but Gerard's mouth had formed a perfect circle from where his saliva came out. Before I knew it, I felt my hands grab Gerard's collar and throw his face into the fence. A slight ring sounded off from the fence as his face bounced off it.

Southside, along with my group, quickly tried to intervene as Gerald attempted to rush towards me with his right hand balled into a fist.

"Come here, you piece of shit. Think you can get away with that?" he yelled as Trump shirt was holding him back with one arm. A piece of the fence had to have had a sharp edge, as a collection of blood started to formulate on his forehead, dripping down towards his mouth.

Sam and Rich managed to step in front of me to prevent any violent lunge. "I'm telling you, the calls here are ridiculous. Try playing a fair game next time and maybe we can finish this," I said.

"You and me, let's go, you're looking to get pummeled," Gerard said back. Trump shirt and the other two boys from Southside did not appear to be aggravated or troubled. They just wanted to play ball. I can respect that.

"Maybe when you're not all riled up. Doesn't look like your boys want to start anything. Let's just enjoy the rest of the day and we'll be on our way. The courts yours for today boys."

Trump shirt released Gerard who appeared to be calmer now. His composure was lost but knew if he tried anything he would be stopped. His biceps appeared to be more formed than mine, which led me to the conclusion that our fight may have been one-sided. Never thought I thank someone wearing a Trump shirt.

"Come on, let's get out of here," Tommy said, as he motioned the three of us to the gate. I could hear Gerard say something behind me, but I chose not to turn around. It wasn't worth giving him what he wanted.

All four of us walked out of the court, heads hung high as we managed to accomplish two things. Play basketball, and watch a douchebag get a new face tattoo.

*

Roma's Deli at the corner of Prince and Salem St. was the perfect place for a celebratory lunch. A nice Italian joint in the center of North End. It had the best capicola in Boston. I mean, that's what the sign outside says. Day by day, it smelled of sliced meat, freshly baked bread, and any spices you could get your hands on. It reminded me of a nice diner you'd see in gangster movies where the owner was protected by "the family." Customers consisted mostly of hardworking blue-collar workers all around town. My dad once introduced me to a guy who lived all the way in Dorchester who comes here every week for a sandwich. The guy actually had his picture taken and framed on the back wall. There were at least thirty photographs hanging there, each in a different colored frame. My father was in a few of them.

I loved the atmosphere. It was the kind of place that made me feel proud of my Italian heritage.

The owner, Roma Gisonni, was a close friend of the Zaccardi family. I'm not sure what the rub is when it comes to naming a restaurant after yourself, but Roma made it fit. I'd like to think it's some sort of unselfish pride, but it may as well be the source of a lack of creativity.

Either way, Roma was as nice as a kindergarten teacher. He was a people-pleaser who never wanted to disappoint anybody. The four of us could see him hard at work behind the counter, slicing what looked to be salami. Roma was in his fifties and definitely showed it to. His black hair was thinning out, plus, the wrinkles that covered his forehead looked like a mountain range. His white t-shirt was a bit tight, allowing his large arms to look more noticeable. As soon as he sees a friend, his voice has no volume control.

"Look who it is! The fearsome four! Get ova here and get some food!" he said, after noticing us in the doorway. "Don't think I'm stupid and realize that it's not Saturday yet. Whatcha doing outta school for?"

"It's too nice outside for that, you know that Roma," I said.

"Your food tastes better than the infected slop at our school," Rich said, as he leaned against the counter.

"Damn straight, Richie boy. You guys playing at Langone today?"

"Nah, I lost my ball yesterday, I think it's their somewhere."

"Ah, it'll turn up. Anyways, schools important you four know that. Education is all we got nowadays; we all need it. If I went to school, who knows where I'd be? Look what you got me doing, I'm lecturing you guys like one of your teachers," Roma said.

"Deep stuff, you should be a teacher. Everybody would listen to you," I said.

"Yeah, yeah. I'll let it slide this time but if I catch you out here again, I'll make you guys' clean dishes in the back."

Roma finished slicing some salami up and handed it to one of his workers. "Hey, Samy, how're your folks?"

"Not too bad. They're off again, Maine I think," Sam said.

"Damn shame, you sure there isn't anything I can do?"

"Nah, it's all good, I'm holding my own. It's actually quite peaceful having them away. I can do what I wanna do."

"I hear ya. Alright boys, want the usual?"

All of us all loudly said yes, to which Roma smiled. He waved us off to go sit somewhere against the back wall and told us he'd bring it out for us. As we all walked back that way, I felt a hand hold my shoulder back.

"Hold a sec, Thomas. Can you do something for me?" Roma said.

"Yeah, what's up?"

"Can you look after Sammy? I know he seems content with his parents gone but it's no way to live a childhood. Marcy and I are working some things out to where he can stay with us sometimes while his parents are off doing God knows what. Whenever you're away from the other two, can you run that by him to see if that's okay? I would myself, but you guys are always together."

His was tone sentimental, a similarity that could be seen from his large brown eyes that looked clear and warranted. I could see that he cared for Sam and wanted the best for him. We all do. This wasn't the first time Roma mentioned looking after Sam. Knowing him, it wouldn't be the last.

"Yeah, I can do that. Thanks, Roma."

Chapter 19

"I'm not the smartest kid at James Middle but there is one thing I do know," Tommy said, a second before he bit into one of the Italian grinders that Roma made for us.

"Roma makes the best sandwich in the entire country, now that's a fact."

"You've never even left Boston. How do we know there isn't another great sandwich out there," Rich said.

Tommy, Sam, and I all paused and then set in unison, "Are you mad?"

"Seriously, I wish Thomas had thrown your face into a fence if you're going to make accusations like that," Tommy said.

"Reckon you could use a nice welt across your face."

"Wanna put that sandwich down and see how many times you can take a hit?" Rich said.

"Ladies, let's all calm down and enjoy each other's company," I said, as I wiped some bread crumbs off my mouth.

"Put your pencils away."

"Pencils? What are you talking about?" Tommy asked. It went silent for a moment until Sam propped his hand on the table and lifted his pinky finger into the air. He started to wave it around and smiled. The four of us started to chuckle at a somewhat contained rate. We caused such a commotion last time with our laughter that Roma almost kicked us out.

"Anyways, what's the deal, are we going out tonight boys? I've spent all of my money again," Tommy said.

"Again? Learn how to save or you'll go broke when you're older," Rich said.

Unlike most middle school kids, we participated in a far more dangerous game at night. I despised my father and my uncles, not just because of what I think, and I know, but what they have forced us to do. My father came up to us, one day, several months ago and offered us a proposition. Like most people in the neighborhood, everybody knows what my dad is. Unfortunately, that includes my friends as well.

My father sat us all down in the back of the bakery and laid out a plan.

"Young people are never suspected. Adults use drugs, which leads the public, and especially the cops, to believe that adults sell drugs as well. Business has been in a rut the past year and I think I've thought of something. You boys like money, right?" None of us spoke up when my father's face scanned our faces for a reaction.

"Well, here is your pathway to the green. Every week, I'm going to give Thomas here a sizable amount of whatever we feel like selling and you boys will be in charge of selling it on the streets at night. I'm talking gas stations, street corners, bars, you name it! Now, I know you're thinking that this sounds dangerous but here's the rub. If you go together, you'll be fine. Not many tweakers or addicts are kidnapping groups of middle-schoolers. Weekends are the best, and remember this, *never* go alone."

It was that quick. We were so blinded about making some money that we had no idea how wrong it was. My dad made Sam, Rich, and Tommy swear to not tell their parents or something bad would happen. Nothing specific was threatened but we all knew what he could do. At first, I felt as if it was a threat against us. '*Sell my drugs or I'll end you,*' type of deal. However, once the money came in, our minds went numb. Every once in a while, I was on the verge of telling my dad that we were quitting but I think we bonded more over it. The few times my dad would talk to was when he was happy that I was bringing him money.

"I don't know guys. The weekend is the most dangerous, we found out the hard way the other weekend," Sam said.

"So, there might be fewer cops than there were that weekend. I'm sure lots," Rich said.

"That's probably not true, there are just as many cops working every night. They never know when something will happen."

"I'm with Sam, I'm not sure I want to either. Let's enjoy the night some other way," I said. I never wanted to go out and work for my dad. It disgusted me, yet I knew if we didn't comply there would be some sort of consequence. The sound of Sam's knees cracking entered my mind as I could picture my father holding the bat.

"Geez, well we always go together so if we're all not in I guess we can wait," Tommy said.

The four of us finished our grinders and then proceeded to leave. As we stood, I was closest to the wall and felt my right elbow hit something. Before I knew what, it was, I heard the crack of glass near my feet. I looked down to see that I had knocked one of the photographs from the wall. After kneeling down to pick it up, I noticed that the crack wasn't too bad. The crack formed a spider web shape in the top right corner. Believe it or not, the picture was one of my dad's and another gentleman in it with a short haircut. He sort of looked like a cop. Figures, sometimes it feels like he's watching me through all of these pictures.

"Hey, Roma! I accidentally knocked one of your pictures down," I said over the crowd of people that had walked in.

"That's alright, Son, just leave it there. Try not to break anything else on the way out!" We both smiled and nodded at each other as I walked out the front door.

The storm clouds were definitely coming in for sure now. The sun was fading fast as you could tell by the sidewalk's brightness starting to fade. I checked my phone to see that it was near one in the afternoon.

"What's the plan now, boys?" Tommy said.

"Good question, basketball was fun, but I'm pretty beat. I might go home and play some Madden if anybody wants to join," Rich said.

"Hell, yeah, Tom Brady is about to rain all over your parade. You guys coming too?" Tommy said.

Both Sam and I declined. We said goodbye to both of them and started to head towards my place. Tommy and Rich both patted us on our shoulders and started to walk down the street. Tommy kicked Rich in the back of his leg just as they were about to cut a corner.

"Remind me again why we hang out with them?" Sam said.

"They keep life interesting. No time for the dullness of human boredom am I right?"

"Yeah, but I don't think parading around in baggy clothes and lacking the need to improve yourself is what we need."

"You may be right. Heck, if it wasn't for you, I'd probably be wearing just a Celtics jersey right now with my pants rolled down to my ankles. Sound sexy?"

"You must daydream about yourself a lot."

"Not as much as Tommy does about himself." We both chuckled for a moment as we crossed Salem Street hoping to avoid being hit by an SUV going over the speed limit.

"How much money you got saved up?" I said.

"That's a random question. Why are you asking about that?"

"Just curious, honestly, I've saved a good bit of mine. Just seeing who I'm competing with."

"Ha, nice. So far, I've got over a thousand."

"A thousand?"

"Yep."

"Dang, do you buy anything?"

"Nah, it's all for savings. Just waiting for the day when I get a chance to leave."

"I remember, your plan to leave us for bigger and better things."

"It's not like that. I just feel like we all deserve a chance to become what we want to be. When I think of what I want, job-wise I have no idea. Location wise, anywhere but here."

Sam deserved anything great that would come his way. The other two had their own faulty aspirations but Sam was smart enough to get anywhere. His home life had to be his drive. Who could blame him to be honest?

"I'll make a deal with ya," I said.

"What's that?"

"In ten years, if you're still here, we'll move away. Just the two of us. After you've gone to college and accomplished so much but still haven't left here. I'll take my dad's money and we'll go anywhere but here."

"Thanks, bud. Glad I can count on ya."

"Anytime anywhere, my friend."

The temperature seemed to have dropped ever since the clouds moved in. A gust of wind came by and almost caused my hairs to become tiny icicles. We were exactly four buildings down from the bakery when we could smell the delicious goods covering the air. When we reached the entrance, a woman with powdered sugar on the ends of her lips walked out carrying a briefcase. Her collar looked like a chalkboard compared to the rest of her black business suit. Sugary sweets are a delicacy I assume.

As soon as Sam and I walked in, we heard Uncle Ralphie shout our names. Somehow, the welcome at Roma's was friendlier.

"Boys, boys. Skipping school, I see. Serves you right, those places are filled with whacks anyways. Wanna come back here and learn a thing or two?"

"No thanks, Uncle Ralph, we just played basketball, we're pretty beat."

"Alright then, your dad's back there, he's a bit hot-headed today."

"Sounds about right," I said under my breath. Uncle Ralphie turned his head as he looked at me, but it was a relief to know he hadn't heard me. Sam and I made our way through the shop and behind the front counter. Ralphie was lifting a tray of dough onto one of the back counters when we opened the back door. Amusing as always, the walls were poorly painted and a few crooked photographs of airplanes from World War II did their best to cover it. Just as we were about to head up the stairs, I heard a voice call out my name. It was my dad.

"You can just head up there, I'll be there in a second," I said. Sam nodded and proceeded to head up the stairs. I took a step back and turned the rusty doorknob into the back room. The same backroom from that awful night. My father was sitting at his desk with a stack of unorganized papers in front of him. He was wearing brown pants and a nice buttoned-up shirt that looked like a checkerboard.

"Yes, sir."

"Who are you with?"

"Sam, we just ate at Roma's and are pretty beat from playing basketball."

"Hatkins? The kid with parents who don't stay put for weeks at a time."

"Yep, the same one you've known for years."

He turned in his seat to face me directly. His hair was combed backward, with a bit of patchy stubble growing around his jawline. Funny thing about my dad, his Italian heritage brought hair everywhere else but his face.

"Watch your attitude, Son, just 'cause you're in middle school doesn't mean you get to mouth off to your father. Look, you need to know something about that Sam boy. I'm sure you know this, but his parents aren't good people. His dad owes people a lot of money. Not to mention, me."

"Wait, what do you mean?"

"It's time for you to start figuring things out. You and your pals are only working for me so that I can gain a profit. But you already knew that. The only reason Sam is working with you guys is because his father offered him to me as a way of paying me back. Yet, he still seems to be falling short. Real piece of work he is. Either Sammy boy is keeping money for himself or his dad is taking it. Shit's bad business."

"Sam's one of the best people I know. You're wrong to accuse Sam of doing that."

That struck something. My father stood out of his chair slowly as if a lesson was about to be delivered. I always forgot how tall my father was. He beamed up like a tower within an old medieval fort.

"I don't know what the hell you seem to be doing, acting out as of late but you need to get one thing straight. I run the town and I run the home. What I say should stick inside that mid-size brain of yours. You're a lot like your mother, never knew when to keep your mouth shut. She's not here anymore for that reason, running off to live with her sister in New York. You act like her you get ostracized. You act like me; you make a name for yourself in the neighborhood. Listen here, Sam and his folks are bad people, you may not see it but he's got some bad genes flowing in his blood. They're going to get what's coming to them soon. Now, leave me before you mouth off again."

Without hesitation, he swung himself around and pretended I wasn't even there anymore. That's what we have, an empty relationship. It's a bottomless pit of differences that never seem to gain any ground. Any time I felt we had something, I found it quickly fading out.

Maybe Sam was right, we need to leave this town.

Chapter 20

"More wisdom from the terror of North End?" Sam said.

"No more than usual."

Sam had already made himself at home. He brought out my desk chair and propped his feet up on the trunk that I had sitting in the middle of the room. The trunk contained sentimental items of mine from when I was younger but also served as an ottoman. My television had been turned on to Sports Center. Several analysts were making their predictions about which NFL teams were going to win this weekend, luckily for us. Tom Brady had a good chance against Buffalo.

Even though my dad was the way he was, he kept my room up to date with the latest furniture and electronics. It used to smell of sweaty socks but that all changed a year ago when Sam arrived with an air freshener he placed on my desk. I remember Sam saying, "My house already smells like shit, and when I come here, I refuse to smell it again." Like most things he was right. If money had the ability to cause a son to love his father, what a wonderful world this might be. Too bad it doesn't.

"I feel drained, how 'bout you?" I said.

"Not too much. I try to get a reasonable amount of sleep at night. If I don't, I'll look like your Uncle Ralphie in a few years."

"Impossible, sleep deprivation is far from his problems. Anyways, I know you've mentioned being a doctor before, and who could forget the time both of us wanted to be archeologists like our hero Indiana Jones, but what would you wanna do to get out of here?"

"Yeah, I remember when we wanted to do that. What, you thinking of coming to now?"

"It's possible, just curious you know? I don't think I want to indulge in the family business."

"I understand that. Better to have a friend than go it alone I suppose. It's hard to tell sometimes. We're still young and we're not even in high school yet. I could see myself becoming a writer or a journalist. Books keep me calm and if they keep me put together, why not make a career out of it? What about you, any ideas going on in the great Thomas Zaccardi's head?"

I knew it was coming but there it came. Sam's a curious fellow and I should have been more prepared for the question, but what kind of kid is prepared for that question? Fireman sounded good at one point, but I heard they sit around most of the day until it's time for the call. Serving the community was the way I wanted to work, whatever altruistic profession I choose would have to help people. A job that would go against what my dad does. It felt obvious but hard to admit.

"Maybe a cop?" I underestimated the pause in my voice after I said it.

Sam's eyebrow went up as he said, "A cop? With the reputation that your dad has, it might be hard to swing. How long have you been hiding this from me?"

"Nah, just recently I've been thinking about helping people. Hard to believe when we sell a sickness to the worst people in Boston. If I even try to ask my father about it, he'll think of something worse. The four of us should never have started this. I know Tommy and Rich just want to make some money, but I feel like we're the only two that see that something is wrong. I'm not accusing you of doing the same thing, but I have to ask. Why did you agree to join in?"

Sam took a deep breath and fumbled his fingers around for a few moments. Maybe I shouldn't have asked him that, I think I already knew the answer.

"I've got to get out of here, Thomas. It's not good for either of us. Save money and never look back."

"Never look back. Sounds like we have something else in common."

Both of us remained silent. We both longed for something more than an unprivileged or unsatisfying life. It was like the weight of the world was on our young shoulders and our legs aren't even strong enough to walk yet. The weight seemed quite literal as I could feel my eyelids start to become heavy. Before I knew it, the room went dark, my ears went dark, and sleep came like a friend pulling me out of this life.

*

Buzz, buzz, buzz. I slowly woke up to a continuous sound that sounded like a bee was inside my head. Not growing louder or calmer, the sound remained steady as my eyes slowly cracked open. It was dark inside my room. The blinds were pulled yet no light came in. I must have slept past dinner. I looked at my desk chair to find that Sam was gone. Must have gone home for his own dinner.

The buzzing sound came from my phone. It was lying near the end of my pillow. I rubbed my eyelids with the palms of my hands before reaching for my phone. Tommy was calling. He'd better not try to get me to go out again tonight.

"Hey, what's going on?" I answered.

"Thomas! Hey, there you are, I've called you several times. Something…something's happened. I, it's too crazy man. Shit, it's horrible." I've never heard him this panicked before. Tommy was the wisecracker who shook off any moment with a joke to ease the pain. There was nothing but doubt in his voice.

"What? What's going on? Did you and Rich go out tonight?"

"Yeah, yeah we did. We're over at Langone. We were going to try to sell to some of the boys in the apartments across the street, but we got blinded by the blue lights."

"Blue lights? The cops catch you?"

"No, no, we're fine. The cops found a body. We can see it from where we are standing. It's a kid. Dammit, it's a kid. Like one of us Thomas."

I envisioned the body of some faceless teenager lying on the street next to the ballpark. There were two bullet holes in his chest, along with a stream of blood coming from each.

"A kid like us? Shit. Is Sam with you?"

"Nah, Rich and I have been calling him but there's been no answer. He picked up once and then just hung up. I don't know it was weird."

"Alright, look I'm headed right over."

I hung up the phone and grabbed my jacket. Thankfully, I left my shoes on and proceeded to head down the stairs. My footsteps were so loud that I must have shaken the house, yet I didn't hear anybody yelling. Where the heck was everybody?

I chose not to find out as I ran out the back door to Langone.

Chapter 21

The lights were blinding. I thought for a second, the only color I would see for the rest of my life was blue. After turning the corner onto Commercial Street, there was a monstrous crowd of people fighting for a better view of something. Tommy and Rich weren't playing some sadistic joke, this was real. I scattered the crowd looking for the both of them when I heard my name. I looked to my far right to see Tommy and Rich motioning me over to their position. They were ducked inside some entrance to an apartment complex that had a brick overhang. I managed to sink half my shoe into a puddle as I made it to them.

"Hey, what's going on?" I said.

"It's definitely a kid. Channel five, six, and seven are here. The police aren't letting anybody through. The doctor, or whoever looks at the body just got here, and he's been walking around the body. It's in the middle of the field so they can't cover it up, or move it without messing anything up," Tommy said.

"Have you guys been able to see it at all?"

"No, not really. The crowd is pretty much blocking our view. Plus, we don't want the cops seeing us and shooing us off. We could try and sneak in through the crowd of the media," Rich said.

"Any updates on Sam? I called him a few times myself on the way over here," I said.

"Nothing, we called again too but there was nothing."

A chill moved through the air, much like something that moves through the night like a raven. There were thousands of kids our age in Boston. What are the odds, it couldn't be true? It shouldn't.

"Sam is always near his phone. It's not like him not to answer. I'm not saying we should be worried but maybe we should get a closer look," I said.

"I agree, I'm on it!" Tommy said. Before we could hold him back, he zipped up his waterproof jacket and ran out into the street. His hair swirled around his head like a hay bell as the wind came with force. Rich and I watched as he moved towards the media vans. He made his way past the channel six van and found the crowd. We saw him move like a snake through a tall field until he disappeared.

"Think he'll get caught?" Rich said.

"Don't think it will matter honestly. The cops have a bigger issue to deal with right now."

I discovered the irritation on my head that wouldn't go away no matter how hard I dung my fingers into it. From time to time it would appear, typically during nerve enticing situations. It itched the night that I heard noises coming from the back room. It itched now, and I couldn't place the feeling.

I felt my hand reach into my pocket. My phone had only half its battery left as I lifted it in front of my face. A slight opening had appeared within the crowd of spectators and members of the media to the point where maybe my camera could zoom in enough to get a look. With it being dark and my focus lacking the sufficiency for a proper line of sight, I almost turned the phone off. The only people near the body at this point were two men. One had gloves on while the other was writing something down on a rather large clipboard. When the one with gloves moved away, I motioned the camera towards the body. It was on the pitcher's mound, granting me a slightly elevated view. I could not make out anything of notice until the camera focused for a single moment of clarity. It was just for a second, nothing much to go on but something that stuck out. I saw green...maybe a green jacket.

When I put my phone down, I looked to see that Tommy was standing directly on the sidewalk. His vacant expression, a slight twitch in his eyebrow gave way to something. His mouth was open, but no words came out. His eyes were blank until they met mine. Before I could speak, he slowly nodded his head back and forth revealing the true nature of his halted persona.

My body became heavy as I felt a sudden pain fall upon my legs.

*

A trembling sensation found my fingertips. Numbness found my knee caps. Both could not distract from the horror of everything. Tommy hadn't moved, along with Rich who stood next to me motionless. I had fallen to my knees and could not find the strength to look towards him. I could feel my face quench up as a single tear started to formulate within my left eye. Rich had finally started to move and started pacing in front of the door into the apartment. We didn't know how to feel.

"Are...are you sure?" Rich said.

Tommy looked as if someone snapped their fingers and brought him out of a trance.

"I could see his face, Thomas. It looked white, too white for someone to look. I, I don't even know what to say." Tears started to part down his face. For the first time in my life, he looked as if he was going to start sobbing.

It was an indescribable fear. Sam, our friend, the most virtuous of us all might be gone. His body lay upon the mound that he loved to pitch every weekend. I could picture him standing there, glove in hand, performing his famous wink as he threw his favorite fastball. I didn't have a best friend anymore. His smile flashed across my mind. This couldn't be true.

Another tear was about to form when something unexpected ran across my brain. Anger. Anger had found me. I felt my trembling fingertips form into fists as I slowly stood up.

That piece of shit. That disgrace of a man that I have the reluctance to call my father.

"Something is wrong," I said aloud to them. Both of whom were still stuck in their own state. "Sam never hurt anyone. He never even would have thought twice given the chance to. He did this."

"Who?" Rich said.

"My father. He told me that Sam's parents were some of the worst pieces of scum he's ever worked with. He said that if they wouldn't pay their dues then…something was going to happen."

"Wait, Thomas, you're not saying that, that's ridiculous. Your father is a piece of work, but I don't think he would kill a kid, no doubt one of your friends," Tommy said.

"I don't know what to think. We have to figure out what happened. He's our friend."

"The police will do a better job than us. Let's just wait for them to figure…

"No. Their process takes too long. We live in the streets of North End; they just patrol it. We'll call the cops when the time is right, but we need to do this."

Just as I was about to go on ranting a bit more, I noticed a car driving past an officer that had just started marking off the street with caution tape. It was unmarked and inside appeared to be a man with a suit on. It was the detective assigned to the case.

I waved Tommy under the overhang just as an auburn-haired woman jogged by.

"Over there, that's got to be the detective assigned to be here."

"Yeah? What is he going to do for us?"

"If we need to call the police, we can get his name so they won't hang up on us if we find anything."

"What makes you think they are going to take us seriously?"

"We lost…" it took a second to get out the words but for some reason, I needed to feel confident. Something needed to push me to figure out what happened to him. One of us had to set things in motion.

"Our best friend. The city will be looking into this starting immediately. They'll take any lead they can get. Rich, think you can lift his wallet?"

"Off a cop? Might as well, this night couldn't get much worse."

Chapter 22

"We deeply regret to inform the citizens of North End that we have lost one our youngest last night in an awful tragedy. Authorities are refusing to release any details on the manner of the death, but we were informed that the deceased was a Sam Hatkins. Hatkins was a twelve-year-old kid who has been a native of North End his whole life. Hatkins was discovered around nine in the evening at the historical Langone ballpark where children play every day. His parents are currently trying to be contacted with no success. If anyone has any information regarding Hatkins or his parents, the authorities would be grateful if you called the Boston Police Department or your Channel Five news station. Both numbers are on the screen now. God Bless Mr. Hatkins and his family during this trying time."

Channel Five news had an image of Sam displayed in the top right corner of Rich's television. Sam's brown eyes looked harrowing despite the smile coming from his sixth-grade picture. His hair was shorter, along with his clear dimples that looked as if you could pour water into them. I remembered that picture. I was next in line that day.

The anchorman, a thin man in his forties, proceeded to switch to another story as he lifted his bone chiseled fingers in the air to present an image of a bus accident from earlier that day. My head laid flat sitting on Rich's couch. Last night, we managed to take the cop's wallet, not to steal it, but to deliver a message to him. It was as ballsy as an idea when it popped into my head. I left a note for him in there stating we should meet up. The chances of him actually showing up was like shooting one of our paintball guns in the dark and hoping to strike the target.

Rich's house smelled of bad Chinese food mixed with pomegranate. Nothing could have prepared me for a smell that unique. My house wasn't my house anymore. It was a darkness, just a pit of apathy and delusive behavior. My father had to know about Sam's death, maybe even ordered it. His scumbag parents were the problem, not their twelve-year-old son. Our friend.

"Think they're on high alert at school? Second day in a row we've given them the slip. It feels kind of nice after saying it out loud," Rich said, as he gorged a bowl of cereal with every word.

"My dad probably gave them an excuse anyway. Doesn't want to cause a panic that his disobedient son ran away."

"You really think your dad had something to do with Sam? He was just a kid. I mean, I know that we sell dope for him every other week but heck, our profits can't be that important."

"His parents owe a debt. Debts must be paid and if they're leaving all the time, the best way to get their attention is to do something abrupt. Sam had to be the…"

The ceiling fan covered for my silence. Rich's gorging continued, and it was as if our conversation never happened. My fingers ran over themselves like a stampede. A beating sensation from my veins started to arise within my left calf. The teal color of my veins looked to be bouncing above my skin. My legs remained stiff, yet my muscles urged to move.

The front door quickly became ajar. Under a hooded figure revealed a familiar face.

"Hey, boys, package delivered. Doubt anybody saw me, I was like an assassin. Not to toot my own horn, I mean, it's already pretty large anyways," Tommy said, looking like a rejected boy band member with his black hoodie and fingerless gloves. He saw that we were watching the news and pulled up a chair.

"What's the next play, Thomas?"

Rich fumbled around on the couch and motioned his body at an angle where I could feel him looking at me.

"I don't know. This is all new to me, the thought of seeing him again. He was our friend, and he needed us and none of us were there for him."

Tommy's eyebrows dropped from intrigue to doubt. His foot that was tapping with interest had also gone silent.

"Let's just think for a minute. What did we do after Roma's yesterday?"

"Tommy and I went to go play Madden here. We were here for probably an hour until he decided to go home. I last saw Sam walking with you back to your place. Where did you last see him?" Rich said.

"Sam and I headed back to my place for a bit. After getting there, my dad called me into his office while Sam went up to my room by himself. Nothing happened to him up there because when I came up after talking with my dad, he was just sitting down watching Sports Center. We talked for a little while until I passed out. I woke up to my phone buzzing. It was Tommy, that's all I remember. When I woke up, he was gone."

110

"Gone? He didn't wake you to say where he was going?"

"Not that I can remember. Even if he did, I was too tired to recollect any of it. Dammit, if I never would have fallen asleep maybe, maybe he would still be here."

"You don't know that. We just need to figure this out like you said. We don't know who is to blame," Tommy said.

The feeling still remained despite his words. This was the second part of sadness I could feel it. First, the tears fell but now I'm in regret mode. What if something could have changed this? Something I could have done.

"Not even a text message from him when he left?" Tommy said.

"Nothing. Didn't you say that he answered your call once but then hung up?"

"Yeah, it was strange honestly. He answered for a few seconds and then he hung up. I could hear some kind of sound in the background, but the wind was blowing too hard to make any of it out. Might have been a voice or something."

"You're saying he might have been with someone?"

"Not sure honestly, but who else could he have been with? His parents are gone, and he only hangs with us?"

The three of us knew something was up. I felt like we were three investigators on a case, despite the fact that none of us knew anything about criminological theory. Just the *Law and Order* reruns we were accustomed to every weekend. The cops probably had it under control but there was something that kept latching on to my brain since last night. My father "owned" North End. Maybe that means, he has some cops working for him. My father probably adds another zero to the end of their paychecks in return for favors. What if I just invited one of those cops to meet with us?

"We need to do something before two. If the guy doesn't even show up, then we're still on our own. Maybe somebody near Langone saw something," Rich said.

"The cops probably questioned everybody on that block. What's the point in asking the same questions?" Tommy said.

"Yeah but cops intimidate people. They're too worried about incriminating themselves to say something useful. I'm not saying it's right but, we could use the sympathy card being Sam's friends in all. They're more likely to talk to a kid anyways."

"Did you just say incriminate? You sitting on a dictionary or something, you look taller."

"Shut up."

Rich stood up and went to the kitchen to clean out his bowl.

Maybe, he was on to something. Rich was pretty bright; it was better than anything that I could come up with at the moment. My mind kept wandering into thoughts I've never even heard of.

How many kids are killed every year? How many feel the cold string of death wrap around their necks until life is gone? For some, it's quick, with no ounce of pain to be felt. Pain was the horror that opened in my mind. Not everyone gets a savior when you need them the most. Sam deserved to be saved, not taken away from the world. He inspired good in everyone he met, and someone took that away from not only me, but the better future that his life would have brought.

I hope he didn't suffer.

My hand brushed alongside my left cheek as I started to stand. After taking it away, I found signs of water upon my hand and dried it out on my jeans.

"You guys can go ask around. There's somebody I need to go see."

Chapter 23

The smells were the same as was the crowd. Roma's was gaining a profit just like any other day. I walked by a man who was here yesterday. There appeared to be a marinara sauce stain on his collar, a much lighter color than the maroon sweater he had on. As I made my way to the bar, I noticed one of Roma's workers becoming agitated with a customer over the state of his sandwich. Too much vinegar apparently was the source of the issue.

My attention went to the back door from behind the counter that immediately swung open. Roma appeared holding a heavy tin. His eyes looked as if they were dragged down by a rake. He lacked the peppiness I was all too accustomed too. When his eyes met mine, he froze. He looked haunted, as if Sam himself was standing before him. He nodded his head and motioned me into the back.

I found myself in his old cramped office that was no more than fifteen feet wide. His desk took up most of the room, along with the chair that one could barely even scoot backward in. Roma stumbled inside and shut the door.

"Hey, Thomas," he said as he removed his apron and sat in his well-punctured chair. The cushions were so flat, the leather from the seats were falling apart.

"Can't believe this is happening, we just saw him yesterday."

"I know. But what could we have done?"

"Been there. Somebody, maybe not one of us but somebody could have been there to save him. He was our Sammy, look what the world has done." For the first time in my life, I witnessed the happiest person I knew to fall into his own hands and cry. I've never seen a grown man cry. I attempted to hold back what I could, but the task felt impossible. My father raised me to be tough, even when it's time to get older. I never saw him cry once. My mother did, it was one of the few things that I did remember about her. Once she left, no one cried in the house anymore.

"I think he did it," I said.

"Who?" he said, after wiping his eyes with such massive hands.

"My father. Sam's parents owed him a debt and I think he killed Sam to prove a message." I was almost afraid he would be angry and disagree. Rat me out to my dad since he was such a good paying customer.

"Look, your father is a tough piece of Boston grind but he's no kid killer. Everybody knows him and he's more the type of guy who knocks a guy's tooth out at a bar at noon. Trust me. I was quick to that assumption as well."

"He likes his debt's to be paid. What makes you think he'd try to change it up this time? My dad is a criminal. Criminals don't even know when they've crossed the line."

"Trust me, some know when to shut up and leave a sure thing that will get them tossed into jail. Your father is protected and narcissistic, but he's not that kind of evil. He represents the original, true crime days that are defined in the old mob movies from the fifties. Child killers are the corrupt agents of evil. Sometimes, they don't even know what they've done, till after it's over."

Roma was more of a father figure to me than my own, but for some reason, I was detached from his train of thought. I felt my head began to itch. The irritation started to increase the more and more I pictured my father.

"What were you guys doing last night?" Roma said.

"Nothing really. We split up after your place. Tommy and Rich went to Rich's. Sam went with me back to my place where we watched TV until I passed out. I was up late the night before; I don't even remember falling asleep. When I woke up, he was gone."

"What about Rich and Tommy?"

"They were together at Rich's. Tommy called me when they found him. We didn't know it was him at first until we got a better look. We saw him, Roma. He was lying out on the field. His arms and legs were spread out like they were moved around. I, I don't understand."

"You saw him? Thomas, why did you look at him? Somebody as young as you should never see something like that. I'm so sorry."

I remained quiet. The horror of Sam's body entered my mind again. I tried to think of a fond memory of the two of them, but all there was his limp body lying on the field where we grew up. Forever a reminder.

"Thomas, I know that you're in a terrible state right now, but you've got to promise me something. Promise me you won't go looking for who did this. The cops will take care of it. If a kid is murdered in Boston, half the force will be out on this. You, Rich, and Tommy are a bunch of kids. All you can do is honor his memory by living for him. Don't go out there and get yourself trapped in something you can't control. I mean it."

"He was our friend. How can I not want to know?"

"It's too dangerous and you are just kids. Please, spare me and even yourself from letting this happen again. We can't lose more of you guys. It's not a suggestion. It's a favor and an order."

The sound of a loud metal sheet just hit the ground outside the door. Roma's didn't even register it as he just stood up and continued to look at me. This was not just a request from a friend, it was an act of caring. Roma was a good man, perhaps even a great one. The thing is.

You can't tell a boy to give up on his best friend.

*

It was past twelve when I walked out of Roma's. The air was cool, and the wind was moving at a light pace. The clouds looked like heavy formations of cement about to burst. They looked like massive mountain ranges that only the birds could climb. Maybe Sam was above them. Maybe he was in a better place now up there than he could have ever been down here. Wondering could only get me so far. I let the unknown wander my brain for a few moments before I started to walk down the street.

I didn't know where to start. The meeting at two might be a waste if the cop doesn't even show. I couldn't help but think about why Sam was even in the fields yesterday without us. He never goes there unless there was a game to play and all it did was rain yesterday afternoon. Maybe there were some other boys playing in the rain, but Sam never plays unless it's with us. When the weather was bad, the field is supposed to be shut down. Mr. Walker. He was in charge of maintenance and upkeep. He had to have been there or seen something.

Adults always see something. Someone had to have seen something in the middle of the day. Second shift workers might have taken their dogs for a walk before the rain. Local boys might have skipped school too, or an elderly couple who likes to take their necessary stroll for exercise because nobody can tell them otherwise. Mr. Walker wasn't my biggest fan, I never knew why. The look he gave me yesterday coming out of Mrs. Kurtz's office was just a fraction of his inclination towards me. The classes I attended of his were compiled of snarky looks and illegitimate accusations of wrongful conduct. I honestly meant the guy no harm.

No matter how he felt, I had to see him.

Chapter 24

Mr. Walker's office was located in building D of James Madison Middle School. The gym, along with the school's production theater, and a janitorial equipment building, were in a sporadic design behind the main building. Luckily for me, there were no fences surrounding the area to keep me out. I walked towards the bus lot, weaving in and out of the buses. They seemed like yellow walls defending some fortress as I finally made it back to building D. I forgot to look at the time when I heard it.

The bell had rung. Hundreds of students were outside of their classrooms. Several of them were leaving and entering the gym as I managed to hide behind a prickly shrub located near the exit to the main building. I saw Paxton Overcash and Sylvia Cluse walking together. Both of them were holding hands, getting closer to my position. His freckled face, along with his curved eyebrow muscles were focused on her intimately as if he discovered what candy tasted like for the first time. They were the classic, cozy couple that everyone knew about. Their expressions proved the stereotypes of middle school romances, their pinnacle form. Love notes, pet names, and deplorable looks marked everything that was wrong with young love before it is adapted into something legitimate. However, just for this moment, I needed them to act exactly the same.

Both were so close, they were within whispering distance of me before their names were called by a few other students. Paxton and Sylvia left, leaving me to release the breath I'd been holding in.

The final bell for classroom change had sounded as once again the back courtyard of the school was empty. Building D was shut and locked as I crept out of the bush and made my way to the northeast corner of the gym. The athletic trainer, coaches, and physical education teachers all had their offices back there. Each door had a keypad or a card reader to allow staff members' access. School security was no joke nowadays. As unlikely as it may be, there is nothing more terrifying than a student losing his or her sense of belonging and deciding to release their anger upon innocent kids.

Fortunately for me, but unfortunately for members of the school, my wandering eyes caught the key code about two weeks ago. Mr. Walker's assistant, Mr. Wilson, a middle-aged man with a receding hairline who always wore the same olive gym shorts with JM stitched on them, had punched in the code one afternoon with me looking over his shoulder. After punching in the code, I heard the click and proceeded inside.

Most of the kids were in the gym. The sound of basketballs continuously being bounced drowned out any type of attention from my sneakers. Several students were involved in pickup games that took up most of the court. A few kids, most confidently the ones who despised physical activity, were all leaning against the walls engaging in conversation. Mr. Stenson was the only teacher out there, making me believe that Mr. Walker must be in his office.

Mr. Walker's office was located on the other side of the hallway, thus leaving me no choice but to cross in full view of the court. Even if a student saw me, I doubt they would say anything. Mr. Stenson was a driven teacher, unfortunately. He was less laid back and more progressive. I took a *leap* of faith and stepped into the open hallway.

Mr. Walker's office smelled of athletic gear and oranges. His skinny fingers were wrapped around a skinless orange as his attention quickly changed to the figure at his door. I stood there, frozen. Having thought about what I wanted to ask, my mind suddenly went blank. He struck first.

"Zaccardi. What are you doing here?" Mr. Walker said as he put the orange down upon his desk and straightened his posture in his chair.

I couldn't believe I said it but an impulse took over.

"Where were you?"

"I'm sorry?"

"The fields, where were you to check the fields? They found him around the time you go check the fields."

The clouds had seemingly swallowed the sun as its rays slowly started to slide down the room.

"Look, Thomas. Don't be assuming something you know isn't true. I had an after-school meeting with some of the school staff. It didn't matter anyway because the field was..."

"Was what? Fine? Sam was lying there, and you didn't check the field until late last night! You could have seen what happened. You could have been there to stop it."

I could not feel the skin beneath my feet. My hands were numb, along with my shoulders that seemed as calm as an ocean. What I felt was far from emotional but more heightened. I almost didn't recognize myself, me a student, yelling at a teacher in his own office. Perception had shifted, and nothing seemed to be as simple as it used to be.

"You hate us, all we do is tick you off. Maybe you had enough."

"I'm a teacher who cares for his students. I may not like all of them, but I would never do this. You need to understand."

"Give me a reason."

"Sam was a great kid. Do you think I would have let that happen to him? I know that you are...were his friend but you can't come waltzing in here demanding whatever it is you are trying to get from me. I heard you weren't even here today. Did you come here just to see me for this?"

"I had to see what you know. You say you weren't there, so I don't even know why I came here. I have to know what happened to him and I won't stop until I do."

"The cops have it now. Half of the town is looking for this guy. You don't have to do anything. You're just a kid. Hell, wouldn't be shocked if the police called your dad to help. He's full of..."

A sound crossed the air that caused him to go silent. It sounded as if it came outside from the open window in his office. His left eyebrow shifted up as both of us heard it. It sounded like a large balloon popping in the sky. Mr. Walker rose to his feet and acted more alarmed than I would have expected. He motioned for the door and walked by me. A familiar smell followed him as it smelled of a flowery sense. It was a custom that I would not have matched with his demeanor or his brash nature. Before opening the door, he looked back at me.

"Stay right here. That could have been anything, but I need to check on it. We're not through here," he said. Like that, he vanished through the door, much like a cartoon character on one of my favorite Sunday morning shows that I never really watched.

Curiosity had crept into my mind about the sound as well.

Chapter 25

I followed Mr. Walker outside into the back courtyard of the school. I could hear Mr. Stenson yelling at some of the students leaning against the wall as I made my way outside. Guess he had enough of their inactivity.

The sun was bright. Its rays were back with a vengeance as I scanned the back of the school. Mr. Walker had headed towards the bus lot. A few administrators had rushed outside, including Mrs. Kurtz. She looked mortified at some hidden incident located behind several buses. I wanted to know more but the closer I tried to get the more likely I would be spotted. As I went to crouch behind one of the freshly trimmed shrubs from before, I noticed that Mrs. Kurtz took a few steps away with her hand up to her face. She was calling someone.

While she was on the phone, Mr. Walker arrived with the other administrators. He was blocking the commotion that was going on. Just as he was about to say something to one of the assistant principals, Mr. Davlin, there was a single scream. It was a girl. She sounded quite young as I looked to see that Mrs. Kurtz and everyone else behind the buses were all staring in the direction of the scream. It came from one of the open windows of the school. My skin felt cold, something awful must have happened. I was about to move towards the edge of the shrub when I heard my name being called.

Mr. Stenson had poked his head out of the door. I'm not sure why he was outside, maybe he saw me this time. He stared at me for a split second and then began to yell for me to come inside. I stared at him blankly, not realizing that my head started to shake back and forth.

I ran towards the street and never looked back.

*

After running for a few blocks, I leaned up against the wall connected to an old barbershop at the corner of North and Sun Court Street. My heart felt like a piston inside of an engine, continuously pumping as if my gas pedal was glued to the floor. I felt a trail of sweat flying down the side of my head, looping around my earlobe on its way down.

That was too close. Mr. Stenson was just an arms-length away and could have yanked me away if he wanted to. He could have stopped me from looking for Sam's killer just by grabbing my collar. But that wasn't what I was thinking about, it was the scream. Its pulsating sound would not leave my mind. I didn't know who screamed but I felt sad for her. She must have seen something horrible, but I knew what it was.

It took me a minute, but after mellowing out and allowing my lungs to catch up, I decided to call Tommy. Maybe he had something. After a few rings, I could hear his voice, followed by the sound of birds chirping in the background.

"Hey, Thomas, where you at?"

"Just left school actually."

"School? I thought we were skipping today."

"Very funny. I went to see Mr. Walker."

"Coach Walker? Wait, why?"

"He was supposed to check the fields around the time Sam was found. I figured he might know something or even…"

"You thought he may have done it and you went by yourself? You should have brought us with you."

"I just needed to know. We just lost one of our best friends, and if there was a chance that we could find who did it. That chance had to be taken."

"Look, I understand, just, we're in this together alright? We can handle anything if we're all there. I mean we sell drugs in middle school for God's sake."

Tommy was right. His illegitimate humor was often too crude to see through but every once in a while, he would prove how loyal of a friend he could be. Together we were strong, but I just felt like a loose string of fabric knowing that Sam wasn't there this time. He was always the reasonable one who helped us find ourselves when life swung us around a blind curve. Now we had to learn to live without him.

"What did the coach have to say?" Tommy said.

"He was more surprised that I was there. I don't blame him."

"What do you mean?"

"I may have started on him quickly. I couldn't help but start off the way that I did. He claimed he had a meeting after school and assumed the fields were fine. He seemed to be as much in the dark as me. He seemed like he was about to give me more when something happened. I think someone got shot at our school."

120

"What? Are you serious?" I could hear him telling Rich about it as his voice started to linger away.

"There was a loud popping sound in the air and Mr. Walker got right up and went outside. Mrs. Kurtz and the rest of the principals were out there, they looked terrified. Then a girl screamed. That's when I got out of there."

"Well, shit. This weekend has already been fucked twice."

"Whatever it was, Mr. Walker still looked surprised that I was there."

"Yeah, that does seem strange. Maybe we can look into him later. Rich and I may have an idea."

"Yeah?"

"You know Twinks right?"

"Yes, our client who never resists the temptation to offer us a Twix bar and claims to eat them by the dozen when he's high. What about him?"

"Rich and I made a deal with him a few weeks ago and I remembered him saying that he and some of his buddies hang out around Langone and most places around Commercial Street on the weekends. Maybe he saw something last night but is too scared to come to the cops. He's probably scared he'll be searched on the spot."

"Not a bad idea. How would we find him though?"

"I got his phone number."

"Why would you save a drug addict's phone number?"

"It's not saved on my phone. I bought a burner phone. I saw it in a movie once, thought it would be a good idea. How do you think I know where most of our clients are? They call me."

A street trick if I'd ever heard of one. "I'm just shocked Twins even gave it to you in the first place."

"Twinks isn't what we call *smart* people. Anyways, I'm gonna give him a call to meet later tonight. Probably not a good idea if we meet in the day time."

"Good call. Where are you guys?"

"About to get a slice at Fernando's if you're down."

"Sounds great, food sounds great right about now. I'll meet you there in fifteen."

Tommy said goodbye and then hung up the phone. It's a shame that it took such a tragedy to unearth his intellect. After everything going on, I forgot about my stomach. Food has been an afterthought ever since last night. I could use a good bite to eat.

After getting off the wall, I decided to head down Sun Court with one hand in my jean pocket while the other grasped my phone. I attempted to look up the stats from last night's Sox game when I could hear my name from behind.

I turned to see Gerard. He was with two of his friends from before. The tall one who held him back yesterday was nowhere to be seen. I clicked my phone off and placed it inside my pocket, preparing for the inevitable retaliation.

"Gerard. This is much deeper into North End than you're used to I bet," I said.

Gerard was wearing a pair of dark jeans with a long-sleeved shirt that looked to be some shade of ivory. His hair was gelled back into a comb-over that was angled towards his left ear.

"Heard this place has some good food when it doesn't want to drop it on the floor. I like my sandwich clean. You know, how I like my basketball." His voice sounded more adenoidal than I remembered.

"If you're still hung up on that then maybe you should get a hobby. I hear photography is great this time of year."

"Funny, not the first time someone smaller than me had a smart mouth."

"Look, if you're trying to bully me or pick on me so matter-of-factly, I'm not interested in squealing." One of Gerard's friends, who had a buzzed haircut, shifted his shoulders as one looked to be hiked up higher than the other.

"If you were playing ball in Southie yesterday and you pulled what you did, your full head of hair there might be a lot less. It's not what I say. It's just what the rules of the neighborhood are."

I started to look around and reply with, "From where I'm standing, Southie looks a lot like North End. We believe in proper sportsmanship here."

"Well, we're not playing basketball today are we," Gerard said, as he started to roll up the sleeves of his shirt. The three of them managed to take a few steps closer. A vein in Gerard's neck had appeared, just one second after I could feel my head start to itch.

"Too bad your three friends aren't here like yesterday. There's three of us and one of you, guess it will have to go our way."

"I do love it when things are fair."

Gerard and I shared a smile when I decided to land one on him. After my fist connected with his lower chin, I vastly shifted my body around and proceeded to sprint back down Sun Court. I made it about ten steps when I felt gravity take a shift and a widespread pressure fall upon my shoulders.

Buzz-cut had managed to catch up to me and slam me backward into the ground. Before I could get to my feet, I felt a ridged force strike the side of my face. Gerard had arrived and delivered a swift kick to it, just above my left eye. My shoulders were still reeling from being slammed to the ground when I could feel my body being dragged by my collar towards what appeared to be an alleyway connected to the street.

As I was dragged closer, I realized it wasn't an alleyway, it was an old garage made for a compact car. The owner had left the garage door open and I started to shake a little as my limp body was being dragged towards it. It smelled of oil but there was no sign of any car. This is the second time I've ever met this kid, I didn't know what he was or what he could do.

The concrete floor was cold as my face quickly met it. My rib cage started to experience a series of toe-focused kicks from the three of them. With everyone that I felt, I could feel less and less air entering my lungs. Yelling was pointless as it would only bring me closer to passing out. Just as I could not take it any longer, and my voice was going to reach a new level that it never has achieved, the kicking stopped. Air found its way back into my lungs as someone grabbed the back of my collar yanked me up to my knees.

The garage was dark, but I could make out some tools hanging on the walls in front of me. They were hanging on green hooks covered in rust. Just as I envisioned myself grabbing one and beating one of them senselessly, I could hear Gerard say something.

"Hold him," was all I could make out. My ears were still ringing. I felt my arms become tighter towards my torso as his no-name friend held my body together and forced my head forward. It was then that I heard the terrifying noise that I heard every day. One of them had unzipped their pants.

I did not know what to feel. True fear had reached me, and it was by the hands of kids maybe a year older than me. It felt like an hour as I kneeled there and took it. Something warm started to hit my face as I could not move. Buzz-cut had my hair held as tight as one would hold onto a bicycle handle.

I didn't scream, I didn't plead. I just took it like someone who had given up. Acceptance was something that appeared in all facets. This one could not be planned nor understood.

After it stopped, I could hear Gerard zipping up his pants and proceed to walk in front of me. He bent down to the point where we were eye-level with each other. "Damn, I really had to go. I hope you were thirsty, the idea just came to me that you might have missed lunch," he said with a grin.

My mouth stayed silent.

"Nothing to say now smart mouth? Damn, I thought that would bring out some kind of response. Guess it is possible to shut you up." A short paused followed. My eyes lifted up slightly. I could see a scab starting to form from where I slammed his head into the fence yesterday. I'd rather take a quick gash than what just transpired.

"Really? Nothing at all to say?"

"Being right sucks," I managed to get out. My voice had fallen hoarse from my lungs trying to catch back up. It took me a second to think about if what I was going to say would hurt my predicament or make it humorous. Just had to take chance, even though the outcome was clear.

"Yeah, what's that?"

"You're as small as we thought."

His sharp eyebrows pointed downwards as if piles of snow were poured onto them. His mouth hung open for a few moments before I felt a sudden pain hit the side of my face.

The familiar coldness reached me again as I started to fall off into a swarm of blackness.

Chapter 26

I found myself unexpectedly asleep for the second time in twenty-four hours. There was a vibration in my left side jean pocket. Its rhythm was steady as my vibrate setting did not let up until someone answered or went straight to voicemail.

Time was telling me to get up, but I just laid there. A throbbing sensation hindered any attempt to completely lift my head. For some reason, I thought about my father. He said the streets were a mean place if wandered without your pack. I felt like a beaten sheep that had escaped its herd and was struck by a pack of wolves. But I didn't picture a wolf, just that damn panther.

After letting the phone buzz a few more times, I managed to lean myself up, pressing my back against the wall. The sun was still out so I must've been out for only a little while.

Rich was calling. I lifted the phone to the right side of my face but quickly jerked it back after realizing what happened on that side.

"Hello?" I said.

"Thomas! Where have you been? Tommy called you five times, and this is my third time calling you. We figured you bailed on lunch to handle some emotional thing with Sam, but we didn't think you'd miss the meeting. It's way past two and we thought something happened," he said. I heard two people walking by having a conversation. Something about what the economy was shaping to looking like in the next five to ten years.

"Yeah, you're right. I ran into Gerard."

"That guy? Did he do something?"

"He, um, he pissed on me and knocked me out." There was a long pause and then I could hear Rich whisper something to whoever was next to him. Before I could add anything more, a new voice came over the phone.

"That son of a bitch. We should have been there!" Tommy said quite loudly on the other side of the phone. "He's dead! First, the detective guy didn't even show up and now this?"

"Wait, what?"

"Yes, the prestigious Detective Michael Bowen who Rich performed an excellent snatch from the other night, did not show up. We did notice a larger man with a funny looking haircut has a badge attached to his hip. Maybe they sent him instead of our guy but I'm not sure. We waited for you to show up, but the fat man left ten minutes ago."

He didn't show up. Is anything going to go right today?

"Where does that leave us now?" I said, not really knowing why I even asked that.

"I'm not sure. Twinks said he'll meet us around 7:30, just after it gets dark."

After saying okay, I slowly got to my feet and found myself looking into a mirror. Gerard and his goons had shut the garage door, but some sunlight was finding its way inside. Like a line drawn in a blacked-out picture, the ray illuminated the mirror perfectly as I could see my own eyes looking back at me. The freckles around my cheeks looked to be faded. My face to me always seemed a tad bland. My cheekbones were not too fluffy but not too narrow, followed by a rounded chin that brought everything together. My eyes were as brown as a cigar. I wiped my hair back and smelled my fingers. A shower might help me think.

"Let's go to Sam's place. His parents won't be there for sure," I said.

"Sounds good. Where you at? I hope Gerard and his boys are there, they won't get off easy for that."

"I'm in some guy's garage. It must belong to somebody who works at the barbershop. I'm surprised no one's stopped by but can you do me a favor?"

"Sure, what is it?"

"Ask Rich if we can meet back at his place. I need to take a shower."

*

The pressurization of hot water felt like the perfect cure for disbelief. Few things made me relaxed within the past day and a half, but a shower definitely fit the bill. After taking what I was later told to be a twenty-minute shower, the three of us headed toward Sam's place.

Rich was a pal. If it wasn't for him, I'd be at Tommy's, hoping my towel wasn't the one that hadn't been washed in five weeks. I borrowed a jacket as well. It was a light-colored jean jacket that had a mustard stain down towards the zipper. A fleece was offered but I declined. After drying my hair, I put on a pair of black socks that Rich offered. As I was walking out, I stepped on something wet. Rich's older brother had left his soaked jacket on the floor, leaving the bottom of my foot feeling mushy. Wonderful.

I walked out of the bathroom to see everybody lounging in the living room. Rich's older brother, Mitch, was sitting with his girlfriend on the couch watching reruns of classic MTV shows. His girlfriend, Charlene or Charlie, was a tough-skinned girl who wore too much mascara around her eyelids. She was fairly skinny, but her knee caps stuck out way too much for my liking. She shot us all dirty looks as Tommy and Rich stood up. The three of us quickly headed for the door as she combed her dirty blonde hair backward and told us not to interrupt their leisure time as we left. Mitch reassured her, yet Rich tolerated the both of them somehow.

"Why do you deal with them?" Tommy said as we headed down the stairs outside of Rich's place.

"Who, tweedle dee and tweedle dum? The way I see it, you can't address every problem. It would drive the world crazy if you did," Rich said. He pursed his lips back as if trying to let out a sigh of relief that they had left.

The three of us were on Cooper Street as a gust of wind found the back of our necks. Almost simultaneously we put our hands in our jacket pockets.

"What do you think we're gonna find there?" Tommy said. "It's just going to feel weird going into Sam's room, ya know?"

"I know, but maybe there is something there that can help. He didn't have any enemies that we know of right? I mean, maybe a teacher who hated us when we cracked up in class but that's not enough to want to kill him," I said.

"Mr. Walker didn't seem guilty enough?"

"He was shocked to see me, like he wasn't prepared for me to come ask him questions. It just seemed, strange."

"Sounds suspicious to me. How do we know that he's not headed home right now, sunflower seeds in hand, and packing all of his stuff up to get out of town?"

"If he ran everyone would know. I'm not saying Mr. Walker is the smartest guy we know but he isn't that stupid."

"Guess you're right," Tommy said as he shrugged his shoulders. I noticed a bit of dandruff falling upon the back of his collar as his hair looked greasier than usual.

"What about his parents? They're never around. They could have come home, made Sam's death look like a serial killer had done it and then left again. They never wanted to have a kid anyways. Remember when Sam told us about the night he hid behind a door in their room when he was looking for some money when both of his parents walked in and his mom confessed to wanting him aborted? We can't cross them out," Rich said. His eyes were dark and jagged, much like a hawk when it's focused in on something.

Sam's parents? I honestly didn't know. It sounded too far-fetched, but his dad was a piece of work. The question popped into my head again, who killed my best friend? That seemed unheard of as well. No friend should feel the way we do right now. Sam should be right here with us, not caring what the future had in store but embrace the undeniable concept of free-will. We were free to commit or go do whatever we wanted, yet now it seemed lost. Sam wasn't free. He's probably lying on some cold table right now with no one who loves him around. He deserves better.

"I can't accuse anyone again unless we find something. We can guess all we want but once we find some kind of lead, we can't ignore any other possibilities," I said.

We turned off Cooper and found ourselves on Endicott. Sam's apartment wasn't too far down but the three of us stopped when seeing the same vehicle parked out front.

"Should have known they'd be here," Tommy said.

A white and blue Ford Interceptor was parked directly in front of Sam's home. *Boston Police* was spray-painted on both sides with a long light bar stretching across the roof. The license plate was orange with a nonspecific display of numbers across it. In what I have come to see, a cop driving an SUV can mean two things. Another officer is being trained or, the officer is simply, oversized.

"Think it's a fatty or a trainee?" Tommy said. Even though we worked on the opposite line from the police, he always seemed to be interested in their behavior.

"Doesn't matter, they're probably all over the place searching his room for prints," Rich said.

I nodded and looked around to see if there were any more police cruisers. Just the one from what I could see. Most of them were most likely here last night after everything went down. After walking a tad closer, I noticed there was bright yellow police tape wrapped around the handrails leading up to Sam's building. The green paint around the rails continued to fall like leaves in autumn. The brickwork surrounding the door frame was growing a congregation of moss that almost matched the green paint job around it.

We crossed the street and mingled our way past a beat-up Chevy truck with a headlight missing.

"New plan?" Rich said.

"Nah, there's something here that will help us," I said.

"Even if we fake a distraction for the cops, one of them will come out not two. Heck, we don't even know if there are two in there."

"Remember the time we had to swipe some cash from my dad?"

Tommy's eyes shot right at mine. A grin started to form as he said, "Yeah, I remember. You distracted your uncle while Rich and I crept in through the back. You can't be serious."

By the look of Tommy's face, he knew I was nothing but that.

"Round two."

Chapter 27

The plan was asinine but confidently planned out. If executed correctly, there would be no heat on our trail. I had my reservations but it was quite simple. Tommy would walk up to Sam's place, simply knock on the door, and convince the cops he was a local boy who claims he saw something. Lucky for Tommy, he looked the part with his lack of hairstyle and his oversized *Foo Fighters* t-shirt within his unzipped jacket. Nothing against the band, it's just that the shirt's neckline hung down farther than his grade point average.

While Tommy was distracting the cops, Rich would stand in the doorway to look up to see if both cops came to the door. If they did, Rich would give me the signal to climb over to Sam's window that overlooked the street.

The fire escape was rusty and on the verge of breaking down. An inspection was long overdue and I'm not sure it would help anyone if flames started to appear out of one of the windows. There wasn't even a ladder to climb up to the fire escape. There was, however, a silver pole that I had to shimmy up just to get up here. After crouching down to get a better look at Rich, I scanned the street hoping there wasn't another police cruiser on the way. Once I thought about it, we really wouldn't have to worry about the neighbors on this street. Endicott Street didn't belong to the brightest, and most of them wouldn't bat an eye.

After scanning for another minute, I looked down to see Rich looking up at me. A blank face looked back and then nodded. I stretched my legs over the bars, using my hands to counterweight my balance. My nervous system started to pump my adrenal glands, as I could feel my heartbeat increase before I looked into the window. After releasing my hand from the railing, I could feel a sticky substance reach my palm.

I slowly looked inside but struggled as the sun's rays were blinding half of my vision. The more I cautiously turned my neck, the more skewed my vision of Sam's room became. All I could do was hope no one was in there. If I remembered correctly, Sam never locked his window and a bit of confidence found me as I was able to lift my fingers under the sill to lift it up. *Thank you, Sam.*

My old sneakers still had some suction as I was able to safely enter Sam's room. The suddenness of what was happening almost distracted me from what this room was now. It was a tomb. A memory locked away in everyone else's mind but the person it belonged to. The adrenaline went away and the air became still.

Not much time.

Sam's room was tidier than most. It's been a while since I've been in here. His comforter was still a darker shade of navy, yet his pillowcases looked more fluffed than usual. His bedside drawer had a miscellaneous set of things spread across it. The dark-brown wood was starting to crack from drinks being left on its surface. I doubt his Andrew Benintendi's baseball card had anything to do with his killer.

Underneath his bed was nothing but a few crumbled up sweatshirts and the worn-out baseball bat he'd bring to Langone all the time. I grabbed it by the grip and observed the barrel. Several black smudges were decorated across it and several chips from countless hours of enjoying the beautiful game could be found at the end cap. I quickly jerked my head loose of the fond memories.

Tommy's voice had started to echo through the hall. It sounded as if he was saying his goodbyes and repeating that he would look around if anything seemed suspicious. One of the officers asked for his name and all I could make out was that he went by Edward. It sounded like a name from Cambridge. I felt my left-hand tremble with the weight of the bat in it as time was running out to find something. I bent down towards Sam's bookcase to find his stash behind three of his books. He had a lot more money saved up than I did. I went to move it around when something purple fell next to my hand.

There was a plastic bag with a purple smiley face sticker on it. The ninety-nine-cent sticker stared back at me as I knew who it belonged to.

Footsteps made my stomach drop. They were slow but daunting with every sound they made hitting the wooden floor outside Sam's room. I grabbed an unknown amount of cash, placed the three books back where they were, and climbed out the window. Without a creek, I slowly closed the window and wisped down the fire escape as fast I could.

*

"You think Twinks knows something?" Tommy asked. His pupils were much wider than usual. His brown irises almost looked nonexistent compared to the amount of interest that he revealed.

"Sam doesn't even like what we do, you think him and Twinks had something on the side?"

"We all don't like what we do. The bag definitely belongs to him though. He likes to be different by having his entire product in the same bag with the same sticker. Makes him feel unique or something," I said.

"He's a weird one."

"Where can he meet tonight?"

"Not Langone, he's spooked out by that place. I mean, I don't blame him. He went on about how there's a serial killer on the loose again," Rich said as he checked his phone.

"He said one of his new spots is in the parking garage off of Hull Street. It's pretty sketchy honestly."

"Did you ask if he could move the spot?"

"Yeah, but he didn't budge. Something about a hangout happening on the third floor. Figured he'd get his fix from us before going up."

'Makes sense,' I thought to myself.

Twinks wasn't the type I liked to hang around for more than a minute. He was the type of deal where you wanted it to go as fast as a prayer before you eat supper.

"Not to worry guys, I've got it covered."

Before my interest had time to peek, Tommy reached behind his waistband and revealed a snub-nose .38. The kind of gun that would make a drug addict laugh if you pulled it out but the kind that reminded everyone that it still could put a hole through your cerebellum. I knew the make as it appeared on an episode of *CSI* one time.

Rich immediately put his phone away and leaned back onto the heels of his feet. His left hand went up to scratch his forehead.

"What the hell is that?" Rich asked.

"It's a gun nut job. You know, bang, don't tell ya motha, I've got some business to do," Tommy replied with a smirk.

"We've never had a gun on a buy before, just the knife that you and I bring. Where did you get it?" I said, appearing to have a bit of sternness in my tone judging from Tommy's taken back expression.

"My dad has one. He hides it in a pillowcase wrapped up at the top of his closet. I found it one day while looking for some money. There is someone out there killing kids just like us, we can't take any chances."

Though rash, Tommy was right. I never even thought about arming myself with a gun. What kid our age should?

"We should go, we've lingered here too long," I said, after leaning off of the cold brick wall my neck was against.

As soon as I was about to take one step, I felt my arm being pulled back, followed by Tommy saying my name.

"Hey, Thomas, look who it is."

After seeing a car door open from across the street, someone familiar stood up eyeing Sam's apartment building. It was Detective Bowen. He was lacking the suit and tie look from the other night but still looked composed. In daylight, more of his features could be made out. He looked much younger than the other detectives I'd seen before, plus, his hair was full and did not lack the stress of the job.

I couldn't help but ponder the thought that he hasn't seen something like this. His youth didn't make me angry, it made me somewhat hopeful. Maybe he could bring something new to the table, a new technique that would actually catch Sam's killer. Boston never did catch the last one we had.

"I thought he would have come here last night after finding Sam's body," I said.

"He probably was at the crime scene for a long time. It's the murder of the year if you think about it," Tommy said. His voice trembled after his last few words. I didn't have to shoot him a look to show that I disapproved.

"We need to see him."

"Wait, what?" Rich said. "We almost got caught just now and you want to go back?"

"Not necessarily, we can improvise."

Chapter 28

The idea came to me. Instead of going back up to Sam's place, I simply fashioned another message. Rich went inside the local department store and obtained some tape and a notecard. I didn't ask how he got them. With the sharpie I kept from the last message, I wrote another one asking Bowen to meet at another place.

It was a dock behind the K-8 Innovation School off of Commercial. The Charlestown Bridge could be seen if you were standing at the end of the closed dock. The school closed it off to students in fear that a kid would fall off. The four of us would go out there sometimes to feel the breeze bouncing off the water. It was serenity for us in a town full of regret and the improvisation of escaping it.

I didn't know where else to go. Cops didn't patrol the dock at night and the coastguard barely supervised that area past five in the evening. Plus, it was about two blocks from DeFilippo courts so we knew the area pretty well in case things went sour and we needed a getaway. It seemed plausible for a good place to meet.

Several hours had passed as we spent the rest of the afternoon walking around North End contemplating what motive someone had for killing our best friend. After having dinner at a pizza parlor, one street away from where we were meeting Twinks, whereas Tommy accidentally spilled some sauce on his t-shirt, we made our way to the parking garage. My phone said it was five minutes till seven-thirty when we arrived. We hooked the corner of Prince and Causeway only to be met with several orange cones shaped into a square. Before us, rested about a five-foot-wide array of fresh concrete that looked as if it was just laid. The cones were about half our size and did a tremendous job of preventing us from stepping in it.

"Heard it takes about twenty-four to forty-eight hours for this stuff to actually dry up. Let's not step in it," Rich said, as the three of us motioned around, trying not to step on the street.

There were two wide openings in the building that were labeled "Enter" and "Exit." The building was painted in a shade of falu red, yet weathered by time and apathy. The paint job looked to be way overdue and there were several hundred traces of heat blistering. The moisture build-up caused the walls to have what I associated with as bubbles.

My father actually told me that this place had a history. Before it was a parking garage, it was the location of the Great Brink's Robbery back in the nineteen-fifties. In the fifties, this spot was taken up by the Brink's Company building. It was a business that professionalized in security and asset protection. Irony has it; my father told me that almost three million dollars were stolen by eleven gang members in an armed robbery, the largest in the country at the time. It wouldn't surprise me if one of my great uncles was a part of it.

We entered the garage and found a staircase to our right. The sun was almost set as several amber lights guided our way up to the third floor. The smell of concrete and other unnamable fragrances entered our nostrils as we slowly walked. With each step, we heard a sound that became louder. It was music, something I could not make out but it was definitely music. Twinks and several other rebels of North End chose the third floor because of the lack of cars that were parked up there. With the music playing, it sounded as if there were dozens of cars up there. Most events in town caused the entire lot to be filled on certain weekends but that wasn't the case tonight.

When we arrived on the top floor, we could only spot out a few cars parked sporadically across the lot. "Lovely," Tommy said under his breath as we made our way towards a group of poorly dressed men in the northeast corner. Around them were close to thirty people, all dressed in either dirty or saggy clothing. It must have been their form of a party as one of them had a speaker box next to a beat-up Jeep Cherokee. It was playing some techno song with no lyrics. It was a lot of people. More than the number of people I felt comfortable with. If Twinks was going to talk to us about our friend, why would he choose such a popular spot? I watched as Tommy scratched his lower back, coincidentally where his gun was resting.

After giving Tommy a quick nod, we spotted Twinks leaning against one of the walls with a cigarette sticking out of his mouth. He reminded me of a sketchy older brother who had plenty of stories of the dangers of adulthood. He wore jeans with three holes around his knees, which looked to be three different shirts, starting with an oversized, black jacket with a pocket missing. His hair was unmade, along with his left shoe being untied. His neck was long and skinny, with his Adam's apple protruding out of it like a rock stuck in an undersized pipe. His face looked like a "V," kind of like a crow. Poor guy, he didn't even appear to be thirty yet and his life was already in shambles.

"Boys, boys! What can I help you with on this dismal day in our great town?" Twinks said, his voice sounding screechy.

"Hope you brought something for us beggars of the community."

"Good to see you too I guess," I said.

"Isn't it always?"

"Yeah, look we don't want to be here long. We just need to ask you some questions about our friend and we'll be on our way," I said.

"In a rush? I don't like that. We always have good times. What happened to Sammy was a travesty but it doesn't mean we can't pal out like we usually do." The four guys behind him, which were dressed in a usual fashion, started to snicker as if he just revealed the opening joke of a sit-down comedy bit. The others, standing around with cigarettes and beers glued to their hands, didn't appear to notice us with Twinks.

"Were you at Langone last night?"

"Langone, nah. We were over in Dorchester trying to score if you know what I mean." A wink followed, as well as a grin from his yellow-stained teeth.

"If we saw something, we would have gone to the cops. Damn shame somebody around here is killing kids. Shawn Stensmore might be out, but he didn't kill kids. Sure it's safe for even you three to be out here?"

An uncomfortable churn in my stomach formed after he said that. Stensmore was a name I saw in the news for about two straight months last year. He was rumored to have killed two people but I don't know if he could… It took me a second to contemplate when someone spoke up.

"We lost our friend and we aren't going to give up until we find him. The police can't find their own ass with a map and a key. You have to get dirty and talk to everyone who might know something. Was there anybody else there that you might know of?" Rich said, as he centered his stance.

"Someone without a badge might get more answers than someone with one."

"Wow, very adult of you guys. Trying to investigate the crime that shook our town. I might feel safe with you guys on the case than some balled up cop who busts druggies for just trying to relax."

"Just trying to relax? That's not what you guys do drugs for."

"Sure, it is. You see, we aren't hurting anyone getting our fix. The cops don't understand. If they leave us alone, then we leave them alone. Nobody has to get hurt for nothin'." Twinks coughed a few times but then added, "So, do you think we had something to do with it? 'Cause, if you do, I'm not opposed to fixing that assumption right now."

"We're not saying that, we only thought you might know something," I said.

"How's that?"

"We found this in Sam's room today, before the police had a chance to find it." I reached into my pocket and displayed the plastic bag with the purple smiley face on it.

Twinks didn't even blink when he saw it.

"Well, what do you know, there is a reason you are coming to talk to me. Sammy's good people, I trusted him the most out of you."

"Why does he have this? We always give yours back."

"Are you telling me that you guys don't know?"

His words echoed in my ears and I presumed Tommy's and Rich's as well. I could feel my face go blank as Twinks caught on. He could see that I was perplexed.

"Sammy was smarter than all of you. He had his own business going down on the side. He would acquire more products for me and I would supply him with more doe. Plus, his dad owed a lot of money. Whatever he made with the three of you, he had to pay off his dad's debt, which meant nothing left for him. He cheated you guys. He sold more than all of you combined just so he could be the proper breadwinner."

"You don't know Sam like we do. He wouldn't have screwed us over like that, you're lying to us just as you lied to your mom back in grade school," Tommy said. His brashness was heard with every syllable.

"Hey, watch it, kid. Look where you are and look where you're standing. You're in no position to say bullshit like that," Twinks said.

"I'm not afraid of you. I've socked kids bigger than you are. What do you think of that?" Tommy's shoulders were tense as I rested my hand on them.

"Know what I think? I think you're one more truth away from breaking my man. Like my ripped jeans here, they look held together but with more pressure, they're going to break. Don't test what you can't handle."

Another silence fell on the third floor of the parking deck. I was reaching my tipping point and Twinks could see it. My facial expressions could be more conspicuous if I knew how to hide them.

"Here's the thing you three. It's a Saturday night, the air is cool and the night just started. Work was hard this week and we need our fix. Now, with that being said, what do you have for us?"

"You're not getting shit from us, not until you start telling the truth about where you were last night. You said it yourself a few weeks ago. You never leave North End unless it's for a Sox game and they played in Tampa last night," Tommy said. His forehead looked to be the color of a tomato, which I doubt was from the cold weather.

"Words, words, words. That's all you got, nothing I want and nothing we need. Sammy was the smartest of you shits. Wish he wasn't dead. Shame he couldn't train you to be reasonable when you're supposed to be."

"That's it, let's switch this up."

The tension seemed to escalate faster than I could move.

Tommy's feet started to shift as his right hand motioned behind his back. In the midst of saying his name, I managed to lunge towards his hand to hold it away but I was too late. Just as he revealed the .38, I closed my hand around his when the ground shook beneath us as a loud pop filled the air.

Chapter 29
The Meet

Delahine and I moved swiftly down the street. In a flash, we were both out of his car with our Glocks held at eye-level scanning the area. The shot we heard was followed by more but spread far apart. Someone was shooting but hasn't found his or her mark yet.

The shots sounded as if they were echoing from the parking garage to our right. A few passersby were standing at the end of the street curious to what was going on. They seem bewildered and shocked when I yelled at them to run for help. I was slightly shocked to see that none of them were taking a video with their smartphones.

"Who could be making this much noise this early into the night?" Delahine said.

I chose not to answer but aimed the muzzle of my Glock at the corner of the parking garage. No one had come out yet. The moment was stifling as I could not fathom the thought of having to fire my weapon twice in one day. As unexpected but welcoming the feeling was Jess entered my mind. I wanted to see her again instead of standing where I was. I shook my head to regain my focus but she still remained there.

Delahine chose to get on the sidewalk as he pressed towards the corner of the building. I continued to follow along the line of cars just a few yards away from where he was. We could hear footsteps rounding the corner along with another shot of gunfire. The shot forced a reactionary duck as I found myself bending down behind a Toyota Camry.

The footsteps quickened as they appeared around a corner. It was a kid, around Sam's age. His brown hair was cut short and had a distinctive face. Despite his frightened expression, a glow of confidence enriched his eyes as if he knew where he was going. Just as I was about to yell out, I could hear a splashing sound followed by a thud. A man cursed aloud, instantly sending my brain into confusion.

Delahine took charge and yelled at the kid to go behind the car where I was. The kid, still in a less convincing daze, did not hesitate and headed straight for me. After letting him catch his breath for a moment, I quickly asked for information about what he saw.

"It's alright, we are police officers. I know we don't look it, but we are here to help. Did you see who was doing the shooting?"

The kid sat huddled up next to the bumper. He was hiding his face behind his hand that was trembling. Was he the one being shot at?

I quickly jerked back up when the sound of two more shots filled the air. I could see Delahine had his back against the wall, before leaning past the corner of the parking garage. He pulled his head back after another shot filled the air. Whoever was shooting needed to be stopped before someone was going to get hurt or something worse.

"Some guy fell in a cement pool and won't stop firing rounds off!" Delahine managed to shout in my direction.

"Can you see anyone else?" I said back, hoping it was just some fool instead of a group.

"The guy looks like a beggar, he's gotta be tweaked out of his mind."

Just as I was about to respond, I could hear the soft trembling of a voice from below. I thought I heard what it said but nothing clear filled my head.

I kneeled down to speak with the boy who put his hand down.

For some reason, I didn't notice it sooner. It was him, Thomas Zaccardi. His cheekbones and eyebrows immediately popped into my head from the picture that Principal Kurtz showed me. There was no smile on his face this time.

"There was a group of them, maybe…maybe five," He managed to say. His voice was still but clear. There was no lie in his eyes that I could find. Fear started to take over as I realized that one wrong move and Delahine could be someone's target practice.

I pulled my walkie out and called in for several units to my location. I didn't mention Thomas, just that two officers were taking heavy fire from an unknown group of suspects.

I stood back up and yelled to Delahine to back off as there could be more. Just as I spoke, Delahine ran towards our position only to be met with a string of gunfire. A second man appeared around the corner and opened fire on Delahine as he ran towards the car. I instinctively raised my Glock and clicked the trigger repeatedly until my finger felt numb. The sound of the rounds shooting off rapidly filled my eardrums with every click.

There wasn't time to count, or to think, just do. Pure instinct took over as the adrenaline in my bloodstream felt like a roaring current during a fall storm.

I could not see the suspect any longer. He was nowhere to be found. The sound of glass breaking caught my attention on the sidewalk as Delahine emerged into view.

I was just about to ask if he was alright when another shot fired off and struck the top of the Camry in front of me, just two inches from my head. Three more shots sounded off when I thought it was the end. Just like a flash of light, I thought my brain had committed its last action.

The shots came from beside me, followed by a loud scream and then silence. The man who came from the corner was now lying in the middle of the sidewalk out of the truck he was hiding behind. I could only imagine the fear in Thomas' eyes right now. The firefight that ensued around him was more frightening than anything I could perceive at that age.

Over the walkie, I could hear Delahine's voice. He called in that one of the suspects was down. I could hear a siren in the distance as the backup was undoubtedly speeding past all lights to our position. Then it hit me.

I wasn't supposed to be here. Burkes was one of the first to be called when an active shooting was occurring in his district. He was either on his way or being informed of everything that was called out on the radio. Thomas was still crouched behind the Camry as I lightly grabbed his collar and brought him to his feet.

"We need to leave, now. Come with me," I said in a tone that I hope didn't sound to commanding.

Thomas nodded and stood close by. The two of us moved across the street to my car when a woman in a blue uniform approached. Officer Switzer, I think was her name. Her blonde hair was put up in a high ponytail that swayed back and forth with every step she took towards us.

"Detective Bowen, Officer Sandoval, what's going on?" she said. Got that wrong. Her voice was light through the air as if a soft melody came from a stereo.

"Officer Delahine is on the sidewalk, one suspect is down and another is trapped in a cement pit. This kid saw the whole thing. He needs to get out of here."

"I can take him, if you need…"

"No, I've got him. He needs to be debriefed right away."

Her expressions could tell all. She was someone who could tell you exactly the way she was feeling just by her animated expression. Her tight-lipped reaction gave me the impression that she was put back. I directed her towards the sidewalk and she headed that way Glock raised high.

Thomas and I found my car. In less than ten seconds, I had started the engine and headed far from Prince Street. This night went to shit real fast. I didn't know what was more distracting, the sound of Thomas breathing heavily or my heart about to bust out of my chest.

Chapter 30

I didn't know where else to go. He would help us, I hope. Thomas was quiet the whole ride as he seemed traumatized or just concentrating on something. I couldn't tell what would help, a reassuring voice or the silence that filled the air. The radio was off. The only sound emanating from the car was the heater set to a blazing eighty-two degrees.

My place seemed too risky. Saturday nights are filled with blue uniforms. Burkes had to have someone staking the place out. I'm sure the report would read something such as "protective lookout." Saturday was, in fact, the busiest night of the week. Our analytical department presented a report to us last week about how many more violent and property crimes are committed on Saturday. If it weren't for the illustrations and the colorful pie charts, I likely would have rendered the whole presentation mundane.

I took a left onto Tremont Street, where the Boston Common was spread out upon my right. The fifty acres of urban park looked peaceful at night, not a bad place to take someone. I should take Jess here to walk around. Since she looked to be in good shape, a jog might not be a bad idea as well. Before I could speculate any further, the quiet came to a stop.

Thomas had grabbed the passenger side door handle and attempted to leave while the car was still moving. I intervened by putting my hand across his chest.

"Thomas Joseph Zaccardi. Twelve years-old, student at James Madison Middle school, and a propensity for delinquency. Yes, I know who you are. What were you doing out on that street corner at this time of night?"

Thomas sat there silent for a few moments. Not a single expression of shock after I revealed who he was and where he even went to school. He refrained from making eye contact by staring out the window. "We were looking for someone."

"What do you mean? Who were you looking for?"

"It doesn't matter. He wasn't saying anything, but you should have been there."

I felt put back. Did I miss something? "Where was I supposed to be?"

"Paul Revere Mall, three o'clock."

Like a chime ringing a clock, I felt a sensation go off in my brain. The moment where something clicks in the most unlikely way. Thomas was trying to reach me this whole time. He knew I was looking into his friend's death.

"You know that I'm on your friend's case then," I said.

"Yeah, we saw you last night walking over to his body. We could tell by your suit. Not many people wear suits so late at night."

"We?"

"My friends, Tommy and Rich."

"Your principal told me about them. Where are they now?"

"I don't know. We got separated when the shots were fired up in the garage. Tommy pulled out the gun he had and tried to threaten someone but accidentally set it off. He was stupid." My eyes caught his hands rubbing together. I could tell the moment must have been circling around in his mind.

"Do you think they're okay?"

"Don't know. I suggested we split up when the firing started. They just started to shoot at us for, for some..."

He scratched his head a few times before continuing, "He was just a guy we met who might know something about Sam. So, we met with him."

"In a parking garage?"

"Yep."

"Sure."

The streetlights faded in and out as I could see merely glimpses of Thomas's face. The boy needed rest and a place where he could get his head on straight. He didn't completely trust me but why would he? Sure I'm a police officer but we aren't exactly a trustworthy bunch these days.

"I need to get you somewhere safe for the night. Trust me, I know a guy," I said.

"No. We need to go see someone," Thomas said directly.

"Who?"

"My baseball coach."

*

Fear had found everything again. The roar of the mind as it meticulously thought about what had happened. I did it once. It's only a matter of time until I do it again. My fear wasn't what someone would think. It's not me who is afraid.

A lion attacks its prey when the moment is right. The texture of the grass had to be just right before it pounces on the inferior creature in its path. The feeling was dark but necessary. Survival is all that I could think about, it just fuels anyone who wants to live on as if nothing has changed.

There was still something left to fix.

Mr. Walker's house was a brown brick housing complex located on West 5th Street. It was the only brick house on the middle-class street of South Boston. I remember coming here before in high school. My friends and I used to play baseball on this street when we weren't at a park like Langone. The sun used to shine bright off the pavement. Years had passed and that familiar feeling of excitement escaped me. Probably since it was the middle of the night and I wasn't wearing my striped tube socks.

After parallel parking at the corner of the street, it took me a second to think about how Thomas even had Mr. Walker's address. After getting out of the car, both of us headed down the sidewalk. Thomas told me about his visit with Mr. Walker earlier in the day and how suspicious he seemed. I couldn't help but listen intently to him as I was quickly running out of leads. Delahine was most likely filling out an officer-involved shooting report at the moment and all of the files he collected were sitting in his car. I was back to the drawing board, but with a small piece of chalk.

After passing a few more houses, one with an outlandish aquamarine paint job to its front door, I expressed my concern. "Look, Thomas. Let me go in there and talk to him. He's obviously not expecting me and I can press him with any questions that you have. Just give me anything that I might be missing," I said.

"Not a chance, he needs to know that I'm on to him," Thomas said back to me as he stopped in the middle of the sidewalk. He had an array of confidence not found in many boys of his age. I was put back by it sure, but it impressed me nonetheless. It seemed different than his father's, not as contemptuous or with the desire to instill fear.

"Do you think, he had something to do with Sam's death?"

"He just didn't seem right. He started to appear more irritated the more we talked before we were interrupted by a gunshot. We were at my school. As a cop, I assume you heard about it."

"Yeah, I believe I did."

Mr. Walker's front door was shamrock, with a rusted golden knocker at its center. An eyehole rested above it, to which I instinctively moved Thomas to the side out of its view.

"Alright, if you insist on coming in let me start us off. You hide behind the neighbor's staircase and I'll give you a signal. You shouldn't even be here so you're lucky I'm even suggesting it," I said.

"What will the signal be?" Thomas said.

"If you're listening, should be easy to catch."

Thomas seemed confused but content on the idea. He raised an eyebrow with the utmost curiosity. Strange, he seemed like someone I knew as a kid. It was a different strength than today's youth had. It seemed molded by experiences not related to school drama or issues with not having an internet connection with a smartphone. His interpersonal demons seemed to be held back, but by something unknown to me.

After waiting for Thomas to hide behind the stone steps about fifteen feet to my right, I walked up Mr. Walker's stairs. After two knocks at the door, it was swung open after just a few seconds.

Mr. Walker stood before me wearing boxer briefs and a gray New England Patriots t-shirt. His hair was unkempt, but he was clean-shaven. His left hand shot up straight into his hair to comb some of the gray back.

"Detective Bowen, what are you doing here? It's late," he said.

"It's fine, tomorrow's Sunday, you get to sleep in."

Before I could add anything, another figure walked past behind him. It was a woman wearing an oversized, baseball shirt. Her long legs looked well-groomed, fairly attractive in the way one of them bent at the knee.

It almost didn't faze me until I noticed the gray hair upon her shoulders.

Chapter 31

It took me a second to hone in on if I identified the right person. Even though her hair was down and not up in a professional manner, it still took me a second after being impressed by the way she looked. Not surprising since similar thoughts found me earlier this morning in her office.

Dr. Kurtz's face looked as if a weight had injected itself into her apple cheeks. Her mouth opened quickly after seeing me in the doorway.

"That's a whole other matter," I said, directly to Mr. Walker.

"Dr. Kurtz, I'm not alone, would you please go put on some more clothes and come meet us in the living room."

She seemed flabbergasted by the request, as she hesitated and then moved quickly up the stairs. I turned back to Mr. Walker and lifted my eyebrow to him.

"It seems we still have some things to talk about. More, if my nose isn't wrong," I said. "May we come inside?"

"Who else do you need in here...wait a minute, you don't have a court order or a warrant, I don't have to do anything. You and your men can leave until you have a piece of paper hanging in front of my face that you can be here by law." His stance changed as he spread his feet more apart for a stronger balance.

"It's an open murder-investigation. I don't want to have to explain it to you but to put it short, if you don't let me, you will be committing obstruction of justice and you can sleep back at the station tonight. Don't make me go on."

A realization spread across Mr. Walker's face as he scanned his thoughts for a response. After nothing seemed to come to mind, he responded. "Fine, bring your men in and tell them not to knock anything over. My buddy is a cop and he almost knocked over my lamp with his holster."

"I'll be sure to mention it. Hey, recruit, you coming?"

After a few seconds, I could hear quick footsteps behind me. After noticing Mr. Walker's face become even more shocked, it was reassuring to know that Thomas got the signal.

"Thomas?" Mr. Walker said, sounding as if his breath was being taken away.

"Coach, nice to see you again," Thomas said as he made his way into the house. He stopped in the middle of the hallway and walked towards what I believed to be the living room. Mr. Walker looked back at me with his mouth half open. I shrugged my shoulders and heard him shut the door behind me after I walked in.

The temperature was dramatically different as I could feel the warm seventy-something degrees hit my shivering hands. Mr. Walker pointed, Thomas and I, in the direction where we both sat down on his brown, beat-down but surprisingly comfy couch. He did not have much taste for interior decorating I could see as most of his walls were covered in sports posters either thumb-tacked on or held by a frame. His couch was a different color from his two other chairs, his kitchen table, and even the rug beneath our feet.

Mr. Walker walked over to one of his chairs and embarrassingly started to put on a pair of sweat pants. Both Thomas and I looked away to elevate the moment from being worse. As I looked away, I noticed a thin wedding ring with a decently sized diamond on the crest. I wasn't looking for one before in her office but damn. We just walked into something worse.

"So, Thomas, what are you doing out so late? What are you doing with Detective Bowen?" Mr. Walker said, as he sat down.

"Not much, but I know what you were doing," Thomas said before feeling me nudge him with my shoulder.

"I'm looking for whoever took Sam away from me. Something you don't seem too keen to talk about."

"I've already said I don't know what happened. You just can't keep repeating the same question and expecting a different answer."

"Mr. Walker," I said. "Thomas told me about the meeting between the two of you earlier today. He informed me that you acted more irritable to Sam's death than he would have expected. You're not being accused of anything. We just need details about what you were doing Friday after school. I know we met last night but anything small could be crucial."

Just as he started to explain his whereabouts once again, Dr. Kurtz arrived downstairs. She was wearing black leggings with the baseball shirt still coming down to her mid-thigh. Her hair had been brushed, as well as some new mascara around her eyes. After seeing Thomas and looking more uncomfortable than she already was, she directed her attention back to me.

"Detective, we can explain all of this. I'm not even sure where to begin. Please, don't judge us on this," she said, as she motioned across the room to the other vacant chair.

"I'm not the one who will be judging, we're here for something else. Mr. Walker was just in the middle of explaining what he knew about Sam Hatkins. If you have anything, please chime in," I said to her. She nodded her head a few times and while flattening her lips. Mr. Walker looked over to her and tried to give her a reassuring face.

"Like I said, Friday was a normal day. I had class from seven in the morning until two-fifteen. It took me a minute to clean the gym but then I proceeded to Rachel's office. She was in the *meeting* I lied about before. We discussed the weekend and well, tonight. Everything else that I said was true. After I met with Rachel, I had a few errands to run and then I went home for an hour or two. I usually check the fields' right after school but I put it off today. If I didn't then, maybe."

"Maybe you would have stopped the guy who did this," Thomas said. He intended for his statement to sound the way it did. I gave him a quick glare and then looked back at Mr. Walker.

"When you check on the fields what does that entail. Just a simple light check and see if there is any trash around," I said.

"Mostly, it wasn't that bad this time since we had the heavy rain. I was able to convince the town board to buy an expensive field cover that I can just detract with the touch of a button. On Friday, I just clicked the button to detract it and went into the clubhouse to make sure no one had broken in. We had an issue the other month of kids hanging in their late. When I came out to check the field, I saw Sam there."

"That explains why no one saw his body, until you found him. Why didn't you mention the cover before?"

"I don't know. It was my first time seeing a dead body. It was Sam's for God's sake. I wasn't ready for something like that," he said as his voice started to tremble.

"This is hard to handle, no one should have to see that. You have more of a relationship with the Zaccardi's than a petty hatred for them don't you Mr. Walker?"

"What do you mean?"

"When I mentioned Thomas and his family last night, it struck you. It struck you more than the average citizen would have reacted. Is there something about them that you are not telling me about?"

His demeanor shot up again, but not out of anger but of something else. Mr. Walker cleared his throat and looked at me, after making a mild glance at Thomas.

"I used to do some stuff for them."

Dr. Kurtz looked as if she had no idea of what was going on. She almost made a motion to leave when I took notice of her uncrossing her legs. She quickly remained still.

Mr. Walker went on. "I was staring bankruptcy down the other year. It wasn't looking good for me, Massachusetts may have the best education system in the country but its workers aren't paid what we should. I made a few costly investments and I was down on my luck. You've heard the same sad story I'm sure. I met Thomas's uncle Richard in a bar and he talked to me about a side-job. I knew him in high school as the guy who never tried but somehow made it by. With so little options, I decided to help them help me out."

"You worked for the Zaccardi's?" I said.

"Yes, it wasn't right I know but it helped me get the money I needed. I even made a little extra and fronted most of the money for the cover over the baseball field. I figured a little bit of giving back might ease the conscious."

"How's that going for ya?"

"Not as well, as I'd hoped. The point is it didn't end well. I backed out on one of the jobs involving assaulting a man in his own house just to find some money underneath his bed. After I backed out, Richard and a few of his friends broke into my house and brought me to the bakery. For what seemed like hours, they beat me. I've never been more terrified. I didn't even know if I was going to get out of there alive with all the stories I've heard. A bat to the head seemed certain until the door creaked open and I thought help had come. Maybe the police were coming but no one knew I was there. Ralphie, Thomas's other uncle, answered the door and I felt the fear come back when it wasn't help."

"You're lucky they didn't kill you. They don't let people go unless a deal is made. What did they propose to you?"

"Ralphie said that my legs were better when they weren't broken. He let me go and said that at any time if they need something, I would have to be ready to go. No choice, no excuses. I haven't been contacted for a year. Maybe they forgot."

"Maybe they contacted you to kill a kid."

A sudden silence filled the room. It was as if the four of us were sitting at a wake just before a funeral. I knew what I did, and the pace of the conversation had to change if the truth would be spilled.

"I've already told you and your Captain, I didn't do it. I just found Sam's... Sam in the middle of my field. I never touched him," he said back to me. His voice was quickened but soft. His aggravation was nowhere near where I thought it would have been.

"If what you are saying is true then trust me, they didn't forget. Sebastian, this is serious. You're one of the few who actually got away. Your information would help us greatly with making sure the Zaccardis are off the street.

"Are you guys forgetting who is sitting in here? This is Thomas's family we are talking about. He needs to have a say," Rachel said. She had remained quiet throughout Mr. Walker's entire story that I almost forgot she was there. "Thomas deserves the right to say something."

I looked at Thomas. He had leaned back on the couch as soon as we sat down but now, he was sitting straight up.

"My family is what you think it is. I grew up ignoring the key signs and pretending that most families were trouble. North End is filled with families who have contributed little to our society, but there are more who make it a better place. One thing has always been clear. My family needs to be taken away."

The room remained silent for a few moments. Thomas appeared to be a kid who has seen it all. He's seen his mother walkout, a family who has no stern moral code, but more importantly, he hasn't seen what a family truly should be.

"It's okay, Thomas, you have the right to say something," Rachel said. "Forgive me for the circumstances that we are in while you are talking about this but you can make a choice."

"I know, and I have. Once we find out who killed my best friend and Detective Bowen can lock them up. My family is next."

Chapter 32

I had to get Thomas somewhere safe now. We just walked in on quite the affair and I didn't even care to resolve it. Another family would be wrecked and our country still puts up with it every year.

I asked Thomas to stay in the living room as I spoke with Mr. Walker and Mrs. Kurtz in the hallway. I explained to them about the seriousness of their current situation. They had to come clean but it wasn't my place to say how or when. Mrs. Kurtz also agreed to write a written statement on Mr. Walker's whereabouts after school. There was no lie in her eye as the look of distaste matched her tone of voice.

I informed Mr. Walker that I would ask my partner to have a unit outside of his house in case one of the Zaccardis came by. In the meantime, I directed him to call me as soon as he heard back from Sam's parents. He clarified that he left a voicemail for them Friday night and did not speak with them directly. All he could recall was that Sam mentioned in school the other day that they took another "trip" somewhere up North, Maine he believed it to be.

Thomas and I said our uncomfortable goodbye to both of them and found ourselves back in my car. The heat was back on, allowing my fingers to be at ease. I couldn't help but think about Officer Warner popping up from the back seat with a wire ready to introduce me to death once again. I shook the feeling when I saw Thomas buckle his seatbelt. One of us had to be the strong one.

"Detective Bowen?" Thomas said.

"Call me, Michael."

"Okay, there is something you need to know."

I checked the time. It was a few minutes until ten in the evening. There was still time for another shakeup.

"What's going on?"

"I was there."

"What do you mean, where?

"The night Mr. Walker was beaten. I was the one who cracked the door open and looked in. I couldn't see who was in the chair. He was in the back corner out of sight. My uncle told me he puts people in the corner to prevent

152

them from falling over. That was the night I knew what my family was...the way they are."

I didn't have the words. It made me freeze, my tongue felt gone as nothing was coming. Before I could muster anything, Thomas continued.

"Sam was my best friend. He was my escape from the life that my father created for me. My friends are my 'family,' not the other way around. I don't know what to do. We have to find whoever did this. Shit!"

Thomas slammed his head back into the headrest of his seat. I felt for this kid. He needed a figure to stand up and tell him it was going to be alright, and actually mean it.

"Hey, this isn't easy. This shit, and it is shit, should never have to be on the shoulders of a kid your age. Not to get too personal because I just met you but my father wasn't the easiest to get along with either. He had strict principles and if I didn't abide by them, then life was rougher. We are going to find out who killed Sam, I promise you. But there is something I need for you to understand."

"What do you mean?"

"We can't just assume your father is responsible for this. The key to a murder investigation is that if you hone in on one suspect, you forget about everyone else. Don't forget about the others, it's almost always the person you least expect."

"But he is the prime one to focus on. Sam's dad worked for mine and wasn't the best at paying back his debts. Killing Sam would have opened his eyes to who he was screwing over. The signs point to him, regardless of how much I hate my father."

"Its times like these you need to really understand that everything isn't so clear."

"What do you mean?"

"When faced with an issue you have to ask yourself two questions. Which fight do we choose, the one around us or the one inside us? If you have a personal connection to this, which you most certainly do, anger can cause even the most confident person to be blind. I will help you with what I can but you need to make the decision that I cannot make."

Thomas didn't say another word until we arrived at our destination. There were not many places to park as the street was so compact that a wide-truck would have undoubtedly taken out a rear-view mirror or two. When both of us got out of the car, Thomas spoke as soon as we started up the stone steps.

"Who lives here anyway?" he said.

153

A sizable feeling of guilt reached my stomach as coming here might be a mistake.

"A good friend."

Chapter 33

Tom's house was exactly what I imagined it to be: quaint and full of character. I remembered him saying that Meredith, his wife, was quite the tidy one who always kept the house in spotless condition. At first, I thought that meant no colorful or personable mementos lying around but their home was full of them. Tom had old movie posters from the thirties, forties, and fifties on the walls. The first one to the right of the door was a Casablanca poster from nineteen forty-two. The poster depicted Humphrey Bogart staring deep into Miss Ingrid Berman's eyes as if they were the only ones left in the world. Bogart at his best.

As soon as Tom's front door opened, I felt nothing but grief. I didn't know where else to go and the feeling of putting them in danger was glued to my conscience. Tom looked frazzled but ecstatic to see me. He said that he was just about to follow Meredith to bed when Thomas and I knocked on the door. It took me a few moments to apologize for our arrival but Tom cut me off right in the middle of it.

He brought us into his living room and implored us to sit down. The living room was decorated with a more modern touch, yet still smelled as if I was visiting one's grandparent's house. A musty smell filled the air as one of the pieces of furniture, most likely the dark wood end table to my right, was most likely the cause of it. A vase with a swan painted on it rested just a few inches from my elbow as I propped it up on the arm of the sofa. The recently vacuumed carpet was a brownish tint that matched the surrounding sofa and guest chairs. Tom's TV was on ESPN's Sports Center. The walls danced with different colors as sports anchors were recounting all of today's highlights in college football.

Tom grabbed the remote and placed it on mute as he nestled in one of his guest chairs.

"So, gentleman, is there anything I can get for ya? Not too often Meredith and I are visited this time of night," he said, with a simple grin aimed at me.

"Not to be rude, but do you have any snacks? I haven't eaten in several hours," Thomas said. His stomach had rumbled a few times on our way here.

"Absolutely, Meredith usually keeps a few things in the pantry in the kitchen right in there. Have a look if you want."

"Thanks."

Thomas soon disappeared into the kitchen. I was just in the middle of taking my shoes off when Tom got to the point.

"Mike, you're a good friend and all but what is going on? Is your father alright?"

"He's fine. This has nothing to do with him. I've got a case going on that hasn't exactly gone the way it has supposed to."

"Does any?"

"This one's different. That kid in there, his best friend was murdered yesterday."

"Lord, you've got to be kidding me. That's awful, where are his parents?"

"Longer story I'm afraid. It's not safe for him right now, he has some bad people after him and my place wasn't an option either. You hear about the shooting at James Middle today?"

"Yes sir, your name has been all over the news. The whole town is in an uproar after finding out that the school resource officer was the attacker. Damn, you've had a day," Tom said before combing his curly hair back with a few of his fingers.

"I'm sorry for coming here but I had nowhere else to go. My boss took me off the case but I didn't listen. Thomas in there needed my help and I can't just sit by and let his friend's killer stay out there."

"Say no more, I understand. You're admirable just like your father was, I mean…is. Not like you to turn your back on a person in need. I see it every night you come and stay with your father. Look, whatever I can do I'm all ears. Meredith will understand, I hope."

We shared matching grins with each other as Thomas came back into the room. He was carrying a rather large bag of Chex Mix in his right hand, while dipping inside with the other.

"Nice to see you found my favorites," Tom said as he reached out his hand. Thomas offered him a handful and the two of them started eating together.

"The pretzels are the only ones I really like. I leave the rye chips for my wife. Lord, help me if I don't save at least twenty for her."

"She sounds rather interesting. I hope she doesn't get too mad," Thomas said.

"Please, my Meredith is the most beautiful girl in all of Boston. Wouldn't trade her for a million dollars or even a million of those pretzels if somebody offered it. Love is a powerful thing, my lad."

I could tell, Thomas didn't know what to say. He sat down right next to me and continued to eat.

"Thomas is it?" Tom said.

"Yes, thanks for letting us come here."

"You are most welcome. It's the least I could do for a friend."

"But I do have a question."

"Please, ask it."

"How do you even know Detective Bowen? You are much older than he is."

I thought for a moment Tom would show signs of being offended but nothing but a smile cracked over his face. "Good question, you're blind if you think I'm older than him, I'm better looking than Mike will ever be. Oh, geez, Mike, I forgot you were here."

It was the first time I heard Thomas laugh. The noise was pleasant in light of why we were here. I'm glad someone could make him laugh.

"Mike and I have known each other for just a few years. His father was diagnosed with Alzheimer's a few years ago, how many was it, Mike, I can't remember?" Tom said.

"Three years to the day," I said.

"Ah, yes, just about three years. I'm his father's caretaker down at the hospital. He's by far one of my most interesting patients. His dad used to be a big-time prosecutor for the city of Boston, locking up baddies ever since the eighties. There is even a plaque with his name on it hanging up downtown in the courthouse. From what I know, he was a great man. Mike here truly knew him the best, as he should."

"Your dad was a lawyer? But you're a cop. You'd make more money if you were a lawyer," Thomas said as he crumbled up the top of the bag and rested it upon his lap.

"This is true. It's not about the money, because if it is, then you might wanna try something else. Cops shouldn't do their jobs for the money, it represents something greater. Maybe you'll see what I mean one day."

"I've actually thought about it but I don't know, my favorite color is green and I don't see a lot of that in my future if I wear a badge."

The three of us laughed together in unison. I could not help but feel a sense of comfortability while being here. Tom presented the kind of atmosphere that was missing from the normalcy that is police work. Safety had its limits as the feeling of guilt soon found me again.

"Now, you two are probably tired and need time to sleep. Let me go check upstairs with Meredith to tell her you are here. Thomas, you'll most likely be up in our guest room as Mike, the couch is quite cozy this time of year. I'll be right back," Tom said.

After he made it halfway up the stairs, Thomas spoke.

"Do you happen to have a phone charger? My phone has been dead for over an hour and I'm sure Tommy and Rich have been trying to call."

"Sure, I brought mine in."

After I handed it to him, he quickly stood up and headed to the kitchen. I'm sure he spotted an outlet in there and wanted a bit of privacy to check on his friends. I hope they were alright as well, it would be worse if he lost more friends over the course of the same weekend. I dangled on the thought for several moments when I felt my own phone buzz in my pocket. I checked to see a message from Delahine.

'I.D. on the shooter: Tavin Goddfrey, goes by "Twinks." He was the one trapped in the wet cement. The one that I hit was Samuel Tarvey. Both have a record of possession and selling. No connection to the Zaccardis or anything. Twinks said that there were other kids there too but they got away. Are you with Thomas? Also, Burkes knows you were here. Might want to give him a call, he's quite pissed.'

How did he know that I was with Thomas? Maybe he recognized his face somehow but I decided to shake the thought and replied back to him. I thanked him and asked if he could stake out the Zaccardi's bakery, I had a hunch about something. As for Burkes, I'm sure a morning phone call would lighten him up.

Thomas came back into the room with the phone charger. He was about to hand it back to me and waved him off.

"You can keep it, mines fine."

"Thanks," he said.

"Any word on your friends? My partner just informed me that they got away. Sounds like good news to me."

"Yeah, both of them texted me back. Told them something has happened and that they should lay low. They didn't agree but it is what it is."

"Smart, they don't need to be out on the streets if they don't have to. I haven't had the chance to ask you yet but, other than your father and your uncles, is there anyone I need to look into who might be connected to Sam's death?"

I could tell that I caught him off-guard. Some of the most important questions have to be asked rapidly to eliminate any signs of fabrication. Most of my largest breakthroughs in a case were the result of quick questions during an interview. Facial expressions, tone of voice, and verbal responses are vital to eliciting the truth. Not that I wanted to think of it, but Thomas didn't seem like a suspect.

Thomas quickly released a name. "Well, there was this guy we met the other day but I doubt it. His name was Gerard. On Friday, we played him and a few of his friends in a pickup game at DeFilippo. It ended with me shoving his face into a fence."

"Sounds like things never change over there."

"Yeah, but it didn't end there."

"What do you mean?"

"Gerard and his friends found me by myself today. I was on the other end of the beating."

That would explain the bruise above his left eyebrow. I noticed it before but assumed it was just the result of some physical activity. Guess I was sort of right.

"Sorry to hear that. You alright?"

"Sort of, I've been hit in the face before but this time it was…different. He pissed on me."

"Pissed on you? You've got to be kidding me."

"It wasn't just that, I just took it. His friends held me down and I fought at first but then my body just gave way. I felt weak for the first time in my whole life."

I took a few hits when I was young but never something like that. This kid has experienced more in one weekend than most people experience in a lifetime. A father figure would have been great right now. I wish that I felt strong enough to fit the bill.

"When everything goes wrong, just assess and move on. You realize that this Gerard will get his one day. I'm not saying that I believe in karma but in the line of work that I'm in, most people's demons come back to face them. You're not weak, I've known you for less than a day and I can already tell."

Thomas nodded but remained silent. Footsteps filled the air as Tom arrived back downstairs. He held a blanket in one hand and a phone charger in the other.

"Heard someone's twenty-first-century treasure was low. Thomas, you're all good to go up here."

Thomas headed towards the stairs and thanked Tom. He turned to give me a nod and then disappeared upstairs. Tom then heaved the charger and the blanket my way.

"I know I don't know much about what's going on but please, don't let anything happen to that kid. Life won't be easier for him after all this is

159

through. Maybe you need to take the extra step and provide him with an opportune future."

"Are you insisting that I..."

"All I know is, you've seen a lot and you're the difference between the successful and the corrupt. Be the role model that everyone wants to be, not just the idea that everyone fails to achieve."

"Always good with your words. Wish I had the gift."

"If you'd come visit me more often than it might rub off."

"It just might, just might."

Chapter 34

The morning came quick. It felt like only a second had passed since I fell asleep. The kitchen was roaring with sounds that were unheard of in my place. Cereal and cold-cuts were abundant in mine but I could smell an aroma of several wonderful delicacies coming from Tom's kitchen.

There was a small window peering into the kitchen where I could see a figure moving back and forth every few seconds. Meredith's long brown hair was tied up into a bun as she moved back in forth in what appeared to be a flower-covered apron.

The smell of freshly made bacon, pancakes, and eggs filled the whole house as I slowly sat up from the couch. Meredith looked in through the window and greeted me just as I was in the middle of a yawn. I decided to stand up and enter the kitchen.

"I just wanted to apologize for barging in so late last night. Tom is a good friend of mine and we had nowhere else to go," I said.

"Honey, any friend of Tom's a friend of mine. He told me about everything, we are willing to help out. Just promise me no trouble is on our horizon," she said, with a rather cheerful voice. Her cheeks were her most prominent feature as her smile only made them grander. She was a woman of mid-weight as she looked rather skinny for her age and knew how to maintain a diet. I noticed a burn mark upon her right forearm with several freckles surrounding it.

"You both are safe. Everything is alright. We just merely needed a place to stay."

"You're a detective Tom tells me?"

"Yes ma'am," I said to her as I cleaned a portion of the counter off with a spare rag.

"You're quite young for being a detective. Most of the ones I see on TV are in their late forties or fifties. Tom tells me you are very bright."

"Is that what he says? He's never told me that before."

"Tom's a wonderful man but has never been direct. Most of the time I hear what he really thinks of everyone. Over the past few years, you've been a consistent topic."

"That's awful nice of him. Your husband is a great man who takes good care of my father. As for me being a detective already, I was one of the few who went to college before joining the department. I sort of had a step ahead."

"Sounds delightful. Glad you have achieved so much."

"Wish it felt like it sometimes, but thank you."

"Wins and losses, that's what I call it, we all have wins during the day but we always have losses during the day too. Friday, I showed up to work on time but forgot to sign a form for a patient, win and a loss. Just make sure there is more weight on the other side of the balance if you know what I mean."

"Can't believe both of you are a dictionary of wise information, is it that natural?"

"How do you think Tom got the way he is?"

Both of us shared a laugh as Meredith moved the food to individual plates. All four were filled to where I could barely see the edges of each of them. Just as if an imaginary bell rang, Tom and Thomas emerged through the kitchen doorway. Both of their eyes were fixated on the plates.

"Good morning gentleman, please don't forget to say hi before you eat," Meredith said, just as kindly as she greeted me.

*

Officer Jones was sitting in his patrol car just one block away from Zaccardi's bakery. He was just coming off a two-day break and had been on duty for a few hours. His legs were a little tired as he stood out on a noise complaint call for ninety minutes as an elderly couple was losing their breath as they screamed in his face about their loud young adult neighbors.

"Shit for brains," he said to himself as he thought about the man who came out arguing that his first amendment right did not violate any noise ordinances in the town.

Jones received a text message from Officer Delahine late last night asking him to sit on the Zaccardi bakery for a few hours when he could spare it. Delahine was a good cop, young and ready to serve. He tended to forget the concept of asking veterans to do things before they even proved themselves. Especially the veteran cops, such as Jones, who were rewarded a black undercover Ford Explorer to remain inconspicuous to the general public. At roll call this morning, Jones and the other officers were informed of a shootout near Prince Street that occurred late last night. Officer Delahine and Detective

Bowen were involved, both young guns who think they are making a difference. What they don't know is that criminals are criminals and there will always be cops chasing after them. Never catching or stopping the threat at large. Anyone younger than thirty think they know the solution to every problem.

Jones took a sip of his Dunkin coffee with two creamers and opened up his laptop to check the call list for today. No calls were waiting as the radio remained silent as well. It seemed to be another quiet Sunday in North End.

Just as he was about to pull up CNN from this computer, out of the corner of his eye he saw the doors to Zaccardi's open. A tall figure walked out with a gray Bedale jacket on, it was Ralphie Zaccardi. Everybody in North End, in fact probably Boston, knew of the Zaccardis. Each of them had their own unique history, especially Ralphie.

Ralphie stood by the street corner, looked around a few times and proceeded to walk on the sidewalk where Officer Jones was. Taking a few looks was an obvious indicator of suspicious activity in his twenty-plus years of police work. Jones put his coffee down and examined Ralphie walking closer and closer to his car.

There was an alleyway directly in between Jones' car and Ralphie. Ralphie kept eyeing it and the man who was currently leaning against it smoking a cigarette. A puff of smoke shot out of the man's mouth as it all but looked like a light bulb to Jones. He was about to catch Ralphie in the act, and he could not help but crack a grin. No back up, just a sole arrest would cement his name in the department.

Just as Ralphie approached the alleyway, he cocked his head at the man to greet him. In less than a second, Ralphie grabbed the man's jacket collar and yanked him into the alleyway.

Jones' adrenaline found him immediately as he leaped out of his car. He scanned the area to see that no one was on the street as he ran for the alleyway. With his right hand on his baton holder, he felt ready.

Just as Jones passed the corner, he noticed both men standing next to each other facing him. Just as he was about to raise the baton out of his holder, the man grabbed Jones' hand and pressed him against the wall. Jones attempted to drive his boot into the man's toe when Ralphie unveiled a silver Berretta pointed directly at his small intestine.

"Not a scream or you'll lose the ability to breathe," Ralphie said. He took a step closer holding the gun low.

"It seems that you were ordered to watch the wrong place today. Not so lucky."

"Screw you Ralphie, I'm a cop. Do you really think you'll get out of this unscathed? Being arrested for assault five times is one thing but attacking a police officer is more years to your stat sheet," Jones said.

"Mighty, brave words coming out of your mouth vet. I've seen you a few times, so I know you know how to make smart decisions. You were picked to watch this place today, but it's hard for us to go out and do our work if we're too busy being watched. Why are you out here?"

"I don't know, I was just asked to stay put for a few hours and keep track of who comes and goes."

"Even the customers? Sounds like a lousy assignment for a vet like you. You know what makes me laugh though?"

"What?" Jones said as he could feel his wrist being turned slowly by the other man who had a repugnant smell attached to him.

"You were so energized to put cuffs on me that you forgot to turn your camera on. The camera upon your chest isn't even blinking. Forgetting simple procedure means so much to credibility. However, given our predicament, you will be the one coming out unscathed."

"Damn you if you think this will end well. I'm tired of this, let me go!"

"Wait, wait we are almost done," he said as he pressed the Berretta against Jones' small intestine a bit more. "Look, we've pretty much already held you here long enough, our job is done. We're simply still here to reward you for your troubles. My partner here, who might need to lighten up on his grip, has an envelope in his pocket. Inside that envelope is north of fifty thousand dollars. Before you start drooling and realizing that that's a year of tax-free salary for yourself, just remember that you are one of the lucky ones who never even receive this opportunity."

"You must think I'm that soft to accept something like that, if you've done your job then just let me go. I don't want your money, I'd rather walk away and have you both arrested."

"Really, with what evidence? There are no witnesses, no camera footage, and no signs of a struggle. If you want, I can take your baton out and hit my friend here a few times to show that you bruised him for no reason. More importantly, what would you do with tax-free money?"

Jones stood there silent. His eyebrows were so heavy that he felt as if they were going to fall off with all of the anger flowing through his nerves. He felt the hand on his wrist weaken but still present. A deep breath followed from his lungs as his mind wandered to a new place, a place that he never wanted to go. He looked directly at Ralphie, and let his eyebrows rest.

"Let's give this guy his money, he's had enough."

Chapter 35

Meredith's meal was the perfect surprise for such a weekend. I haven't experienced this amount of supremely cooked food since Burkes invited me and a few of the other detectives for dinner one night. The bacon had a unique and wonderful sensation every time it hit one of my taste buds. I'm sure my facial expressions gave off a clear indication of how much I enjoyed their food.

For over thirty minutes, the four of us talked and laughed at each other's comments.

Tom told us stories about the hospital as Meredith would embarrass him about some of their first meetings. My favorite was when Meredith spoke of the time where Tom tripped walking up the steps when he proposed to her outside the steps of her beloved childhood restaurant. It was humorous because it just didn't sound like Tom. At work, he was put together and well-affirmed with his confident attitude. It was nice to see another glimpse of what he was at home.

Thomas was rather quiet when not laughing at Tom and Meredith's stories. It wasn't that he seemed out of place, it was just he might not have any stories like that to share. I couldn't imagine what his day-to-day life was like while living with one of the most notorious criminals in all of Boston. Tom and Meredith did their best to make him laugh, for it was more than I felt like I could do.

After finishing our meals, Thomas and I volunteered to wash the dishes. Meredith frowned upon the use of the dishwasher as she claimed it was a waste of water and jacked up their bill the more times, they used it. It was a simple philosophy, for I found it quite comical. Thomas did not complain once as he dried each dish that I handed him. When we were finished, I informed the couple that we had to be on our way. It was around nine in the morning and this case had to be solved for me to return to my home without others watching it. My thoughts lingered to what Tom had said about Thomas last night.

"It was a pleasure having both of you here this morning. Both of you are handsome young men who will make any lady happy one day. You've certainly made this one happy. As for you," Meredith said, the last part directed at Thomas as he was following me out the front door.

"Me?" He said, acting rather shocked by the comment.

"Yes, you seem very bright for such a quiet lad. I believe that you are more talkative with other people than you were with us this morning. Meeting strangers is one thing but just think, everyone could use a nice conversation one day. You never know how much they will appreciate it and what it does for them."

"Yes, ma'am."

"Goodbye to the both of you, and please be careful. I hear detectives tend to find the nastiest bunch when they are least expecting it."

Thomas and I said goodbye to her when Tom came out to shake my hand.

"Mike, be careful. You too, Thomas. If you need anything, I'm scheduled with your father later today so just stop by. Nothing a joke from me and a visit to your old man can't solve," he said proudly.

"Thanks, always appreciated. I can't thank you enough for what you have done. I'll repay you for this I promise," I said.

"Just come see me again, you don't always have to reward good behavior."

With that, Thomas and I walked down the steps. We entered my car and quickly started the ignition to get some heat going. The morning was bright from the oncoming rays of the sun but the wind still blew with force. As we buckled up, a thought came over me. I had no idea where we were going.

"Where to?" Thomas said.

"Not sure, you could break into Sam's room again if you want," I said.

I could feel Thomas turning his head towards me. It was a guess but I figured it had some weight.

"How did you know?"

"Residue from the fire escape was found on the floor of his room. It suggested that someone had recently broken in, either to hide or get something. So, which is it? Did you hide something back in there or did you steal something?"

"Neither, I found something that didn't add up."

"And?"

Thomas's hands fumbled back in forth as he started to rub his thumbs together in his lap. "My dad makes the four of us sell drugs for him. One of the guys we supply to has a signature bag that he likes to put his pot in and I found it, in Sam's room. We went out looking for him and that's when you found me. Twinks was the one who was shooting at us."

Father of the year. "I can't imagine having to do that. What was so peculiar about Twinks's bag being in Sam's room?"

"I didn't know what to think of it until Twinks told us that Sam was making money on the side. He said that Sam was making more of a profit than the three of us but I could understand why."

"Why's that?"

"He wanted to get out of this place. All the money he was making with us had to go to paying his father's debt he had with mine. He had to make money on the side so he could save up to leave here. I was the only one who knew about him leaving."

Seems that a lot of people work for the Zaccardis in this town. It's truly disheartening to learn about these things coming from another source. I'm a cop, this news shouldn't be shocking to me, yet here I am, confused by it all.

"How were Tommy and Rich when Twinks told you guys this?" I said.

"I'm not sure, they looked put back but it's hard to tell. The shooting started before I could do anything. Tommy was stupid."

"Do you guys get along all the time?"

"Yeah, we rarely fight about anything. If we do, it's probably over something that Tommy did. We were really close to getting Twinks to talk more but he just had to pull his gun out. First time I've heard a shot. It's not what I expected."

"It's never what you expect." I could see that Thomas was still pondering the memory of having a gun fired at him. I had a feeling it would the memory would stay there for a while. "Alright, I know where we have to go."

"Where?"

"To the field, it's making a little bit of sense now."

"Wait, what do you mean?"

"Whoever killed Sam had to have lured him out to the field and surprised him somehow. Nobody could see his body for hours, but how? I think his body was underneath the cover the whole time."

*

"Have you ever enjoyed a day off?" I said.

"Not since meeting you, I'm afraid," a tired Delahine said on the other line.

About halfway to Langone, Delahine had given me a call. He most likely just woke up a few minutes ago, as sleeping in became quite different when you're a cop. Waking up before five in the morning every day impacts your days off. Seven-thirty becomes the new ten-thirty.

"What's the plan?" Delahine said, as it sounded like he was moving something around in his kitchen. "You still got the kid?"

"Yeah, he's with me. A lot smarter than most kids his age."

"Must be nice. I finished writing the report from last night's shooting. Burkes has given me a few days' leave, followed by a wonderful counseling visit to the department's favorite therapist. Apparently, they take shootings seriously here."

"As opposed to?"

"Ever been to Texas?"

"Not to my knowledge cowboy. Thomas and I are headed to Langone now. We're trying to connect some theories."

"Be careful, I'm sure some units are driving around the place more periodically. Last night I heard Burkes saying that if anyone saw you then to report it right away. He said it sort of kindly."

"Sounds great, thanks for the heads up. What did Twinks say last night when you left him?"

"Nothing that would amuse you, unless you're into immaturity. Stubborn and smelly is the best way to describe it. It was hard to be in there with that guy, he repeated every question back to me like a child. He even licked his own hand to show how clean he *really* was."

"Anything of substance?"

"After fifteen minutes of trying to entertain me, he finally realized I wasn't leaving. He told me that he's been buying from Thomas and his friends for several months now. He said the victim made more money than the rest of them and that he respected him the most. He ranked them, Sam, Rich, Thomas, and Tommy. He also said that Langone was one of his spots to hang but he wasn't there the night Sam was found. I checked his record and it says that he's worked at several gas stations in the area. His last date of employment was in October, just been cruising since then I guess."

"Interesting, any correlation with any of the sex offenders on the registry?"

"Not that I could see, there are thirteen that live within a mile of Langone Park. Three of them are less than half a mile. I was going to check out Mr. Panza on Charter Street later today. Maybe one of them originally tried to kidnap Sam but panicked and killed him."

"Maybe, it would be hard to articulate how one of them could straddle…or do what he did in the middle of the afternoon," I said while hoping that Thomas was still zoned out looking out the window. He probably heard it.

"It's your day off. You're not supposed to even be out anyways."

"Coming from…"

"Good point, just be careful. This isn't exactly on the books this time. Don't do anything unlawful, I'm still working out of my means as I go."

"We're not suspended. Just think of it as being temporarily unavailable. Most undercover units are technically not signed on to a shift."

"Interesting way to look at it. Thanks for all of your help, nice to know there aren't any tattle tells in the department."

"Please, Burkes is on the other line now. I'm getting a big paycheck ratting you out."

"Nice, call me if anything happens."

By the time I hung up the phone, we arrived at Langone. Thomas had shifted in his seat and I could hear a deep breath being exhaled.

Time to pick up the pieces.

Chapter 36

The field was open. The covering remained retracted towards the visitor-side dugout. The sun's rays lit up the whole field as there were several patches of brown scattered out amongst the green. The wind was coming down a bit. Nice day to play ball, if it wasn't for the police tape wrapped around the field entrance.

This place was a reminder of the past. It revamped a plethora of memories that I had here. I could not help but think Thomas was feeling a different feeling as he stepped out onto the green. Every few steps, I became paranoid and would scan around to see if anybody was watching. Out in the open during a murder case never seemed too appealing.

I tried to run everything in my mind. Thomas told me that they ditched school Friday to play basketball at DeFilippo and ate lunch at Roma's. Afterward, he said that he and Sam went back to his place for a little but soon passed out from being tired the night before. There was supposedly a two-hour window from when Sam left Thomas's and was murdered at or near Langone. There weren't many secluded areas around the ballpark. Unless, he was killed in an alleyway or one of the clubhouses, which happened to be locked and could only be opened by the person who had the key: Mr. Walker. As suspicious as I felt, he still didn't fit any description of a child killer.

I took a few steps to the mound and stood in the same position where I first examined Sam's body. I crouched in the dirt to see if there was anything I might have missed. Maybe it would look to Thomas that I actually knew what to do next.

"Why are we here again?" he said to break the silence. His tone gave way to the idea that he was unsettled.

"Things aren't adding up. I need to trace everything back. You last saw Sam when you fell asleep Friday afternoon right?" I said, wiping dirt off of my hands.

"Yeah, I was tired from the night before. Sam must have left sometime after that."

"We didn't find his cell phone that night, did he have one?"

"Yeah, he did. It wasn't a nice one but at least he had one."

"Do you know what service he had, like Verizon or AT&T?"

"I'm not too sure but maybe Verizon, why do you ask?"

"I might have an idea but it won't work unless we have the correct phone company. How many times do you guys come out here a week?"

"Maybe three, sometimes four times. Homework really isn't our favorite after school activity. Except for Sam, he always found a way to complete his." Thomas walked around kicking the grass below him.

"Did you ever see anybody who, maybe a hooded figure or someone who wore sunglasses to hide their face, standing around while you guys played? Lots of people walk around here, it's okay if you can't but try for me. It could lead to anything."

Thomas stood silent for a moment. "Not that I can remember but there was, yeah, there was this one guy who came out from time to time. He always wore a plain black, sometimes navy sweatshirt with his hood up. He'd smoke every now and then but he would just stand by the home dugout near the street. We waited around one time to see if he was the dad to one of the kids but no one ever walked over to him."

"Ever see what direction he walked in or if he went into one of the apartments across the street?"

"We were curious but never that curious, sorry."

"It's cool, what did he look like? Not that you might know anything."

"All I can say is that he was white, and was rather on the skinny side. Not too skinny, but lengthy. It's not like the wind would blow him over or anything."

"I understand, thank you for all of that. At least it's something to go on, maybe."

I stood back up and felt like some traction was on its way. Why would someone kill a kid in the middle of the day, but why would anyone kill a kid? Sexual predators kept coming to mind but there were no signs of sexual assault on the body. Well-respected at school, with friends, and apparently within the drug community, this didn't make any sense. Maybe this was a crime of jealousy? Most of the time a wife will discover that her husband or boyfriend is cheating on them with a "younger version" of themselves. Jealousy kicks in, as does the knife set in the kitchen.

I could feel my head start to itch once again with the stress of not knowing the next step. I was about to look towards Jess's apartment to feel a sense of calm when Thomas sounded disturbed.

"Who, who is that?" He said, as I could see him backing up a few steps.

I turned to see a man in khaki pants with a dark blue sweater approaching us. A ball cap covered what I knew was a head of hair that was losing its natural brown tint.

"Someone who wants to help I hope," I said.

It took a few steps for Burkes to crack a smile over his face followed by him shaking his head. Here it comes, the end of the line.

"Mike, I figured you would show up here sometime this weekend. I've driven here about five times today. Every good detective goes back to the scene of the crime at least twice. Glad I know I can still pick the best," he said.

"Not that I appreciate what I think is a compliment, but are you planning on taking us in captain?" I said.

"Haven't made up my mind yet. Is that Thomas there? He looks a lot older in the school photo we have of him."

"Acts older too. He might as well be as smart as one of your admin type. He's scared but driven, quite unheard of for a kid his age."

Burkes gave Thomas a small wave in which Thomas returned with a half-broken smile. "I know I specifically told you not to keep working on this case but as it is, what have you got?" Burkes directed back at me.

"I've...we've got a timeline," I said, pointing back towards Thomas, "Sam had about a two-hour window where his whereabouts are unknown. I've listed three sex offenders off the registry to check on today. I'm not thoroughly confident about the three on my list but it is something to go on. Sam's parents have been the two most elusive parents in the history of this job as I still have heard no word from them. They weren't at his place..."

"That you visited without my approval."

"Yes, but you said it yourself I had to work on this all weekend."

Burkes knew I had him but he was the boss. Better keep the shots to a minimum at this point.

"I'll disregard that last part, any suspects lined up yet? Timelines are good but unless we have some sort of list to go on, we are like a deer in headlights when the press starts crawling up again later today. I've already received thirty emails this morning asking for information."

"We have a few so far."

"You, the kid, and Dehaline. Yeah, I know you guys have been at it together. He's a good cop, reminds me a lot of you but be careful. This kind of case can break a career, and not in the promotional way. Who ya got?"

I proceeded to tell him about Mr. Walker's involvement in everything. I included his whereabouts during the day of the murder and the circumstances for how he found the body, plus, the few details about the cover that he neglected to mention when Burkes was there. I even told him about his relationship with Zaccardis and how they have a history. I added nothing about Dr. Kurtz. It wasn't the kind of attention I felt needed to be shared.

Francis Zaccardi came up next as Burkes was already expecting that one. I told him about Sam's father owing him some money and how his father had a tendency to not stay true to his word. His mother had no ties to the Zaccardis that we know of but had a few instances of possession of drug paraphernalia according to her record. I told Burkes that the only angle that I could find on Francis was that he decided to kill Sam to prove to Sam's father that he was serious about his dominance. Killing the youth wasn't typically Zaccardis' style I told him, but it was an angle, to say the least. I finished by telling him that Twinks might be a suspect and that he was the one who committed the shooting last night. He caught his breath when I told him that Thomas and his friends were there. He apologized to Thomas who solemnly nodded his head. Just as I was about to say more, Burkes busted with a question that he appeared to be waiting to express.

"Francis do that to you?" he said motioning towards the bruises on my face. "Those are fresh ones from the look of it, not the ones from Warner yesterday."

"Yes, about that," I said, as I squeezed my lips against each other in preparation for what I was about to say. "The Zaccardis took me yesterday, blindfolded me and knocked me cleanout. I woke up in a dark room with Francis there. He asked me lots of questions about what was going on. It was terrifying, but quite informative as he revealed to me that he wasn't going to kill me. He told me he had no idea where Thomas is and that the only reason, he was keeping me alive was to find him. I figured if I find Thomas, then I could get the facts I needed to get closer to who killed Sam."

"That son of a bitch, you're an officer of the law and he kidnapped you? We have enough to lock him up now. It's about time he did something stupid."

"Wait, we shouldn't do anything yet."

"Why not? We have physical bruises, GPS on your phone, and the testimony of a trusted Boston Police Detective. Mike, this is the break we've needed. Did you at least record the conversation?"

"No, they turned off my phone, sorry boss."

"Dammit, we still should have enough. We need to act now."

"Captain, I certainly can't tell you what to do but I just need you to listen. If you move on Zaccardi now, then we might lose the bigger picture. If Zaccardi really did kill Sam or if he knows who did it, he's going to do something about it. He went out of his way to entrust me to find his son, mostly because he knew my father and for some reason thinks I'm trustworthy. Zaccardi is going to slip. If we take him off the ice before he can, we might be headed back to square one. Give me the rest of the day and then you can move in on him. Please sir, just give me a chance."

Burkes stood there. I could see his hands moving around in his pockets as the wind started to pick back up. His nose was turning the color of a tomato and his nose was on the verge of dripping. I turned around to look at Thomas who seemed in awe of the whole conversation. I gave him a quick look of what I envisioned as hope and returned to face Burkes.

"I don't like this, I really don't. Dalworth and Riosky are on call if you need them, which judging by the way you have been handling things I doubt you'll need them. Whoever killed this boy needs to be found and we are way past the forty-eight-hour mark. Less than ten percent of these things are solved by now."

"You trying to encourage me or cause me to deflate?" I said, with a grin.

"Just trying to remind you to be careful. It's putting me a little at ease that we might have an edge on Zaccardi but with him still out walking around, I'm afraid he's got the edge on *you*. At least take the kid somewhere he can be safe, type of business only leads to more trouble."

"I can't go anywhere sir, he's my best friend," Thomas said. I wasn't expecting him to speak. "I'll stay back but I have to see this through."

"Noble and courageous, don't let it go to his head Mike," Burkes said after a quick sigh. "Be careful, the sun is out right now but the weather is reported to get worse. Just stay in the clear. And Mike?"

"Yes, sir?"

"Not that I'm the king of advice or anything but, just listen. Great men know the rules, but the right man knows when and where to act. Don't forget the need to do what is right. Watch your back and don't let anybody get killed."

Not another word was spoken as Burkes walked back to his car and drove away. A cloud had removed the sun just as Burkes' car went out of sight.

Chapter 37

After walking back to my car, Thomas and I found ourselves in silence while I looked up the address to one of the registered sex offenders within the vicinity. As I typed, I thought to myself about how I forgot to mention to Thomas that his father kidnapped me yesterday. Or that I did not mention the history between my father and his. He's a smart kid but the idea that he felt betrayed kept coming to mind.

I partially shook the thought off when I got a name from the NSOPW website. Victor Rardar, a thirty-two-year-old guy living at the corner of Commercial and Foster. His roommate, Gavin Smith, was the other occupant. Most likely a friend who is helping him stay on his feet. Guess whoever Smith's landlord was didn't do a thorough job of allowing a sex offender to live too close to a public playing area for children. He was about a five-minute walk from our position. Mr. Rardar was arrested for a sexual assault on his girlfriend in 2015. No jail time, just a few years of having his name on the list and an impeccable amount of community service. I ran his name through the BPD system, and after a few minutes of slow internet connection and a sudden freeze of the laptop, his records came back. The only thing besides the sexual assault was a speeding ticket the year prior. Hard life.

I pulled my Glock from my holster. My jacket was doing a decent job concealing it but I just wanted to check it before knocking on a sexual predator's door.

"Hey, Mike," Thomas said, as I was just finishing with my gun.

"What's up?"

"How do you know my father? You told your captain that my dad knows who you and your dad are."

Here it was. "Yeah, I probably should have said something sooner. Didn't know if it mattered or not. My dad was a lawyer back in his heyday. He was one of the most successful criminal lawyers Boston had in a long time. Your father, Francis, was one of the guys my dad tried to put away. A priest was found dead with cocaine in his system when the forensics report came back. At the time, the police thought your father supplied him the cocaine and was the reason he died. My father was the prosecutor on the case and failed to put your dad away. It was one of the few losses my dad actually had as a lawyer. Zaccardi never forgot that, and neither did we."

"Were you there?"

"Yep, I saw your dad that day. He looked guilty, even from a mile away. Sorry if that's too harsh, he's still your dad."

"My dad deserves to be taken down. He should have never gotten away with any of what he has done. I want him gone. My mom tried to stop his ways a few times. As you can see, it clearly worked."

"Where is she now?"

"Don't know, she just left. Haven't seen her for a few years now. She did okay as a mom. She made sure I got to school on time, did my homework, and even introduced me to some of my friends. Tommy's mom knew her and that's how we met. It wasn't all that bad but, I guess she couldn't handle the pressure of being married to my dad. I don't blame her but I can't agree with her leaving me to deal with it."

"You shouldn't have to deal with all of this."

"Where's your mom?"

I pictured her pushing my hair back from my face. A slight warmth hit me. It was just for a moment, until I realized that it was a trick that I had brought upon myself. "She's gone too. Not dead gone, just gone."

Thomas remained quiet. He looked out the window but then looked back at me. "My father can't keep doing this to people."

"He'll get his, I promise you that. My captain is right. This whole thing isn't going to end with a simple hook of the handcuffs. We need to be ready for whatever we find or if we find anything. I don't know what's worse."

"Yeah, so what's the plan? I'll do whatever you need."

"Great, stay here and don't go anywhere."

*

Thomas didn't much like the idea of staying in the car but he had no choice. Going into Mr. Walker's house was one thing but bringing him to the house of a charged sex offender was out of the question. Mr. Rardar's apartment was on the first floor one house down off the corner of Foster Street. The walk was rather quick as I rounded the corner from where we parked in just under a minute. The street was filled with Sunday morning joggers and elderly individuals who took to strolls as a relaxation method. Two women ran by wearing some innocuous running gear as the cold weather limited their opportunities for wearing anything more revealing. Jess entered my mind as I

176

realized that this Rardar guy lived right across the street from her. I walked by her place looking up at her window. Maybe she would be looking out at the same time I was and she could halt everything that was going on so that I could be with her.

The idea quickly died as there was no one on the other side of her window. As my footsteps found the road away from the sidewalk towards Mr. Rardar's place, I made a common error when examining a case. I already created a predilection that Mr. Rardar was guilty and he should be someone considered to be dangerous. It was a common mistake with where I worked. When the idea of being a cop first came to me, I tried to tell myself that I wouldn't let it change me. As a whole, I've remained content with everything but every now and then I find myself falling in line with many other cops who already assume they know a situation before they get both sides. This guy had a choice, either he tells me his side of his story or judge me as soon as I would begin with my first question.

After letting a jogger pass by, I reached the front of Mr. Rardar's steps. When looking up at the door, something odd caught my eye. When I reached the top of the steps, I noticed that the right door handle had been smashed and the hinge had been pried. There was no sign of a crowbar on the ground after scanning the platform. I looked into the side window of the place to see nothing but complete darkness. I turned to see if anyone was jogging by but saw that the only person in view was an elderly man whose back was turned to me.

My conscience was trying to reach me as picking up my phone for an additional unit was protocol. I blindly ignored the ethical side of myself and pulled out my Glock.

I held the Glock in one hand while slowly pushing the front door open with the other. After seeing about halfway through the opening, nothing but darkness laid before me. I lifted my flashlight from my back pocket and crossed it under my other hand.

When the light illuminated the darkness, I almost expected to jump back. I closed the door slowly and looked around. Mr. Rardars and Mr. Smith's place was pretty tidy. A front hall dresser could be found with photographs of different family members. Dust could be seen flying in the air when my light flashed over the dresser. I couldn't hold out any longer, I had to try.

"Police! Is anybody here? If so, have your hands up and come out slowly with no sudden movements," I said loud enough for anyone to hear.

No answer.

I took careful steps down the hall while looking around into the different rooms. The house seemed well kept but still ominous at the same time. To my left was a lounge area with a large flat-screen hanging over the fireplace. The place smelled of ashes and some air freshener that I could not figure out. My gun started to feel a little heavy as I continued to keep it at eye-level.

I repeated my previous words aloud in case someone did not hear me. Once again, no one answered. As I was about to turn around and head for the stairs, I heard metal cling to life from the left side of the hallway. My light shined towards the corner of the hall where a kitchen counter could be seen through a doorway.

"Hello? Is anyone there, I'm a police officer, please come out and you will not be harmed," I said, arriving at the door. I slowly started to inch farther and farther in front of it, with my flashlight illuminating more of the kitchen with every step I took. My heart started to beat a little faster as I could see nothing but a blue granite counter with several silver dishes lying out across it.

I lowered the light to see a shoe. The shoe was a white sneaker and wasn't alone. It was attached to a leg that disappeared in the darkness behind it. I lifted the flashlight and was face-to-face with someone lying on the ground. A distressed pair of eyes looked back at me as the body started to gesticulate uncontrollably. Frightened would be an understatement as he started to screech in fear as if death himself wearing a cloak walked through the doorway.

After a few seconds, he started to plead for him not to hit him again, or pull it back out. He repeated it over and over again. I turned my light off and flipped the switch I found on the wall. When the lights came on, the man became fully visible. It was Mr. Rardar, or some defenseless form of him. His blond hair was long and was failing to hide the bruises upon his forward. His right eye was bloodshot, along with a gash over his right shoulder. He was rather skinny, with his tank top barely wrapping itself around his body.

"Sir, sir, I am a police officer I'm here to help. What is going on?" I attempted to take a step forward but he jolted backward, almost knocking himself out when his head hit the wall.

"They came, they came in here. I was just sitting in the living room and they busted through the front door," Rardar said. His voice became clearer with every word that he spoke. He noticed that he was drooling and quickly wiped it off with his forearm.

"Who, who came in here?"

"Two guys, two big guys. They knew who I was, what I'd done in the past. They started asking all these questions that I had no idea about."

"What did these guys look like? Tell me everything so we can find them."

"They looked similar, like same hair color but different faces. They could have been related, for all I know. As soon as they broke in, they found me and threw me to the ground and started…hitting me. One of them hit me while the other asked the questions."

"What kind of questions?"

"They started asking me about that boy who was killed in the park across the street. Wait a minute… I know you. You were on TV about the case, you're the cop. Is that why you're here? Do you think I did that?"

"It's not what you think. I'm here to check something out, nothing more. What about the kid, did they ask you about?" After kneeling down, I realized that I put my flashlight away but still had my gun out. Rardar's eyes glanced at it before I was able to put it away.

"They asked about where I was and if I did it. They seemed like they were looking for someone, but they were too busy focused on beating the hell out of me."

"I'm guessing you said no."

"Of course, I said no! I would never harm a kid like that. It's not in me, man."

"Any reason they decided to leave you alive?"

"The one who hit me the most said that I should be left alone to live the life that I already have. A sorrowful one."

I stood up and could not help but think of who came in here. I knew, at least there was a high percentage chance that I knew, but confusion once again came back. Why would Zaccardi send his brothers to do this when all they are doing is looking for Thomas? There was no lie in every word that Rardar spoke and if he did, then I should just hang up my badge. Was Zaccardi looking for someone to blame?

"How are you feeling?" I said, as I wiped my hands across my face.

"Not too good, I feel like one of my eyes is clogged up and every time I breathe something is resisting me from inhaling correctly," Rardar said, as he straightened his posture against the wall. He winced with every move he made.

"You probably have a broken rib. I'm going to call you an ambulance, just sit tight."

As soon as I pulled out my phone, something clicked in my brain. It felt as if someone had broken in and left an unwanted thought. I wasn't the only one checking for sex offenders today. The thought sat there oozing in my head. My eyes lingered to the wall next to Rardar as I caught his eyes on me. Just as I was about to reach for my phone, Rardar disappeared. The whole room did.

The lights were off. Either a power outage or something had caused it. I could hear Rardar wince a little.

"You prone to power outages?"

"Never had one, this is the first," he said. "This is a good place. We've never even had water damage of any kind."

"Lovely, just sit tight. Let me call an ambulance for you." One of my knees popped as I straightened myself out. Just as I turned on my phone, a thud sounded off. It was quick but sounded rehearsed. Another one came and then ceased.

"That you detective?"

A voice pierced the air like an arrow being shot through the hallway. I knew that voice. Apparently, Rardar did too as I could hear him move around on the floor.

"Seems to me like you're not listening," Ralphie said, "My brother Francis trusted you to find Thomas, not keep dicking around in places you don't belong." Everything still remained dark, with no sign of light from anywhere. I chose not to say anything.

"Don't waste your time with the gimp in there with you. He bruises like a peach, just like you if I'm thinking about it." Ralphie wasn't shouting but was still loud. He must be in the hallway or near one of the front rooms. He knew where I was, guess it wouldn't hurt. I brought my flashlight back out and started to head back towards the hallway.

"Won't be needing that anymore. I'll be gone by the time you even get the chance to see my sexy face," he said.

"I'm on to you guys, aren't I?" I said softly.

"You think this is going to be like one of your other big cases do ya? A young guy just like you should know better than that. You're swimming up shit's creek, you're not getting any warmer. We have our consequences, don't forget about what's left."

"Not sure I understand what you mean." The hallway was empty after I shined my light upon it. There was no sign of him. Nothing had moved or made a sound when I entered. Nothing had fallen or shattered, only the dust in the air danced as my eyes raced around the room waiting—wanting to something to move. After a few moments had passed, I knew that he was gone.

Chapter 38

After calling in an ambulance to Mr. Rardar's house, I left his apartment and started for my car. His answering machine had picked up twice on my way out the door. Fear had found me again as I could not contemplate the fate that might be in front of him.

I arrived at the car to find Thomas tapping on the dashboard. I quickly opened the door and started the ignition. In less than five seconds, I sped us onto the road and through traffic avoiding all the cars in my way. Thomas jumped in his seat when the sirens located within the front fender of the vehicle were initiated.

"What is going on? Was he the guy?" Thomas said. Acting quite dumbfounded of how the world around him felt so rushed.

"My partner might be in danger," I said. "Just hold on."

I picked up my radio and called in any unit in the area who could report to Charter Street right away. An officer in danger call would have snapped any unit squatting around doing nothing as I presumed many units would answer the call. Just as I finished my time on the radio, three other units responded and were headed to that position.

After taking a hard left onto Jackson Avenue, I took a quick notice of the Copp's Hill Terrace and the impressive stonework before directing my attention to the vehicles currently in my way. After speeding around a red pickup truck going ten miles under the speed limit, Charter Street arrived a little unexpectedly with the speed I had attained. The walls felt like they were closing in and the road in front of me down Charter became nothing but a thin line as I sped to the address. Tell me it's not too late.

Just as I arrived at the intersection of Charter and Salem, I mounted the car on the curb, whilst avoiding a woman and her German Shepard walking right at the corner. The sirens scared both the woman and the dog as they fled down the street. I signaled on the radio that I was there and heard another unit say the same as I got out of the car. Thomas looked at me as if he already knew what I was going to say to him. He didn't even unbuckle his seatbelt.

The other unit who confirmed over the radio arrived from the east on Charter. An officer that I did not know exited his vehicle and quickly ran over to mine. After examining his tag, it read: Officer Taylor. The sun's rays were blazing upon the man's bald head as he reached my position.

"Sir, what's going on? Where is the officer?" he said, while frantically looking around on the street. I could tell he was worried about the crowd that had gathered to see what was going on.

"Officer Delahine is supposed to be here checking the residence of a current registered sex offender. He hasn't answered his phone, something just feels wrong. The address is that one over there," I said to him while pointing to the brick building at the top of the "T" of the intersection.

"What floor?"

"The second," I guessed. I couldn't remember the exact number but I knew what building was the correct one.

Another unit showed up as Officer Taylor and I entered the intersection. It was Officer Jones. As soon as we made it to the other side of the sidewalk, we lined up directly adjacent to the door leading into the complex. I looked around to see that Delahine's car was not even parked anywhere. Was he even here?"

"Bowen, what's the play?" Jones said, as he had his weapon drawn.

"Not sure, we're here for Officer Delahine but his car isn't even here. Just give me a second." I paused my brain for a moment to figure out what was going on. If he wasn't in there, then we were busting down a door for no reason. The thought of Delahine being beaten entered my mind until a break in thought interrupted it all.

"Screw this, if there is one of our own in there, we should be in there," Jones said as he left his position against the wall. He centered himself in front of the door and was in the process of kicking the door in when I saw him.

Delahine had arrived unscathed running up to us. He looked more confused than interested at the sight of the three of us about to initiate what appeared to be an unnecessary breach. Just as I noticed Delahine, I leaped towards Jones and accidentally knocked him down when not realizing that all of his body weight was on one leg. He fell to the ground hard, landing mostly on his hip. The profanity coming from his mouth told me right then how he felt. I apologized and quickly helped him up.

"What's going on here?" Delahine said. He was wearing a nice, winter jacket along with a pair of blue jeans that had lime green paint stains on them.

"I thought they had gotten to you, it was a rash moment of just thinking of the worst," I said.

"Who would have gotten me?"

"Not sure it will shock you when I tell you."

"Not that you haven't noticed but I think the weekend would disagree with you."

*

It took about ten minutes for Officer Taylor and Jones to remove all of the interested parties surrounding the area. They commented the crowd by saying that it was a training scenario, even though half the crowd looked at them as if they knew it was false. After several more minutes of waiting for people to leave, I waved Jones and Taylor off thanking them for their help. Jones barely cracked a smile as he looked to be staggering in his steps a bit.

Delahine and I made it back to my car where Thomas was standing outside of his car door.

"Quite the show you just put on. Almost had me for a loop," he said with a grin.

"This Thomas?" Delahine said.

"Yours truly," I said to him.

"I like him."

"Great, we'll all get along then. Thomas and I checked out the guy living on Foster. It went south almost as quick as last night."

"What do you mean? It was just supposed to be a simple knock and talk."

"Tell me about it." I proceeded to tell him and a curious Thomas about my venture into Mr. Rardar's place. Thomas's mouth dropped when I told him about Rardar's condition and the ludicrous accusations coming out of his mouth. I spared some of the description about the way he looked but focused more on what he said. Details were crucial and this guy might be another way we could bring the Zaccardis down.

"You think two of the Zaccardi brothers did this? How do you know for certain?" Delahine said.

"I know it's them."

"How?"

"Ralphie was in there." It wasn't hard to notice a shift in Thomas's facial expression as he took a step closer to me.

"What? My uncle was in there with you?"

"Yes, he was there for a reason. He beat Rardar to make a statement. He wasn't trying to kill him."

"Then why beat this Rardar guy? Why didn't he try to kill you?"

"I don't know, but I think they know we're getting close. Not you Thomas, they must think I haven't found you yet."

183

"This still doesn't make sense though," Delahine added. "The Zaccardis are bad-shit crazy but they don't bust into sex offender's houses just to get their violent fix for the day. Either Rardar had to of known something or the Zaccardis are looking for, wait, maybe."

"For what? I said.

"A fall guy. Someone who they can pin Sam's murder on."

"It wouldn't be a bad play, hell, I'm sure they've gotten away with it before. But, why Rardar, why a sex offender? There are plenty of guys they might know who could take the fall but instead, they chose this guy."

"Maybe he met up with some of the other guys like him?" Thomas interrupted.

"What do you mean?" I said.

"I'm just thinking, if all these sex offenders or whatever you call him, have the same kind of issues and problems. Don't they have therapy groups or something where they can talk about everything? Maybe this Rardar guy was a part of one and might know someone who was struggling to not do it again."

Delahine and I both looked at Thomas. Damn, this kid continues to surprise. It's as if a *Law and Order* episode script just spilled out of his mouth and he memorized the most climactic scene. I thought of the possibilities and lifted my cell phone out of my pocket when a thought hit me. Maybe we should get him out of here.

"Maybe, that's not a bad thought detective," I said before directing my attention back at Delahine. "Maybe we should get Thomas somewhere safe until this blow over. People are going to get hurt and we can't have him being in the middle of it. You and I both know poking around a sex offender recovery meeting isn't the best way to make friends. Do you have a place he could lay low?"

"Wait just a minute. I think I have a say in what should happen to me," Thomas said. "I have more stake in this than the both of you and I'm not going anywhere until we find who did this. I know these things may take a long time but I'm here to see it through."

"These things often aren't even completely solved, you know that, right?" Delahine said, "Mike isn't saying that you don't have the right to be here. He is just saying that he wants you to be safe so we don't have another murder on our hands."

He was right, this whole weekend I continued to forget the common similarity that haunted most murder cases, they never get solved. Every case is different within every measure of morality or violation of the law. Sam's death could go down as just another murder, never completed, never fully resolved until we found the closure this town needed. We had to figure this out. We have the necessary cause flowing through our blood to see the task through. It came to me like a steady stream of water that completely escaped the stillness of being frozen. I had a plan.

"Thomas, I apologize if I hurt your feelings but if you are going to tag along, you will do *exactly* what we tell you. This isn't just like a scrap on the basketball court, this is life or death. Everyday cops have no idea what we are getting into. It may be nothing and it may be everything, all we can do is prepare for what is difficult. Do you understand?"

"Yes, yes I do," he said. With a haircut and some shoeshine, he could have passed as a new recruit coming in for his first roll call.

"You trying to be a cop one day?" Delahine asked when Thomas was just about to cross his arms.

"Depends on if we find the person who killed my best friend."

Chapter 39

Sunday mornings were the most challenging day of the week. She lied there in her bed contemplating if she could make it. If she lifted herself out of bed now, she could shower, clean up, and be at the door ready for the latest service that was offered. For three years now she has experienced the same dilemma every Sunday.

Jess decided to lift her body up where she propped her back on the two pillows wedged against her and the wall. She took a deep breath and watched as the fan above her continuously rotated. Her predicament felt like a continuous cycle with no end. Her parents lectured her on the importance of faith and divine reward for most of her adolescent life. Spirited Catholics who attended church every Sunday, even on Wednesday nights, her parents were two of the most morally righteous people she knew. Both of them lived in Virginia. Her father was a mechanic for the local Honda dealership while her mother was an elementary school teacher. They always pleaded with her to embrace *His* love as it would never falter, even if it was hard for her to commit to the same lifestyle they had.

She never disliked the faith, she just struggled with consistency. Every week she propped a book about "Returning to Catholicism" on her desk as a reminder that she would go back to its studies. As of now, she coasted through her life praying from time to time with no fear of losing her love of the faith. Most of her friends growing up were strict Catholics who devoted themselves to its practices and a love for God that seemed greater than her own. Most of her adolescent life she spent with people who did not share the same thoughts as she did. Until, she met Mike.

She thought back to when they first met at the dining hall at BU. It was a Friday night. She was just wrapping up her chemistry test from that day when she decided to get a quick bite before spending another night buried in a book. While she was in the line, she remembered how the lasagna looked and how it almost caused her to drop her tray to walk out. Before she gave it another thought, she could feel a presence beside her. Then it spoke.

"Do you think the lasagna is real our just a figment of your imagination?" a low voice said. She remembers expecting to see some fraternity brother with a gelled hair cut with an unnecessary button up on for eight-thirty at night. When first seeing him, her thoughts quickly changed.

He had a gentle face. His cheeks were circular with a small dip on the sides. His brown hair was cut moderately short with a few curls arising in the front. He seemed lean but someone who knew how to take care of himself. He was wearing a BU t-shirt with the red eagle flying over the city of Boston. A popular shirt found in the student store.

"If it was real, I'd be home with my mom helping her make it. Whatever this is, it can't be real so no one around me is real as well," she said back to him.

"I see, two things then I assume."

"Is this one of those pickup attempts we college students love to dream of?"

"That's a little forward. I was just trying to point out two concepts often missed by the ordinary individual. You don't seem just ordinary. I'm assuming you know what I'm talking about."

"And, these two concepts are?" she asked him as they moved further down the line to a pile of somewhat appetizing breadsticks.

"Repellant or fear."

"What?"

"When a guy, that being me, starts a conversation with you there are two different thoughts going on if you are not interested in speaking with the opposite sex. Either you have an imaginary 'don't talk to me' sign hanging around your neck, that being the repellant, or…"

"Or? You were really on a roll there."

"Or you're afraid that some guys just want to talk and nothing else."

"Interesting, you already think you know me after one phrase. Wow, you must be quite the psych major."

"Please, I nearly failed the first test. I've just observed a lot of girls rejecting my friends. It's a shame really. Courage can only get a guy so far."

"You seem to have more than your friends."

"Maybe it's the fact that you haven't left yet."

Both of them made their way to the end of the line. Jess stood there, fidgeting with the napkins and the forks until the guy came over to get his. Once he did, he gave her a quick smirk and reached over to grab his utensils. Just as he did, he turned to walk away.

"Good point, I'm Jess by the way." He heard her words and slowly turned around. Just as she noticed one of his curls falling upon his forehead he spoke.

"Mike, nice to meet you."

*

Jess decided that ten-thirty would have been pushing it. She rose out of bed and found herself craving something to eat. Her kitchen was well cleaned as she just dusted and wiped the place down yesterday. The areas that could be seen by visitors were her most prominent focus as she indulged in cleaning the living room, the bathroom, and the kitchen as often as twice a week. Her bedroom, though always smelling of Febreze, was neglected as it could simply be hidden by closing the door.

After finding a banana, and heating up some oatmeal, she took a seat on the couch to watch the morning news. The anchorman was speaking about the upcoming Patriots game today when the focus turned to a harrowing story from last night. Referencing the shooting from Saturday morning when a police officer was assaulted in the bus lot of James Madison Middle school, the anchorman displayed an image of another shooting taking place several blocks away from Jess's apartment.

She almost dropped the half-eaten banana in her hand when she saw that it happened in a parking garage that she happens to run by just about every week. She listened as the anchorman said the following:

"Boston Local News is bringing the public an important update. Investigators and reporters have informed us that last night another shootout has struck North End. Occurring around eight in the evening, several people walking in the vicinity of the parking garage claimed to have heard shots fired. The incident, though being kept in secret by law enforcement, has been labeled as an isolated incident. However, our investigators here at BLN were able to obtain actual video footage of the incident sent in by an anonymous source. Please advise, this may be inappropriate and difficult to watch for younger viewers. Keep children away if you do not want them to see or hear gunshots. We believe someone has been murdered in this video."

Jess turned the volume up and looked in disbelief at the anonymous video footage. The camera was shaky as it was undoubtedly taken by someone's handheld device. She could see two figures running down the sidewalk. One looked to be a short boy of maybe thirteen years of age and the other was a man in baggy clothing. Bursts of light were coming from the large man, followed by loud noises until they stopped. The man had fallen into something and cursed out loud. Something temporarily blocked her vision as whoever was taking the video was hiding behind a metal trash can of some kind. The view came back as the boy could be seen running behind a car still several feet away from the guy stuck in some hole. Why doesn't he keep running she thought?

As the person holding the camera moved around a bit, two more men appeared in the video as one was backing up against the building. An instant wave of fear came over her as the man attempted to look towards the man who was stuck. More gunfire ensued as she looked to see that the boy had found another guy hiding behind the car. Before she could observe who, it was, another man rounded the corner just as the man who was being shot at left. More gunfire ensued as no one could be seen except for the new man who had just run out. Jess watched in horror as the man was suddenly lying on the floor after more shots had been fired off. Heavy breathing from someone who sounded like a woman followed, and there was no movement. The video wandered away from the body as the boy and the man he was with were running away from the scene, and then the video ended.

How horrible, Jess thought to herself. Although, when the video ended, she could not help but think she noticed something. She rewound the video and returned to the image with the boy running away with the man. She stood up and walked closer to the screen.

Was that... Mike?

Chapter 40

Unity creates the possibility of attainability, yet there remained an ounce of guilt swarming around in my stomach. I could feel an unwarranted pressure running through my mind as I continued to think about this case and everyone involved. A boy's best friend has been murdered, an officer is choosing to risk his career not on paid time, two parents have lost their only son, and I just ignored my captain's request to lock up the most dangerous man in Boston. This is turning out to be one hell of a weekend.

Just before he got into his car, I asked Delahine to call anyone who might know about a sex offender therapy session of any kind. He said it might be a while but everything he has been doing has been more than enough. He gave me copies of the files from last night right before he left in his car.

As I fumbled through a few police reports, Thomas sat twisting his fingers. I could not help but wonder what he was thinking. He offered a pretty good idea before but I know he felt like he could be doing more.

"What are your friends doing?" I said.

"Not sure, I told them to sit tight and lay low this weekend."

"Think they listened to you?"

"Not a chance."

"Not that I'd approve of asking your friends to help but it would be a little hypocritical as you are still here. Why don't you give them a call to see if they thought of anything helpful?"

"Not a bad idea, anything else captain?"

"Good one rook."

"Just learning from a fellow smartass. It's nice to know adults still have a sense of humor."

Thomas got out of the car and walked a few paces towards the corner of the apartment building we were parked beside. I caught myself grinning as the kid ignited a different kind of spark. Middle school kids were supposed to be terrors but this one wasn't half bad. Not every kid has a sociopath as a father.

Now would be a good as time as ever before Thomas would get back. I pulled out Sam's crime scene photos as the black and white images of his lifeless body brought me back to that night. His white face with his mouth open would be ingrained in my brain forever. Maybe there was something that I missed.

His arms and legs were stretched out except for his right leg that was not fully extended. Why would, whoever did this, arrange Sam's body like that, for what purpose? They would have had to kill Sam, brought him there and then hidden him with the apparently expensive water-resistant cover. The case had no correlation with other cases that I had ever worked on. The pain and the promise of finding who did this continued to resonate after every thought. Even after something positive, the pain remained.

After flipping through a few more of the photos, I could feel my phone start to buzz as it was coming from my personal phone. My interest honestly fell flat as I looked to see that it was not Jess on the other line. The phone read *No Caller ID.* I ignored the call and looked back at the images.

To my discomfort, my phone came to life again. Once again, the caller I.D. was unknown and I found it rather odd. I picked up the phone, deciding to answer it out of curiosity.

"Hello, this is Mike," I attempted to say in a professional manner.

"Hello, I can't but remember the deal we had yesterday. This is Mike Bowen, the detective who felt my fist pound against his skull multiple times correct?" said the other voice on the line. Couldn't forget that voice.

"Ah, Francis, nice of you to remind me of one of my favorite memories. What seems to be the reason you are calling?"

"According to BLN, you've found Thomas. Can't help but notice that he's not currently next to me and my phone has zero voicemails from you. Damn, I hate unlucky predicaments."

"BLN? I'm quite lost."

"Some idiot with a video camera happened to record the firefight that my son was at last night. You know the one in front of the parking garage on Commercial. The video showed two courageous cops coming to my son's rescue and wouldn't you know it, your young self just happened to be featured in it."

"No kidding, how'd I look?"

"A little shitty, you've looked better. Back when I thought I could trust you."

"I hate it when times change. Makes our youth look like glory days."

"I'm in my glory days. Now, I'm going to make this as clear as I told you yesterday. Bring my son to the bakery and get back to solving your case. All I care about is Thomas and if he is safe then we can go back to the way it was."

"I'm not sure Thomas feels the same way." I took a moment to check to see where Thomas was. He remained on the street corner with his phone pressed against his ear. "He wants to find who killed his best friend. Know anything about that?"

"Still think I had something to do with it I see."

"Well, Sam's dad did owe you quite a lot of money I've heard. I've also heard and read about what you do to guys who don't pay you back. Lots of history to lean my finger towards you."

"If you have knowledge of whomever you've read about, you should know that you are now qualified as one of those individuals. Police aren't exempt from the rules."

"Police have handcuffs and the authority to do what you cannot."

"Funny, when was the last time you heard someone talk about how courageous the police are? Always willing to save the innocent, are they? Police don't run North End, that leadership belongs to someone who lives amongst the people with the proper cause."

"I see, even willing enough to go as far as killing a kid to make his father pay up?"

"You can accuse me all day but at the end of it, you have nothing. No evidence to threaten me with or anything of the sort. Now, once again, bring Thomas back to me or I can tell the news that my son is being withheld from me by police. It wouldn't look too good after one of your officers tried to kill you this weekend."

"Thomas doesn't want to come live with you anymore. If you want, he can tell you that himself once this case is over with. They still let the sons of notorious criminals come visit their fathers in prison."

"So, it's like that. Everybody makes wrong choices. Your father made one when he tried to put me in jail, look how that ended up. Failure is hereditary. I'm just glad I get to see father and son go down together in the same lifetime."

"Afraid history will not repeat itself, but I do have one more question before I ignore your threats." I waited for a moment as Zaccardi remained silent.

"Why are you so interested in finding who killed Sam? It can't be just because you've lost some money right, there's something else going on."

A chuckle followed as Zaccardi acted quite amused by that.

"You are smart, Mike. Wish you were smart enough."

The phone call ended. Zaccardi had hung up without another word. I sat there contemplating what was going to happen next. I couldn't help but think he wasn't looking for us before, but now he is. I had to get Thomas away from here, somewhere he could be safe. Just as the thought crossed my mind, the passenger car door opened.

Thomas sat back inside and gave me a quick wave.

"Your dad called; says he misses you very much."

Chapter 41

After explaining to Thomas about his father's phone call, I decided to take him to the police station. Since Burkes gave me the rest of the day to work a miracle, my presence at the station would not be as monitored or even denied as it might have been before. When we arrived, it was a couple minutes past eleven o'clock.

Thomas and I entered through the back way as the front office was closed on the weekends. The civilian workers behind the front desk had it made only working from Monday to Friday. Thomas looked around either in awe or curiosity as we made our way through the main hall. His attention was directed towards the framed historical photographs and the awards along the walls. His gaze lingered on an old photograph of three captains including Burkes, who had accepted a community service award from the town of Boston. When we arrived at the elevator, I let Thomas call for it pressing the button on the wall.

"What did your friends say?" I said, while scanning to see if there were any officers in the building.

"Rich said he tried to look for Sam's phone at his and Tommy's place but couldn't find it. Tommy wondered if it was in my room but I didn't remember seeing it when I left that night. I honestly didn't look around too much since I was in a hurry. Other than that, they said they were staying at home since I told them I was with you. Knowing them, they've been out looking for anything they can find."

"Sounds like you have some good friends."

"Either that or they are just looking for trouble."

"Trouble finds the strongest of us. Idiots look for trouble."

The elevator dinged and the doors opened. I usually don't go to the office on the weekend and here I was stepping back in here for the second time. It felt like a deserted courtyard. The investigative floor on the weekend was like a clock with no cogs.

Thomas hardly looked amused as he looked at all of the empty desks. We made our way over to my desk. Once we arrived, I pulled a chair out for him. I turned the computer on and waited for it to load. All of the files from Delahine were now lying across my desk. An unexpected sigh came from my mouth as I sat down.

"Everything okay?" Thomas said. Saw that coming.

"This case is like water Thomas. Whenever we find something it slips out of our fingers. Sam was your best friend. His killer could be watching us right now and we wouldn't even know it."

"This place is a graveyard if you ask me. Does anybody work here?"

I could not help but laugh. Thomas shared one with me as a sense of comfort fell over me. Like this morning with Tom, something bright was able to creep back into the darkness that I manifested. Somehow, the pressure felt a little lighter, but the seriousness remained.

"I just need to think a little clearer."

"Sounds like you need a beer."

"A what? Did you forget how old you are?"

"No, it's just what adults use as the solution to stress. My father and my uncles do the same. When's the last time you had a drink?"

"Not since college."

"Aren't you like thirty?"

"Yep, just never felt the need. There are other ways to handle stress."

"So, if you don't drink, what's with the bottle in your desk?"

I looked down near my leg to see one of my cabinet drawers cracked open. The only thing that could be seen was the blacktop of a bottle sticking out of it. I leaned forward to open the cabinet. It nearly slipped out of my hands as I pulled it up.

"This is for something else, not stress."

"Not for bad habits I'm guessing."

"Not exactly. It's for the day when my father passes."

A dramatic shift fell upon Thomas's face. I continued on. "Yep, he's got Alzheimer's. I usually don't disclose something like that to someone I just met a day ago but I honestly don't feel like dancing around it anymore. This bottle here is for the day he passes and I can drink for him...or to him. Whichever mood I'm in that day."

"How long does he have?" Thomas said.

"I don't know actually. Doctors say it could be in a month or in a year. The inability to predict the future holds true yet again."

"Yeah, I'm sorry about that. No one in my family lives past sixty really. I'm pretty sure you can guess why."

"Sadly, I can."

"What was your dad like? I can't seem to remember the last time mine was actually a dad and I'm only twelve."

The room felt darker as the sun hid behind the clouds. I only turned one set of lights on when we walked into the room. Should have thought about the sun moving away.

"My dad was different. He was sort of bi-polar, know what I mean?"

"Not really, does that mean he has mood swings?"

"That's one way to look at it. He was a man with strong principles and if you were to violate one then you were scolded. Don't get me wrong, he was probably the best provider a kid could ask for but when it came to being sentimental, he stumbled out of the gate on several occasions. My youth was fine, but once I started high school he shifted. He demanded success and would not allow me to waste any opportunity that came my way. Sounds alright on the surface but it felt different."

"Sounds like our dads are the same. Except yours was on the opposite side of the law and offered better opportunities. The only thing my dad offered me was a way to make money. I guess that's an opportunity."

"Why didn't you say no?"

"Say no? Just kill me now why don't you," Thomas caught his breath and scratched his forehead. "Can't believe I just said that. But, saying no with my dad was like saying no to a judge when they decide to throw you in jail."

"Trust me. Your father is no judge. He may think he is but we all know he's not."

"Tell me about it. He told me it was a way for me to provide. He thought bringing my friends in to help would develop a sense of 'teamwork.' Sure, we made some money but we had to give most of it to my dad. If what Twinks said was true, I should have started to do what Sam was doing."

"Selling drugs as a kid, never thought I'd run across that in this part of town. For curiosity and I guess for my job, how does a kid your age get away with it? People who buy drugs aren't the most dependable. What stopped them from knocking you out and taking all that you have?"

"My name," Thomas said. "Once I say my last name, they become dogs with their ears peeking up. When the four of us would walk around with the product in our pockets, and not in bags, we would find a spot that my dad said was popular for buyers. We mainly worked at night, weekends were the best. Once we found a group or even one person, I would take lead to introduce who we were and who we represented. We tried to target large groups to make more money but some nights were slow. I know what we did was illegal but it got my dad off my back. Plus, I was able to save some on the side for when I was older. Sam wanted to leave this place, and up until the other day, I was going to go with him. Now, I feel like I'm stuck here."

I remained silent for a few moments. Images of Thomas and his friends selling drugs entered my mind. The images were difficult to fathom with their young faces entering into a dark reality many choose to endure. Not because it seemed that it wasn't the kind of reality that we live in today but just the lack of parental care. Even the most ruthless criminals want what is best for their kids. I've seen abusers and professional dealers admit they were only committing crimes because they felt like they were meant for nothing else. Parents shouldn't force their child into a life like Zaccardi has.

"Sam seemed like a great friend. I'm sorry you had to do all of that. It's going to be different now, even if we don't find who killed Sam. We will bring your father down. You can't live like that anymore."

"I agree," Thomas said as he was standing up. I could tell he needed to pace around for a bit as I left him with his thoughts.

There was a TV hanging on the back wall. I walked over to the desk next to mine and picked up the remote. After turning it on, it took me just a few clicks to find the news. I figured if they were still showing it, I'd see a glimpse of what Zaccardi mentioned. BLN was apparently still covering the video from last night. I felt a presence to my left as Thomas had walked up behind me.

I was hoping the anchorman listed the incident as "isolated" compared to the one at James Middle. Luck would have it, he did not. The footage in some sort of fashion revealed my face on the screen. It was a bit blurred but Thomas and I were definitely running together at the end of it. The anchorman said the following after freezing the image of my face:

"Our sources have now confirmed that the man at the end of the video with the young boy was, in fact, Detective Michael Bowen of the Boston Police Department. Detective Bowen, was indeed the same detective involved in the shooting at James Madison Middle School just several hours before. Bowen's partner, Officer Leo Delahine, was the other officer seen in the video. Both Delahine and administrative staff have repeated that Bowen and the young boy's whereabouts are unknown. The child has yet to be identified."

"What kind of an idiot records a shooting on the side of the street?" Thomas said, with a bit of irritation hanging on the edge of his words.

You and me both, I thought to myself.

I was just about to turn the TV off when Thomas spoke. "Wait, don't turn it off yet."

I looked back at the TV to see a familiar face. Officer Warner's departmental photo was being shown. His gray hair and his toothless grin took up half the screen. I could feel my hand moving across my neck as I could still feel the bruise below my jaw.

"What is it?"

"I've seen that guy before," Thomas said. He hesitated for a moment before I cut off his thinking."

"Yeah, he was the resource officer at your school. You probably saw him all the time."

"That's not it. He was in a picture at Roma's he was with…"

"Who?"

"My dad."

Chapter 42

The next hour was perusing through paperwork. After Thomas told me about the framed photograph of Francis and Warner, I immediately started checking any police reports that could tie the two names together. Thomas said Warner looked fairly young in the picture, which lead me to assume that maybe Francis got to him when he was starting out. A sleeper agent from an old spy movie was the first depiction that came to my mind.

While I was reading, Thomas took the liberty of searching through the crime scene photos taken of Sam's bedroom. I assume when he broke in earlier, he was in quite the rush and failed to look around as much as he liked.

I texted Delahine the information. He didn't seem shocked as he was currently in the parking lot of some Episcopalian church near Fenway. He said that his contact had mentioned that there was a gathering of addicts or "victims of the system" that met every other Sunday. The meeting didn't start until twelve. I looked at the time. He still had a few minutes. I told him to keep me posted before putting my phone back in my pocket.

"Anything interesting in the photos?" I said.

"Nothing out of the ordinary," Thomas said, "He was clean. His room was the only one that wasn't trashed. Sam said his dad came in one day and got so jealous that he trashed Sam's. You should meet that guy. He's nothing short of trash himself."

"I've been trying to. Both of Sam's parents can't be found."

"Sounds familiar."

"What's the deal with that anyway? When I visited his home, everything was a mess but they look like decent people."

"Looks can be deceiving. Sam's parents leave anytime they want. Both of them can't keep a job to save their life. His dad works for my dad. That should say it all."

"Child services should have been called already. Do you know if anyone was trying to?"

"Not that I know of."

"I'll write that down then. Once, or if his parents contact me, they will get an earful. Parents should never leave their children to fend for themselves." I looked back up at the TV.

"Where was this picture of your dad and Warner again?"

"Roma's, the sub joint."

"Yeah, I've been there once or twice. He makes good Italian food, the way it should be made. Does he work for your dad?"

"No, no. Roma is a good guy. He knows about my dad but tolerates him so that he doesn't lose his business. He would never do anything illegal."

"How do you know this for sure? We can't leave anybody out for consideration for this. No matter how painful it will feel."

Thomas exhaled deeply as he lifted his head up from the photos. "You don't understand. Roma is a great person. He looks out for the four of us. He's like the visiting uncle who would be a better parent than someone's actual parents."

"But he has pictures of your dad in there. They must be close somehow."

"No! Roma is not mixed with him." The wrong cord had been struck. "Roma was going to adopt Sam."

I stayed silent.

"Roma and his wife already went to child protective services and were in the process of having agents come in and see how Sam was living. It was going to happen until...until you know." I could see that Thomas's eyes were starting to turn red.

"Hey, I'm sorry to push like that. I guess my curiosity doesn't know when to shut up sometimes." I patted him on his shoulder and turned back to my desk. Swing and a miss, Mike.

I sat there for a few minutes pretending to read. Thomas made a few sniffles with his nose and wiped his eyes. I could hear the photos being turned again.

After reading the names attached to another police report, I stumbled upon a report written by Warner in ninety-eight. It was in late August around six in the evening. Warner reported that he was the only officer on the scene. Judging by the time, he was close to the end of his shift. The report was a larceny by vehicle report of an SUV in North End. The driver-side window had been shattered and several items were listed as stolen. Over one hundred dollars in cash was recorded as taken, nothing else. The plate came back as up to date but that wasn't what interested me. The name attached to the car appeared in front of me.

The car belonged to Francis Zaccardi.

The parking lot of the Episcopalian Church only had about ten cars parked in it. Most of them were beat up cars that needed some restoration. Two of them had expired license plates.

Delahine hopped out of his car. The air was getting cooler despite it being the start of the afternoon. He zipped his jacket up towards his sternum. He scanned the parking lot before making his way towards the back of the church.

The church was covered in gray stones in an assortment of different sizes. The front had three different glass windows with a blue tint coming from any direct light. The tower above it was topped off with a large cross. Its arches were circular around each entrance. Delahine made his way towards the back where he found a half-open door. There were no signs on display as he was sure the public would love to know the location of an addict's meeting. The dark, wooden door had a black circle as its knob. He pulled it backward and went into the dark hallway.

He could barely see a thing as he looked back and forth. Down the hall to the left, he could see a faint white light upon the floor. As he walked towards it, his steps could be heard across the stones as he wished he wasn't wearing shoes.

Once at the door, he paused before crossing through it. He decided to peer around the corner, revealing just half of his face. Inside he saw a poorly lit room with several chairs lined up in rows. A table with donuts, muffins, and coffee could be found up against the back wall. The smell of coffee beans trumped all of the other aromas as it circled the room. The ten cars in the parking lot did not reflect the number of people in the room. After a quick headcount, he discovered that there were at least twenty-five people sitting down.

Guess a few of them have expired licenses. Delahine looked towards the podium to see a man with a gray-stained beard standing up. It was hard to comprehend what he was saying behind his slurred speech but Delahine could make out something along the lines of how he was tempted to drink two weeks ago in a sports bar.

After listening to a few more of the man's words, Delahine scanned the seats to see if he saw anyone familiar. Just as he was eyeing a guy in the back corner with the brim of his hat laying low something nearly made him reach for his holster.

"Can I help you, Officer," a voice said from behind him. The hairs on his back all jumped in unison as he turned to see the outline of a woman in the darkness. She stepped into the light of the doorway and raised her eyebrows.

She looked to be in her mid-thirties. A few wrinkles were over the top of her eyebrows, but could easily be hidden by the long brown hair upon her scalp. Her face was thin, but comfortably thin. She had minimal makeup on. The area around her blue eyes was untouched. She appeared to be in good shape as her black dress accented the curve of her hips soundly. Her legs were thin, as her shoulders looked lifted.

"Officer?" she said once again.

"Sorry, you just caught me off guard. I was listening for footsteps on the stone floor and you have none," he said.

"Ah, I know," she said with a smile. "As a kid, I put more pressure on the balls of my feet than the heel. It's always been quieter. Now, are you with probation or are you police?" Delahine noticed a sense of confidence behind her voice.

"Police, and you are?"

"Kate, I'm the director of the meeting in there. I'm part of AWAC, Addicts With A Cause. We have several meetings spread across the city."

"Officer Delahine," he said as he reached out to shake her hand. They were surprisingly rough within her palm but her fingers were soft. "I've heard of you guys. Hope you're making the impact you want."

"More or less. Some of these guys, and girls I should say, just don't care about their identity enough to change it. We have names for those individuals."

"Which are?"

"Residual idiots."

Delahine expressed a quick snicker as he caught a glare from Kate's sunglasses hanging from her collar. He glanced at her breasts but quickly looked back inside the room. "I won't be any trouble. Just hear observing a lead."

"Is there anyone that you need to find?"

"Not in particular but I guess I could ask you something."

"Anything you need."

"Do any of your attendees seem to be more unstable than usual?"

"Unstable is every other Sunday. Acting out is a different story. Most of the people who come in here are usually polite and want to be treated with respect. The few residual idiots in the room have an outburst every once in a while, but nothing violent."

"Have any of them been skipping lately?"

"We have a sign-in sheet but recently in the past month, we've only had one guy disappear on us. It's a shame, he was on the up curve when I got the call his body was found in a dumpster in New York. I guess he tried to flee and some deal went bad."

"That's interesting, what about names? Have you seen the list today?"

"Yes, I generally browse through it before the session begins. I went off to get something from my car in the lot across the street before I came across you here. I don't like parking in the same lot as them. I bet that sounds judgmental."

"I don't blame you. Do you ever remember a guy with the last name Rardar on the list?"

"Not that I'm aware of. I would have recognized that."

"What about Walker, Zaccardi, or Goddfrey? Any of those sound familiar?"

"No, not...wait, Zaccardi, I know that one. He comes here every other Sunday. He never misses a meeting."

Delahine could feel something churn in his stomach.

"What's his first name?"

"Jack, Jack Zaccardi. He's here now actually."

Delahine stared at her for a moment. His focus had shifted. "Can you point him out? I may need to talk to him."

"Sure, let me just take a look." She faced the open doorway and scanned the room. Delahine could see the back of her hair as he found himself glancing at her ponytail. After a few moments of looking around, she announced that she found him.

"There, the man with the hat on in the corner. He's wearing the brown jacket, unzipped," she said.

"Thank you," Delahine managed to say as he entered the room. After taking a few steps, he realized that every one of them made an echo every time his shoe hit the ground. A few heads turned to face him. Jack was one of them.

Jack's eyes widened as he saw Delahine. Then he looked down to see the shiny piece of metal attached to Delahine's hip. Without any cause of delay, Jack was quickly out of his seat and running for another exit. Delahine had no choice to dart after him. He could feel the rush coming. It was starting in his brain, slowly flowing down the rest of his body as he went out the door.

Delahine found himself in the dark hallway once again. Several other doors were creaked open with a little bit of light. Dust could be seen floating in the air and quickly circulating every time Jack passed one of the doors. Delahine followed and was now two doors behind him. The hallway seemed like a dark passage that would never end. Just as he thought Jack had found the end of the hall, it kept going. The darkness grew darker until a large beam of light lit up the right side of the hall and the heels of Jack's feet could be seen leaving the building.

Delahine almost tripped himself as he came to a stop. He drew his Glock out of his holster and held it at eye-level. His eyes were like a laser locked on the open doorway. He took slow steps one in line after the other as he arrived at the door. He looked on the outside and then quickly jumped through the threshold. Jack wasn't there.

He looked around the exterior of the building and it was if Jack had vanished. Delahine listened for a car to be started but there was nothing. He cursed aloud and slammed the door behind him as he walked back into the church.

Chapter 43

"Jack Zaccardi was at the meeting at the church. The director said he hasn't missed a meeting in like two years. I went to talk to him but he fled," Delahine said on the phone. I could hear the roar of his car's engine in the background.

"He got away?" I said.

"Blame our training for that. I was just about to catch him in the hall when he opened a door to the outside. I pied off the door slowly as he was getting away. I wasted too much time and he got away."

"It's alright, just leaves more questions for us now."

"I guess I shouldn't be too shocked to find a Zaccardi in a treatment meeting, they all have the wrong kinds of addictions."

"He's probably the first one to ever try and identify that he has a problem."

"True, any luck on your end since I blew chunks on mine?"

"Well, a few things have happened. Not sure if you've turned on a TV on but our shootout is all over the news. Zaccardi called, he knows I have Thomas and won't give him up. Also, I just found a police report linking Officer Warner to Zaccardi back in ninety-eight. Things are going swell."

"Damn, think Zaccardi has a guy at your house?"

"If so, he's probably parked far away. WCVB, BLN, and others are probably parked outside my house. Not every day a cop in their city gets in two shootouts in one day."

"The first one wasn't really a shootout. Not to calm your fire or anything."

"Good one," I said, closing the Verizon website on my screen. "Last night your first one?"

"Second. There was that one in Dorchester last month. I picked up an off-duty at a festival and some genius thought it would be nice to fire off shots while they were serving lunch."

"That was you there? I remember that. The thing is, I can't get back home and sooner or later they're going to I.D. you. Zaccardi probably knows you've been working with me as well. Maybe you should lay…"

"Don't even say it. I'm seeing this through, for Thomas and his friend. Whoever did this has to be found and two cops work better than one."

"Appreciate it. I'm at the station now with Thomas. We've been through files for over an hour. My eyes have lost too much water looking at this screen."

"I'll bring some sandwiches and we can have lunch. Roma's okay?"

"Perfect, can you do me a favor while you're there?" Not that it was my place but maybe I had a chance to do some good for Thomas. Can't hurt but to try.

"Whatcha need?"

"Tell the owner Roma, that Thomas is okay. Apparently, he and Roma are really close. Figure it would be nice for him to know that he is in good hands. Be careful though, one of the Zaccardis might be snooping around."

"If it's Jack we're going to have some words. I can do that for ya."

"Thanks."

"No problem."

I swiveled my chair around to see that Thomas was on the phone with someone. I waved him over and he hung up.

"My buddy has food coming if you're hungry," I said.

"Thank God, I'm starving," he said.

"Glad to hear it. Who were you on the phone with?"

"No one, I tried to call Tommy twice but he didn't answer. That guy is always on his phone, weird he hasn't answered. Rich too, both won't pick up."

"I'm sure they'll call back. He's a teenager, they always use their phones."

"Are you an expert on teenagers now?"

"Not really, juvenile crime isn't my forte. The law changes too much. Do you label yourself as a juvenile?"

"Only when I feel like it."

"And when is that?"

"School, preferably. I struggle in that place."

"Well, I hope you are enjoying your vacation from it."

"It's a lot more interesting than solving math equations."

"Hopefully, you'll be back to school soon. We're going to find out who killed Sam so that your life can become normal."

His life shouldn't be this complicated. Homework and girls should be his main focus right now. Shame it had to happen to a kid his age. At least, he was safe here for the time being. I looked outside towards the window to see that the clouds were moving in. The sun was covered as the last ray of light looked to be erased from the sky. A strange feeling came over me as I found myself itching my head again. I continued to look out the window when I could feel a buzzing sound coming from my pocket. I reached in and answered.

"Tom? Hey, is everything alright with my father?"

"Yeah, he seems fine. I just came into my shift and found that he had a visitor and was wondering why you came to see him today."

"I didn't come to see him today."

"Really? That's odd."

"Yes, said he was an old friend. He left a name, a Mark Scofield? Do you know who that is?"

The name sparked nothing to me. I searched my brain but the name had no significance that I could think of. Was he an old lawyer friend or a guy he played golf with on the weekends? I had nothing. "Can you do me a favor, Tom?"

"Sure, whatever you need."

"Can you ask security to send me a clip of the video? I'm just curious. His name isn't ringing any bells."

"Not a problem."

"Thanks, Tom, keep a closer eye on him tonight will ya?"

"Two eyes, my lad."

Tom hung up the phone. He left me with another puzzle for the day, but one that could wait. My father was a popular man. He used to have several visits a week until his condition worsened. The bottle on my desk, the one for him was three years old. It's still never been used, as it has been sealed for longer than most bottles of that price are. Sooner or later its time would come. Sooner seemed better than later at this point.

I felt another buzz hit my phone and pulled it out. I turned back to Thomas with a wave.

"Foods almost here."

Chapter 44

"Are you sure that these were the guys that attacked you?"

"Yes, I'm definitely sure. One good eye still works."

Delahine, Thomas, and I had finished with our lunch. Delahine had a good taste in sandwiches as he brought us grinders and a few Cokes. Just before leaving, I printed out mugshots of all of the Zaccardi brothers, including Francis. It took us almost half an hour to get to Mass General Hospital. There was a wreck involving a minivan and motorcycle on the way, thankfully no one was hurt.

Rardar was on the second floor of the emergency room, number 212 to be exact. Once we arrived, the nurse attendant explained to us that he had four busted ribs, a lacerated blood vessel in his right eye and several broken fragments of bone in his cheeks. The Zaccardis surely did a number on the guy and would certainly get the bill once they've been charged.

"They both had masks on at first but then took them off as a scare tactic," Mr. Rardar said, as he tried to find a comfortable position in his bed. The floor was covered in white tiles, much like the walls that were also painted white with a single navy striped painted across the middle. A few beeps could be heard from the heart-rate monitor next to Rardar's bed. The hallway was noisy with nurses discussing their patient's conditions as Thomas decided to shut the door, cementing some privacy for us.

"Scare tactic?" I said.

"Yeah, they said it should matter who did this to me. No one goes against them in this town and they said if I ever saw them, what was I going to do? Try to kill them myself? Look at me. I'd get shot quicker than your first time in bed with a girl."

"You won't have to worry about that Mr. Rardar. We have a case going and you won't have to see them on the streets anymore. I can promise…"

"Spare me. Every cop in a blue moon comes around saying they are going to protect us, cure us, or whatever the hell you guys think you can say to make us feel safe. Men like, like these in those pictures, they're never gone. Look around, if someone on the street doesn't look like they are capable, then watch a little more. Everyone has thoughts of beating someone up or being with another person they aren't already with. It's human hypocrisy at its finest. Spare me your testament of justice. We'll never see the day when people like me aren't beat to a pulp."

"Not everyone is like you, remember that," Delahine said. "Most people don't go around assaulting children just because they can. Thinking about it is wrong but actually committing it, that's immeasurably dark. The world is screwed up, doesn't mean the mess gets to complain about being messy."

"Cops are worse than the public. Haven't you seen the news lately? Baltimore would be a great place for you."

"You would be laying somewhere else then. Not in a hospital."

I turned to look at Delahine. He wasn't blinking as he looked upon the battered Mr. Rardar.

"Alright, not that you guys haven't been amusing but that's all we needed. Anything else you'd like to mention before we leave you in piece Mr. Rardar?"

Mr. Rardar wiped his good eye with his hand. He had a tube running from his inner forearm that was filled with spots of clear liquid. A handheld remote was lying next to his thigh. Time for some morphine as soon as we leave.

"There was one thing, could be nothing," he said.

"Whatcha got?"

"The one who was yelling at me must have messed up his words but I don't know. While I was being beaten in the kitchen. The guy standing over top of me was repeatedly asking me if I knew where he was. Like I said, I had no idea what they were talking about. During his yelling, he slipped up and yelled 'where is it?' It may have been a slip of the word but the guy caught himself after a few seconds and tried to shake it off." Interesting, not much to go on, it could have just been a casual slip of the tongue.

"Thank you, Mr. Rardar. Have a good rest. I'll make sure some uniforms are outside of your room tonight," I said, standing up from my chair.

"Sure, they'll be thrilled to be guarding a registered sex offender," he said.

The three of us didn't answer as we left. I saw that Thomas was the last to leave as he managed to give Mr. Rardar a nod just before we left.

*

"Think that was just a simple slip of the tongue? Could the Zaccardi's be looking for something besides Thomas?" Delahine said.

The three of us exited the hospital out the same exit I take when I visit my father. We were only one building over from him while visiting Mr. Rardar. The wind picked up as I felt the breeze run across my fingers. Rardar looked as if he had nothing to lose. A person with nothing to hide generally tells the truth and analyzes every comment around them. I couldn't be sure, but maybe he was telling the truth.

I pulled my keys out and fumbled them around. We motioned for the car when Delahine stopped me.

"Hey, Thomas, go wait in the car for a second, I have to talk to Mike about something," he said.

"You guys falling in love?" Thomas said.

"You jealous?"

"Ha, not in the slightest, enjoy your talk."

Delahine and I watched Thomas cross the street as he headed for the parking garage. Just as he was out of hearing distance, Delahine spoke. Nothing was coming to mind about what he wanted to talk about.

"Not to step on anything, but I just wanted to ask you something."

"What is it?"

"What you've been doing for Thomas has been great. Keeping him away from his father is what is best for him but I just, I just don't know if you've thought this through."

"If you mean about his safety, I can protect him it's not like that. I…"

"No, I know that. It's about what happens when this end. If we find who killed Sam then that's great and what we want."

"But?" I noticed his feet kick against one another, followed by a sniff.

"This isn't going to end with a simple click of the cuffs, you know that, right? This will never stop. The Zaccardis are like a stain on a carpet. They won't go away unless you get rid of the carpet."

"That's what it means to throw them in prison. There is plenty of space in prison for a fresh carpet."

"You know what I mean. Zaccardi, Thomas's father, is not going to let you put handcuffs on him and bring him into the pen. This will end with gunfire and I hope you are ready to be the one who fires first."

"Look, Leo, I know what you are saying but the Zaccardis will be put in jail. We have evidence on them and we just need a little more. They will be tried. If we go into this thinking a firefight is coming then we might as well be having our guns out through every door we enter. I've only had to shoot first once and that was when a man tried to strangle me at a damn middle school. We will play it smart. No one has to die when this thing is over."

"They pay off everybody Mike. He knows too many people, too many strong people. He's going to get away just like before. Your father was close, but he just gets away. Yeah, I read about your dad and him, shame the evidence didn't stick."

"My father tried his best. He just tried his best and lost. It happens to us all."

"It doesn't matter how it happened; it still did. Boston doesn't need them anymore. I know I'm young and there is a lot I don't know about how problems should be fixed in this world but I can't think of anything else. We can call someone else to help but the Zaccardis are just going to hurt more people until we do something. A choice is going to have to be made and it might come to you. Are you going to be ready for that?"

"Would you?" I looked away towards the parking garage, hoping Thomas would walk out to interrupt the conversation. I still trusted this man but he would not let this idea go.

"Leo, look," I said. "Last night, when you shot that man, how did you feel, pain or relief? You shot someone and ended whatever kind of life they had. That had to make you feel something, didn't it?"

"Is there a wrong answer?"

"There is when you have to ask."

Chapter 45

It wasn't long ago. I heard a man, sitting down in a coffee house, having a conversation with someone. Both were in polished suits, without a wrinkle upon their sleeves. Politics, what crafts of beer they liked, and their overall view of society spewed into the air as their forks and knives scratched their plates. Ideas of what to do and what can never be done filled my ears. The two men discussed issues about abortion, Planned Parenthood and whether or not it should be funded by the state. Or if convicted felons recently released from prison should be implanted with a homing device to track his or her movements for the rest of their life.

These men were educated but also cruel. By their expressions and tone of voice it was obvious they were raised in a life of affluence. Prosperity was just a word for them. Never realizing the true struggle it was to achieve it. Work hard and expect more work was their output. Their college rings from their distinguished universities rested on their fingers, frequently clanging against their plates as well. I remember fumbling with my finger pretending I had one while they spoke.

It wasn't until they started speaking about the death penalty when my ears perked a little wider. I figured this topic would circle around sooner or later.

"It costs more money to kill a man than keep him alive, can you believe this system? A simple stick of the needle or a wrap around the neck apparently costs more money to house a convicted murderer that killed a family of three," One of the men said.

"You know it's not about that right? It's the prep and trials for it. It takes months, sometimes several years for a death penalty trial to even conclude. A few years ago, it took one guy's trial over a hundred months to be concluded and sentenced to death," the other man said just before filling his mouth with another fork filled with eggs.

"It took the Boston Marathon bomber what, two years? Sounds like the opposite of swift justice. Our high-class trials take several weeks at most."

"That case had more publicity than the Super Bowl, that's why the courts cleared that one fast. Apparently, if you were part of the trial team it would have been sooner."

"Damn straight. There is plenty of low-life in this town that deserves a quick death for us to have a little breather. If one more person gets shot, raped, or God knows what in Dorchester or Southie, I'm going to have an aneurysm. I know I've been doing this job a long time but when does it stop? Or, hell, freeze for a moment."

"The Zaccardis fit into that?"

"At the top of the list. They'll get their day, if we can't, someone will."

"Hope so, but like you were saying. When it comes to will it stop? Never, seems the consensus of us all. There are the few here who keep us happy and that's what we count on. Boston isn't just a city, it's a community of people who know there is shit around the world and without tradition, we'll just let it happen."

"Some say Boston's a shithole."

"Yeah, if we are, then at least we are a classic shithole. Go to Fenway and tell me we don't have unity. The Marathon proves that we are a city ready to fight back against anything in our way."

"Wish it was as simple as it was back then. All we had to worry about was when New York came to town. No one knew who was getting shot that night." Laughter followed as I continued to listen.

"What does your boy think of all this? He's a college boy, they've got opinions. Let's hear it."

"What will it be, Mikey? What do you think of people dying so that others can live?"

I turned to see my father's brown eyes looking back at me. The light above us flickered as I sat straight up. Richard Bowen, the best prosecutor to ever see Boston was asking me a question. I felt more like a coworker than a son.

"I believe that killing is synonymous with taking. Taking someone's life away is too great a decision, we can't make that call. Those who commit acts deemed criminal by society can't be silenced swiftly. It takes work to bring someone back," I said.

There was a moment where I thought no one was going to speak. It was as if I just justified every murderer in the country.

"Well thought out, son. College is treating you well as I can see it. Don't be pushed into something that you don't believe. I'm sure everything we've been saying hasn't been to your liking," my father said, as he drank his glass of water

"Richard, are you serious? Your kid thinks that rehabilitation is actually effective. When was the last time our recidivism rates dropped in the past ten years? If more news broke out that felons are getting the needle, we'd have less work to do at the office," my father's work associate, Frank said.

"Frank, Frank. My son simply has a different opinion. I may not agree with some of them but I can't disagree with him right off the bat."

"Now I see why you don't call for as many objections as I do. You let all of your opponents talk as what, some kind of respect to their argument? I guess it works with the record you have."

"People are given the opportunity to speak, just like our First Amendment says so. If we don't let them speak, we look like bullies who want nothing but personal gain."

I almost jumped back at the words coming out of my father's mouth. He was a man of strict action but too few were there glimpses of his side of respect for another person's opinion. He knew how to push, and today he felt like easing off the peddle. Memories of his worst push came to mind before he spoke again.

"Frank, learn from my son here. Once he graduates, he might be a lawyer just like his old man," he said.

"Can't wait to have two of you in the same office," Frank said.

"You forgot to smile when you said that."

My father looked at me with the grin I was accustomed to as much. Maybe this was a façade, a show he was putting on in front of his friend. To make him look like the perfect dad. In some ways he really was, but when he scolds me for not being good enough or when the alcohol takes effect, the good thoughts began to fade.

My father looked back at me.

"Know what I mean son?"

"Yeah, dad. I know what you mean."

*

I looked back at Delahine like I was looking at a familiar face. Neither of us felt like we were wrong, but who can judge that? Who with a clear conscience and no bias attached could ultimately make the decision to end someone's life? It was a question I've fought ever since that day with Frank and my father.

"Look, I'm not trying to say that either of us is wrong. We just have to prepare for how this is going to go. You're probably right, we may have to be ready to shoot first but it doesn't mean we have to aim to end. We can't lose sight of what we vowed to do," I said, just as I felt a buzz in my pocket.

"I understand. You know better than most that these guys won't fall when they hear somebody tell them they are under arrest. I just want us to be ready. I don't want to have to see one of us put a bullet into someone that he used to love."

"Neither do I. Let's just go back to our cars and figure out what to do next. I called Verizon. Sam's phone has been inactive for a day. The customer service agent said we had to go to an actual store to check his last calls or texts."

"For a day? That means someone still had it on up until sometime yesterday."

"That's what I was thinking too. We need to get his last few calls. It's time to get ahead of the game."

"'Bout time we have some kind of trail. I was thinking..."

Delahine stopped in the middle of the street as we were walking. He had his phone held up to his face. "Shit, you've got to be kidding me."

"What, what is it?"

"How the hell did the Zaccardis get by my lookout?"

*

Jess was wide awake now. She could not stop thinking of Mike and seeing him on TV. Her phone was resting on the counter but she feared calling him might put him at risk for something. She imagined him staking out a place somewhere local trying to be silent. The ring of her phone call potentially eliminating any source of surprise put a hint of fear within her fingers. He was back in her life only a few days ago but she felt like everything needed to be fixed. Everything that he was uncertain about needed to be known. She had to tell him the truth. There was something she had to do first.

In less than a minute, Jess was in her closet frantically searching old files to find what she was looking for. After dumping a pile of old tax returns, a throw blanket from her grandmother, and several worn-out records, she stumbled upon a folder. The top of it had two letters "MB" marked on it. The sharpie still held up after all these years. The surface still felt smooth across her fingertips as she opened it.

"Mike was inside this folder," she thought to herself. She stumbled upon old photographs of the two of them back in school. Several of them were from campus during their study breaks. Her hair was a bit fuller then, less cut and cleaned as it was now. She was a little thinner in them, as the lack of motivation hit her from time to time in her thirties. Mike still had his curls in one of the pictures. He was sitting on one of the benches with a grin across his face as he was holding a graded paper from one of his classes. She found a note written for her as well. He didn't like to admit it back then but Mike knew how to write a convincing Valentine's Day letter.

She caught herself smiling. She hadn't stopped since opening the folder. As she made it to the back, she found what she was looking for. It was a newspaper article dated three years ago. It was almost three years till the day she noticed after reading the top. She flipped through it until she found the desired page.

Jess sat there and started to read once again about the father of the man that returned back into her life just a few days ago.

Chapter 46

Delahine offered to drive to the Verizon store. It wasn't as far his GPS revealed but he said he would take care of it after speaking with Officer Jones. He sped out of the parking garage leaving his right turn signal on.

I sat back against the hood of my car. The day was closing in every minute and nothing seemed to fall in line. Some bruises, broken bones, and the testimony of a registered sex offender wasn't the dream line of evidence I was expecting to bring down the Zaccardis. It would help, but this wasn't about them unless they had something to do with Sam.

Mr. Walker and Francis popped in my head. They were the only two people who I could attempt to connect to Sam. Baseball coach turned killer would be compelling but he appeared to have no hatred towards Sam, just the Zaccardis. But, the Zaccardis claimed they would call him again, I wonder if they already have.

I could go over all of the claims against Francis, it's just, why kill a kid? He was a teenager not even paying taxes yet. Money was replaceable. Francis didn't care about a loss that much, did he?

The car felt warm as I sat back inside. Thomas was sitting there, with his red hand over the vent.

"It's only fifty degrees outside. I'm starting to think if we need to buy you gloves or not," I said.

"I hate this, I live in Boston. We are supposed to adapt to the cold quicker than a kid learns how to pitch for the first time. Anyways, what's next?"

"I want to talk to your Uncle Jack."

"What?"

"Your Uncle, Delahine found him today at one of those meetings you thought about. We need to speak to him."

"He's not going to talk. He's the quietest of them all, what makes you think he'll even talk?"

"You, you're his nephew. You contact him and he'll come running if you say that you need him."

"If I do that, then won't my father come looking for me too? We're already being *hunted* and you're the police. Nothing makes sense right now. Why can't we have SWAT bust down my dad's bakery and start searching the place? There has to be thousands of dollars there."

"Hundreds of thousands, I'm willing to bet. We can't just barge into their house based on an assumption."

"It happens on TV. What's stopping us?"

"Warrants, we need a signed paper from a judge to search the place. If we go for one now, the process will take too long and my captain's pulling the plug today. I need you to do this. I'm sorry. We're running out of options."

Thomas wrestled around in his seat. He took a deep breath and pulled his phone out of his pocket. It wasn't what he wanted to do, but his eyes gave in.

"What do you want me to say?"

*

Thomas played his part better than expected. Jack answered after a few rings, to which Thomas almost went white in the face. I wrote down a few things to say on a piece of paper to which Thomas only looked at once. He left the phone on speaker.

Jack sounded quite shocked and hesitant. It was clear to me that this uncle could not fathom the thought of making his own decision. Fastidious in his speech, Jack held a long pause after Thomas asked a question. Thomas started off by saying that he needed to see him and felt like he could not trust his father or this other uncle. Jack seemed put off by his tone but continued to press Thomas for more information.

He didn't give off any impression that he was not speaking his own words as Thomas was able to get him to meet us somewhere. He said nothing about my presence as instructed and hung up the phone just as Jack was about to ask another question.

"Sounds important if you hang up," Thomas said as he buckled his seatbelt.

Park Street Church was the destination. I chose it for its ability to throw off the scent of any criminal, especially Francis. I was willing to bet that church wasn't on his schedule for a Sunday afternoon.

When we arrived, there were only a few cars parked on the street. We parked directly adjacent to the Granary Burying Grounds off of Tremont Street. I could remember walking on the stone paths as a kid. Its historical significance to the town was worthy of recognition. My father took me when my mother was still with us. In his boisterous presentation voice, he would go on about how since 1660 this site has contained the burial sites of some of

Boston's greatest citizens. Paul Revere himself was buried here. It was one of the graves my father frequently loved to lecture me on. It was one of the prime places he would take me if I needed to be reminded again on how to cement your name in history. My father meant well with his speeches but often turned me off with my stubbornness.

Jack said that he could be there in thirty minutes. That was twenty minutes ago by the time we arrived at the church. Thomas and I exited the car and proceeded inside.

The church could fit a small plane in its arches. The cathedral looked to be four stories high, but the architecture of its stonework could easily fool the eyes into believing it was much larger. It smelled of furbished wood, accented with the dust-stained carpet. The air seemed contained but not in a restricted way. Not even echoes could be heard. The only sound in the room came from two men sitting in a pew towards the front of the altar.

The sign outside said there wouldn't be another service until four. Plenty of time for a quick talk. I scanned the room for someone to remain hidden when Jack would arrive. Thomas agreed that if he would see me with him then he would fly right of here. Both of us walked down several rows of pews when an idea struck me.

"Here, sit in this row. Whenever you hear the door open, knock on the pew in front of you twice to signal that it's him. If it's not, knock once," I said.

"Where are you going to be?" he said.

"I'm going to take a nap." I didn't turn to see Thomas's face as I assumed what it might be like. Two rows down, I propped my legs across the pew and lied down.

"You can't be serious. You're going to look ridiculous."

"Not with this face I won't. Let's not talk until he gets here. Don't forget to knock."

Several minutes had passed without the door opening. I could hear footsteps coming from the front of the altar. The two men talking once before walked by to see me lying across the pew. I gave them a polite wave as they walked off. A few seconds passed and the doors opened, to which I heard a knock.

It was no less than two minutes when I heard two quick knocks. The carpet was light but I could make out gentle footsteps towards us. My heart started to quicken as I continued to listen for more footsteps. Only Jack's could be heard from where I was.

"Hello, Thomas," I could hear Jack say as he made his way into the cue. It sounded like he was sitting in the one next to him, but I couldn't be sure.

"Uncle Jack. Thanks for coming. It's been a long weekend."

"Of course, I'm sorry about your friend. Sam was a good kid. It's a shame for what happened. I couldn't imagine losing a friend at your age. It's too young ya know?"

"Yeah, not my favorite weekend. Thanks for coming alone, I'm not really talking to my dad right now."

"Yeah, I know. Ralphie and Richard are out looking for you right now. They were at your Detective friend's place for a little while, hoping you'd show up. I have no idea where they are right now. Where is Bowen anyway?"

"He had to go with his partner. I guess he thought it would be safe for me to be in a church, dad has a problem with these places. I figured I could go along with it until he comes back."

The tweeting of some birds could be heard from some of the windows before I could hear anyone speak again.

"Thomas, you need to come back to your dad. He's going crazy looking for you and he's afraid. He wants you back."

"Afraid? Afraid of what, that I'll get hurt on the streets that he makes dangerous."

"It's not like that. If there is somebody out there who killed your friend, they might be after you too. Francis wants you back to protect you."

"How can he protect me if he might be the one who killed Sam? I know that Sam's dad works for him, and owes him quite a lot of money. I can't trust any of them. You've always been the more understandable one, that's why I called you. Until I find who killed Sam, I can't come back with him until I know for sure." A pause followed as I could not tell what it meant. Was Thomas running out of things to say? "Do you know if he killed him?"

I guess not. Jack didn't say anything as I assumed, I heard his foot tapping on the carpet below him. "Your dad had nothing to do with this, you have to believe me. He's out there right now trying to find where you are. He's trying to find out who killed Sam too. He managed to look up all of the sex offenders in the area to see if they knew anything. Your dad is doing his best to find you and whoever killed Sam. If you come home with me, you'll see."

"Beating people up until they can't breathe anymore isn't how you track someone down," Thomas said. The statement went over Jack's head as he didn't even question how Thomas knew that.

"He is doing what is necessary. No one is going to talk to someone if you don't have a badge on. It's hard for even cops to talk to people about a kid dying in a public park."

"Kindness can go a long way. None of you know that. All our family does is use their fists to earn our money. The bakery is a front, everyone knows that. Sooner or later, my dad, you and everybody else is going to get caught."

"Look, things are more complicated than you think. Your dad is going farther than before to get what he wants. If you come home, we can figure something out. I know I'm not thought of as the smartest but I've got something that can help us out."

"I've heard this from before. Our family is too far gone. I don't want to hear anymore excuse until I find out who took Sam away from us."

"Thomas, if you just listen I can…"

"Can I make a suggestion?"

I rose up from the pew to see a white in the face Jack looking back at me.

Chapter 47

"Fancy seeing a Zaccardi who actually follows the rules. I'm glad you could make it Jack. It was nice seeing you the other day," I said, as I carefully placed my Glock upon my lap.

"Thomas was supposed to be alone," Jack said while shifting in his seat a little bit.

"We just want to talk. Don't worry, I'm not going to arrest you, I forgot my handcuffs."

"What do you want?"

"Answers to our curiosity. Do you have a minute?"

Jack didn't answer.

"Why did Ralphie and Richard visit Mr. Rardar? We just visited him in the hospital, said two guys who looked a lot like brothers broke into his house and questioned him. Thomas here just got you to answer one of my suspicions, but what does Francis want?"

"I just told him, they want to find Thomas."

"What else are they are looking for? Something that Francis doesn't want us to know about?"

"What do you mean?"

"Ralphie asked Rardar for something. We don't know what he was talking about, maybe you could tell us?"

"I'm not worth beating a guy to death like that," Thomas said.

"I don't know any…"

"Stop it," I said. "I know they treat you like a servant and that you're just a piece of meat but you have the opportunity to help your nephew here. We're not going after Francis unless he had something to do with Sam."

"Okay, I don't know much you're right. Francis handles the finances while Ralphie and Richard are the muscle. I assist in keeping the bakery running, plus doing whatever else they ask of me. Last week Francis came in pissed off one day. More than usual, he even cussed a customer out he was so rattled. Could have been anything but he is typically good had containing himself. Thomas was out with his friends so he wasn't there. I went back to ask Francis what was wrong but said they he lost something, something that could ruin us if we didn't get it back."

"It couldn't be money could it?"

"No, money comes and goes. Francis once lost twenty thousand dollars in an hour and replaced it, plus more in less than two. He's a magnet with money. I don't know what it could be but it must be important. Maybe enough to point the police in his direction."

"We are always pointed in his direction, might as well have a BPD tattoo on his forehead."

"That's not what I mean. He didn't mention you guys."

I remained silent for a moment. Alcohol law enforcement and state police might be after them for a plethora of reasons but they've slipped from them before.

"The Feds?" I said.

"Think so," Jack said. "I know you'll keep asking but I don't know what it could be."

"We'll see. Anything else?"

"After he came in pissed off that day, he made us do something. Well, I was the third guy, he brought in two others."

"What did you have to do?"

"We had to take…some people. Francis thought they may have whatever was *taken* from him. I didn't physically help. I was in the getaway car."

Thomas's head jerked up straight after he heard what his uncle said, "I didn't know who or why, it was quick. It happened the same night after he came in on his tirade."

"What did they look like?"

"They put bags on their heads. One was a skinny guy, the other could have been a woman. I didn't get a good look."

"Does Francis still have them?"

"I don't think so. I thought I heard him say Thursday that he was letting them go but I can't be sure."

"How do I know that you are telling the truth?"

"He's telling the truth," Thomas said. "My uncle here is not a good liar. He taps his foot when he isn't being truthful. Being short has its advantages when you grow up in a family of criminals. I would look down at their feet a lot. He hasn't tapped his foot once."

I looked at Thomas and gave him a nod.

"Jack, if you are telling the truth. We need to act now if Francis has them. Will he kill them?"

"No, he won't, not unless they royally piss him off. Francis has been off all week so I think they are still alive. I can go look but it might not end well for me."

"This is your family we are talking about. Why are you even talking to me about this? This could be just one big ploy. I don't understand what you are trying to prove."

"Being loyal to your family doesn't mean you have to agree with everything that they do. I'll call Thomas about what I find out."

"You an addict, Jack?" I asked him just as he was about to get up.

"What?"

"An addict, do you have an addiction to anything?"

"No, not as bad as some people."

"My partner saw you at a meeting today. Said you ran off before he could speak with you."

Jack's face turned another shade of white as he looked at Thomas. He looked unsettled despite being in such a holy place. He exhaled as he looked back at me.

"I drink too much. For a few months now, I've had it under control but the meetings help me. Seeing everyone else suffer like me makes it feel less lonely. Francis has no idea, this is something I'm doing for myself."

"Then why run?"

"I thought I was going to be arrested."

"Only guilty people run, Jack."

"I was afraid you connected everything and were rounding us all up. I didn't know what to do."

"What do you mean connected?" The answer seemed clear while I even said it.

"You know what I mean. You know what my brother has done, what we all do. I know we are going to get caught one day. It would happen on a Sunday; we don't deserve to rest on this day."

Jack combed what little hair he had and started to stand up.

"This has to end. Francis is coming for you and he won't back down until he gets Thomas or finds whatever he is looking for. Get Thomas out of here before it gets bad. I'm surprised you haven't started walking for the door."

Like a confident poker player after making his last move, Jack turned and headed toward the door. He was different, he spoke like someone else.

*

"Any word on your friends?" I said.

"Nothing, they usually respond by now," Thomas said as he dug his heel into the wooden floor.

"I'm sure they're alright. We can go look for them if you want?"

"Maybe, I'll wait a little longer. Delahine get back to us?"

"Nothing, he hasn't, well would you look at that."

A text had come across my phone, it was from Delahine.

'Jones is a piece of shit. Found him with over fifty thousand dollars in cash in his car. Burkes came out and oversaw everything. He's headed to the station now. Jones said Ralphie got to him, he didn't know where the others were. He didn't have his camera on so we have no real evidence, just his word. The Zaccardis could be anywhere, lookout.'

"Shit."

"What?"

"Your Uncle Ralphie managed to convince one of our officers to take money in exchange for not recording who left your house. Your dad isn't at the bakery as we thought. He's out there somewhere."

"Shit."

"No kidding. Every time it looks like we are getting ahead something has to happen. Do you know the names of his contacts? Like known associates who work for your dad?"

"That list is too long. My dad would call people all the time asking them to do something for him. He only trusted a select few, besides my uncles."

"Any names?"

"Cub is one. He's a greasy mechanic in Southie with a large scar across his forehead. Maxie and Derrick are two brothers who live somewhere around us. They come around sometimes. They came into my room one time to play Madden. I was too young to even care. They just walked right in and acted like my friends.

"Maxie and Derrick Romez?

"I think so."

"Both bad news, especially together. We arrested them a year ago for a nasty fight outside a gas station. They fought four guys by themselves. Their bail was paid by an anonymous donation."

"You don't need me to figure that one out."

We walked out of the church. There were people walking in and out of the local gelato place across the street. A family of five walked out, each with a different flavor as they walked in our direction. Thomas had pulled his phone back out. His neck was perked forwards intently.

"Do you think my dad has them?" he said.

"I don't know. I don't want to lie to you. It would be a smart move by him since they mean so much to you. The only hope that is causing me not to think about it is that he hasn't told us yet. That gives me hope, how about you?"

"I guess." Thomas didn't look as though I made any difference. He walked the rest of the way to the car by himself.

This had to end.

Chapter 48

I looked over the pier. The water was dark, placid as it appeared. Nothing wrong, nothing capable of disturbing it as it just swayed back and forth. The light from behind shined across the water causing white stripes upon its surface. I held his hand as we looked out upon it. The hard-working hero before my eyes. I felt nothing but peace between the both of us, until it happened.

As soon as I got in the car, I decided to check my phone. Thomas was sitting quietly in the seat next to me. It took me a few minutes to get back in the car as I looked around the block, pretending I was pondering something important.

I saw a notification from my email after turning my phone on. It was an email from Tom. Guess he found the video footage. I clicked on it only to be met with an unknown number calling me.

"I once heard, if you answer an unknown call, it might link your account to a cybercriminal. You'd think a cop would know better." Francis's timing this weekend was just as dreadful as he was.

"I thought you would have found us by now. Guess you're falling off. Is old age getting to you?"

I could feel Thomas looking at me. Maybe it was time he heard what dad really was. I lowered the phone down and pressed the speaker.

"Your smart mouth has an expiration date. Might as well be today, it's as good a day as any," Francis said.

"You keep thinking that but you're not as lucky as you think you are," I said.

"Do tell?"

"You'll know soon enough. Can't give away my hand too soon, it's not fair for the game."

"Tom might have something different to say about that."

Forget about what I knew about having something under control. I looked at Thomas. His forehead creased at the sound of his father's words.

"He's fine. He almost seems nice, too nice if you ask me. I see him right now. He's speaking with another woman at a desk. For a nice guy he's got

227

quite the glare, he must really not like me. I'm so likable aren't I Thomas?" A shift by Thomas in his seat gave Francis everything he needed. "There's my son, I figured he'd be listening in."

"Why are you harassing him?" I said. "He has nothing to do with this. Please, leave that man out of this. He has done more for me than you could possibly know."

"Mike, Mike. I'm not harassing anyone. You know, harassment is a funny thing, everyone thinks it's one-sided. One person aggravates another and everyone thinks that both sides are innocent. No one is innocent…

As he kept talking, I felt an itch forming around my scalp when I had an idea. I went back to check to see that the video had loaded. After pressing the button to view it, the grip on my phone grew tighter. I saw him, at the front counter, talking to Margery. My eyes started to become hindered. I could feel the water and anger falling out of my eyes.

"Francis, you have no right going to see him, you…"

"Ah, you are a detective. He's a friend of the family, am I not entitled to a meet and greet?"

"Get out of here now or I'll call half the cops in this town to come yank you out of there. You are there without any sort of permission, and I would have a case against you being there with your history. Leave now and I won't do that."

"If you were here right now, I doubt you'd feel like you had any say at all. Your father likes shiny things, I can see. Buttons seem to be a favorite of is, plus he keeps staring at my metal belt buckle. Might have some other issues if you ask me. There's something freshly shined and cleaned in my hand underneath a pillow. He seems to be fascinated with that."

I felt so angry. I almost threw the phone at my windshield.

"Let me set the rules here," he added on. "You and Thomas will be here in thirty minutes. We'll have a quick chat, maybe discuss where you have been and who knows, maybe we can solve this big case of yours. I'll see you when you get here. Oh, and don't cause a commotion when you get here. I haven't had to press the trigger for some time now. I'd hate to prematurely end your father's life."

Fear has never attached itself so well to the end of a phone call.

*

The parking lot was more confusing than she had anticipated. She researched Mass General on the internet and found the address for the Memory Unit. Alzheimer's was a disease she had no experience with. Her parents were still here and still moderately healthy. Her grandfather died of lung cancer two years ago but that process wasn't as long. Stage four is already pretty late in the game. He might not even recognize me.

Jess decided to park her car next to a truck that was almost out of the lines. When she made it down out of the parking garage, she turned to see a pair of signs pointing her north to the entrance. After speaking to a generally nice receptionist, she found herself in an elevator. The Memory Unit was on the third floor on the other side of the building. She could smell sanitizer in the elevator as two doctors were standing in front of her. One of them was discussing a clogged aorta that he was struggling with an hour ago. She thought about the stars and alignments she studied during her time at work and wondered about the complexity of their issues compared to human anatomy. The thought of life intermingled amongst the stars lifted her spirits. She knew her work was important, but could not help but compare her career choice to the two white coats in front of her.

After both of them exited the elevator, she found herself walking down a different hallway than them. Her footsteps felt heavier the more she walked towards her destination. She could see it labeled above the doorway. It was written in sterling silver lettering that would remain there for many years. Many people behind that sign and in those rooms would never remember it.

"I'm here to see Richard Bowen. I'm not on any visitation list, but I'm just an old friend," Jess said.

"Mr. Bowen? May I have your name, please?" the lady said as she began to move quickly with her pen.

"Jessica Clark."

"Miss Clark, may I see some identification?"

"Sure."

Jess handed her driver's license over to her. She peered at it for a few moments and then handed it back. After spending several minutes on her computer, the lady handed Jess's license back to her with a smile.

"He'll be in the lounge quarters. Just make sure you tell his attendant that you will be here. He's been one of our most sensitive patients."

"Thank you."

Jess smiled back to the lady as she made her away around the front desk. The thick, wooden doors before her clicked as she opened them. Inside, she saw a new hallway with lighter colors on the walls. On the walls hung framed pictures of either a sunset or inspirational quotes from an anonymous author. One had a sailboat on it resting easily on water with the sunset not far from its bow. She couldn't help but smile as she continued to look at it.

"Are you Miss Clark?"

Jess turned to see a man in green colored scrubs. His dark skin looked brighter under the fluorescent light above him.

"Yes, I'm here to meet Mr. Bowen."

"Wonderful, he doesn't have guests that often. Just his son every other week. Let me lead you to him, he's in the common area. We were trying to play checkers but he isn't in the mood," he said.

Jess followed him through another hallway when he spoke again.

"I'm Tom by the way. How do you know Mr. Bowen?"

"I used to date his son actually. It's been a while since I've seen Richard. I bumped into Mike the other day and it made me think of coming to visit his father."

"I thought your name sounded familiar. Mike's mentioned you before. More than I'm sure he would be willing to share with you."

"Nothing positive I bet."

"You'd be surprised. He told me about what you…what you did. Not that it's any of my business but he doesn't seem like a man who's looking to retaliate."

"Nice to know he doesn't hate me."

"Like I said," Tom said as he pointed to a man sitting in a chair across the room. "This isn't my business nor am I an expert on these kinds of things but the best thing to do in your situation is to talk. I'm afraid we men struggle with that."

Tom smiled at her and proceeded to talk with another patient that walked by them. Jess walked towards the man on the couch. His hair was fading but still rather full. He was wearing a brown sweater with a lighter tint of brown khaki pants. Years could be seen added to his face as she looked at him. As soon as she crossed in front of him, his eyes looked up to hers. He looked as if a new sign of life had shined upon him.

"Mr. Bowen, I know it's been a while but I thought it would be nice to come see you."

He opened his mouth but nothing came out. Only a few words that didn't make much sense came out but were impossible to string together.

"I know it's been a while since the last time we met but I felt it was important to come see you. Our talk that we had, back then, it's all that I've thought about the past few days. You were right about Mike. He seems to have achieved success doing something greater than most, just like you said. He's done it all on his own, without me there to distract him as you once said. You told me that if I stuck around, I might slow him down. Maybe you were right."

She wiped her cheek as it started to feel wet. "You gave me a choice to leave him or stay. Maybe, me leaving was a good thing. I tried to put you and him behind me so I wouldn't ruin anything for him. I don't know why I'm telling you this because you know it already. I just wanted to come by to say that I saw him the other day. He sparked something in me again and I thought maybe if I come see you then I could figure out what that was. Since you can't speak this has become more difficult. I'm... I'm sorry."

Jess started wiping her cheeks with her hands as she headed for the doorway. She did not look back as she quickly passed Tom sitting down behind a table with an elderly woman coughing into a napkin. She could see his puzzled face but did not linger to speak with him. She made it past the locked wooden door and was almost put back as she almost ran into a man in the doorway. His large trench coat was draped over a well-ironed suit. Jess quickly looked up at the man and apologized.

He returned with a smile and said, "Oh, that's alright. Seeing old friends is hard to do."

Chapter 49

Thoughts of my childhood quickly began racing through my mind. Staying out late with friends and being scolded by my father when I arrived with fresh bruises or stains upon my shirts. He wanted what was best for me and now, he was in the opposite position to do anything about it.

I ignored every stoplight in my path as I glued the gas pedal to the floor of my car. Thomas had his seatbelt on but struggled to be still as I weaved in and out of cars. My adrenaline was taking control of me now. My hands felt as if they were stitched onto the steering wheel as my eyes did nothing but search for different routes around cars. My pursuit training from the academy started to come back to me now while I was able to manipulate pressing on the gas and break in a corrective way for my vehicle not to skid.

In less than ten minutes, I made it to Cambridge Street. I calculated that in less than thirty seconds, I would be closing in on the entrance into the hospital. I thought ahead, running up the stairs looking frantic as the other doctors around me looked in confusion. The thoughts almost took me completely when Thomas started to raise his voice asking where we were going.

I turned the wheel, making a hard-right turn onto North Grove. The entrance was several hundred feet ahead as I sped towards it. Several people were walking along the trees to my right when I glimpsed at a small boy holding his father's hand with a bandage over his forehead.

I parked the car near the bottom of the roundabout, directly in front of the parking deck. I felt for my Glock in my holster and whipped my head towards Thomas.

"Listen to me. I need to go in there. Your father is holding someone important to me hostage and it's a trap for you. You need to follow my instructions carefully."

"I can come with you, my fath—"

"Your father is ruthless and will not hesitate to hurt anyone. He will not take you, I promise you that. Now, listen. When I get out of the car, you need to drive it up to the highest floor of the parking garage. There should be spots, so don't worry about that. Take my phone and call Delahine. Tell him where you are and he will come get you. The password is the number sprayed on one of the pillars on the fourth floor of the building, you can't miss it. If he asks about me, tell him Francis has my father hostage and I'm trying to deescalate the situation. My phone is the key, don't lose it."

I left the keys in the ignition and shut the door behind me. My eyes did not wander back at him in hopes he listened to everything that I told him.

The doors felt weightless as I pushed through them, only to find myself looking bewildered by all of the faces glued to me. Too much attention might cause something. I rubbed the back of my head and started to hastily walk down the hall towards the elevator. It arrived as soon as I pressed the button. The doors opened and my mouth almost dropped.

"Jess, what, what are you doing here?"

"Mike, hi. I don't really know how to say it but I came to see your father."

"My father? Is everything alright?"

"Yes, yes, I just felt like I needed to see him. I'm glad you're here, I wanted to tell you something."

"Jess, I'm sorry, there's something I need to take care of. Did you see anyone after you left my father in the visiting center?"

Her face looked put back but still cognizant of what I asked. "I'm not sure. There were a lot of people."

"Nobody looked strange to you?" My voice must have elevated as her facial expression changed frantically.

"I'm not sure. There was a man in a trench coat wearing a nice suit when I was leaving but I don't know if that matters."

"It just might. Look, can you do me a favor and just wait here. I can't explain but I will tell you everything. I need to do this."

I instinctively kissed her forehead and squeezed past her into the elevator. The action caught her off guard, even to me as well. Her wonderful face looked back at me in confusion as the doors shut. She had to be away. Why was she here, during all of this?

I arrived on my father's floor quickly as the elevator made no stops. My pace quickened as I walked down the hall towards Magarey's desk. She was about to say hey before she noticed my face.

"Open the door please," I said, making for the door. "This is an emergency, don't tell anyone. I can't say anything but help will be here soon."

The door clicked and I thrust myself through the threshold after opening the door. The hallway seemed friendly as usual while I made the turn into the common areas. Tom was there. He was bending over a desk talking to another attendant when he jerked up dramatically when I entered the room. His movement caught the attention of the man sitting in the chair just a few feet away. I recognized the back of the man's head as he was sitting directly in front of my father. The man turned his head and smiled.

"There is the prodigal son."

Chapter 50

It was just after nine in the evening when we got out of the movie. My father took me to see *The Shawshank Redemption*. At eight-years-old, I really didn't understand Morgan Freeman's wisdom as the character Red. He spoke with great precedence, as if he read a book about the world and understood all facets of it. Several times throughout the movie, I asked my dad questions about it. He would often seem annoyed but willing to give me a quick answer in order for him to enjoy what uninterrupted scenes he had.

When the movie ended, we exited the theater. He took me to Loews Theater down on Tremont. It was one of the most popular theaters in all of Boston with its neon lights tethered around the corners of the building. Inside seemed like a light show from some futuristic movie. It lit over half our path down the block as we walked to our car. My dad decided to break out his brand new 1994 Lexus SC for the occasion. Its black exterior was almost fully illuminated by the lamp post it rested under. I honestly was shocked to even be going to a movie as late as it was. My dad was usually too drained from work to want to take me anywhere, especially on a Friday night.

"Did you enjoy the movie?" he asked as he unlocked the car doors.

"It wasn't bad, the only exciting parts was when a fight broke out or when that greasy-haired guy got shot for no reason. The whole movie had too much sitting around and talking," I said, after sitting down and buckling my seatbelt.

"That's the thing, Son. Life isn't all about the action. It's the in-between stages that deserve the proper attention from people. Words have the power to do more than anyone could ever know. A punch to the face doesn't send the message that deserves to be sent."

"Is that why you work in a courtroom, Dad?"

"That's right. I know you're young but everyone needs to know that being in that courtroom, opposite of me is never a good thing. Never do anything stupid, never get arrested. That's one of the reasons I wanted to show you this movie. The world keeps going while men like them rot behind bars. You are going to be part of our new world, and there is no need for you to be locked up in a place without hope. Just listen to me and I'll guide you the right way. Do you understand son?"

"I do."

"What's your favorite soda again?"

"Coke, it's been my favorite since I first had it with mom before she left."

A minor silence filled the air. "Well, just think of it this way. They don't serve Coke in jail. If you want to experience the things you love, don't let them be taken away from you."

I watched as several lamp posts streaked by through the passenger side window. Each was as bright as before. I could do nothing but look up at them in amazement. It was impressive to see the amount of consistency on every street that we drove upon.

"Can I stay up a little later when we get home?" I said.

"What for?" he said.

"Just want to play a game or two. Sam told me he invented a new card game and wanted me to give it a try."

"Sure, but we aren't going home yet,"

"Where are we going?"

"Somewhere with a nice view."

We hooked a right turn into Sargents Wharf Parking lot. The lot was located directly next to Boston Harbor. Next to the Pilot House Park, the parking lot overlooked the dark body of water that stretched out farther than my eyes could reach. After getting out of the car, my father said nothing as he led me down the pathway towards the water. The night was cool, with just the right amount of wind to keep it jacket-worthy. The trees were dancing with the sky as several leaves started to fall in front of us.

We arrived at the harbor walk. I looked down to see several different shades of rock being hit by the current. I was just about to step closer towards the edge when my father pulled me aside.

"Here, let's go on that dock over there. We can get the perfect view if we go out there."

It was an interesting moment. He seemed nervous but intrigued at the same time. The last time I saw him act like this was the time he brought home a fresh set of ties for me. He was proud of professional wear, but it mainly represented what he hoped I would wear in the future.

The beginning of the dock was metal but then later became weak wood. It creaked with every step that we took but still, my dad made us walk on it. A bright light from a post behind guided us. When we arrived at the end, I realized something. The sight was something worth seeing.

I looked over the pier. The water was dark, placid as it appeared. Nothing wrong, nothing capable of disturbing it as it just swayed back and forth. The light from behind shined across the water causing white stripes upon its surface. I held his hand as we looked out upon it. The hard-working hero before my eyes. I felt nothing but peace between the both of us, until it happened.

The world became cold. Water had found its way into my shoes and filled my pockets. Instant stiffness found my fingers as I could not fathom the world around me. My head became submerged under the water until I rose to the surface. The light from the lamp post was all that I could see. Once I turned, the outline of my father was hovering over the edge of the dock.

"C'mon son, swim back. You can do it, adapt to your surroundings. Find a way to swim."

Coldness filled my ears as I could barely make out his words. Everything felt distorted as my body continued to rise and fall within the water. Memories of my mother trying to teach me to swim at the age of five began to arise. Every attempt proved to be a failure. She gave up early each time. I haven't touched a pool of water since then.

I furiously kicked at the darkness below me. My muscles began to cramp the more I swung my arms around to stay afloat. I cried out for help but my father watched on. He wasn't going to jump in to save me. He stood there watching to see if I could achieve what I felt like was his goal. His figure continued to disappear as my head would sink below.

Nothing but the black. Nothing but the cold and blackness filled my body as it continued to fail. At first, it was just a large force sucking me down. Once my resistance began to falter, it changed its form. The bubbles and current around me felt as if a pair of hands were encircling around me. I closed my eyes and heard a loud splash.

For a split second, time had jumped forward. Life had skipped the shaking, the heavy breathing. I found myself in the back seat of his car. The heater was on, but coldness still latched on to my chest. My hands did not shake, nor did my teeth chatter. I continued to breathe.

He was wet too. His jacket was soaked as he continued to drive without looking back. Life must have skipped him talking as well. Did he say anything, did I even care?

I looked at the man who tested my limit. With one push, he managed to shatter the night I started to trust him again. No words found my mouth as I refused to speak. Something was different about me, I could not explain it but nothing felt the same.

The lights shot by the outside window while the world pressed on.

Chapter 51

"The man who is going to *bring* me down. How are you, Mike?"

I sat down in the chair opposite of him. My father was in the chair next to me. He was wearing the nice sweater I got him for Christmas last year. It looked better on him that it would have on me.

I turned to look at Francis. My hand moved across my body to move my jacket back.

"I see that you came prepared," Francis said. "Let's not be stupid and make a mistake. I told you, I'm a little antsy with this thing, haven't shot one off in a while."

"Yes, I remember that." I could feel my right eyebrow start to twitch. His whole presence agitated me, unlike any feeling I've ever had. "What is it that you want?"

"I just want to talk. Family reunions are my favorite and its bout time we had one. Don't you think?"

I turned to my dad. He was looking at Francis now. Maybe he knew who he was.

"Look at him," Francis said. "Still the fighter I remember him being. I couldn't be rude, and lose any sort of manners my mother taught me so, I wore this. Do you recognize it? It's the suit I wore on the day your father failed to lock me up. It's a little tight but I must say it does feel quite memorable. In a justified kind of way."

"Why are you here?"

"Because your daddy's here. I knew you wouldn't turn down an opportunity for us to meet. You might even follow directions for once but seeing as though Thomas isn't here, I guess not. Tell me, where is my boy?"

"He's not here. He doesn't want to go back with you."

"Clearly, but do you think that gives you the power to withhold my boy from me? I simply asked for my boy back so that we can discuss the valuable insight that I might have. But it appears that you are more likely to get him killed in a firefight then bring him to me safely."

"I found him there. He was out looking for who killed his best friend. He's fixed on you, any reason I should believe him?"

"Fixed on me? Damn right you should take his word into consideration, he's a Zaccardi. His instincts are more profound than the hunters in a jungle. His blood is my blood, with that, comes intelligence that the public still doesn't seem to understand. Since you've been with him for a while you could see that. Thomas is smart. Of course, he thinks I did it, his father owes me…wait just a minute."

Francis shifted in his chair revealing the gun his hand, it was an M9 Beretta. It was black, but still looked shiny as the light from the ceiling reflected off of it. "Please place your cellphone on the table. No need to run the risk of having you recording our conversation. Didn't think I'd think of that one did ya?"

"Please, according to you, you're a natural. Here's the thing, I don't have my phone," I said.

"No phone? No need to lie so early in the conversation. Give it up, now."

"I don't have it." Francis lowered his eyebrows. I could see that his patience was starting to wear.

"Where is it then?"

"I gave it to Thomas. He's supposed to call my partner if anything happens to him."

"So, you left my boy alone. You know there's a killer on the loose right? Killing boys my son's age, didn't think that one through did you, Mike?"

"He's safe. This is between you, and me getting you the hell away from my father."

"Easy there, you better lighten up if you want Richard here in well, better health than he is now. Honor isn't earned by provocation. You have to respect it before you can go about setting it off."

"You don't even know what honor is. Tell me what's going on. Why did you try to have me killed at James Middle, worried I was getting too close?"

"Damn, 'bout time you figured that one out. What gave it away?"

"I'd rather not say."

"Really now? Protecting someone I see. It had to be Thomas, wasn't it? They've had Bill's face all over the TV for over a day now. Tommy boy must have recognized his face from Roma's. I nearly forgot about the picture still hanging up until I asked him to take care of you. I told Jack to go take it down but maybe he didn't get to it. Did you know that he's working with someone?"

My dad moved in his chair, as did I after Francis's words. Jack with someone?

"Jack? I haven't seen him since your bakery yesterday."

A quick silence filled the air as Francis quickly jumped on it. "Park Street Church has a service at four I believe. Any chance you and Jack will make it back there?"

Shit.

"I've had my suspicions of my brother for a while now," he said. "My gut told me I was right when he just let you walk into our backroom when you came in with your questions. He wanted me to trip up."

My mouth opened but no words came out. I knew what Francis was thinking, that's why he tried to take me out.

"You've got the wrong play here," I said. "I don't know what you're on about. My man saw Jack leaving a therapy session today. Jack has been nowhere near this."

"Trickery doesn't seem to be your strong suit. Making an ass of yourself with your mouth seems to be your true calling. You can't look me in the eye and tell me that Jack isn't working for you."

"I can and I will. Jack isn't working for me, if he was, I'd have you in cuffs already."

Jack came to my mind. If he could be with someone, who with? Burkes would have told me if we were running him. Informants were confidential on every level of the department. The importance of this case and what it was, Burkes would have shared it with me.

"Look, you need to understand. My family has been doing our thing in North End for years. It's about time one of us cracked because they weren't getting enough attention. If I was Jack, I'd want to find a way out too. It appears after years of cleansing my town of cheats and in few cases, cops, I've learned something. Something, I could not understand when I was on the lower end. Our fate is to pretend. We have to pretend to have the life we want until we actually achieve it. Police officers, teachers, down on their luck gamblers are victims of it. One stack of money can help them stop pretending. I do this town a service every day, without even having to lay a finger on anyone. If someone acts out, then you know what has to happen. Check your police reports, you know what I've done."

"People like you get caught. Check every history book. It doesn't end well for the ones on the opposite side."

"It does if you choose the right side."

My hands began to sweat more as I thought about how quick I could reach for my gun before Francis would fire his. His hand was already wrapped around his, with his finger likely on the trigger. In my head, I could see my name near the top of the firearm scores at the BPD academy. I was near the top but I wasn't that good. It would be a waste.

"You don't understand, do you? I said. "Unless you had anything to do with Sam, I'm not here to arrest you. Someone is out there right now thinking they can kill again. You wouldn't have sent Ralphie and Richard around harassing sex offenders if you weren't looking for who this is as well? Sam was paying you for his father's debt but you wouldn't go through all this trouble to kill me and track down Sam's killer over a sum of money. There's something else, something that's been hidden but has found its way out into the open. Tell me, what are you looking for?"

"What are you talking about?"

"I'll make it clear. I don't think you killed Sam, but I think you are looking for whoever did. Somehow you think Sam had something that belonged to you and finding who killed him might lead you right to it. I... I don't want to say it but maybe we can help each other."

"Help each other?" Francis said, followed by a quick laugh. He almost lifted the gun up from his pillow as he seemed jubilated. "Look at your father now, he might be proud but pretty pissed off if you're turning to me. I would say go to him for help but look at him, he hasn't helped you in years."

I could feel my hands turn to fists. "Stop it. Let's get back to it. What is it that you are looking for? Maybe if I knew I could help you."

"Ha, please. I'm not telling you anything. Why don't you ask Thomas? I'm sure he's told you plenty about what my brothers and I do."

"We spoke with Sebastian Walker. Did you have him kill Sam?"

"Walker? Please, he's definitely the type to take a fall but we haven't called upon him in a long time. Piece of work that one is. At least he's better than Sammy boy's dad. James never pays us back in full. That's why I recruited Thomas and his friends to work for me. My workers weren't producing as much as I'd liked them to. Kids are good workers. They're not smart enough to figure out how bad the consequences can really be."

"I wouldn't count on that. Thomas and his friends are more capable than you realize."

"I've been thinking the same thing. Never thought one of them would be stupid enough to do what Sam did."

"What, keep a share of his money?"

"I knew he was doing that. He stole something important. A classified piece from me. I couldn't give a damn about the amount of money he hid, unless it's a great deal."

"That why you have Sam's parents locked up somewhere?"

"Damn again. You are as sharp as your father. I bet you've been getting pretty suspicious why Sam's own parents haven't been blowing up your phone with questions. Probably because they've been trying to answer my own questions. I was going to take Sam next but, you know what happened with that. I know what you're thinking. Why did I just go off and tell you that? Here's the thing, when this blows over, I'll let them go. They won't say a word because like I said, they're part of the pretenders. Money has the power to ignore morals in a heartbeat."

"They give you the answers you want? I'm willing to bet that was a no, since your brothers are out doing your dirty work."

"Richard, yes, but Ralphie is doing something else for me."

"That is?"

"Have you forgotten what he looks like? He was right downstairs standing next to a beam watching you go into the elevator. Of course, that was before you were immediately stopped in your tracks by the breathtaking auburn-haired beauty in the elevator. Ralphie took a picture before he temporarily escorted her away."

There it was, my hatred had ignored my conscience. Anger had penetrated my heart and decided to take over what little control I already had.

I stood up swiftly, only to be met with the Beretta in my gut. I could hear several of the attendants and patients cry in horror. It could happen within a second, the end of everything. It wasn't fear that had me. It was an anger that made my body feel numb.

"Mike, don't do anything rash. She is quite lovely."

Chapter 52

I could feel the bruise from Warner's wire around my neck like a snake that would not let go until my neck snapped. My muscles tightened as Francis dug the Beretta deeper into my stomach, pressing it against my lower intestine. I looked around to see Tom calming some patients down. A middle-aged blonde woman with scattered hair had fallen back in shock at the sight of the gun. I shook my hands at him to get everyone out.

Within a minute, the room was emptied. The three of us remained silent. My father still sat in his chair, not fazed by his son having a gun pointed at him.

"I didn't want things to go this extreme but hell, where's the fun without more obstacles?" Francis said.

"There are cameras in this place, don't you see that no matter what happens you'll be locked up now," I said.

"Ah, so here's the thing. You see that camera back there?" He motioned with his eyes, while cocking his head back. I stepped to the side to make out a solid black camera with a beeping red light hanging just over the doorway.

"That camera," he said, "is fixed on one angle of the room. It does not move or rotate, which as you can see, my back is to it. It cannot see what is in my hand. The only thing this camera has captured is you standing up and me standing with you."

"You must be out of your mind. No one is going to believe that a faulty camera angle will deny the testimony of everyone in this room."

"Patients with Alzheimer's? Yes, detective, they truly are our society's best luck when identifying wrongdoing in this great city. But, worst case, I can just shoot the camera and find the footage. You'd be long dead anyway if I get to that point."

"You're a man who doesn't like to be told what to do, most of us don't. But whatever you decide to do, just don't hurt her. She was never involved with any of this."

"Warms my heart to hear a man plead like that. Do you know the great thing about self-control? I know who I can hurt and who I want to." He took a

243

step backward but did not look away. If he looked hard enough, which I'm sure he was, he could see my forehead in a strain. He continued to smile.

"Just don't, I'll talk with you," I said.

"I won't, as long as you just sit the hell down so we can finish talking. Shit, it's more difficult talking to you than it is a millennial with a phone in their hands." Both of us slowly sat down. Francis took great care of making sure that his gun would not show up on the camera.

"Where is she?"

"She is safe. She won't be if Ralphie doesn't get a call or a text in the next ten minutes. Now, listen to me carefully or you won't be able to listen to my theory."

"Theory on what?"

"On who killed Sam. I'm sure I'll find what I'm looking for soon enough but you, what you're looking for or, who you're looking for, is much more elusive."

"What do you know about Sam? Thomas told me you never asked about his friends unless if it was about payments."

"It's not what I know about him, it's about what everyone knows."

"What are you talking about?"

"Sam is a teenager and at that age, it's hard to understand the world around them. You and I have seen how the world works. The streets are dangerous, yet forgiving to those who work hard. You think I'm a monster for what I've done but I've been molding them into something more."

"You mean breaking the law?"

"Breaking the bonds of the people who tell them they can't do anything. Teens are easily influenced but they latch on to something more than we do, friendship. Thomas probably didn't mention the pep talks I would give them before they would go out. I would make them sit down for several minutes as I explained to them what they were really doing for me. Learning strength and self-sufficiency were the ideals that I lectured them about until I saw fit that they were ready. Kids their age would never get the opportunity that they have if I did not think they were ready.

"You're hysterical if you think selling drugs is a way to become self-sufficient. No wonder your son doesn't want to live with you anymore." One of Zaccardi's eyes twitched. He looked frustrated but still maintained calm within his words.

"Thomas and I have our own demons to fight. His mother leaving was one of them but you don't know us. Leave your nose out of it or I won't give you what you need. Anything helpful you'd like to add?"

I remained silent. Francis continued to speak after waiting.

244

"It was strange. My first thought was Sam had a deal that didn't go well. But then I realized that a kid isn't killed unless something else is involved. The kind of people they sell to are too weak or scared to do something like that. Depravity can take many forms but nothing is worse than killing someone who hasn't had a chance to understand the world yet."

"No one should get away with that."

"Finally, something for us to agree on. Thomas, Sam, Rich, and Tommy have all been childhood friends. Together they are strong, but separated, they become something different. Thomas took the lead most of the time and made the decision that they all go out at the same time. In doing that, they would have to split profits. It seemed an intelligent decision at the time but greed can take over when no one is looking."

"What are you trying to say?" The clock on the wall ticked off another minute. Francis had four minutes to contact Ralphie.

"Jealousy and greed can only go so far. Sam was the studious one with a brain on his shoulders, but I never spent too much time with the other two, Rich and Tommy. Both seemed bright and eager to make money for me, regardless of the danger that Thomas and Sam stressed to them. Sam and Thomas were smart, strategic in what I had planned for them. Rich and Tommy looked more like followers. As you have seen with Jack, some followers start to…change the way they see things. Followers only like to be followers for so long. Sooner or later, friends become enemies."

My stomach turned over at his words. These kids were too young to contemplate such an act. It can't be what he is saying.

"Rich and Tommy have been with Thomas looking for Sam's killer," I said. "They've been together this whole time, if they were jealous of Thomas and Sam, they would have killed your son already. Sam's body was placed in a position that didn't seem accidental. Someone knew what they were doing, a psychopath or a hired gun. This seems too heinous to be jealousy."

"Maybe, but you're overlooking how old these kids are. They are influenced by what they see, not what they can understand. To them, actions can be quick and easily forgotten."

"Killing is an act that no one forgets."

"Doesn't mean you don't understand what you've done."

Chapter 53

Stay in the car. Don't move.

His words kept going around in my head. Michael was a smart man but my father did something to him that I could not understand. He seemed off-edge, as if some poison had returned into his brain. I sat in the driver seat of his car with his phone in my hand. I forgot to look at the beam with the number on it.

Unknowingly, and without thinking, I managed to park the car in a spot that blocked my view of the beam. He told me to get the code and call Delahine. After resting my hand over the vent producing warm air, I turned the car off and got out. The air was still cool. Not as much wind was getting through but just enough for me to instinctively put my hands in my pockets.

As I walked to the beam, I thought about Sam. His friendship was one of the things that kept me glued to sanity. My father was a mess, and the teachers at James Madison were too focused on test scores to actually indulge in a conversation with me that mattered. Rich and Tommy were good friends but they just didn't ponder the things that I did. Sam was different. He was the one I went to for things that I was too embarrassed to bring up with anyone else.

He was gone now. The tears that I had the night we saw his body were nothing compared to the weight it added inside me. My best friend had been taken from me. In a town where kids break the law every day, he was always there to dig into my brain that we could make it out and make something out of ourselves. Different from what everyone around us believed, we, two boys from North End, could branch out to accomplish whatever we wanted. Sometimes, I saw it as nothing but a dream. But Sam talked as if it was coming faster than we could expect. Time was bringing us closer and all we had to do was be patient. Patience was a virtue that I struggle with a lot, but Sam acted as my teacher when I could feel myself falling back.

If only we had more time.

I arrived on the other side of the beam to see the numbers: 4218. I entered it into Mike's phone to see if it worked. After seeing that it did, I headed back towards the car. I looked out towards the sky above and saw a few hummingbirds flying by. They were peaceful as their wings flapped along the current of the wind. Effortless it seemed as if they were flying along a line. Just as I admired them, I heard the echo of a sound. I turned but saw nothing.

My fingers felt the handle of the car door as I made it back. I unveiled my phone to see that I had yet to receive anything from Rich or Tommy. What could they be doing? Regardless of this weekend, both of them always had their phones.

I punched in Mike's code and proceeded to call Delahine. After a few rings, he picked up.

"Hey, Mike," Delahine said.

"It's Thomas. Something's happened," I said, holding the phone tightly against my ear.

"What's going on, where are you?"

"We're at the hospital. My dad is with, I think Mike's dad. He sped over here and asked me to park the car at the top of the parking garage. He said he was trying to calm the situation so I'm assuming he doesn't need help yet."

"He went in by himself? Do you know what part of the hospital?"

"No, I'm sorry. He just told me to stay in the car and call you. He said his phone was the key to something, do you know what he meant by that?"

"I'm, I'm not sure. Just stay there and I'll come find you. Don't go anywhere. I need you to be safe. Lock the car doors and lay low."

He ended the phone call. A sudden tiredness fell upon me. The feeling was odd, I could see a patch of sunlight shining over the glass but fatigue still had a hold on me. If I slept, I would be vulnerable. The panther could find me again and bring me roaring back to this reality. There was no reason to nod off now, I would just come back. Mike's dad was in danger and we still felt nowhere near close to finding who killed Sam. Yet, I still felt tired.

I could feel my eyelids become heavy. As the light around me soon became dark, I could feel my head fall back against my seat. Everything felt still. Then I heard a tap.

The tap sounded again. I looked up to see the barrel of a gun against the window. It was pointed right at me.

Then I saw who was holding it.

*

Another one. Another lecture from Thomas's dad who never knew how to keep his mouth shut. This man actually thinks that he is creating better men. He gave us the opportunity to sell drugs, not go to college. Profit was his goal, not to label himself as a man with principles. We were not pubescent teens anymore, we knew right from wrong. We knew that selling drugs was wrong but we were also smart enough to know who Francis Zaccardi is.

"Men, that is what you are now," Francis said, and continued on. "For months now I have seen you boys come back with more profit than most of my guys ever could obtain. I'm proud of you. Thomas truly has some trustworthy friends to get the job done. You have proved that age is just a number. Not many kids your age could accomplish what you have so far. The best part is there is still much more to be done. Don't you think Thomas?"

"Yeah, whatever you say, Dad," Thomas said. It was easy to tell that he never cared for what his dad has been doing for us. Just the other year Thomas had discovered what kind of a man his father really was. It was eye-opening, but a learning point. His father had more money stashed away than he ever thought a corner bakery could accomplish.

"Don't forget what I'm doing for you and your friend's son. You're learning how to make money and become more independent. The world doesn't give you what you want, you have to go out and grab it yourself. I'm just giving you a little nudge out of the door."

"Filling the streets with more drugs does sound lovely, shame I haven't been a better son." A common outburst that he never seems to lock away.

Mr. Zaccardi gave Thomas a glare and proceeded to talk with the rest of us. At first, it felt like we were bonded in another way. It wasn't until I started to figure out what was really going on.

The four of us were inseparable but rather separable. The past few months proved to be the defining line. Thomas and Sam were together more than all of us were together. They felt like the leaders. Their arrogant attitudes towards decisions made things worse. From time to time it would show. This feeling of, anger or deception had never come over me the entirety of our friendship. It's as if our childhood was modified, with Thomas and Sam writing their own new entries.

Everything became worse when I found out what Sam was doing. One night, after we left an alleyway near the Coastguard Base, we all decided to split up and go home. Almost halfway home, I felt in my pockets to find that my keys were missing. I decided to turn back and returned to the alleyway. When I arrived, Sam was there. He was with Twinks. Both of them were discussing something and then Sam revealed a plastic bag with Twinks's sticker on it. It was then that I put it together that Sam was selling more on the side to ensure that he would make more money than the rest of us. On the walk back, I ran it over in my mind. A little extra money didn't hurt anything but something just didn't feel right. He was going behind our backs. He and

Thomas might be in on it together. The anger spread within me that I broke my own window that night just to get inside my room.

I let it go for a week and decided not to say anything. Days pressed on and we continued to enjoy our time together. Certain times throughout the day, I was able to block all of my thoughts in order to have a good time. It would become worse when I was alone. Even at home, with my family around, I could not shake what I was feeling. Walking back from school one day, I overheard Thomas and Sam talking about something.

"I can't wait to get out of here," Sam had said. "We can do more than North End. I know I don't talk too much about it but once we graduate high school, I think it would be a good idea for me to get out town."

"Really?" Thomas said.

"Yeah, you know my parents. They will never leave this place. I can't be stuck in a hole that will only get deeper the more I stay."

"Your parents wouldn't even bat an eye if you left."

"Exactly, sooner or later I need to leave. You should come with me? We can go wherever we want."

"I'm not sure. North End has been my home. Where else would a kid like me go? I'd honestly have to think about it."

Each word infuriated me. Thomas was feeding into Sam's idea of leaving us behind without any inclusion. Thomas didn't even stand up for us. They both were plotting to live a life that did not include the four of us. I had to speak with Sam. This could not go on anymore.

On Wednesday, after convincing Sam, we decided to ditch school on Friday. Typically the skeptical one when it came to delinquent acts, Sam took some convincing but he finally gave in. The afternoon was enjoyable. Playing a pickup game with some boys from Southie turned out to be a nice representation of how strong we were as a unit. A rift occurred when Thomas and one of the boys almost started an all-out brawl. Afterward, we decided to have lunch at our favorite sandwich shop.

The afternoon ended with the usual turn of events. Thomas and Sam went off together while I was left with my feeling, the one that continued to grow. The agitation still remained inside me for some reason. It was a bite mark that wouldn't stop itching. I couldn't take it anymore, I had to do something.

It was just around when school would be letting out when I called him. He answered the phone pleasantly. I asked him to come to the baseball field to help me out with something. After agreeing, I waited for him near a bench that overlooked the field. It was raining pretty heavily at this point so I decided not to sit down. When the rain fell, it was as if the outside world had shut down. The field was a place where a lot of us would pass the time, ignoring our homework. This was a great place to get Sam to talk. I fabricated some story to him about how one of the guys we played ball with, out here, had left his glove on the mound. Sonny Sisto, his name sounded like the main character of a children's television show. His glove was always cleaned and ready. Sam believed me when I told him that he left it near the mound and forgot about it after Mr. Walker had closed the field with his expensive cover.

After twenty minutes, Sam arrived. He was getting soaked in his fleece jacket while smiling as he saw me across the street. He can't even understand what I'm going through. What he was doing to us all. Up until I would tell him how I was feeling, he was the successful one screwing everything up.

"Sonny left his glove? Sounds like we hit the jackpot," he said as we made our way onto the field. We headed towards the clubhouse, only to find that it was locked. I wasn't sure why I was hesitating to tell him how I felt. The words just weren't there. Just as I was about to patch some together, Sam brought about a suggestion to go underneath the cover and look for the glove.

We were able to lift the cover with ease. We had to crouch to get around as the weight of the cover was too heavy to fully stand. Sam went first as I followed behind him. I finally had him alone and the words continued to escape me. We took a few more steps forward when I managed to find a few.

"Can you believe we almost got into another fight today? I knew Southie was bad, but who knew they wanted to leave such a wonderful place," I said.

"Yeah, glad we avoided that one. Not that my parents would notice, but I'd rather not get another black eye," Sam said as he took a few more crouching steps.

"Funny thing is, I never get tired of the almost fights or the ones that turn ugly. We're all together for each one. It's a team effort, ya know?"

"We can't always be doing the same thing forever. Fights become more frowned upon the older we get."

"What do you mean?"

"We have to figure out what we want to do after all of this. Enjoying this time now is important but we can't forget about what's ahead. We have to desire something more."

"You mean, moving away from here?"

"Probably, I see more opportunities out of this town than in it. I don't think I have the strength to put myself through this place anymore."

Like a curtain fading to black, my mind went numb. It wasn't anger, but solace. The cover felt like a blanket around me, its material rough, but welcoming. Sam's words penetrated me with an epitome of acceptance, as in he really meant what he was saying. I truly hated what he said. His plan, his vision for what would become of us did nothing but fuel it. The fear that one day we would all be separated, with him taking Thomas away, tearing us up for him to live out his dream of success outside of our home. The thoughts swayed in my head like a pendulum of repetitiveness. Just as I was about to scream, my eyes became clear, the darkness had gone.

Sam was at my feet. His eyes were open but he did not move. My hands trembled as I put into focus what happened. The fear had dissipated as I saw Sam lifeless at my feet. At first, I felt as if I would panic, yet my hands fell to my side. Still, the shaking had stopped.

I grabbed Sam's ankles and dragged him onto the mound. I extended his arms and legs to make it look like it was by design. The strange idea of manipulating his body came to me quickly, without a second thought to combat it. Just as I was about to extend his right knee when a thought popped into my head: his phone. I was the last person to call him. It would arouse questions if the phone were to be found. I reached into his pocket and found it. After quickly placing it into my own, I took a few steps back. The thought occurred to me that maybe someone saw us go in.

After lifting the cover off my head, I felt the clear air return to my lungs. The rain was still beating down. There appeared to be no one around, as the rain painted the worst picture for taking an early afternoon stroll. Something smooth filled the air as the rain seemed to mask anything that had happened. Relief struck me as I walked home.

The walk wasn't rushed or slowed. It was general. I made it back to my house in the typical fifteen minutes. I patted my pocket for Sam's phone and entered in the house. I waved at my mom as she was sitting on the couch with her knees brought up to her chest. She gave me a smile, just like usual. Everything seemed the same to her, nothing out of sort.

"Hey, honey, how hanging with your friends was?" she said over the television.

"Fun, just like always. We all get along just fine, you know that."

"You boys are my favorite boys, you know?"

"Yeah, Mom, I know." I waved her goodbye as I went to the bathroom.

The hot water felt refreshing on my face. A few splashes did the trick before using the towel next to me. I looked into the eyes looking back at me. In my head, I knew what I did. Yet, the feeling of loss or fear seemed absent. It was…welcomed.

I could feel my stomach tearing back at me. A snack sounded good I said to myself as I took off my brother's jacket and left it on the bathroom floor.

Chapter 54

"I've got to get to Thomas."

"Wait just a moment, you need to hear the rest of what I have to say. Do you understand?"

I sat there, unnerved. Thomas was by himself, vulnerable to the knowledge that he did not have. He could be talking to one of them right now. His father was going to get him killed.

"So, what happens now?" I said.

"This has to end of course. Your father here spent most of his career bringing me down, if we can help each other, you'll value my insight," Zaccardi said.

"Insight into what?"

"Let's just say, there are a few fall guys looking to have some shiny brass across their wrists."

I looked directly into Zaccardi's eyes. He didn't blink after pronouncing every word. He was firm in what he was proposing. But why?

"You're willing to give some of your guys up, for what exactly?"

"A chance for you to make a pretty big arrest, with your name all over it. The best part, you won't have to worry about me getting involved. I've already lined up who the head guy is."

"Let me guess, you walk away as if nothing happened. Some lucky guy, who you have fabricated some form of evidence against, will be your Corleone?"

"Bingo."

"What makes you think I won't come after you after all of this is over. Sam's murderer might be discovered he might not, but that doesn't make you an innocent man if it isn't you. You're right, I have read your police reports. I know about the man you proposedly beat to death while making his son, a boy close to Thomas's age watch. You used a crowbar to rid the earth of that boy's role model. What makes you think an act like that can be put aside because you give me a handful of guys who are a fraction of you? You can't think I'm that young to take a deal like that."

Zaccardi closed his mouth for several moments. He tinkered with the Beretta in his hands, moving it back and forth. He lifted his phone from his pocket and formed a grin.

"Well, look at this. One minute until Ralphie has his way with your pretty little girl. Says her name is Jess. Damn, what a sexy name for a girl like that. Now, listen, Thomas needs you and Jess does as well. If you don't agree to this and back off of me, you'll be risking two other lives. Can you live with that?"

"You won't hurt anyone here. I know where Thomas is and if you don't let me go, he will be in danger. You're a bad father, but you're not that inconsiderate."

Zaccardi let out a laugh. It haunted my ears as he went on. After he was done, he lifted the gun higher and stopped laughing as if a switch was pressed. "Listen to me very carefully, if I don't send this to Ralphie, he will do exactly what I instructed him to do. Want to hear? Of course, you don't, but that's the point. He's going to take her away, either in his car or even in one of the closets on the bottom floor. He has a rag in his right pocket that he's going to use to tie around her mouth. A slap or two might be necessary but depends on how resistant she is. Once he's got her in a good spot, he's going to pull her pants down to her…"

"Just stop! You don't know when to stop, do you? Your son is in danger and all you want is to make sure your name is unscathed. You are the scum you employ. I'll take your deal, just send the damn message."

"That a boy," he said as he pulled his phone back out. He sent the message and placed the phone back into his pocket. "Don't worry, I'll send you the names in due time. Along with where to find the, what's the word you use, oh, incriminating evidence against them. I like that word, it's sophisticated. Damn, maybe I should have been a cop."

As he proceeded to stand up, he started to place the Beretta behind his waist when I saw the opportunity. I leaped towards him, straddling his hand. As I forced it into his side, Zaccardi let out a loud curse. His strength far outmatched mine as I quickly began to think of what was going to happen next. I decided to go against a vital rule when wrestling someone. Never take them to the ground.

I released my left hand from his and swiped my feet against both of his. While pushing his back with my free hand, we both fell to the floor hard. Somehow, after the impact, I found my hand gripping the handle of the Beretta and flung it across the floor. After bringing my hand back for a strike, Zaccardi was already halfway standing up. The tip of his right knuckle struck my temple with great force.

I felt my skull jolt back to the ground as Zaccardi stood hovering over me. The room around me appeared to be in fragments as I felt my collar being yanked up. I resisted by trying to hit his hands to find some sort of release, but nothing came. Instead, he struck my face again. It was different, he did not hesitate. Something different fueled him this time. I hoped that every strike would be his last, but he continued on while speaking words I could not match together.

Acceptance had taken me now. The strikes felt like a further numbness that would never go away. I didn't know why, but I started to smile. Then, the strikes stopped.

"What the hell are you smiling about?" he said, while I could hear him gasping for air. "You think this is funny? I hope you know there isn't a deal anymore, I'm going to kill you now."

"You don't get it, do you? This is all you are ever going to be. A father who couldn't love his own son and the man who will never have respect. Every swing of your heavy fist means more of what makes you who you are. A waste of air."

Zaccardi began to raise his fist back again when a quick shadow passed above him. He dropped to the floor with his hand holding the back of his head. I blinked a few times to recover from the dimness my eyes could not shake. A figure began to form in front of me.

It was Tom. He was holding the serving tray that my father's favorite steak would come on. He was breathing heavily as he stood over Zaccardi. Just as Zaccadi looked as if he was about to lift his body, Tom reared back for another strike.

"Wait," I said. Using my father's chair, I lifted myself up while trying not to give in to the heavyweight my head was bringing about. When I got to my feet, I saw two of the most frightened eyes I had ever seen.

My father was sitting there, mortified. I'm not sure if he knew what was going on but he must have been frightened by all of the movements. I found myself placing my hand across his cheek, bringing our foreheads together.

"I forgive you," I said, aloud. His face remained frightened but he had to know. The push, every push he gave me was forgiven. He was the father that everyone should have, but maybe not the one everyone wanted. He was the great man I always knew he could be.

I stepped back and noticed that Zaccardi was still on the ground, wincing in pain. After looking around, I found his Beretta next to a table leg. I walked over to pick it up and returned within a few steps of him on the ground. I lifted it and then felt the kick.

Zaccardi was now screaming. He held his right leg as if it was being ripped from its tendons. I stepped closer and pointed it right at his forehead. My finger was sweaty as I could feel it slipping across the trigger. Zaccardi quickly remained stiff and looked up at me. Just as I thought about it, and what he would look like with his blood on the carpet, I took a deep breath. Everything could end here, the opportunity to rid him from Boston was just a click away. The moment had replayed in my mind several times this weekend, but something was different now that I saw him wincing in front of me. He didn't deserve a swift send-off. He needed to understand what it felt like to live a life as he did. My father would have wanted to see him rot behind metal bars contemplating all the mistakes that he made. It became clear.

The butt of the gun connected right above his ear, sinking him to the floor. The screaming had stopped and his wound started to bleed across the carpet.

"Thank you, Tom," I said as I handed him the gun. "Tie him up and clean that wound. He can't die on me yet."

Chapter 55

Tom looked frightened but reliable when I left him. A few security guards had followed in right after. Hopefully, he would be feeling more comfortable with them around.

Jess was my focus now. Hopefully, Delahine was already up in the garage keeping Thomas company. Everything was probably still fine, one of his friends couldn't possibly know where we were. Both of his friends circled around in my mind as I started to speed down the stairs. Could one of his friends really be out to kill him? If so, then which one?

Just as I made it past a few nurses carrying fresh needles upon a silver tray, the door to the lobby felt like air as I shoved it open. The room was full of people. Several receptionists were gathered at their desks helping patients at each of their individual windows. A man and his wife were sitting together at the end of a row chairs looking at me after hearing the door slam open. My eyes caught nothing unusual. They were not here.

A few more people walked by when two figures emerged from one of the back hallways. He was dressed in a black, leather jacket with his hand tightly gripped around Jess's arm. Her auburn hair was down, but not enough to cover the obvious restraint before me. Ralphie was hurrying them to the exit. He kept swiping his head back and forth scanning the room. I stayed behind them as my pace began to quicken. They were about to pass the reception desk towards the exit.

Once I was within a few feet of them, the thought hit me. Just like Francis, Ralphie weighed well over my 190-pound build. If my head found its way in between his arms, he could snap my neck like a toothpick. One strike to the back of his head had to discombobulate him, it was my only chance. One of the receptionists wearing a rather large pair of glasses noticed my quick pace. I could see the back of Ralphie's head look in her direction. It was all he needed.

In what felt like a millisecond, Ralphie had turned around, pushed Jess away from him and leaped for me. His hands went up first as I instinctively managed to bring my fist up, catching the underside of his chin. It didn't faze him as I could feel both of his hands clamp down on my shoulders. Everything looked out of sorts as he managed to toss me towards the waiting area. I could hear some of the nurses' gasp just as my body went flying over a table filled with magazines. Several people started to move away as Ralphie came right towards me once again. I could see Jess just past his leg looking horrified leaning against a pillar.

Just as I managed to get on my feet, Ralphie was already on me. He jammed his knee into my pelvic bone, followed by his forehead connecting with the top of my own. Now I felt discombobulated as I tried to jam my hands upon his deltoids holding him back. I felt like a tractor trying to hold back a mountain of gravel falling upon it as Ralphie was clearly using his size to his advantage. Just as my arms and legs were about to give, he grabbed me by the shirt and thrust me towards the pillar next to us. I prepared for another blow when Ralphie was being tackled to the ground by a quick figure. The figure's presence caught me off guard until I saw who it was. Both Delahine and Ralphie managed to quickly stand up, each of them taking a step back from the other. Ralphie looked at both of us and produced a grin similar to the one Francis had given me upstairs.

"Two against one. You cops always like to make things unbalanced," Ralphie said in between his heavy breathing. "Not that it will matter anyway. You two are skinnier than most of the guys I deal with. No guns now, want to keep things fair."

I could see that Delahine was already thinking about it as his right hand started to move towards his belt.

"Too many people," I said to him as I looked around the room. Everyone still had the same panicked look on their face. There were no guards around, most likely due to the fact that Francis had a hole in his leg upstairs.

Delahine gave me a nod and directed his attention back to Ralphie. With both of our fists raised high, we went in. Ralphie swatted my fist away and swung his elbow towards my face. Before it was able to meet my cheek, Delahine used both of his hands to shove Ralphie against his sternum. Stumbling a few steps backward, Delahine and I took our chance to grab both of his arms to pin them around his back. His arms held true to their size as I could barely hold the one I had back. I managed to deliver a jab to one of his ribs but quickly regretted it as he managed to grab my neck when one of my hands left his forearm. The bruise from Warren's grip before felt reactivated as Ralphie's grip instinctively caused me to release his arm to try and peel back his fingers. My eyes wandered to Delahine who noticed that I failed to hold Ralphie's arm back. Delahine took one look at my neck and then at Ralphie's. Just like a page from our arrest techniques course at the academy, Delahine dug the tip of his thumb into Ralphie's hypoglossal nerve right underneath his chin. Ralphie's face immediately turned a different shade of red as I could feel the grip around my neck loosen.

Ralphie let go of me and then started to drive his now free fist into Delahine's gut several times. Just as Delahine let out several shouts of pain, I grabbed Ralphie by the collar and pulled him towards me over the couch. We both fell over together as I could feel my head hit the floor, thankfully, without Ralphie's body on top of it. I rolled across the rug where my back felt up against the adjacent couch. Ralphie's back was to me now. He was starting to get up when I saw Delahine leap across the couch. Delahine had managed to lift both of his legs into the air and struck the heels of his feet against Ralphie's chest sending him back down to the ground right into my lap. Without hesitation, I placed both of my arms around his neck placing him into the tightest chokehold I could muster.

My grip remained steady for a few moments as Ralphie aggressively tried to break free. His elbow caught my rib twice before I could hear the door to the stairs being swung open. A security guard wearing a white buttoned-up shirt walked through the opening. He scanned the room immediately and lifted his Taser at eye-level once he saw us in the waiting area. Just as he took a few steps closer, Delahine looked at him just after he sunk a hook across Ralphie's left cheek and shouted, "On the ground being held down. Shoot him, now!"

The quicker the security guard stepped closer, the younger he looked. The twenty-something guard almost froze when he saw that my grip was weakening. Just as Ralphie used the back of his head to hit my forehead again, the guard shot his Taser releasing two wires into the air. The prongs struck Ralphie in the chest as he let out a loud yell as his gyrating body fell back to the floor.

After the programmed five-second shock time ended, the guard's eyes started to widen as Ralphie was in the process of standing back up. To the disillusion of both of us, I could not believe what I was seeing either. Before Ralphie got the chance to get up, Delahine came right up to him and struck him in the face with his heel yet again, only this time his assailant did not get back up.

Nothing but heavy breathing filled the air for a few seconds after Ralphie was rendered unconscious. With everything that had just transpired, I thought of Thomas. Delahine was not with him, he was alone.

"Leo," I managed to say as I held my forehead up with the center of my wrist. "Go to Thomas. I can clear this up. Go make sure that he is okay."

"What if he gets back up?" he said.

"Then our new friend here will jolt him into submission again." The young guard looked at me and tried to crack a smile, but he was still standing in disbelief. Delahine even revealed his badge to ease his calm.

"Okay, we'll stay up there until you are done," Delahine said. He took a few more deep breaths and then started to walk towards the exit.

"Don't forget to tell them how brave I was."

He held his own and I could not have done that without him, that was for sure. I lifted my handcuffs from my back pocket and threw them towards the young guard. "Cuff him before he gets back up. I don't think you want to help me if he does." He caught the cuffs with one hand and slowly started to place them upon Ralphie's behemoth wrists.

Instead of remaining with the guard to make sure he was alright, I broke away. He wasn't the one I was worried about. I found her against the pillar, she was still curled up in the same position. She looked up at me as if there was only one person she was expecting. Behind the bruises, and the aching across my temple, I could not help but crack a smile. She was beautiful. It didn't matter what she was going to say or where we would be tonight, I didn't want to let her go again.

Jess managed to stand up, her left hand was shaking. I took it in mine and rubbed it gently until the shaking stopped.

"Hi," I said. My voice sounded as if a squeaker box had found its way into my lungs. Ralphie must have smooshed them when he fell on top of me.

"Mike, I'm so sorry. That was, that was horrible. Who was that?"

"Someone you won't ever have to see again."

"Is Richard okay? Does this have to do with him?"

"My father is fine, and don't worry about him. It's you who needs to be okay. I shouldn't have let you go so easily back then. When I saw you the other day, it was like those ten years had been erased. I'm sorry. You should never have been here, you deserve to be safe."

"I am now, right?"

"More than you know."

Just as I could feel her warmth wrapped in between my arms, several officers came barreling in through the front door. Each of them with adrenaline pumping through their eyes expecting the world to come crashing down upon them. Officer Gonzalez was one of them. He scanned the area and noticed Ralphie on the ground. The young guard was still standing over him waiting for any sign of movement. Gonzalez gave me a nod and went over to the unconscious Zaccardi brother. Jess and I watched them for a few minutes. The threat was gone, she had to know that now.

259

Her embrace felt like the medicine I needed. Just as I was about to open my mouth to say something else, she beat me to it.

"What's that?"

"What?"

"Your pocket just buzzed me." I managed to smile at her again until I picked up the phone and saw the message across the screen.

This couldn't be possible.

Chapter 56

I looked down the barrel of the gun again and blinked to see if this was real. After temporarily seeing nothing but the dark for a split second, he was still there. The gun moved back and forth as he motioned me out of the car. The door handle felt cold as I pulled it open. I placed Mike's phone in my pocket and slipped out of the car. I took a few steps away from the car and then just stared into his eyes. It…it didn't make any sense.

"Rich?"

"Keep your hands down," he said. "Don't do anything stupid."

"What are you doing?"

"Finishing what you and Sam were trying to do."

My fingers stopped trembling and balled into fists. I thought of my best friend being taken from me and the hatred that flowed through my body. I could see Sam's face, lifeless and alone in the field. Then, I could see what I couldn't before. The figure that was walking away from his body, the one who knew what everyone did not. He had a face now.

"You? You took Sam from us?"

"Don't act too shocked. He had it coming with everything that you two were planning."

"Rich, what are you talking about? We haven't been planning anything."

"Sam wanted to get away. Get away from us and this town. He didn't realize that this town is who we are and everything we've been through. You can't throw away that, we're friends. Friends don't plan to leave, but that's why he asked you to go with him. Tommy and I are the outsiders, the ones who will be left to rot with no hope of success. Did you really think that you and Sam could go away without telling us?"

"It was an idea, something to think about later. You haven't had to deal with the life that Sam has. His parents are never there, he practically lived by himself. You know what he's had to do, why? Why take the best of us away?"

"The best of us? All of us are the same. We grow stronger with each other, why can't anyone see that?"

"He knew that this place is a hole, one that can't be climbed without someone to push you. He was my push, but we weren't going anywhere yet. We're too young to go anywhere, what could we possibly do?" My fists became sweaty as anger and fear felt like they were being jammed together immeasurably with every word he spoke. Just as I took a step forward, Rich held his gun a little higher, directly at my face.

"Sam went behind our backs and made more money than all of us. Twinks really did buy more, I saw them together."

"Is this why you killed him, because he was making more money than us and trying to get away? I know we're young and stupid, but dammit Rich. How could you be so sick?"

Rich lowered the gun a little back towards my chest. I've seen that gun before.

"Where is Tommy?"

"Now you care about us? It's not your problem to care. None of this will be anymore."

"Tommy, where is he? Have you done something to him too?"

"Him too? What do you think I am, the friend who became jealous and killed all of his friends? Sam was our disease. He represented what was weak about us and saw us as beneath him. You were his best friend who would have served as his servant, nothing more."

"I'm sorry, Rich. You've got it all wrong. Sam would talk about all of us all the time. We were his family, the one that he could depend on. Not his real parents who left him. Just admit it. You lost it when you killed him, and could not handle the truth that he was the one who looked out for us. We needed him and you took him from us."

"Stop, I can't hear this anymore. You don't know what's about to happen, do you?"

"You're going to kill me?"

"Back up to the edge."

"What?"

"Now. Back up to the edge."

Rich took a few steps closer to me. His eyes never wandered away with each step. I knew him well, but this was not the friend I remembered. Something had broken off, nothing that I've seen before from him. When he was about four steps from me, I started to slowly step backward. I wasn't sure how far away I was from the edge but after what felt like over thirty steps, I could feel the cement hit my back.

My hands were instinctively held up just below my shoulders. I didn't know what to do with them, it just occurred to me that having them up was better than having them in my pockets.

"You got me. I'm against the edge, you going to shoot me and toss me off?"

"Of course not, you're going to jump."

Obscurity, for some reason the word popped into my head. I heard Mrs. Kurtz use it the other day and for some reason, I pondered what it meant. It was a strange thought but Rich changed something.

"Couldn't handle it," I said.

"What was that? He said, his voice sounding irritable.

"I couldn't handle it, right? If I jump from here, it's going to look like Sam's death was too much. The pain is too much, Rich. Nothing compares to see you standing there. You, of all people."

"If only you were smart enough to figure out what Sam was doing to us."

"He was trying to get away from his life. Not from us, why can't you see that?"

"It's not my fault if I can't get you to understand. Turn around, and face the ledge. Don't make me ask twice again."

I felt what seemed like a bee had stung my collarbone as this couldn't be happening. Maybe that's what it would feel like. It would be a sharp pain that lacked the ability to linger. Once it happened, nothing could continue. My father once told me that the weak only killed in the quickest form to eliminate the lingering of pain. Maybe I would die knowing that Rich was weak, but then I could see Sam in front of me. He was sitting on top of the ledge, feet hanging over the side. He turned to look at me. He smiled back at me as I stepped up to look out to see the town. The sun was being hidden by the clouds, but the day still remained. I could hear Sam's voice. "Like a bee sting, quick and painless. You said it yourself, maybe two seconds of pain. It's not so bad, at least we can finally get away. I did, now you can too."

Sam's voice echoed in my head. I took a deep breath and didn't feel it anymore. Maybe after I would see him, waiting somewhere. My father never stressed studying the beyond. He thought we'd all end up in the same place. If he were right, Sam would not be far. Anything was better than living in this life where he wasn't.

"Ready?" I could hear Rich say. He had taken a few steps forward. I could feel his presence as if my shadow had become his. I decided to stay silent. Words meant nothing now. I placed my hands on the cold cement and proceeded to lift myself up.

"Thomas! Stop!"

Rich and I turned to see Delahine standing there. His gun was drawn and his face had confusion painted all over it, as if an artist brushed it with a multitude of strokes. I looked at Rich. He had temporarily frozen. Then he spoke.

"Stay back, this isn't about you. I don't know who you are but you need to leave. Leave now."

"Afraid I can't do that," Delahine said. "So, you're the one we've been looking for. You're just a kid."

"Don't call me that. Does it look like I'm a kid anymore?"

"Clearly, you're not yourself. Rich, right? I saw a picture of you guys yesterday. You were there the night of the shooting, right?"

"If Tommy hadn't screwed things up then there wouldn't have been one."

"I heard. Not to be too oblivious, but what are we doing here?"

"What does it look like? Thomas and Sam were trying to undermine the group. Unity was all that we had in North End. You know what this place is like. The Zaccardis rule it and ultimately end up like their parents. As a group, we could have broken the trend, but Thomas and his *best* friend shit on that. Tommy and I are the only ones left."

"What would Tommy say if he knew what you did?"

"He won't. Thomas here is going to jump, making it look like he couldn't take it. You're a cop, cops don't kill kids."

"Not often. Your wrists, I'm afraid, can fit in my cuffs. Looks like you have a decision to make."

"It looks like you have a decision to make," Rich reinstated as he took a step closer and dug the barrel of Tommy's gun into my back. The barrel shifted to the right as it moved past my spine. Rich added, "I know what I'm going to do. You're the one who is unsure."

I turned to look at Delahine. He seemed perplexed. Rich had caught him with his words. There were only two ways Rich was leaving here, shot or in handcuffs around his wrists. I could see that Delahine wanted the latter, but the way he held his gun said otherwise. I wanted to say something but the words did not come from me.

"Delahine, we have to think about this," said another voice. I thought I heard footsteps a few moments ago but the gun digging into my back was quite distracting.

Mike appeared behind one of the columns. He must have taken the stairs that were located at the corner of the parking garage. His face was masked with fresh bruises across his left cheek. A line of dried blood rested just below his eye. He was breathing heavily by the time he made his way over behind Delahine. When he saw me, he nodded and for a moment, I felt at ease.

"Rich is it?"

"Am I going to have to introduce myself again? Don't you idiots talk to each other?"

"Fair. This doesn't seem like you. Thomas told me you were the reasonable one of the group. Yes, your friend there with the gun pointed at his back. When it came to the decision-making, you were always the one who seemed trustworthy. I don't know how you are seeing this but we can help."

"Reasonable? Not the word I would have chosen of late. Thomas here wouldn't make a decision unless his precious Sam gave him the nod. What I am doing here, this is helping. Sam was the naïve one who couldn't see something coming. Thomas is too much like his dad. He would have seen something like this coming. I had to start with Sam first."

"I'm sorry that you feel that way," Mike looked around for a second and then asked the question that never popped into my mind, "Rich, how did you know Thomas was going to be up here?" I chose not to turn my head, but the question quickly grabbed my attention.

"Chance. I was walking around and saw your car speeding by. It wasn't hard to miss both of you as your lights were blaring down the road. I just left Tommy's, he didn't realize that I had taken his gun. I'm shocked you didn't see me."

"That's because we weren't looking for you."

"Sounds to me like you were too slow. Look where we are now."

"Not that you will believe it, but I want to be honest with you," Mike said as he lifted his hands up towards his mid-section. I could see his gun attached to his belt. "This is going to go the way it will. Whatever happens, we cannot let you leave freely. You know that, right? The scenario you have built in your head, it's not going to go the way you think. Not that you should be shocked, but I just have one more question before you chose to do whatever it is you are going to do. Tell me how you killed Sam. I'm just curious about how you killed one of your best friends without him being able to fight back."

Silence had filled the air. Nothing but the sound of a few birds. I could see them in the corner of my eye but I was more curious about the question that still hung in the air.

"It wasn't planned. If you want the truth, it was not what I wanted to do first at all," Rich said. "I wanted to talk to him. Several nights ago I saw him and Twinks making a deal behind our backs. Sam was making money on the side, and didn't tell any of us. That was after the bond that started to form between him and Thomas. For weeks they acted like the two friends who would survive, leaving the others to crumble. At first, I thought it was harmless. Then Sam mentioned to Thomas about leaving this place, just the two of them. I, I couldn't understand what made them forget about us. It was like a movie. Something that was only found in a theater, not on the streets you grew up on. So, in order to figure out what was going on, I decided to talk to Sam. It was raining and I came up with some lie about how a kid we knew had forgotten his glove at the field."

"Sisto?" I said aloud without even knowing it.

"Yes. Sam believed it. Like I said, he was naïve. He couldn't predict something bad happening to him if someone were to walk up to him with a Yankees cap on. I just wanted to talk to him but the words never came. I had him by myself and all I had to do was ask him what he was doing. He gave me the moment, but I couldn't find it. I told him that the glove was on the pitcher's mound. The rain was coming down hard as we went under the cover. He started to talk about leaving and that's…that's when it went black."

"When you killed your friend," Delahine interrupted. His gun was still raised high and he did not lighten his grip.

Rich looked at him. "That was when I broke his neck. He let me do it. He wasn't as strong as Thomas thought. I may have blacked out through most of it but I could feel the life go away. He fell to the ground and that was it. I didn't cry or sink to my knees. He found himself there because of what he was doing to us. It's not like the movies where one character is always innocent. Everyone has something they regret. I fixed his."

"You're a monster in a kid's body," Delahine said. "He had a future and you ruined what he could achieve." He started to take a few steps when Mike said something.

"Leo, stop. You're being baited by a kid. He wants you to do something stupid. How do you think this will look? If we kill a kid, how would this case look? You're the one holding the other gun, not me. You have the decision to do something, or nothing."

I turned to look out across the wall. The cold of the cement had become numb to my fingers. My fingers were pressing against it hard enough to wear my fingertips were white. Sam wasn't there. I looked across the edge of the wall and could not see him anywhere. He wouldn't want this.

"Take your shot. What do you have to prove?" Rich said. "Try having your world separated by your best friends. Something had to be done. Sam was the disease that needed to go away. Thomas would have eventually figured it out, that's why he is going to jump. Killing Sam, was just…"

It happened in a blink. The world didn't fall into black, but a bright white. A loud sound cracked above us as it echoed for a moment but then fleeted. I used all the strength that I had and thrust him as far as I could. I screamed as I did it. The pain and the strength that came were almost too much. My chest had risen and sunken quicker than ever before. They saw it but I did not. I didn't even want to look. Their footsteps approached me as my back leaned against the wall. Its coldness was absent. My eyes looked forward and not behind me as I could not think of anything else.

Everybody loses someone.

Chapter 57

The Light

Everyone around tried not to look at him. His body dared not to move.

Only a select few looked at his body that day, those who had to. I took one look as I helped Thomas back into Delahine's cruiser. I gave Jeff a quick nod and lingered a few seconds as his team was covering up the body.

We gave Thomas a few days until he had to come to the department. He stayed at his friend Tommy's house in the meantime. I trusted him when he said he felt comfortable there.

Wednesday came quickly as both of us were sitting in two uncomfortable chairs. The Internal Affairs Office was what everyone thought it was: uncomfortable. Lies and deceit stood no chance in this room. For some reason, its psychology delivered on the ability to root out corruption in a place built on enforcement. I told Thomas I'd only been to this part of the building once. It was nothing major, just a rookie cop who forgot to tag some counterfeit bills in connection to one of my cases. The story didn't materialize as much to Thomas as I would have hoped.

A low, three-pronged ceiling fan hung above us. The walls were painted an off ivory. Many years ago, it looked to be. There were small windows on two of the walls, with the blinds half dimmed. We were facing one of the windows and noticed two uniforms chatting over a manila folder between them. One of them was Dalton, an officer that I remember being in the academy with. He seemed to be the one running the conversation. A door opened to our left and two men walked in.

Internal Affairs Investigators Brian Richardson and Kevin Conaway sat in front of us. Conaway had closed both of the blinds while Richardson started to open his briefcase. It took them a few moments to disperse their paperwork across the table. I recognized the BPD insignia across one of their binders as it was identical to the one, I was handed a year ago. Instead of accumulating dust, Conaway was putting his to use. They introduced themselves to Thomas and started to ask him several procedural questions. Thomas was stiff in his answers. He divulged very little as they pressed on. I could tell he wanted no part in this.

"I know you're going through a hard time but we just have a few more questions, Mr. Zaccardi," Conaway said.

"Don't call me that," Thomas said.

"Okay, Thomas. Were there any signs that your friend was capable of such a violent thing? Our reports say that you've known him most of your life. Was there any behavior that was deemed as…disturbing?"

"Disturbing? One of my childhood friends turned out to be the one who killed my best friend. He was like me. We broke the law, we skipped school, and we talked about girls. Any of that behavior interest you?"

"Thomas I…"

"No, he didn't show any signs of killing Sam," he said as he uncrossed his arms. "Look, he was my friend and he did something unforgivable. He's gone now, so what's the problem? Why are we even here?"

"To gain a little more perspective. Now, your friend, Tommy. Where does he fit into all of this? Reports show that it was his .38 found on your friend's body. Any thoughts on that?"

"He wasn't my friend anymore. Tommy helped me find Rich. Of course, we didn't know we were looking for him at the time, but he was with me almost all weekend until Twinks started to fire at us. We were separated after that. I called him once or twice but that was it."

"Are you saying that Rich stole Tommy's gun from him?"

"Yes, that is what I'm getting at."

"You don't think he gave it to him?"

"Are you serious?"

"Is that too far out of relevancy? Seems to me that Tommy didn't report it missing at the time. Does that not sound odd to you?"

"Rich took it off him before Tommy had a chance to notice. The police have already talked to Tommy and answered all their questions. Are you telling me that now you are interested in him too? Is this why we are here, to try and take another friend from me?"

Richardson put his head in. "Thomas, Detective Bowen is being investigated for his decisions to keep you around during his investigation. Even though you two were able to stop your friend, his actions must be investigated to obtain clarity on his decision to put you in harm's way on multiple occasions. Not every story has a clean ending."

Thomas remained silent. He didn't know what to say as his one of his fingers started to tap the underside of the table.

"I chose to keep him around to protect him. His insight was helpful, but his protection was of my main concern," I said. Conaway and Richardson remained silent. Thomas and I shared a look while waiting for their response.

"Mike, we know where your heart is in this but from our standpoint, you could have had another kid in a body bag. The Feds have been here for three days and they want every end cut. The string is getting shorter and shorter every day. This just happens to be one of the last things on their list," Richardson said.

"Yeah, I'm sure."

"We would like to interview Thomas alone for the rest of our questions if you don't mind."

I glanced at Conaway. He folded his mouth and lifted his wrists off the table with his palms facing up. I felt an elbow dig into my bicep.

"Get out of here," Thomas said, "I can handle these guys. They're not as tough as their suits look."

I gave him a smile and nodded. "Gentleman," I said, while leaving the room.

The door shut slowly behind me. Dalton and the other officer were gone as I could hear other voices around the area. The first time I met Thomas entered my brain. He was scared, looking for an escape. As that door shut, I knew that I did not leave him feeling the same way. Death surrounded his life, and this was the first time he knew about it. He deserved another chance, a chance to live a life with opportunity around him. His father had committed the greatest disservice to him. He lacked inspiration.

Just as I was about to sit down, I felt my phone buzz. I reached in my pocket to look at my personal phone.

As the screen shined back, another smile came across my face.

*

Francis had been arrested the same day he threatened to kill my father. It took four cops to lift him onto a gurney with both of his wrists cuffed to it. He went without a struggle. It was over now. A concept that I believed Francis never knew how to understand until now. He didn't matter anymore. Only the girl waiting for the world to change again.

I remembered how much she shook as I held her. I couldn't count the number of apologies that came out of my mouth. Even though one of my eyes had swelled up to the point where half of her face was a blur, tears still managed to find their way out of them as I held her outside of the hospital.

I refused to let go of her all night. She stayed at my place that night and her soft skin felt like it never left as we lay together for hours. It was what I've wanted for many years. We didn't have sex but did not hesitate to kiss each other whenever we wanted. Her touch traveled throughout my whole body.

She told me everything. She told me about the conversation she had with my dad back in college. She stressed that my father wasn't trying to ruin what we had but to ensure that my potential would not be shaken. More tears followed as she spoke of the car ride. I assured her that I wasn't angry, just upset that we spent the last ten years wasting our time away from each other.

The next day I had to leave her. The FBI had come in to handle the Zaccardis. They needed my insight for the arrest. Before leaving the crime scene where Rich was laying on the ground, I handed Burkes my work phone. When Zaccardi kidnapped me the other day, they took my personal phone but neglected to check my shoe where I had managed to slip my work phone. In the car, before the widow's peak knocked me out, I managed to open my phone and activated the video camera. When Zaccardi sent me out to find Thomas, I waited a moment to see that I had over an hour of black footage with our dialogue at the very end. It ended my suspicion that Widow's peak used to be in law enforcement.

Francis and everyone that could be connected to him were arrested for a range of different crimes. Conspiracy to commit murder and possession and selling of narcotics were two of my favorites. The FBI had secured a search warrant to upturn Zaccardi's bakery. A plethora of evidence was obtained, not to mention enough money to finance half of the department's 401K plan. Mountains of cocaine and heroin were discovered in the basement, along with an arsenal of sawed-off shotguns, handguns, and even a few assault rifles. Two of the pistols found were connected to a murder investigation in Dorchester.

One of the last crimes to be entered in the report was kidnapping. Sam's parents were found in one of the storage units that Francis used to dispose of or hide materials he didn't want anyone to know about. Each of them had bruises somewhere on their body. Ralphie's prints and trace DNA were found all over their clothes. After spending two days in the hospital, they were allowed to return home. Neither Thomas nor I have gone over to the house to talk to them about Sam. I sent a few officers to retrieve their statements but never read them myself. The news did plenty to spread their word. At first, they were hailed as parents who lost their angel and were given donations for their troubles. Like most things, their true nature was unearthed, and the news took an ax to their recovery. Maybe they didn't deserve it, but maybe it was all that I could agree upon.

I tried not to smile when I got the news about the FBI's informant. Nothing was more surprising then when Jack Zaccardi walked into the police station with a fresh cup of coffee in his hand. He greeted one of the FBI jackets as if they had known each other for years. His face was clear and for once he did not smell of cigarettes. Francis was right when he suspected a mole within his house. He was just wrong to assume that I was running him. The FBI had picked him up over a month ago. It was a risky choice I thought as I knew that Jack had little responsibility within Francis's operation. Jack was slow at first to acquire what they asked. One of the agents told me they almost dropped him when Jack informed them that he could get it.

I didn't believe it at first, but the surprise was nice.

Francis had a book, one with names. In its pages contained the aliases, and the identity to every man he had ever worked with. Satan's guest list was rumored to be the nickname after one of the officers on the scene took a glance at it in the evidence room. It was a monumental discovery, the kind that lasted on the front page for a week. The list proved to be jaw-dropping. Two lawyers in Suffolk County were brought in, as were a few patrolmen. Warner was one of four to be connected. A DEA agent was listed as well. A real thorn in the FBI's side as they realized their paperwork clip was about to break. The dates of their jobs were recorded as well. It was impressive, to say the least. Francis knew who he could pick to be a fall guy whenever he wanted to. Jack was on the list as well. His record would be expunged for the most part, except for a few hours of community service that would look good on his case report.

Jack revealed that he located the book in one of Francis's drawers one day when looking for something incriminating against his older brother. When he found it, Ralphie had almost caught him, causing Jack to hide it. He mistakenly placed it somewhere in Thomas's room to avoid suspicion. After Francis revealed to him that something precious to him had been taken, everyone who had been in and out of the bakery was being investigated. Sam was one of the last ones to be in their house, which prompted Francis to start a full-on investigation to who killed Sam. He thought, whoever killed Sam, might have taken the book as well.

It was the wrong place for a kid to be.

Chapter 58

After a few weeks, Thomas had informed me that Mr. Walker and Dr. Kurtz had stopped seeing one another. Nothing public was announced but he never saw the two of them together again. Dr. Kurtz had brought him into her office during lunch to disclose the news. She confided in him that he must never speak of anything.

Mr. Walker had moved away. He left no clear inclination from where he went but Dr. Kurtz claimed she had no idea. She chose not to say anything further. Thomas was sent back to class without being called back.

Thomas told me he did not agree with her about not telling her husband. Some decisions cannot be made for someone else. Life would go on, with the truth or without it.

Captain Burkes was hailed as an investigative genius. He produced his crooked smile at every high-profile press conference about the case. I did not care for the attention and let him speak about everything. I'd never seen the man excited to see the press. Our Chief even promoted him to oversee another investigative unit. His career showed no signs of dimming after Rich's body found the concrete. It felt strange, how can men prosper when two kids have been taken from us? Then I thought about the monster that used to rest in one of them.

He pulled me aside the other day and apologized for doubting me. I almost laughed him off, but he seemed compassionate in his words. I never saw that side of him before but it was leveling to see. He showed me that we were two men in the same job, not higher in the mind than the other.

"Tell the auburn beauty that you owe me a dinner date," he said, while walking back into his air-conditioned office.

Tom and Meredith watched the news for several days straight after everything came out into the open. Tom was recognized by BPD as a decorated citizen and even received an award for his bravery. He said that Meredith was beyond exuberant when she found out that he was okay.

Tom remained my father's primary caretaker. I owed him more than he could ever know but, yet he still acted as if nothing had happened. He continued to impress me with every visit. I always reminded him how much of a pleasure it was to see him taking care of my father. He often told me to tone it down and wanted to see Jess more often than he did.

Thomas and I have dinner with him and Meredith every Sunday night. Jess has been there every night as well. Her presence has definitely shifted almost every conversation at the table. Just as every Sunday passes, once thing never changes when we arrive through the door. Tom can't stop smiling.

Roma's business remained the same. It profited as much as a local sandwich shop could. Thomas brought me in to meet him. I remember eating at his shop a few times but never met the man himself. He was kind, and it was clear that he cared for Thomas and his friends. I recognized the kind of smile he showed them. Tommy came with us. He was quite the character.

Roma actually took a few minutes to sit with us as a large crowd walked in.

"So, you're the super cop," he said.

"Not exactly," I said. "Thomas is the one who showed the most bravery out there."

"Shame, it came to what it did. I'm sorry to you two boys. I know I've already said that but none of this should have happened. You deserve better."

"Maybe it was meant to happen," Thomas said. He made the three of us freeze as we waited for his response. "Sam was going to go on to be something great, I know that. Life had another plan for him. Maybe he's in a better place. Someplace where he can't be hurt but the life that let him down here. Boston is great, but maybe he's a part of something greater."

"I hope you're right," Tommy said.

"Trust me. He's doing just fine wherever he is."

Delahine struggled for a few days after he pointed a gun at a twelve-year-old. Several of the officers on his shift said he wasn't the same. One of them told me that Burkes had approached him about taking the detective exam. Not even that news managed to lift his spirits.

I visited him in his apartment in South End. A few liquor bottles aligned themselves on his kitchen counter. I was expecting his place to look a lot worse but only one pair of jeans were on the ground when he let me inside.

The department gave him a couple of days' leave after everything. After seeing the weight under his eyes, he needed them. He had no idea how much of a help he was to me.

"I'm not going to ask how you're doing. I can see it fair enough," I said. I took a seat in one of his chairs next to his television that had just been muted.

"Thanks for that. My maw calls me every day to check. I've heard those words more than I'd like."

"Funny, I kind of wish I could hear my dad ask me that." I almost regretted saying that after Delahine fell silent for a few moments, until he came back.

"But you're here to check on me? Make sure I haven't put a bullet to my head instead of a helmet?"

"Something like that. But I came here for something different."

"An enlightenment?"

"The opportunity to thank you. I know I may have been hard when talking about when to kill and when to walk away. Without you, we would have never closed this case. You were there for me when Burkes closed off everything to me. Even when he trusted me again, I still went solely to you. Not to pat yourself on the back too much but you deserve to know how big a part you played in all of this."

"I almost shot him, Mike, I almost pulled the trigger. His back was to me and there was nothing he could have done about it. Thomas would not have had to kill one of his friends if I just shot him."

"You made a choice. I wish Thomas didn't have to do what he did, but you don't have to live with killing a kid. Rich made the wrong choice, you didn't."

"How can you be sure?"

"I don't know everything. With the amount of times I asked for your help, that is recognizably clear. In this job, our choices affect more than just us. It affects the people around us. My father kept a gun in his drawer when I lived with him and even after I moved out. He believed that there was a time and a place to act. For over thirty years that gun rested in his drawer. He didn't know how he would have reacted if the moment came where he had to use it. But he knew one thing. The opportunity was there, and he had the choice to change something. Sometimes you have time to think, sometimes you don't. Our instinct tells us when to fire our weapon and you decided not to. Don't regret the decisions that help make you who you are." I couldn't tell if my words did anything to help. Delahine sat there, looking towards his wall.

"Thanks, Mike. Thanks for coming down here. I guess you've been spending time with Thomas's therapist?"

"Ha, yeah. I just want to make sure you're alright."

"I will be."

"Good to hear," I said as I stood up.

"Think I have a chance at the detective's exam?"

"Not a chance but go get it, Sherlock."

I patted him on his shoulder and left out his door.

Everything seemed to be going the way my father had wanted it to go. Not that I did much, but Francis Zaccardi was getting the life he had earned for himself. My father deserved to see this. I brought him the newspaper with the story on the front page. His eyes, maybe, looked at it once. Maybe his brain could read it but failed to communicate. After folding it up and putting the paper away, I looked at him to find that it didn't matter. The fact was that it was over for him. Francis would never step in his path again.

I readjusted my tie, making sure all my buttons and my belt buckle was hidden. We sat there, waiting for time to move. My visits with him felt different now, as if a large weight was no longer strapped to my angles every time, I moved closer or away from him. He was not an easy man to know or to love. I tried to picture his conversation with Jess in my head every time I came to visit. It was difficult to imagine the man she talked to. Either it was the caring father or the resolute attorney reaching for a goal. I realized that it didn't matter. Jess was waiting for me at home and that was always going to happen from now on regardless of the talk they had those years ago. It was a sign that we were going to be together, no matter the obstacle.

He was the father who wanted what was best for his son. His methods may have been hard to understand, but it didn't distract him from his goal of providing the life he wanted me to have. I was on the only one in this world who could call him what he truly was, my father.

Chapter 59

"Dammit, the Red Sox lost again."

"Hey, watch it. We have a lady here. No need for such language." I felt like my father when I once cursed at a Sunday brunch with some of his associates. Thomas and Jess were hardly the stern type at that table.

It was now just over two months since Thomas and I had met. The three of us were sitting in my living room. Everything around was a bit cleaner since Jess started to visit more frequently. It was a pleasant touch. She and Thomas had hit it off. She had translated some of her kindness to even buying him some decent clothes.

"Am I expecting a new sweatshirt soon?" I said, as I took a bite of my strawberry jelly covered toast.

"I might have to. Look at the hole below your arm, might be able to fit a whole quarter in there," she said.

"I'm a medium, sometimes large."

"I'll keep that in mind."

"This one is soft, I like it," Thomas said, after putting down his phone and rubbing his sleeves. "I cannot wait for my last session to be over. I don't know how many times I have to tell this guy what I experienced was hard but not impossible to get over. Sam will always be my best friend. Nothing can take that away from me."

"As it never should."

Thomas had been seeing the same therapist every week since his father's arrest. He complained every time he went. The doctor has been practicing the psychology of Boston's youth for ten years and was evidently thorough. Thomas told me that he once connected his loss to a bag of sand with a hole in it. Strength eventually runs out, but all of it never leaves.

"Don't worry about it," I said. "He'll have you out of there early if you're lucky."

"I thought it was a mandatory hour."

"Saw past that lie I see. I need to work on that."

"Do you even remember who my father is? He lied every second of every day."

"Good point."

"I know I'm good, but it's nice to be reminded."

Jess had let out a light laugh and collected her plate. She finished washing some eggs off her plate when she turned to Thomas.

"Mike tells me that you like baseball. Your father ever play catch with you?"

"Not that I can remember. He never even came to watch me play. I had games every weekend when I was little. My Uncle Ralphie came to some, but my dad only drove by once."

"That's a shame. From what your friend, Tommy, told me the other day, I heard you're pretty good."

"I'm not too shabby. Tommy is just jealous that he can't play second as well as I can."

"I'm sure. Hey, Mike?"

"Yeah?" I said.

"Promise me you'll take Thomas out to throw the ball around with him. I'm sure he'd love that."

I stared at her for a moment. Her forehead rose as she expected an answer. I decided not to give her one and headed for the living room. Within a closet that contained my vacuum and a few other cleaning supplies, I reached up to find the box I was looking for.

When I came back into the kitchen, both of them looked exactly the way I envisioned.

"Way ahead of you," I said, placing the box down in front of Thomas. The Boston adoption center document attached to our refrigerator nearly swung off when I walked by. A smile came across my face when both of our signatures entered my vision.

He gave me a look and started to open the box from its corners. He reached in and lifted a brand-new Wilson baseball glove. Its shiny brown leather reflected off the light above. A smile instantly fell across his face.

"Mike, what is this?" he said.

"C'mon, you're smart enough to know what that is."

"Yeah, but you didn't have to. This is over a hundred dollars. Like, real money spent...on me?"

"Not sure if it's better than Sonny Sisto's."

"I love it, but now everyone is going to be after me now. You've pretty much painted a bullseye on my back."

"You could take this one." I brought about a much-tenured version of the new one in front of him. "My dad gave me this one. I haven't used it since I was about your age. I doubt my hand can fit in it but I'm sure you'll be able to use it just fine."

"Yeah, I think I'm going to stick with this one."

Both of us laughed for a bit. A pair of birds rested on a branch outside our window. Their chirps were pleasant as the three of us sat there. It took me a few seconds to put together that the birds' chirp was a sign.

"Want to go test it out?"

"Absolutely."

Thomas shot outside the front door onto the sidewalk. I followed close behind with a beat-up baseball in my right hand. Just as I landed on the sidewalk, I tossed it to him. We managed to toss a few back and forth when Jess followed us out. She sat on the steps watching us, smiling every time Thomas caught the ball. The morning sunlight upon her skin made me realize that she was sitting in the perfect spot. Not just on the step, but with me. The past ten years of our lives were put on hold it felt like.

We discussed it for hours one night over dinner. Within those years, we decided that we may have tried to have a child. When I brought the idea to her attention, she did nothing but smile. Thomas deserved a second shot and it felt as if we did too. I'll never forget the bewildered but accepting look Thomas gave us when we told him. Thomas would let us take a picture, no matter how happy he secretly was.

"If you're lucky, maybe I'll coach you one of these days," I said.

"I'm not trying to lose my talent if that's what you're suggesting," he said just as he dropped a ball.

"Clearly you don't need it."

Thomas laughed it off. He was my chance to leave an imprint. A chance to find meaning in the work that I do. Every case has a different outcome. It just so happens this one left me with something to look forward to.